Hey, Whiskey

NEW YORK TIMES BESTSELLING AUTHOR

KAYLEE RYAN

ONE

Saylor

SITTING ON THE edge of the mattress, I survey the room. Boxes neatly labeled surround me. I saved this room for the end; I didn't know how to let her go. I still don't. The pain in my chest from losing her is unbearable. She was the only family I ever knew. My phone rings from its place on the dresser; I stand, rushing to grab it before it goes to voice mail.

"Hello," I say my voice rough from tears.

"Say."

I sigh at the sound of my best friend's voice. "Hey, Tara," I greet her.

"You should have let me come over and help you," she scolds me.

"I'm good, really. It's just so final, you know?"

"Yeah, are you sure you want to do this? This is a big decision, and it's only been a month."

One month—thirty days since the only mother figure I've ever known passed away. Elaine Phelps saved me from a world unknown. One of pain, hunger, and fear. When I was twelve years old, she became my foster mother. "It doesn't feel right being here without her."

"That's your home, Say. The only real home you've ever known," she says gently.

"It's not home without her. I'm sure this is the right choice. Besides, Pete and I have talked about this. Our life is in West Virginia now."

"I know, and I'm happy for you guys. I just don't want you to make a rash decision that you'll eventually regret."

"No regrets. It's not home without her. She was what made this place home. I was lucky to have her for eleven years. Her memory and everything she taught me, gave me, is all that I need to remember her. Not this house. Besides, I have a few mementos that she insisted were mine in her will."

"Is the sale final then?" she asks.

"Yeah. I have until Friday to be out, but I'm leaving here in a few hours. They offered me more time, but it's a young couple expecting their first baby. I'm sure they're eager to get settled before the baby comes. I've donated the furniture and most of her clothes to Goodwill. There are a few things I'm keeping other than that, just my clothes and a few personal items."

"If you need me, you call. I wish you would let me help you."

"I'm fine, really. I'm sorry I didn't get to see you before I left. This was just something that I needed to do on my own."

"I get it. I just worry about you."

"I'm doing as well as can be expected. Pete and I have dinner plans, so I'm loading up my SUV and heading back."

"Drive safe. We need to plan a weekend, and soon," she insists.

"I agree. I'll call you in a few days." Ending the call, I start the heavy lifting, moving my remaining boxes into the back of my SUV. I don't have much, just some clothing I left behind and a few personal items of Elaine's. My heart aches at the thought of what life is going to be like without her.

I do one final walk-through of the house, making sure there is nothing I've missed that I want to keep and take with me. The house is almost empty, but it's like a final goodbye as I make my way through each room. I let the memories of my time here wash over me. The first night she brought me home, our first holidays as a family. Although she never adopted me, Elaine was adamant that I was her daughter too. She always said I had two mothers who loved me more than anything. She saved me, made me who I am today, and I will forever be grateful for her.

"Goodbye, Mom," I choke on the words. "Thank you for all that you did for me. I miss you so damn much." I pick up the one final item that I plan to take but couldn't pack away. Her old gray sweater, the one she wore practically every day. Bringing it to my face, I discover it smells like her. Sadness tears through me. Life is so unfair. Why of all people did it have to be her? Why did I have to lose her too, the only real family I can remember?

With one final fleeting look, I close the door, making sure it's locked, and head home—my new home, the one I'm building with Pete. He and I met sophomore year, both attending the University of Cincinnati. I was working at a local pub, putting myself through school, against Elaine's wishes of course. It was illegal for part of the time I worked there, being underage and all that. She offered to pay, but I couldn't let her. She'd already given me so much. We compromised with me living at home rent free and hot meals each day. I busted my ass working full-time and earning my education. My time at the pub was worth it. I made great tips from all the drunk frat guys. Pete hated it, but he didn't have a say in the matter. It could have been worse; I could have been stripping—not that there is anything wrong with that, it's just not my thing.

The three-hour drive home feels like an eternity. I don't bother with any of the boxes, deciding to do it later. Instead, I grab my phone, keys, purse, and the gray sweater and head inside our house—well, Pete's house. Sure I live here, but it doesn't actually feel like home to me. Not yet. These last six months since graduation have been a whirlwind. I don't feel like I've had the time to settle. I took a job at Pete's families real estate firm as the human resources manager. I've been learning the ropes, and I was just starting to feel like I was getting a grip when I got the call that they were rushing Elaine to the hospital.

Heart attack.

Since that day, I've been reeling, trying to find something, anything to ground me. Pete's been extremely patient with me, but even I'm getting fed up with myself. I need to snap out of it and move forward. She gave me opportunities, which I would have otherwise never been given. She would be devastated to know that I'm drowning in my sadness and not embracing life. I know that, and still, I can't seem to shake this feeling, this loneliness that has seeped into my bones. It's just like the years pre-Elaine, where I bounced from foster home to foster home, never feeling grounded, never feeling safe. Of course, it's ridiculous. Pete and I have been together going on four years. I have security in him, I know that, but there is this nagging feeling that says things will never be the same.

3

Rushing up the stairs to our bedroom, I strip out of my dusty clothes and hop in the shower. Pete will be home within the hour, and if I know him, he has already made reservations. He's a planner; every move is thought out, calculated. With my hair pinned on top of my head, not having enough time to wash it, I rinse off the grime of the day. Pulling a pair of leggings and a sweater from the closet, I quickly dress. I'm tempted to wear Elaine's sweater, but I'll save that for another day. She wore it around the house, just lounging. I can feel the smile tilt my lips as I picture her curled up on the couch, sweater wrapped around her, throw over her legs as she read. Along with the smile, a ping of sadness lays heavy on my chest. I miss her. Shaking out of the thought, I let my hair fall free and run a brush through it. Glancing at the clock, I see I don't have time to add a few loose curls, so straight it is.

I'm just grabbing my ballet flats when Pete calls up the steps for me. "Coming," I yell, grabbing my shoes and rushing down the stairs.

"Hi," I say, hoping on one foot, trying to get my shoe on. Slipping the shoe over my heel before walking toward him. Leaning in, I kiss him. "How was your day?" "Good. You ready?" he asks. His tone is clipped.

"You okay?" He seems… off tonight.

"Yeah, just… we need to talk, Say."

"Okay, you want to do that now? Or wait until after we eat?"

He sighs and runs his fingers through his dark blond hair. "At first, I thought after would be better, but now…" He closes his eyes. "Can we sit?"

"Sure." I agree and follow behind him into the living room. Pete takes a seat on the couch and pats the cushion next to him. "You're scaring me," I tell him.

"I know, and I'm sorry." He releases a heavy breath. "Listen, Saylor, what I'm about to tell you is wrong. It's going to hurt you, and for that I'm truly sorry. I don't even know how it happened, just that it did, and when Elaine died, I held on a little longer, but then…"

"Just say it. Whatever it is, just say it."

"I'm getting married," he blurts the words. His eyes hold mine, never wavering, never looking away.

"M-married?" I look down at his hands, and he's not holding a ring. "I'm going to need you to explain that statement," I say, trying to keep my anger in check. Maybe he's nervous, and he's botching the proposal, but then he said it would hurt me. Oh God. I place my hand over my mouth to keep the sob from escaping. Instead, I swallow hard, fighting back the emotion.

"I'm so sorry, Saylor. I didn't mean for this to happen. Tabitha and I were working late, and one thing led to another. And, well, she's pregnant and it's mine, and I have to marry her. I have to take care of them."

"Pregnant? Married?" I mumbled the words as questions. I'm struggling to comprehend what he's just told me. "How long, Pete? How long have you been fucking her while you were fucking me?" I ask through gritted teeth. My heart drops to the pit of my stomach. How did I miss this? How could I be so stupid?

He lowers his head. "Six months," he mumbles.

I stand and pace back-and-forth in front of the couch. Pete keeps his head down, no longer willing to look at me. "Six months, you've been cheating on me? Six fucking months!" I scream. "The exact time we moved here. I fucking moved my life for you!" I pace back-and-forth, back-and-forth. "Is she clean? Jesus, Peter, do you realize what you've done? Thanks to you, I've slept with that slut too," I seethe.

"Saylor, come on." He finally looks up, and to my surprise, he looks devastated.

"What? You're getting married to the girl you've been sleeping with behind my back for six fucking months. Six months. And thanks to you, I get to go have my lady bits poked and prodded to make sure you and your slut-of-a-fiancée baby mama didn't give me the fucking funk!" I yell.

"I care about you, Saylor, but she's pregnant. I have to do this."

"How long have you known?"

"What?" he asks.

He's clearly avoiding. "How long have you known about the baby?"

"She just passed her first trimester, so about six weeks."

"You let me sell the only home I've ever known." My mind is racing. The house is sold. I have no family. What am I going to do? "You knew, Peter. You fucking knew!" I can't stop yelling at him.

"I did. The night I was going to tell you, Elaine died, and I just couldn't."

"You're a fucking coward, that's what you are." I stop and look at him. My glare is menacing. "I can't be here," I say, turning to look for my purse.

"Saylor, come on. I want us to be friends; I care about you."

"Seriously? Do you hear yourself right now? You're fucking delusional if you think I want anything more to do with you." I spot my purse, keys, and phone sitting on the table beside it. Elaine's sweater is laying on the same table. Stalking toward them, I gather it all in my arms, hands shaking uncontrollably. "I have to get out of here," I mumble to myself.

"Don't be like that," he pleads.

I scoff. "I'm leaving. I'll be in touch with a time to gather my things. I would appreciate it if you were not here when the time comes. I won't touch anything that's yours. I just need my clothes and what few personal items I have. I'll leave my key on the table, and you can forget you ever knew me."

"I'll call you. Once you calm down, you'll see this is what I had to do. It doesn't matter what I feel for you; I have to take care of my kid."

"That's admirable, Pete, really it is. But you're missing a big piece of the puzzle." He stops in front of me, waiting for the missing piece. "If you would have kept your dick in your pants, this wouldn't be happening. You're a coward and a cheat, and I never want to see you again. Have a nice life," I say, stalking toward the front door. He's there in an instant, but the look I give him halts his steps. Opening the door, I step onto the porch, slamming the door behind me.

"Saylor, we'll talk soon," he says, standing in the now open doorway.

"Fuck off!" I say, climbing into my SUV, the one that is still packed with my life from Ohio. My mind races with what I'm going to do. Tonight, I'll be going to a hotel, and then after that? Who the hell knows. I have no family, my heart is shattered, and now I'm homeless. Still clutching my phone, I'm startled when it starts to ring. I assume it's Pete, but a quick glance at the screens tells me I'm wrong. It's Tara.

"H—" I clear my throat. "Hello," I finally say.

"Saylor?"

"Yeah." More throat cleaning.

"Why do you sound funny?"

"I'm fine. What's up?"

"I just called to make sure you made it back okay."

Her words cause the dam to break, and the tears fall from my eyes. I can't fight back the sob that breaks free. "Yeah," I choke out.

"Say, what's going on?"

"It's been a shit day," I tell her, avoiding the question.

"What happened?"

"Pete—" A sob breaks free from my chest.

"Did he hurt you?" Her voice rises, and I know she's about to panic. My best friend is a worrier.

"No, not physically. Listen, I'm okay." I take a deep breath. "I'm going to check into a hotel, and I'll call you once I'm settled in the room. I need to drive, and I can't do that and tell you at the same time. I need to focus on driving."

"I'm on my way—" she starts, but I cut her off.

"No. Tara, it's fine. I'll call you in about twenty minutes. Let me just get settled. I promise I'm not hurt physically."

"Is Pete?" she asks hesitantly.

I laugh. "He's perfectly fine with his baby mama," I say without thinking.

"Holy shit," she whispers.

"Yeah, so let me call you in a few. I'm good, I promise. Don't come here. I'll explain it all soon."

"Drive safe, and if I have not heard from you in an hour, I'm heading your way."

"Okay. I'll call soon," I say meekly. Dropping the phone in the cupholder, I rest my head against the steering wheel. *Six months, pregnant, married,* his words keep flashing through my mind. How could I be so stupid? How did I not see it? Needing to be away from him, away from this house, I lift my head and buckle my seat belt, place the keys in the ignition, and back out of the driveway. I let the tears fall freely. I cry because I miss her, I cry because my heart is aching from deceit and lies, from the loss of my family. When I arrive at the hotel, a glance in the rearview mirror tells me I look like hell. My eyes are red and swollen, my makeup smeared. Grabbing a few napkins from the glove box, I try to make myself a little less scary before going in and securing a room.

Room key in hand, I watch the elevator door close. My reflection staring back at me has me closing my eyes. So much for looking less scary. I keep my eyes closed until the door opens. A quick glance up tells me this is my floor. Stepping off the elevator, I follow the signs until I reach my room. Inserting the key, I step inside and place the Do Not Disturb sign on the door. I drop my purse, keys, and room key to the small table and fall back on the bed. Taking a deep breath, I lift my phone, unlock the screen, and dial Tara.

"How are you?" she asks in greeting.

I scoff. "You mean before my cheating boyfriend decided to drop the bomb on me that he has a fiancée who is pregnant?" I ask, fighting back another round of tears.

"Holy shit! Start from the beginning," she says. I can hear her moving around, no doubt settling in to listen to my nightmare. Tara has always been there for me since that first day of eighth grade. I was the new girl in school, and she took me under her wing. We hit it off and have been inseparable ever since. "Saylor," she says, reminding me she's ready for me to tell her what happened.

So I do. I tell her about my conversation with Pete, how he's been cheating on me and is now getting married. "You know he kept saying he cared about me and that he would talk to me soon. Why would I want to talk to him?" I ask, even though I don't expect an answer.

"Come home and live with me," Tara says immediately. "Colin and I have a spare room; we have that apartment over the garage that we've been meaning to fix up. We can do that, and you can have your own space."

"Tara, I can't. I just… I need to figure out what's next. I need to get my stuff, and oh God, what am I going to do about work?"

"How often do you see him? See them?" she amends.

"Enough that I know I don't want to work there anymore."

"All the more reason to come home."

That's the problem though. Where is home? It used to be Elaine, not her house, but her. Then I had accepted that home was going to be with Pete, and now…

"Saylor, just come home," she says again.

"I don't know where that is," I say softly.

"Say," she whispers. "What can I do? You're welcome here. Hell, I'll be there in a few hours, and we'll load your stuff tonight."

"No. I need to figure this out, Tara. I appreciate your offer, but I need to just… figure this out."

"Why can you not do that here, close to me where I can help you?" she asks.

"I don't know who I am, Tara. I don't know where home is. Where do I belong? Where do I fit in?"

"What can I do?"

That's what I love about my best friend. No matter what, she's there unconditionally. She's there for me.

"Give me some time. Just be there if I need you. I promise, if I need a place to stay long term, I'll come to you. Right now, I just need to regroup. Figure out my next move."

"Okay," she says hesitantly. "You promise, Say?"

"I promise. I'll call you in a few days." I end the call and toss the phone on the bed beside me. Staring up at the stark white ceiling, my mind races. I need to find a place to stay. I need to find a job. The sale of Elaine's house is final in a couple of days. I close my eyes and remember the reading of her will. It was just me, the lawyer, and his assistant. She had written me a letter. I can still remember her words.

"Everything I am, everything goes to you, my daughter, Saylor Keller. As far as the house, sell it, live in it, I don't care. Use it to purchase your first home, something of your own. Use it to continue your education. Use it to live, Say."

After a couple of days of talking it over with Pete, we decided that selling was the best option. Our lives were in West Virginia. The entire time we were discussing it, he knew. He knew he was leaving me, getting married, having a baby with her. He knew, and he still let me go through with it. He convinced me to do it.

Sitting up, I grab my keys, purse and phone and head out. I passed a bar on the way here, and that's where I'm headed. I refuse to sit in this room and stare at these four walls feeling sorry for myself. He doesn't get to have that power over me. I've been through worse and weathered the storm. This too shall pass. Wiping the tears, I school my features. No more crying over him. He's not worth it. Besides, I'm so new to the area, it will be good to get out a little. I've been engrossed in my job, learning the ins and outs, and then Elaine passed, and I've spent the last month driving back and forth from here and Cincinnati. It's time I checked out the local haunts. I'm giving myself one night to not think about tomorrow. Then it's time to figure out where I go from here.

TWO
Rhett

MY EYES ARE crossed. I've looked at these production reports all damn day. Sitting back in my chair, I turn to face the window. Leaning back, I place my hands behind my head and close my eyes. I just need a minute.

"Mr. Baxter," my receptionist, Carrie, buzzes the intercom, causing me to groan.

Swiveling around in my chair, I push the button, "Yes, Carrie."

"Mr. Baxter has requested to see you."

You heard her correctly. The Mr. Baxter she speaks of is my father. Rhett Baxter the second. My grandfather and I are subsequently numbers one and three. "I'll be right there." Standing, I grab my phone and head down the hall to his office. I wave at Betty, his longtime receptionist, before lightly knocking on his door. "You wanted to see me?" I ask, walking on in, not waiting for him to give me permission to enter.

"Have a seat, son," Dad says. His jaw is locked, and his eyes are somber.

"What's wrong?"

"It's your grandfather. He's taken ill."

I move to the edge of my seat. "What happened?"

"Looks as though all his years of smoking like a freight train have caught up with him. He's been diagnosed with emphysema and subsequently fallen ill with pneumonia."

"How is he?"

"Same old firecracker, but he's going to be out for a while. We're going to need to have someone step in until then, and well, he's saying he doesn't need the help, but I know better. Your mother and I discussed and we want you to go."

"Me?" I ask, although I shouldn't be surprised. I spent every summer with my grandfather. Mom and Dad would come and visit every other weekend, and Mom always tried to convince me to come home. I always refused. I loved every minute of every summer I got to spend with him.

"Yeah. I know you're in the middle of the quarterly reports. Brief me on where you are, and I'll take over."

"Okay. Carrie's aware of where I am with all of my projects as well. She's actually very knowledgeable, you can lean on her as well."

Dad nods. "I'm sure we'll have to do that. Your mother and I will take over your workload for now."

"Is that a good idea?" I ask. My mom is recovering from a recent car accident. After several surgeries, she's finally able to walk on crutches. A drunk driver T-boned her coming home from the grocery store. That made big headlines. *Owner of Baxter's Brewery, hit by a drunk driver.* It was weeks before the vultures, who make up the press, moved on to something else.

He shrugs. "You know your mother. She's been itching to come back to work for weeks now, and I've been able to hold her off. When we got the call this morning about Dad, she wouldn't take no for an answer."

"Stubborn as ever," I say with a laugh. My mom is one of the greatest people I know. Both of my parents are. They always made time for me, and I admit, growing up, I was spoiled, hence the reason they let me stay with grandpa all summer. Being their only child, they hated being away from me but knew that both me and Gramps valued those summers we got to spend together. The compromise was their every-other-week visits. Excessive yes, but it wasn't a hardship for us. Sometimes they would drive, making the eight or so hour trip from Tennessee. Usually it was a flight, so they could get back to the brewery on Monday.

"Looks like you're moving from beer to whiskey." Dad grins.

Did I forget to mention that my grandfather owns Baxter's Distillery? My dad, as headstrong as ever, thought he knew better, more than Gramps, and branched out on his own. He and my mom opened Baxter's Brewery. Dad and Gramps had a few rocky years when I was a baby, but by the time I was old enough to understand, all has been right in our world. They now share ideas and even marketing for both businesses.

I chuckle. "Looks like it. I miss that place. It's been years since I've spent any time there. Summer before college, I guess."

"Sounds about right," Dad agrees. "Your mother and I are leaving tonight to go see him. I booked you a flight for Monday morning. That gives you today and tomorrow to wrap up and delegate anything here. Allows you the weekend to get ready to be gone for a few weeks. That enough time?" he asks.

I mentally run through it all. Nothing at home; I'm a single guy living alone. As far as work goes, I can make it happen. "Yeah, that works. Tell Gramps I'll see him in a few days."

"Will do."

After a quick goodbye, I head back toward my office. "Hey, Carrie, I have to go out of town for an undisclosed amount of time. My mom will be coming in to cover, as well as my dad." I still refer to them as Mom and Dad here at the office. It's a family run business after all. However, our staff never refer to them that way when speaking to me. They always maintain full professionalism.

"What can I do?" she asks immediately.

"I'm going to wrap up these quarterly reports, and can you make sure Dad gets them? I also have a few meetings on my calendar. Can you reach out and let them know they will be meeting with my mother instead. Don't want anyone getting pissed off because they're caught off guard."

"Done. You need me to book a flight?"

"No, that's done. My gramps is ill, so I need to go fill in for him while he's recovering. I'm not sure how long I'll be gone. Two weeks or so, maybe longer. You can e-mail anything that comes up that you're not sure about. Mom has a good handle on the operations, so I don't foresee any issues."

"I put the Big Marketplace contract on your desk. There is a counteroffer."

I sigh and run my fingers through my hair. "Thanks. I'll look it over and make my notes. Can you make sure Dad gets it on Monday? They're leaving tonight to go see Gramps."

"Sure thing, Mr. Baxter. Anything else?"

"Uh… not yet, but I'm sure there will be. Thanks, Carrie." I head back to my office, and before I dive into the Big Marketplace contract, I pull out my phone and text Jake. He lives in West Virginia. His uncle was a local bar owner and did business with Gramps. Every day during the summer, he and I were out getting into something. We've kept in touch over the years. As a matter of fact, it was last year about this time he brought his now fiancée, Molly, to Nashville and we met up.

> **Me:** Hey, man. I'm going to be in town next week and staying for a few. I'll hit you up when I get settled.

> **Jake:** I was just telling Molly that I needed to get ahold of you. How's he doing?

Of course, Jake would already know about Gramps. Gramps and his uncle Jerry are best friends. The four of us spent a lot of time together during my summers in West Virginia.

> **Me:** Okay. My parents are flying in tonight. He just needs rest, so I'm filling in until then.

> **Jake:** You always said you would take over one day.

> **Me:** And you said you would run the bar. How's that going by the way?

> **Jake:** Good. Molly and I are kicking ass and taking names. Made some changes.

> **Me:** All right, man. I'll reach out next week after I get settled.

> **Jake:** You know where to find me.

Placing my phone on the desk, I open the thick manila file folder sitting in front of me. Time to bust this out. One less thing Dad will have to take care of while I'm gone. I get lost in the reports; numbers this quarter are good. It's not until Carrie knocks on my door to tell me she's leaving for the day that I even realize the time. Just about another hour and this is done. Grabbing my phone, I send my buddy Doug a quick message. We are supposed to meet up for drinks tonight.

Me: Hey, man. I'm here for at least another hour. Bump it back to 8?

Doug: That works.

Tossing my phone back on my desk, I push through the final numbers and call it a day. Gathering up my computer and a few files I can work with remotely, I head home. I have a list of things for Carrie that I can send her this weekend.

Reaching my condo, I drop my bag on the couch and make my way to the shower. My intention was to be quick, but the hot spray feels fantastic on my sore muscles. Sitting in front of the computer screen all day, staring at numbers, has my shoulders tense.

Quickly dressing due to my long-ass shower, I grab my phone, wallet, and keys before rushing out the door. My stomach growls, thankfully the pub we're going to has great food. I can cook, but cooking for one seems like a waste of time. Besides, this is our guys' night tradition.

Pulling into the pub, I park next to Doug's Lexus. He's a big shot engineer. I swear, when we met in college and he told me he was an engineering student, I didn't believe him. Long hair, ink, and always the life of the party—I was sure it wouldn't last. I was wrong. He met Dawn, his now wife, a few months later, and suddenly he was on the straight and narrow. She's good for him. He's lucky. He found one of the good ones. Doug comes from money too. His father owns the biggest development company in Tennessee. When girls find out we have money, they're like vultures. His wife is a saint for dealing with it. They're not deterred from his wedding band. Sure, when I was younger, not that I'm an old man at twenty-five, but in my college days, it made pussy easy. I never had to work for it. Now, it's getting old fast. You never know who you can trust and, honestly, easy pussy just isn't doing it for me anymore.

"Baxter!" I hear my name called as soon as I walk through the door. Looking to the back corner, I see Doug in our usual spot.

"Hey," I slide into the booth across from him.

Doug turns to look across the room before he acknowledges me. This could only mean one thing. Dawn is here for girls' night too. "Hey," he finally says, taking a big sip of his beer.

I motion with my head to where Dawn and her friends are sitting. "They can join us."

He doesn't hesitate to slide out of the booth and stalk toward his wife.

I watch him go and immediately see what the issue is. Two guys in business suits are chatting up the table of four women. Doug is territorial over Dawn, as he should be. I'm sure she would disagree with that statement, but you can't let another man mess with what's yours. Not even a minute later, Dawn and her friend, Tessa, join us. I slide over in the booth, so Tessa can sit. I try not to groan that she's the one that joined us out of the three. Tessa is a good friend to Dawn, at least that's what Doug tells me, but the girl is relentless with her pursuit to get me in bed. I've came close a few nights, too much alcohol swaying my decision, but I always come to my senses before it's too late. Tessa is one of those girls, the vultures that want to latch on and never let go. I'll pass.

"Hey, Rhett," she coos. Yeah, she cooed, and let me tell you, it's not attractive, not at all.

"Hi." I take a drink of my beer, not wanting to give her any ammunition.

"Thanks for the invite," she says, her voice is husky, but not naturally so. She's trying to be sexy, and it's not working for her. Not even close.

"Dawn is always welcome," I say, looking up at her. "Hey, D." I wink.

She laughs, and Doug gives me the "don't wink at my wife" look. I just chuckle under my breath. He's too damn easy to rile up when it comes to her.

"Long day?" Dawn asks with soft laughter.

"You could say that. I have to fly out to West Virginia on Monday."

"What's up with that?" Doug asks.

I ignore Tessa beside me hanging on every word, trying to find her in. "Gramps is sick. He needs to be off a few weeks, and he's been running things all on his own. He's kind of a control freak."

Doug laughs. "You mentioned that. That's why your dad went out on his own, right?"

"Pretty much. At least that's what they tell me."

"Oh, you poor thing," Tessa says, her small hands and tiger claw nails clamping around my bicep.

Seriously, do woman think mile-long nails turn a guy on? I mean, I'm all for some scratches on my chest and back, not a man out there who isn't, but those things, fuck me, they'll put an eye out. No thanks. I shrug her off, not even caring that I'm being a dick. She needs to back the hell off with those torture devices.

16

"So yeah." I turn my attention back to my best friend and his wife. "I'll be there a few weeks or so. He's been diagnosed with emphysema and has a pretty bad case of pneumonia from what Dad says."

"Why doesn't your dad go?" Doug asks.

"They have a good relationship now, but I still think, even after all these years, there are hard feelings when it comes to their respective businesses. Not to mention, Dad doesn't really want to leave the brewery. Makes more sense for me go. I used to spend every summer with him. I'm sure, just from hanging around the distillery, that I know it better than my old man."

"Whiskey, huh?" Doug asks.

"Yeah, the concept is the same. The formulas are different."

"I'm sorry to hear about your grandpa," Dawn tells me.

"Thanks. He's a tough ole bird. I'm sure he's going to be right back to his old self in no time." I say the words and hope they're true. Gramps has always been bigger than life; I'm not so sure I'm prepared to see him sick and frail.

"So we should celebrate tonight," Tessa says, again with the fake huskiness to her voice. How is she even doing that?

"Celebrate my Gramps being sick?" I ask, giving her a hard stare.

"N-no, I mean since you're leaving."

"Not happening," I tell her. Looking back at Doug and Dawn, I say, "I'm starving. Have you two eaten?"

"Yeah, I cooked dinner." Dawn looks up at Doug, and he leans down and kisses her.

"Not yet. We should get out of here," Tessa tries again.

"Look." I turn to face her. "It's not happening. Drop it," I say, keeping my voice hard. She opens her mouth as if she's going to speak, and I hold my hand up to stop her. "No."

"Tess, why don't we let the guys talk and go see what the others are getting into?" Dawn offers. Doug leans in to kiss her with a whispered "Thank you," and then they're gone.

"You all right, man?" Doug asks.

"Fine," I say through gritted teeth.

"I can tell," he says with a laugh.

"I'm over the dumb shit, D. You don't know how good you have it with Dawn."

"What's this? Rhett Baxter's ready to settle down?" he mocks me.

"Fuck off," I say, not able to hide my smile. "I'm not opposed to it, but fucking hell, man. Not going to happen with chicks like her."

"Truth." He holds his beer up, and I do the same as we clink them together. "Here." He slides me a menu then signals for the waitress. "Order some food. Maybe it will help this piss ass mood you're in."

I don't need the damn menu. We've been coming here for years. The waitress appears, and I order enough for an army. The rest of the night goes smooth. Dawn comes back over once Tessa and the other girls head out. Apparently, she realized tonight just wasn't her night. Hopefully she understands it's never going to be her night, not with me. Once last call is announced, it's time to head home. I say goodbye to Doug and Dawn, and as I watch them walk away, I tramp down the envy I have for my best friend as I head home alone.

THREE

A WALK IN the cold November weather did me some good. I'm hoping my cheeks are not as puffy. I'll be able to pull off the redness, blaming it on the cold wind, should anyone ask, not that they would since I don't know them. When I reach the bar, the Corner Pocket, I stare in through the window. It's busy, which is a good thing. I hope to be invisible. I just need a drink, or twenty, to forget this shit-tastic day.

Taking a deep breath, I wrap Elaine's sweater a little tighter and pull open the door. To my relief, no one turns to look my way. Everyone is too engrossed in what they're doing to pay attention to me. Seeing an open seat at the end of the bar, I slide into it, placing my phone on the bar and rubbing my cold hands together.

"What can I get for you?" a girl who looks to be close to my age with long blonde hair asks with a smile.

I point to the bottle of Baxter's original on the shelf behind her. "Make it a double," I say.

She smiles and works on getting my shot. "You want a tab?" she asks.

I nod, pouring back my first shot. The burn instantly warms me from the inside out.

"Another?" she asks, still holding the bottle.

"No, thank you. A beer, anything on tap is fine."

She smiles. "Let's stick with the tradition, shall we? We have a Baxter's Lager on tap."

I nod, letting her know that's fine. Sitting back in my stool, I focus on letting my body relax as I thaw out from the cold. Thoughts of Pete and his betrayal are buried deep, and I refuse to let my mind go there. The bartender places my beer in front of me with the promise to check on me again soon.

Taking a swig of my beer and grabbing my phone, I start looking for a new job. I hate that I've just gotten comfortable where I am, and now I have to leave. It can't be avoided. I can't work with them. I scroll through pages and pages of human resources jobs and flag a few to apply to when I get back to the hotel.

"Job hunting?" the bartender asks.

I look up, startled. I didn't realize she was standing there. "Yeah, unfortunately. Boyfriend decided to have a baby and marry someone else. We live and work together. It's actually his family's business, so I'm definitely in the market for a new job." I clamp my hand over my mouth to stop the word vomit. I don't know what's wrong with me.

She laughs. "What do you do?" she asks, pointing to my now empty glass.

"Refill?"

"Yes, please. My degree is in human resources, but I've been where you are too. I slung drinks all through college."

"Really? Where?"

"Cincinnati. Tuff's little hole in the wall, cheap beer, and college students," I say with a laugh.

"Sounds like my kind of place. We get some college crowd too. We have a good mix here."

"Are you the owner?"

"No, well, not really. My fiancé, Jake, owns this place. He took over a couple of years ago. His uncle used to own it."

"This might be out of line, but the alcohol is settling and my filter is, well, not filtered." I chuckle. "But you're close to my age, right? Twenty-two?"

"Yep. Care to tell me how you slung drinks all through college?" She smirks.

"Funny story, the owner was not one of the… legal variety. He was good with paying me under the table, and I took it. I was careful, and if anyone came in who looked like they could be there for reasons other than throwing a few back, I went to the kitchen or stocked the bar. I was never working alone, which made it nice."

She whistles. "You got lucky," she says.

I shrug. "Yeah, I guess so. Looking back, I can see it was a bad move on my part, and his. At the time, I was in need of a job with no experience and a college class schedule to work around. It worked."

"Well, I'm glad it worked out for you."

"Yeah, hindsight is twenty-twenty, isn't that what they say?"

"Who is they?" She laughs.

I can't help it, this causes me to laugh too. "I have no idea."

"What's your name?" she asks, once her laughing subsides.

"Saylor," I say, holding my hand out for her.

"Nice to meet you, Saylor. I'm Molly." We shake hands. I let mine drop, but Molly is still watching me. "You know, we're hiring," she says.

"Really?" I ask. "For?"

"Bar, you're legal now." She winks.

"I just might have to apply. I also need to find a place to live. Boyfriend is moving in his baby mama, aka future wife, I'm sure. I have to go there tomorrow and get all my stuff, only I have no idea where to take it. You think the hotel will look at me like I'm crazy if I bring in a ton of boxes?" I ask, running off at the mouth again. I'd like to blame it on the alcohol, but I haven't had that much. It's the drama in my life that's causing it. Pete, he caused me to be where I am at this exact moment.

"I might be able to help you with that too. We have a garage apartment. Needs some paint, but we could work out a price."

"Are you my guardian angel?" I ask her. She laughs, but I'm dead serious. Funny how Tara's offer of her garage apartment wasn't appealing, but Molly's is.

"No, but I have good instincts, and I can tell you're good people, just shit luck with the dick boyfriend."

"Hey, babe," A tall, dark-haired, inked-up god says, placing his hands on Molly's hips and kissing her neck.

"Jake, this is Saylor. Saylor, this is my fiancé, Jake. I was just telling Saylor here about our opening for bartender. She's got experience, but she also just so happens to be looking for a place to stay. Long story, but boyfriend screwed her over and she moved here for him."

"Hey, I didn't tell you that part," I say, confused as to how she would know.

Molly shrugs. "I guessed. Why else would you need a place to stay unless you had no one else in town?"

If she only knew how true that statement is—not just in town, but in life in general. I have Tara, but I can't go home to Cincinnati. With Elaine not being there, it hurts too much. I'd rather risk running into Pete and his baby mama than go back to where everything reminds me that my only family is no longer there. Placing my hand over my chest, I try to rub the ache away that appears any time I let myself think about my foster mom.

"Nice to meet you, Saylor," Jake rumbles, offering me his hand.

Reaching out, I take it. "You too."

"We have a garage apartment," he tells me.

Molly grins and winks.

"Let's talk rent. I'll need to find a new job. I can't go back to mine," I tell them.

"What? You don't want to work here?" Jake places his hand over his chest as if he's offended. I worry until I see the grin tilt his lips. "We need a bartender." He points to the window behind me. Turning, I see the help wanted sign. "When can you start?" he asks.

"Just like that?"

He wraps his arms around Molly again. "My girl thinks you're good people, that's all I need to know."

"Wow. I can't... I don't know what to say."

"Say 'I accept the job, and when can I move in?'" Molly grins.

I've never been one to believe in fate, being in the right place at the right time, and all of that. Life sucks. It's hard and messy, and bad things happen to good people. But there are those times when good things happen to good people too. Like when your social worker gets tired of seeing you bounce from home to home and takes you in herself. Or the time you're in a random bar after a life-altering revelation from your boyfriend.

"Saylor?" Molly says.

Looking up, I see they're both watching me. Waiting. "I accept the job, and when can I move in?" I smile at them.

"Let's get you moved in first. Like I said, it needs some paint. How about you meet me here tomorrow morning around eleven? We can go pick out paint and get started. We need to get you out of that hotel. Once it's painted, Jake and I will help you get your stuff from dick's place."

"Dick?" Jake asks.

"Her ex," Molly tells him.

"Suits him," he laughs.

"His name is Pete, actually. But I have to agree dick fits."

"Okay, so tomorrow. Let's get you moved in and settled, and then we'll get you behind the bar."

"Are you sure? You can hold the job until then?" I ask.

Molly waves me off. "We're fine, Saylor."

I grab my purse and pull out my debit card. "I guess I should get going." I hand Molly my card. "I can't thank both of you enough for this. I don't... thank you," I finally say. I was about to release more of my woes, but they don't need to hear that. They've helped me more than they will ever know.

"It's on the house," Jake says, pushing my hand away. "Consider it a social interview."

"Really, I insist." I hold the card out again.

"Your money is no good here." He gently pushes my hand away again. "I got to go check on the other side." He kisses Molly, this time on the lips, waves to me, and off he goes.

"Molly, really, I feel terrible. You're doing so much." I try to hand her my card.

"Nope." She grins. "Be here in the morning, Saylor. We've all been there, fell on hard times. We're happy to help."

"Thank you. Thank you so much," I say, shoving my card back into my wallet.

"You driving?" she asks me.

"No." I shake my head. "I walked from the hotel just around the corner."

"You want a ride? It's cold out there."

"No, I'm good."

"It's late. You don't need to be walking on your own. Let me drive you." She walks away and says something to Jake, and he nods. Instead of Molly, Jake is the one who walks toward me.

"I'll take you. No reason for a woman to be out late on her own." He pulls his keys from his pocket. "My truck is out back, come on." He motions for me to follow him, and I do.

I don't know what it is, but I know I can trust him, both of them. I wave to Molly and mouth "thank you" as I follow Jake past the bar, down the hall past what I assume is his office, and then a few more doors to the back door. He holds it open for me, and to my surprise, his truck is running.

"Remote start." He holds up his key fob.

"Nice. Thank you again for everything," I say once we're in the truck.

"It's a two-minute drive. It's not a problem, Saylor."

Like he said, the ride is short. I take off my seat belt and open the door. "Thank you, Jake, and thank Molly for me too."

"I'll see you tomorrow, Saylor." He waves and drives off as soon as I have the door closed.

Once I'm back in my room, I realize I have nothing. I have a few clothes that I left at Elaine's when I moved here, but it's late, so going down to my SUV to dig through boxes isn't an option. Instead, I kick off my shoes and pull back the blankets. My phone is about to die as well. I'm out of sorts, yet I feel like there is hope. Hope for the future that a few short hours ago looked bleak. Hope that life moves on, you keep moving forward taking baby steps one day at a time.

I wake to the sound of the neighbors in the room next to mine getting in the shower. This is a nice hotel, but as with most, the walls are paper thin. Took me a while to fall asleep last night, and a quick glance at the clock on the nightstand tells me it's too damn early to be up. I don't have to meet Molly for five more hours, I'm the type of girl, once I'm up, I'm up for the day. I lived in foster homes that I had to be up for chores before school. Getting up early is something I've always done even when I lived with Elaine. Old habits die hard and all that. There were a few times when I tried to convince Pete to just stay in bed all day, but he shot the idea down faster than I could finish getting the words out of my mouth. You can't make money sleeping in. Or in his case, you can't knock up your employee sleeping in. He was always out of the house early, coming in late. Hell, I never once questioned him.

Live and learn.

Climbing out of bed, I slip on my shoes, grab my room key, and head down to the parking lot. I need to either go buy some clothes or find something in my car that will work for today. It's a chilly morning, and I can see my breath as soon as I step outside. I jog to my SUV, unlock the back door, and start to dig through boxes. I find an old faded pair of jeans with holes in the knees. They were always my favorite, but Pete never liked them. I can't remember his exact words, something about dressing below my grade. Just another shit thing to say. Looking back, there were several. I'm not sure why I stayed with him as long as I did. No, that's not true. I do know. I cared about him. He was the first guy to show me affection, and I latched on like a spider monkey. During the early years, we were good together. Yeah, there were offhanded comments and he was particular about things, but I wanted to make him happy. I didn't think much of it. Today, I'm seeing things in a whole new light. He was using me. All this time. I'm sure Tabitha, AKA, baby mama, isn't the first. I shudder at the thought. Time to call and make an appointment to be tested.

Jeans in hand, I dig a little further and find an old Def Leppard concert T-shirt and an Ohio State hoodie. Digging a little further, I find a sports bra, some cotton panties—the kind Pete hated and complained every time I wore them—and a pair of socks. Luckily, my old tennis shoes are in a reusable shopping bag. I empty the bag of shoes, leavening my Nike's and adding my clothes. That's everything I need, except for my cell phone charger. Locking my doors, I rush back inside. The girl behind the counter greets me with a cheery "good morning" as I enter the lobby.

"Good morning," I mumble my reply and hightail it to the elevator. In the room, I empty the bag on the bed and lay the clothes out. There are enough wrinkles in them as it is. Sure, there's an iron, but that's what Pete would expect. Today, I'm rolling with it. Besides, I'm just going to buy paint and, hopefully, start painting. Stripping out of my clothes, I head to the shower, grabbing the complimentary shampoo, conditioner, and soap off the sink. I take my time, letting the hot water beat down on me. My mind races with the last twenty-four hours, and a sob breaks free from my chest. I hate him and care for him at the same time. I loved him, I did. I thought we were happy, and I guess we were. I just wasn't enough for him.

I wish Elaine were here. She was always my calming voice of reason. I stressed over leaving her and moving here with Pete. She insisted that I needed to live my life for me, and here we are six months later, she's gone and so is he, and that leaves me… alone. My legs tremble. Resting my back against the shower wall, I slide to the floor, burying my face in my knees, and let the tears fall. I cry for Elaine, for Pete, for the life I thought we were building.

Nothing ever stays the same.

FOUR

STAY IN the shower until the water runs cold. Slipping into my old comfort clothes, I dial room service and order some breakfast. I choose comfort food, biscuits and gravy with a side of bacon. I'd never had it until I went to live with Elaine. It quickly became my favorite. I make a mental note to pull out her old recipe and work at perfecting it. Breakfast finished, I grab my keys, phone, purse, and head toward the Corner Pocket. I'm going to be early, but I'd rather wait on Molly than her wait on me. She's given me a place to stay and a job; I owe her everything.

To my surprise, Molly is already at the Corner Pocket. She's sitting in her car talking on her cell phone. She waves, and I motion to let her know that I'll drive.

"Thanks," she says, after opening the passenger door and climbing in. "You want to see the place first, get an idea of what color paint you want?"

"Honestly, it could be shit brown with bright orange polka dots and I'd be good with it. Thank you so much, Molly. Really," I say for emphasis.

"You're doing us a favor actually. We've been meaning to get it together and just haven't done it."

"We need to talk about rent," I remind her.

"Why don't we go take a look first. Then you can decide if you think you can live there."

"I don't have the option to be picky right now."

"I'm sorry. I can't imagine what you're going through," she says softly.

Just like last night, the word vomit erupts. "I moved here for him, with him actually. We went to college together, and he was from here. We both work for his family's real estate business."

"Wait? What's this guy's name?"

"Pete Victor, you know him?"

She scoffs. "Yeah, I know him. He's an ass. We all went to school together. He thinks he's entitled."

"Yeah," I say softly.

"Saylor, I'm sorry. That was insensitive of me."

"No, you're right. I just wish I found out a little sooner, before I left it all for him."

"What about your family? Is moving back to Cincinnati out of the question?"

I hate talking about it, about my past. Molly is nice and has kind of taken me under her wing. Since I'm going to be living above her garage and working for her and her fiancé, the least I can do is tell her my background. "No family. I was in foster care until I was twelve. Well, I mean, technically I was still in foster care, but only one home. Elaine, she took me in. She was my social worker. She was my only family."

"Was?" Molly asks gently.

I swallow the lump in my throat. "Yeah, she passed away last month."

"Oh, Saylor." She places her hand on my arm. "I'm so sorry for your loss."

"Thank you. She was amazing. So, yeah, no family to speak of. My best friend, Tara, lives in Cincy still. She offered to let me stay with her, but I just can't go back there. Everything reminds me of Elaine. She was home, not the town."

"So you left there to come here after she passed?" she asks.

"No. Pete was always moving back home to work for the family business. He begged me to come with him. Convinced me it was the next step for us. I moved out of Elaine's house and moved here. I feel so damn guilty for leaving her. He fucked me over, and she was alone when she died." I feel the hot tears as they prick the back of my eyes. I blink hard, trying to keep them at bay.

"He's an ass. Elaine loved you, Saylor. I'm sure she was thrilled to know you had a good start at life, a job, your education. She would be proud of you."

"Would she? I mean, do you think she would be happy that I left the only home I've ever known, the only family I've ever known, to be left by my live-in boyfriend who is marrying his secretary/baby mama?"

"She would be. You know why?"

I don't answer her. My emotions are too strong, and my grip is slipping. I'm about to lose my shit in front of my new boss/landlord.

"She loved you first of all. Second, look at you. You're not sitting in that hotel room wallowing in self-pity. You're standing up, dusting off, and moving forward. She raised you to be strong and independent, and she would be damn proud of you for it."

"You didn't see me in the shower this morning, losing my shit," I whisper, but she hears me.

"True, but your entitled to break down, multiple times if necessary. Hell, how long did you say the two of you were together?"

"About three and a half years. We started dating sophomore year in college."

"See, that's a long damn time. You're human, Saylor. You have to grieve the loss of what could have been, but not the loss of that asshat. You deserve better."

I can't help but laugh at that. "Thanks, Molly."

"You're welcome. Turn right here." She points to the next road. "First house on the left."

"Wow, this place is nice," I say, looking at the sprawling brick ranch.

"Thanks. We bought it about two years ago. We remodeled it ourselves. Well, Jake remodeled it himself. I just assisted." She laughs.

"It's beautiful."

"Thank you, we like it. Pull up next to the detached garage." She points in front of us. "The people we bought it off of had a son in college who wanted his own space. They built him this apartment over the garage. It's pretty sweet."

I park in front of the garage like she said, and we both climb out. I follow Molly up the side steps and wait for her to unlock the door.

"Here we are, home sweet home." She grins.

"Wow, this is great and bigger than I was expecting."

"Yeah, it's like nine hundred square feet or something close to that. One bedroom, one bathroom, living room, eat-in kitchen, open concept as you can see." She waves her arms across the room. "It's all yours."

"How much?" I ask. I really want it. It's better than anything I could afford from an apartment complex.

"Jake and I talked about it last night, and really we're just happy to help you out. How about you buy the paint, and we'll call it good for the first month's rent?"

"Molly, this place is great. Where does it need paint?" I ask her. The walls are a cream color, and they look immaculate to me.

"The bathroom and bedroom need to be painted. So what do you say?"

"That's hardly fair. That's what, a hundred bucks in paint?"

She shrugs. "A hundred dollars a month it is. You're hooked up to our water and electric, so a contribution to that, say fifty a month? I can't imagine you would use more than that."

"Seriously? One fifty?"

"Sounds good to me." She holds out her hand for me to shake. I take it and smile at her. "Now, let's take a look at those two rooms and go get some paint. I'm helping. I got a ton of experience from our remodel."

"Don't you have to work today?"

"Nope. Jake has it under control. He knows we're painting, and then we're going to go pick up your stuff. So go ahead and call asshat and let him know we'll be there later and he shouldn't be."

"Molly, you don't have to do this."

"You're right, I don't have to. I want to. Come on, I'm good at it." She gives me a big goofy grin.

"I can't thank you and Jake enough for this, I mean…"

"You just did. We're glad to help. Now come on." She grabs my hand and pulls me first to the bathroom and then the bedroom.

She's right, they both need to be painted. "I think the cream works. Keep it neutral that way the next person doesn't have to paint again."

"Moving out already?" she asks.

"No." I laugh. "Just thinking ahead. It's my thing, you know. Nothing ever stays the same."

"I have a feeling things are about to change for you."

"Really? What makes you say that?"

"I have this feeling. I can't really explain it. I'm not psychic or anything," she says when she sees my not-so-convinced facial expression. "I'm a good judge of character, situations, and things like that. I'm usually right. Ask Jake."

"Yeah, right. He's going to agree with you regardless. He knows who keeps his bed warm at night."

"True story," she says with a laugh. "But for real, I see good things for you, Saylor."

"Let's go get some paint, crazy girl." I grab her arm and pull her out the door. I like Molly; she's easy to talk to and reminds me a lot of Tara. I need to think of something nice to do for her and Jake. They have saved me so much worry and stress. I'll think of something. I invested the money from Elaine's house so without the job at the bar, I'd be hosed. It was Pete's idea and although it was a good one, now the money is tied up and I can't access it for a few years without giant penalties.

"Did you text asshat?" Molly asks as soon as we get in the car.

"No, but I'll do that now."

Me: I'll be there later today to get my stuff. Don't be there.

Pete: Come on, Saylor. Can we not be adults about this?

Me: I don't know, can you? Were you acting like a responsible adult when you stuck your dick in Tabitha? Don't be there.

Pete: What has gotten into you? You're better than this.

Me: I know. You did me a favor. I'll text you when I'm done, and you can come back.

I toss my phone into the cupholder. It's time to get paint, a new coat for a new chapter in life.

FIVE
Rhett

"**B**out time you get here, boy," Gramps rumbles from his bed.

I chuckle. "How you doing, Gramps?" I ask from where I stand leaning against the doorframe in his bedroom.

"I'm fine." He coughs. It's one of those deep coughs that make you cringe because you know it hurts just from the sound.

"I can tell." I step further into his room and take the chair beside his bed.

"I don't need a sitter," he grumbles.

"I agree." He looks shocked.

"Well, then what the hell are you doing here? I told that son of mine and your mother that I didn't need no help."

"You might not, but who is going to run the distillery?"

"I can do it from here."

"Really?" I sit back in my seat and cross my arms. "You're going to run meetings barking like a seal?"

"I've done it before."

"I'm sure you have, but, Gramps, the doctor says your emphysema is getting worse and pneumonia on top of that, it's not good. Dad said they

33

wanted to keep you in the hospital but you refused."

"I have a—" He breaks off with a deep cough. "I have a business to run," he wheezes.

"How about you let me do that. I'll report in each day; you just worry about getting better."

"You know beer," he states matter of fact.

I try like hell to hide my smile. He's grumpy as fuck in his old age, but this illness is making it worse. "I know beer; I also know whiskey. It's been a few years since I've been here, but I know that place like the back of my hand."

"Things change," he says, defeated.

There, now we're at the heart of the issue. I'm a prick. I went from spending every single summer with him to none at all. I've been back for a few days here and there since college, but nothing like I used to. "I'm here now."

"So it seems." He coughs again.

"Can I get you anything?" I ask.

"I've been doing fine on my own."

He's really pissed, as he should be. I make a mental note to let Mom and Dad know that, once he's better, I'm going to stay a few more weeks, spend some quality time with him once he's feeling like himself again. "I'm sorry it's been so long," I finally say.

"Hmpf." He closes his eyes and turns away from me.

"Look, I'm here to help you get better. I'm not going away anytime soon. It would be a hell of a lot easier if you would just tell me where you are with things down at the distillery. Otherwise, I'm going to have to go down there and start digging to figure it out on my own."

"The hell you will, boy. You know beer, not whiskey," he says again.

"I know you. I know how you run your business. I can figure it out, and what I don't know, I have you to help me. So, which is it going to be? You going to help me out or am I going to have to jump in feet first and wing it?"

"I don't need you here," he grumbles. "I can work from here."

"I'm sure you can, but not efficiently. Not and run the distillery the way it needs to be ran. Let me do this for you, Gramps."

"I'm tired, please leave me be," he says, still facing the opposite wall.

With a heavy sigh, I leave him to rest. Back down stairs, I grab my bags that I left in the foyer and head to the west end of the house. That's where the room is that I always used to stay in when I was here. Pushing open the door, nostalgia falls over me as I take it in. The same full-size bed with the blue and white checkered comforter sits in the center of the room. My old ball glove and bat are sitting on top of the bookshelf. So many memories. Walking further into the room, I take a look at the corkboard above the desk. A picture of me and my old buddy Jake, Gramps, and Jake's Uncle Jerry, all of us holding our fishing poles, is still pinned there. I don't remember exactly which summer it's from, but I remember those fishing trips fondly. I'll have to ask Jake if he and his uncle want to get together once Gramps starts feeling better.

I make quick work of unpacking before jumping in the shower and washing off the travel. My plan is to head over to the distillery and check on things. Dad didn't when they were here, leaving that for me. I guess, even though they get along, there is still some animosity about the distillery between the two of them. Gramps is grumpy as hell, and although some of it is his illness, the rest lies on me. I'm a prick, have been anyway, but I'm going to make it up to him.

I check on him one more time before leaving. He's sleeping, so I leave him be. I'm just going to go in for a few hours and see where things are. I assume Dorothy is still his assistant. Sharp as a whip, that one. I'm sure she can catch me up to speed.

The drive to the distillery is a familiar one. Things have changed, yet remain the same. What used to be a huge lake in my eyes as a kid, is now just a really big pond in my eyes as an adult. Baxter's Distillery is located on over one hundred acres, and Gramps has all kinds of perks for his employees, the pond being one of them. There's also a park and a full gym with twenty-four-hour access to employees. There is a full-time cafeteria, and one weekend a month, he has family day. You can bring your family to tour the facility, enjoy the park, the pond, and all the other amenities. As I drive to the main building that houses the offices, I take in the fall scene; it looks like a damn postcard. Gramps always used to describe it to me, but I've never been able to see it. I was always in school, and by the time we would come to visit for Christmas, all the leaves were gone. I can still hear him telling me to always enjoy the beauty of nature. Gramps is one of a kind for sure.

Pulling my rental into the spot marked reserved for Rhett Baxter, I can't help but grin. Gramps used to say this was reserved for me when I came to visit. For years, I believed he had the sign there just for me. As I got older, I caught on of course. This is the first time I've driven and parked in this spot. I may not be the right Rhett Baxter, but my lips tilt in a smile all the same.

Inside, I take the elevator to the top floor, where I know I'll find Dorothy sitting outside of Gramps office.

"Well, I'll be," she says as soon as I step off the elevator. "Rhett Baxter, you get your little hind end over here and give me a hug." She stands from her desk and walks around to greet me.

I laugh. "Hey, Dorothy, how have you been?"

"My goodness, you're not so little any more. It's been too long." She playfully smacks my arm. "I'm good, dear. How is your grandfather? The last time I spoke to him, he had his undies all in a bunch. I assume that's why you're here?"

"I guess you could say that. He needs rest, doctor's orders, and well, he didn't want the help, but Dad overruled him and here I am."

She studies me. "How do you feel about that?"

I give her a smile, the one that usually gets me what I want with the ladies. "It's been too long, and you're more beautiful than ever."

"Oh, hush you." She waves her hand in the air before taking her seat back behind her desk.

I chuckle. "I miss this place. He's not impressed that I'm here."

"He misses you." She says is so matter of fact, that I feel like an even bigger tool for not visiting sooner.

"So, where are we? Staffing, production times?" I fire off questions.

"How much do you know, Rhett?" Concerns laces her voice.

"What do you mean? How much do I know? About running the distillery?"

She shakes her head, a solemn look on her face. "No, child. He's been ill for a while now. He swore to me that he told all of you."

I stand stock-still waiting for her to say more. I'm not even sure I'm breathing. When she doesn't elaborate, I find my voice, although it's rough. I ask, "What are you talking about, Dorothy?"

"Oh dear." She places her hand over her heart.

"Dorothy." I say her name with authority.

"He's going to be angry with me, but you need to know." She takes a deep breath. "Two years ago, he was diagnosed with Parkinson's Disease. His symptoms are getting worse to where he loses his balance. It's hard for him to even hold a pen."

"Parkinson's," I repeat.

She nods. "Afraid so. That stubborn old coot refused to tell any of you, and lied to me about it. And now with his emphysema and the pneumonia on top of that, it's taking a toll on his body."

Needing to sit down, I take a seat in one of the many chairs reserved for guests who are here to see my grandfather. Why didn't he tell us? Even more so, I should have fucking known. If I'd visited, I would have seen the signs. I should have been here. Fuck!

"Can he… I mean, what do we do now? Has he seen a specialist?"

She nods. "Yes, dear. There is nothing more they can do. He takes medication that helps with the tremors most of the time. The pneumonia is a setback, and a serious one. Many his age, who fall ill to pneumonia with Parkinson's, well, they don't seem to come out on the other side of the illness," she says as gently as she can.

Her words sink in. This could take his life. I've been living it up, partying at college and then engrossing myself into the brewery, too damn busy being me to come and see the man who shaped who I am today. He was my best friend growing up. My heart is racing, as is my mind with what I can do. I need to speak to his doctors, get their credentials, find another doctor who can help him.

"Rhett." Dorothy's raises her voice, bringing me out of my mental debate. "We've taken him to the best doctors. He's receiving the best care. What he needs is to not stress about things here. You being here, that's what you can do for him. Make sure this place flourishes."

"I wish he would have told us," I say, fighting back the emotions that are fighting to break free. Dorothy is like a grandmother to me and has been with Gramps for years. Her and Grams were best friends before she passed, at least that's what she's always told me. It was before I was old enough to remember her.

"He's a stubborn man, that one. Now, go on in." She points to his office door. "I have a few items that need taken care of. I also have a few contracts for you to sign. There is no governing board, as he is the sole owner, and I know as sure as I stand here that he would agree with letting you step in. His feelings are hurt, but he knows deep down this is the best until he's better."

"You think so? Is he going to be able to come back? How bad is he?"

"I don't know, my dear. He has good days and bad days, but this has really got him down. I'm glad you're here, Rhett, for him and for the business." She gives me a small sad smile and points toward the office door again. "I'll be right behind you."

Feeling like a kid again, I do as I'm told and wait for her in his office. Sitting behind his desk brings back memories of times I would sit here and spin around until I was so dizzy I couldn't walk. Gramps would just laugh that deep belly laugh of his and tell me that I looked good in his seat and that someday maybe it would be mine. He has three framed pictures on his desk. One of Grams, it's of their wedding day, one of me and my parents, and then one of him and me. It's of the two of us sitting in the grass around the pond, both wearing big grins. That was my last summer here.

"Ready?" Dorothy asks.

Looking up, I see her arms loaded down. I stand to help her, but she just shakes her head and drops the load on the desk.

"Right, let's do this," I say, grabbing a pen from the desk drawer. For over four hours, Dorothy and I comb through reports, contracts, staffing, and what feels like a million and one other items that needed approval. Production is low, product is on backorder. Apparently, there is a machine down and no one wanted to bother Gramps with the order to sign off to fix it.

Dorothy packs up her stack and stands now that we've been through every piece of paper. "I'm glad you're here, Rhett. We needed you. He needs you." Those are her parting words as she carries the mound of paperwork back to her desk, leaving me alone.

SIX

Saylor

OLLY AND JAKE are godsends. Last week, Molly and I picked up paint and had ourselves a little painting party. Wine was involved. It was a good time. It's been a week since I met them, and I feel like I've known them for years. I only broke down once at the end of the night. Molly, being the sweetheart she is, just hugged me tight and assured me everything was going to be okay.

Turns out she was right, but I wouldn't be this functional without her and Jake. Within two days of meeting her, I had a freshly painted, fully furnished apartment. All my stuff was picked up from Pete's, and to my surprise, he wasn't there, just like I asked him not to be. He left me a dozen roses on the counter with a note saying he was sorry and hoped we could be friends. Funny thing, when we were together, he never sent me flowers. Not once.

I insisted that I start work on Saturday night. Molly told me to take some time, but I didn't want more time to sit and think and feel sorry for myself. I knew I had to keep moving, keep pushing forward. That night, the three of us, Molly, Jake, and I, worked the bar. By the end of the night, they deemed me able to work on my own. Slinging drinks is slinging drinks, and I just so happen to be good at it. I worked my ass off to pay for college. Elaine used to tell me that working hard for what you want is an honor. You have to put the blood, sweat, and tears in to appreciate all that you have. Those are words I try to live by, even with my previous failed relationship.

When I got here tonight and found out that Anna had called in because her kid was sick, I pushed Jake and Molly out the door. They had both been here all day. I was sure I could handle it and promised that if things got crazy I'd call them and they could come rescue me. It's just a short ten-minute drive to their place—well, and now mine.

Tonight, being a Monday, is slow as usual in my experience. Most people went back to work today after the weekend. It's not usually until mid to late week when the evenings start picking up. It's as if the entire world tries to be responsible the first half of the week, but true to nature, the stress of life, jobs, family, and whatever else plagues them brings them in for a drink. Most just a few to relax or shoot the shit with friends, others as their only means to unwind.

This evening there has been a few regulars, who I've already learned in my short time here. Those are the customers that come every day regardless of what's going on in their lives. Some might have an addiction, others no one to go home to. Some just want a beer to relax before going home after a long day.

I'm wiping down the bar, trying to stay busy or at least appear to be, when the door opens, bringing in a chill from the cold November air. Looking up at my next customer of the night, my breath hitches. Holy shit, this guy... he's tall—well over six feet—with dark hair, longer on the top and a mess as if he's been running his fingers through it all day. He's built, if the way his black dress shirt clings to him is any indication. He smirks when he sees me looking, so I avert my gaze and lift the bowl of peanuts that I've already wiped under what feels like a thousand times tonight. It's not until he takes a seat at the bar, right in front of the bowl of peanuts that has my full attention, that I look up at him.

Damn.

Those eyes.

Brown as if the sunlight were shining off a glass of whiskey. They seem to sparkle as I stand before him, just staring at the brown orbs that seem to have me mesmerized.

"What can I get you?" I ask. My voice is clear and professional, regardless of how I'm lusting after him. In a word, he's... pretty. I know it's not the word you would use to describe a man, especially a man's man, you know, the rough rugged type, not that I know that's his type, but first appearances and all that.

"Whiskey." His voice is deep and the rumbles race through me, sending shivers down my spine.

"That's vague. You have a preference?" I ask, still maintaining indifference even though I feel anything but.

Those warm brown eyes, so much the color of the drink he's just ordered, capture mine. "Baxter's, any of them. Make it a double."

All right then. Baxter's it is. It's a local distillery, and Molly tells me it's a local favorite. I'm not new to Baxter's; we served it at Tuff's too. Although not as much as here at the Corner Pocket. Turning my back to him, I grab the bottle of Baxter's that I've served the most in my short time here. Grabbing a tumbler, I pour him a double. Setting the bottle back on the shelf, I take a deep breath before turning to serve his drink. "Here you go. You want a tab?" I ask.

"Do I look like I need a tab, Short Stack?" he asks.

Asshole! "Not my place to judge, just to serve. It's six dollars for the whiskey." I turn and walk away to refill the beer of one of the locals, Bart. He's been here every day that I've worked. He's a nice older man. Molly told me he lost his wife a few years ago. He comes in and sips his beer for the companionship. "Another, Bart?" I ask.

"Sure thing, girlie, this is my last of the night," he says.

I pour his beer and cash him out, ignoring the pull of this sexy stranger's intoxicating eyes. I take my time wiping down the opposite end of the counter, trying like hell not to look down at the bar at Whiskey Eyes. And who does he think he is with that nickname? Short Stack? I'm short, at five four, but not terribly so. Of course, from the looks of him, he's a good foot taller than I am.

"You keep whipping that counter, it's going to crack," he says, throwing back the rest of his whiskey.

"Crack?" I ask, confused. "Another?"

He shakes his head. "Yeah, crack. You're going to rub it thin." He smirks. "You're good at that, rubbing," he adds.

Great. He's one of those. I've heard more sexual innuendos to last a lifetime. Disappointment washes over me. Figures, with his looks, he's also a jerk. I know his type—entitled, never want for anything because it just falls at his feet. Sure, I'm a little jaded on the male species right now, but this guy is making it easy. I ignore his comment and keep wiping down the counter. It doesn't need it, but the alternative is striking up a conversation with this guy, and well, I'd rather make myself look busy. He slides a ten-dollar bill across the bar.

"Thanks, Short Stack," he says, bringing the glass to his lips and swallowing the last little drop.

I watch his lips—full kissable lips surrounded by a dark beard. My vocabulary is seriously lacking as the only word I can come up with is pretty. The corner of my mouth lifts as I try to keep from grinning. I wonder what Whiskey Eyes would think of me calling him pretty? A shot to his ego, I'm sure. The phone rings, pulling me from my thoughts. "Corner Pocket," I say in greeting.

"Hey, Saylor, it's Molly, just checking in on things."

I smile. "I've got it under control. Poor Harold is bored to tears in the kitchen," I tell her.

"Good. Well, not good being slow, but good you're doing okay. Oh, you know what I mean." She laughs.

"That I do," I say with a chuckle. "Did you all go out to dinner like I told you to?" I ask her.

"We did. Nothing fancy, just pizza, but it was good. We're actually on our way back. Want me to bring you the leftovers?"

"No, I'm good. I think I'll have Harold grill me a burger or something. Don't want him feeling like we don't need him."

"Good plan. All right, call if you need anything."

"Will do." I end the call and turn to take in the bar. Everyone is gone now except for the sexy asshole. I do my best to ignore him and busy myself putting glasses away.

"Jake around?" he asks once I've finished. I know he was watching me; I could feel his eyes.

"Nope," I say, ignoring him as I walk from behind the bar and clean the two tables that were occupied tonight. When I get back to the bar, I see that Mr. Brooding is walking toward the door. Grabbing his glass, I see his cell phone sitting on the bar. "Hey, Whiskey!" I call out, not knowing his name. He stops abruptly and slowly turns to face me. The look on his face is one of resignation and maybe… bitter? I hold up his phone. "Forgetting something?"

He stalks back toward the bar. Reaching out, he grabs his phone, and my skin tingles where our fingers touch. He pauses, those whiskey-colored eyes boring into me. He doesn't say another word before turning and walking away. I watch him as he goes—trust me, if you were me, you would too. He fills out those jeans like it's his job. My body is tingling from his brief touch. Arms to the side, I shake them out, as if I can rid myself of the feeling of his hand on mine. Whoever that sexy stranger is, he's not for me. I wouldn't ever survive him.

SEVEN
Rhett

WITH MY PHONE clinched tight in my hand, I stalk out of the bar. As soon as the cool air hits me, I stop and suck in a deep breath. After a long day of travel and getting caught up to speed at the distillery, I just wanted a drink and maybe to shoot the shit with my old buddy Jake. Sure, I should have called, but I still needed that drink. What I wasn't expecting was that little spitfire behind the bar. Hair black as night and eyes as blue as the sky, I noticed her the minute I walked in. She didn't know me from the next guy and treated me so. I liked it, more than I would have ever imagined. I like the fire inside of her and how she's not afraid to speak her mind. Usually women tell me what they think I want to hear. They fawn all over me and are willing to drop to their knees and suck my cock. All I have to do is say the word; some try on their own. Sure, I've enjoyed it. What single guy wouldn't? But it's getting to the point where I don't know who to trust. I'm far from celebrity status, and it's grueling to date when people know who I am, who know my family's background. I can't imagine what the A-list celebrities go through. No wonder there are so many divorces and prenuptial agreements in Hollywood.

When she called out for me, calling me Whiskey, I froze. Then I remembered there is no way this girl knows who I am. It had to be because of the drink I ordered. She doesn't strike me as the type to be a gold digger, or one of those women who are looking to be a trophy wife. Definitely not. There is too much sweetness lurking beneath the surface.

She's a tiny thing. My cock twitched at the anger in her eyes when I called her Short Stack. Sure, she's short compared to my six feet four, but she's also stacked. Firm, round tits behind that T-shirt. The name fits her. Maybe if I'm lucky, she'll be working the next time I stop by to see Jake. I'll need to make that happen soon.

Real soon.

I call a cab, which in this town will cost me an arm and a leg, but driving isn't an option. That's all either company needs is a scandal with me being caught driving drunk or worse. Not going to happen. Leaning against the building, I pull out my phone and scroll through my e-mail while waiting for the cab to arrive. I'm barely through my reply to Carrie to answer her long list of questions when the cab pulls up. I'm pleasantly surprised and relived. I'd contemplated going back inside to wait, but I don't trust myself to not pursue the sweetness that is the bartender. Not tonight anyway. Sure, she was full of piss and vinegar, but I could work that out of her. Adjusting my thickening cock, I climb into the back of the cab and give him the address.

Back at the house, I kick off my shoes and head upstairs to check on Gramps. He's awake, watching television. "Hey, you're up," I say, stepping into his room.

"I'm up," he confirms.

"How you feeling?"

"Fine."

"Can I get you anything?"

"No."

He's still being short with me. "I went to the distillery this afternoon. Met with Dorothy and went over a few things."

He turns to face me. His face showing his age, the wrinkles around his eyes, the lines across his forehead. He looks as though he's aged twenty years since the last time I saw him. It was last Christmas, but it's been years since I've been here to stay and visit outside of a holiday. Shame hits me in the gut.

"I told you I have it under control."

"You did, but I'm here, so you might as well let me help you."

"Go home, Rhett."

His voice is void of any emotion, causing a tightness in my chest. This isn't my Gramps. This isn't the loving old man who was so full of life and would take me fishing. This man, he's frail and angry. I can't help but think that I caused this. He and I were two peas in a pod until I changed the dynamics. I let life, college, and work take me from what matters most.

Family.

"Gramps, I'm here. I'm not going anywhere. I'm here until you don't need me anymore. Maybe when you get to feeling better, we can take the boat out," I suggest.

"I don't need you." With that, he turns away from me, ending our conversation.

I take him in as he lies there. His breathing is labored, but I don't know if that's from anger or the illness. He's yet to cough tonight, so I'll take that as a step in the right direction. "Night, Gramps. I'll see you in the morning." Standing, I place my hand on his shoulder and give it a gentle squeeze before slipping out of his room.

The house is eerily quiet as I make the walk to my room, which depresses me even more. I never remember Gramps's house being quiet. Even if it was just the two of us, there was always a game on the television or music. Gramps is a fan of old bluegrass and always had it playing. Now, it's just quiet.

In my room, I strip out of my clothes and head straight to the shower to wash away the day. The distillery has taken a back seat, and the production numbers show it. I wish I would have known sooner. Then again, if I was reaching out and visiting more, I probably would have known. Resting my head against the shower wall, I let the hot spray rain down on my back and neck, hoping to ease some of the tension. I stand there until the water runs cold, which is starting to become a habit. Snatching a towel and quickly drying off, I rummage through my suitcase to find a pair of boxer briefs. If I were at home, I wouldn't bother, but if Gramps happens to need me in the middle of the night, I want to at least have the family jewels covered.

Climbing into bed, exhaustion hits me. Grabbing my phone, I set my alarm for six in the morning. Gramps always was an early riser. I want to eat breakfast with him before heading into the distillery. He might say he doesn't want me here, or need me, but I know better. Even more so, I want to be here. I just need to prove it.

Startled awake by the alarm on my phone, I slip my arm from underneath the covers and slap at the nightstand until I feel the offending device under my fingertips. Lifting my head, I open one eye and work to turn off the alarm before letting my head fall back against the pillow. I fell asleep as soon as my head hit the pillow, but it feels as if that was only minutes ago, when in reality it was a little over six hours. Rolling onto my back, I force both eyes open and stare up at the ceiling. It's still dark outside, my room lit with only the dim light of the moon. Remembering that I want to eat with Gramps before heading to the distillery, I climb my tired ass out of bed and get dressed for the day.

As I get closer to the kitchen, I hear movement. I'm ready to yell at Gramps to get back in bed when I round the corner and see Rosa. She's been my gramps's housekeeper for as long as I can remember. "Rosa."

She jumps and turns to face me with her hand clapped against her chest. "Rhett, boy, you scared the life right outta me. Come here and give me a hug." She opens her arms wide.

I can't help the grin I'm sporting as I make my way toward her. Bending, I wrap my arms around her and hug her tight. "Nice to see you," I say, standing to my full height.

"It's been too long, child. Come, sit." She points to the island. "Look at you all grown up and handsome."

"I agree, it's been too long," I say, taking a seat. "How have you been, Rosa?"

"Oh heavens, just fine. Spoiling my grandbabies. I've got four now." She beams with pride.

"Four, wow, so Gabbie or Rick?" I ask, referring to her two children.

"Both. Gabbie has two little girls, and Rick a boy and a girl."

"Congrats, Grandma," I say, smiling at her.

"Thank you. What about you, dear? Married? Kids?"

"No to both." I'm ashamed that she doesn't already know this. Just another reminder that I haven't been here. What's worse is Gramps knows these things. He's not been talking about me. Sadness washes over me when I realize how selfish I've been.

"You work too much. You need to visit more often; he needs you," she scolds me.

I'm hit again with the reality of how my actions have hurt my grandfather. "Yeah, I let life get in the way, but I'm here now," I assure her.

"How long are you staying?"

"It was just going to be until Gramps gets better, but I'm thinking it would be nice to hang out, you know, spend some time with him once he's better."

"Can you do that? What will your parents think? You work for them, right?"

I nod. "I do, and it doesn't matter what they think. It's what I'm going to do."

"But who will cover for you?"

"They'll be fine, Rosa. Mom is taking on my role until I return. She's enjoying it, trust me," I say with a laugh.

"How about some breakfast?" she asks, taking my word for it.

"I was actually going to eat with Gramps. I assume he eats up in his room?"

She nods. "That he does. Today he's having oatmeal and wheat toast."

"That sounds great. Can I help? I'd like to take it up to him if you don't mind."

Her smile is soft and comforting, reminding me so much of my childhood. "You just sit there and keep me company. Won't take but a few more minutes, and I'll have you all set."

For the next five minutes, we talk about her grandkids, and she asks how my parents are doing, how I like my job, just catching up.

"Here you go," she says, setting a tray with an oatmeal breakfast for two in front of me. "Now, he's a little surly, so just ignore him."

I laugh. "Yeah, he's something all right. He's angry," I say, picking up the tray.

"Rhett, he misses you."

I sigh. "I know. I've missed him too. I realize now I should have visited more. That's on me, but I'm going to fix it." With that, I stand and head for the stairs to eat breakfast with Gramps.

The door is cracked, and I see the glow of the television. "Knock, knock," I say and push the door open with my hip. "I thought we could eat breakfast together." I set the tray on the side table beside his bed.

"Where's Rosa?" he asks.

"In the kitchen. She made this." I scoot the hospital-style table closer so that it's over his bed and he can access his food.

Once I know he can reach his, I grab my plate and begin to eat. "Did you watch the game last night?" I ask, referring to the highlights of last night's NFL game playing on TV.

"No." The one-word answer is all I get as he stares at the TV.

"Are you not going to eat?" I ask.

"Not hungry."

"Come on, Gramps. Rosa went through all this trouble." I set my plate back on the table.

"Good morning," Rosa says cheerfully from the doorway.

"Rosa," Gramps greets her, and the change in his voice and attitude is obvious.

"What's this I hear? You're not hungry?" she asks, fussing with his pillow.

"I'll eat later," he tells her, continuing to ignore my presence.

"Nonsense, you two used to do this all the time," she gushes. "Brings back good memories." Rosa picks up his plate and hands it to him. "Now, eat up." She holds it out for him until be begrudgingly takes it from her. "Much better. Now, I'll be back in a few with your medication." With that, she leaves us alone.

"Anything you need me to take care of today at the distillery? Anything you want or need updated on?"

"If I do, I'll call my staff and handle it. You can go back home to your beer."

"Look, Gramps, I know you're upset, and I understand why. I should have been here more than just a holiday here and there. I'm sorry. I'm here now, and I'm not leaving no matter how indifferent you are to me." I watch him as he stares straight ahead at the television. No reply, no facial expression, just... blank stares. Releasing a heavy sigh, I grab my dishes and leave him be.

"Where are you going?" Rosa asks as I pass her in the hallway.

"To work. He refuses to talk to me. Keep me updated, will you, Rosa?"

"He'll come around, child. His feelings are hurt, but he misses you."

I nod. "I'll be home later. Thanks for taking care of him." I give her arm a gentle squeeze and head to the kitchen to drop off my dishes and head into work.

EIGHT

'M WORKING ON finding my new normal. Each day, the pain of what Pete did to me fades just a little. He's called me a few times, and I've ignored every single one of his calls. However, the voice mails are rather entertaining. He gives reasons such as "calling to catch up" and "we get to find out the gender next month." I've started deleting them without even listening to them. He's a selfish asshole, and I honestly don't know how I didn't see it before now. Tara's theory is that I just latched on to the security of being in a relationship. Maybe she's right. She suggested that I talk to someone, a therapist, but honestly, I'm okay. Pain no longer slices through my chest when he calls or texts, and I no longer wake up missing him.

It's been two weeks today, and I'm finding that I'm okay. I expected it to take longer, but honestly, when I look at the bigger picture, he wasn't my soul mate. Hell, I'm not sure they exist. Tara and Molly tell me otherwise. I'm still on the fence. Even so, I'm not sure it's worth the heartache and pain when it ends. In my experience, it always ends. I lost my parents, Elaine lost Henry, I lost Elaine and Pete. I could even go as far as saying I lost Tara. Sure, we're friends, but honestly, how often am I going to make it to visit her?

The pain of losing Elaine, well, it's there, as I fear it will always be, but each day I learn to cope a little better.

Live with the loss.

Live without her.

My mind goes to the phone call I had with Tara last night. Colin received a job offer, a transfer within his company. They're moving to Oregon of all places. She was adamant that the offer stands for me to go with them. She even offered to buy me a plane ticket to fly out next week for Thanksgiving. They leave this weekend, as Colin has to report on Monday. His parents are from Oregon, and they're staying with them until they find a place. I had to reassure her that I'm good here. I have Molly and Jake to thank for that. I don't know where I would be if I didn't wonder into the Corner Pocket that night. I would like to believe it was Elaine that led me there. Maybe it was fate. Whatever the reason, I owe them so much. I've been working as many shifts as I can and saving tips. I need to get out of their hair, even though they assure me that they wouldn't even notice I'm there if it wasn't for my SUV in the driveway. Still, I know I can't lean on their kindness and generosity forever.

Being alone on Thanksgiving is not the ideal situation, but it's one I have to get used to. Having a family is a dream, one I can honestly say I don't know if I'm brave enough to embark on. I've had enough loss and pain in my life. If the alternative is spending the day lounging and watching the parade on my own, I can live with that.

Looking around the apartment, I try to decide what to do today. It's just a little after seven in the morning, and I don't have to be at work until three. The apartment stays clean with just me, and I picked up groceries yesterday. My running shoes are sitting by the door. I used to run every day before moving here. Today is as good a day as any to get back in the habit. Quickly, I change into some cold weather leggings, grab a hoodie, lace up my Asics, and I'm out the door. I decide to drive to the park to run on the track. I make a mental note to talk to Molly and see if there are any other local places to run.

The November morning air is brisk, but I know once I get started, I'll be wanting to shed some layers, especially since it's been months since I've been for a run. Locking my SUV, I strap my phone to my arm, pull up my playlist, place my earbuds in my ears, and I'm off. I can feel the smile tip my lips. I love this, and the park is beautiful. Letting all the worries and all the pain fade away momentarily, I just enjoy feeling like me again.

Just past the half-mile marker, the paved trail dips down into a small valley with trees; most are void of leaves, but the few that remain are beautiful fall colors. The sun shines bright over the tree line. Closing my eyes, enjoying the feel of the heat on my face, I inhale and take it all in. My eyes are closed for mere seconds, but that doesn't matter. Before I can open them, I'm running into something tall and, from the feel of my hands on his chest, muscular. My eyes pop open. "I'm so sorry. I... " I suddenly lose my ability to talk when I see it's him. Whiskey Eyes from the other night.

"Careful, Short Stack." He glares down at me. His hands are on my shoulders to steady me, keeping me from falling on my ass.

Once my feet are grounded, I pull my hands from his chest and jerk my earbuds out of my ears as I back away. "I'm sorry, I wasn't watching where I was going."

"Why in the hell were your eyes closed? Do you not understand how dangerous that is?" He's scowling at me.

"It was maybe five seconds. If you knew my eyes were closed, you should have moved out of the way," I fire back.

He laughs. "Right, this is my fault. Noted." He shakes his head.

"Yes, it is. You knew my eyes were closed, you could have stepped to the side." I place my hands on my hips and glare at him the best that I can. I try like hell not to melt from those whiskey eyes that seem to be boring into me. Damn, he's a gorgeous asshole.

"Whatever you say, sweetness. Word of advice. A woman running alone should always be aware."

He's pissed, and yeah, he's got a point, but I'm pissed too. This could have been avoided if he just stepped out of the way or went around me. "Noted," I throw his words back at him. "Catch you later, Whiskey." Shoving my earbuds back in my ears, I don't look back as I continue on the trail to finish my run. My happy mood is gone as I think about the way he acted. Sure, I should have had my eyes open, but it was merely seconds, and he didn't need to be a jerk about it. It was an accident.

By the time I'm back at Molly and Jake's, or I guess my place, I'm still fuming.

"Hey, Saylor, go for a run?" Molly asks as I climb out of my SUV. She's coming down the front steps and walking toward her car.

"Yep." I say it with attitude, and I don't mean to. Closing my eyes, I take a deep breath. "Yes, sorry, just irritated."

"What happened? Pete?" she asks.

I walk over to her where she's standing by her car. "No, this jerk. He was actually in the bar my first night I worked alone. He was an asshole then, not sure why I expected anything different."

"Saylor, focus." She places her hands on my shoulders. "Did he hurt you?"

"Who hurt you?" Jake asks, walking up behind Molly.

Great. "No, I'm not hurt. He didn't hurt me; he's just an asshole." I go on to explain the story.

"So you were running with your eyes closed?" Jake asks.

"Yeah, and he'd seen that. He could have moved."

"Listen, Say, I happen to agree with him. Maybe his delivery was off, but it's not safe. I know it's daylight, but there are some crazy motherfuckers out there. If you're running alone, even if you're not, you need to be alert. Do you have mace?" he asks. I can hear the concern in his voice, see it in the way his brow is furrowed.

"I agree," Molly says. "Jake bought me some mace for when I run. I would have gone with you," she tells me.

I exhale a heavy sigh. "I know you're both right, but this guy, he was pissed like me even being on the trail was an issue."

"You said he's been in the bar?" Molly asks. "Was he bothering you then? You don't think he followed you, do you?"

"No," I say quickly. "Both incidents were coincidental, I'm sure. He's just... so damn irritating."

"If he bothers you again, or if this is a pattern, you need to tell me. You both need to be alert," Jake says, pulling Molly back against his chest and kissing her temple.

Jealousy slams into me. Just a twinge, but it's there all the same. Even when I was with Pete, I never had that—the affectionate, loving, and concerned boyfriend. Jake is definitely one of the good ones.

"We're headed to the grocery store. You need anything or want to come with us?" Molly asks.

"No, I went yesterday. I'm going to go shower and maybe take a nap before work tonight."

"We'll be there tonight as well, so we can all ride together if you want,"

Jake offers.

See, one of the good guys. "Thanks, I'll see you guys later." With a quick hug from Molly, I head to my garage apartment. After a shower and a bagel with cream cheese, I settled on the couch. Curled up under a throw, I grab the remote and flip through the channels. Nothing. Daytime TV leaves much to be desired. Frustrated, I turn off the TV and settle in for a nap before my shift, still trying to find my new normal.

"So, what are you doing for Thanksgiving next week?" Molly asks a few hours later. We're both serving drinks tonight, while Jake is in the back working on the order.

I hesitate, not wanting her to feel sorry for me. "Tara invited me to Oregon, but I passed. I figure I'll just have a lazy day lounging around the house."

"You're going to be alone?" she asks softly.

Molly knows my history, but I don't know if she really understands how alone I really am. "No family." I shrug, as if saying the words doesn't cause an ache deep in my chest.

"Saylor," she whispers.

I hold up my hand to stop her. "I'm good, Molly. I promise. I've never had a large family. It was just Elaine and me. This is normal. It's all I've ever known." It's true, I've never known anything different, but it still hurts. The emptiness is still there, still new, and the pain still beats in my chest from the loss of Elaine, the only mother and the only family I've ever had.

"You're not alone, Say. Not anymore. If you won't go see Tara, you're going to be with us. Jake and I, our families are not conventional. I don't speak to my parents. They're not happy with my life choice." She laughs humorlessly. "I was supposed to marry a politician, follow dear old mommy's footsteps and marry up. I'm not good enough for them." She pauses to collect her thoughts. We've talked about her family, but not much. "They say Jake isn't good for me. They refuse to see the way he loves me, the way I'm his first priority. I've never been happier. I don't need them to live a full life. Sure, I wish I had them in my life, but they made their choice." Closing her eyes, she takes a deep breath. "What I'm trying to say is that family is what you make it. Jake's upbringing was not anything to write home about. He has his uncle Jerry, who actually raised him. We've made our family with friends and people who look out for us, who care. It's not just blood that makes a family."

"I know," I whisper. "Elaine, she was… everything. I miss her," I admit.

Molly steps toward me and wraps her arms around me in a tight embrace. "Of course you do," she says softly.

"What's wrong?" Jake asks.

I can't help but laugh. He always has perfect timing.

"Nothing." Molly smiles up at him. "Saylor just agreed to spend Thanksgiving with us," she tells him.

"Molly!" I scold her.

"My uncle can cook, Say. You're in for a treat," Jake says.

"I don't want to impose."

"You're not," they both say at the same time.

"You're not," Molly says again. "We want you there." She leans into Jake. "I'm supposed to call Jerry tonight and finalize plans. I'll let you know what time to be ready."

I shake my head. It's hard to argue when I can see the sincerity in her eyes. Maybe this is my new normal.

NINE
Rhett

THESE LAST TWO weeks have been hectic. I'm not even sure Gramps knows the extent of what has been going on at the distillery. Numbers were down due to mechanical issues he said he would handle when he got back in the office. It's been weeks since he's be in. Thus, production is down, which leads to low sales. We can't keep up with the demand. Finally, this afternoon, the line was repaired, and we are back up and running. I've approved overtime to anyone who wants it to try to get our numbers back where they need to be. Two months the line has been down. That's a hell of a lot of production time, considering we run three shifts around the clock. Luckily, Gramps has a great staff and the volunteers are plentiful. I can only hope that having all hands on deck helps. It'll make tank clean-out faster, hence production times increase. At least that's my thought process.

When I pull up to the house, it's dark. I assume Rosa has gone home and the night nurse has taken her place. Gramps is recovering slowly but improves each day. He stays in his room—at least when I'm home that's where he spends most of his time. I still go to his room to eat breakfast with him every morning. I talk and hope he's listening. I get grunts every now and then and the ever constant, "You can go home," and "I don't need you here." I love the old man, but he's pissing me the hell off. I've admitted I should have been here, but damn it man, he's holding this grudge and taking this too far. I'm running his company, and he refuses to talk to me about it.

My phone vibrates in the cupholder. Shutting off the car, I grab it, seeing Dad's name on the screen. "Dad," I greet him.

"Son," he chuckles. "How are things?"

I sigh.

"That good, huh?"

"He's pissed. I get it, I do, but he needs to let it go."

Dad laughs. "I know his stubborn side all too well. I know we kept most of the drama from you, but why do you think I'm here in Tennessee at the brewery and he's there in West Virginia?"

"I've never seen this side of him." I rake my hands through my hair. Why does the old man have to be so fucking frustrating?

"You wouldn't." He chuckles. "He was your hero, next to me of course," he boasts.

"How long is he going to be like this?" I know my father can't really know the answer to the question, but I'm grasping at straws here.

"Hard to tell, son. He's always been stubborn. When I was younger, I felt it was easier to leave, start over on my own. I love him, he's my dad, but to work with him, I don't think we would have been able to pull it off. That's why I sent you. If anyone can get him to pull the stubborn stick out of his ass, it's you."

"Thanks for the vote of confidence. I think."

"You're a lot like him, Rhett. You've always known what you wanted and never stopped until you achieved it. It's in our blood as Baxter men."

"I should have been here more, I get that," I admit.

"Maybe. You also can't live your life for anyone but yourself. I'm just as guilty, but you two, you always had a special bond. He'll come out of it. It's only been two weeks."

"How's Mom doing?"

"You know your mother. She's loving it. Misses you, but she and Carrie are two peas in a pod. Taking the brewery by storm."

I can hear the affection in his voice. Mom has always been his biggest weakness. "And I'm sure you're letting them." I know he is.

He chuckles. "That I am, son. She's my light, and she gave me you.

She can do and have any damn thing she wants."

I shake my head, a smile on my face. "Sappy old man," I tease him.

"You just wait, son. One day you'll understand. In the meantime, just try to be patient. He'll come around."

"Tell Mom I love her," I say, knowing I need to get inside and see Gramps.

"Will do. Take care, son."

With that the line goes dead. Climbing out of the car, I head inside. There's a note from Rosa on the counter.

Rhett

He's had a good day. There's a pot roast in the Crock-Pot. He hasn't eaten. See you on Monday.

Rosa

Without the note, I would have found dinner. The entire house smells so fucking good it makes my stomach growl. Rosa is a fantastic cook, and I'm suddenly starving. Serving up two bowls of roast, potatoes, and carrots, I grab two bottles of water and head upstairs. "Knock, knock," I say, entering the room. "Rosa made her famous pot roast."

Gramps looks at me, no expression at all, then turns his attention back to the television.

"I hear you've had a good day."

"Hmpf." That's the standard reply I've been getting the last two weeks.

I busy myself setting his bowl and water on the table and move it over the bed so he can reach it. Grabbing mine from the dresser, I take a seat and begin to eat. "So, we got the line back up and running today. Finally. I approved overtime, so hopefully production numbers will go back up. It will take us a week or so to get back to where we were."

Nothing. No reply. He does however pick up his fork and begin to eat. I'll consider that progress.

The landline on the nightstand rings. "You want me to get that?" I ask. He grunts, so I take that as a yes. "Hello," I say.

"Who's this?" a gruff voice asks.

"This is Rhett. Who's this?"

"Rhett number three, is that you?" the gruff voice asks.

Immediately I smile. "Mason, how have you been?"

"Good. Good. You know, living the dream. Number one around?"

"He is. Hold on." I hold the phone out to Gramps. "It's Mason."

He reaches for the phone and puts it to his ear. At least I know he hears me when I talk. Or maybe he tunes me out and was just interested in who was calling to talk to him. I eat my food, and it's just as good as it smells. Eventually he hands the phone to me. I have no idea if Mason hung up, so I put it back to my ear. "You there?"

"Yeah. He's got a thorn in his ass, I can see." Mason laughs.

"Yep." No use in defending him. These two have been friends for years.

"Well, I'll tell you. We're coming there for Thanksgiving this year. We alternate his place and mine every year. This year it's his turn, which is convenient since he's not well. He doesn't need to be out and about. We keep it small; it'll be nice to have you here with us this year."

"Yeah," I say wistfully. "Should have done this sooner."

"You're here now, that's all that matters. I talked to Rosa earlier when he was sleeping. She's going to do all the shopping, and we'll do the cooking like always. We'll eat at one. I'll be there the night before to start the bird. Number one usually does it, but he's in no shape. I'll see you then."

The line goes dead. Mason has always been like a fucking hurricane, full of energy. I would have thought he would have slowed down in his old age. Apparently, retirement is good. Gramps places his empty bowl on the table in front of him. "You want more?"

"No." He coughs, turns off the TV, and rolls over.

Dismissed again. I gather our empty bowls and close the door lightly behind me. Needing to wash off this day, I head to my room for a hot shower. I stand there until the water runs cold, and it's not lost of me that this is definitely my routine. When I step out of the shower, my phone is ringing. Quickly, I grab a towel and rush into my bedroom to answer.

"About fucking time," Jake, my childhood friend, says as soon as I pick up.

"I was in the shower, dick," I fire back.

He laughs. "So what's the deal? You've been here for a few weeks now, and I've yet to see you in my bar."

"Two weeks, not even a full two weeks if you want to get technical, and I've been there, but you were not."

"When?"

"The day I got here. It was a hell of a day with Gramps being pissed and it being my first day at the distillery. I needed a drink."

"You shitting me?" he asks.

"Nope. I met that hot little bartender, dark hair, blue eyes, chip on her shoulder."

"Ah, you were here. That's Saylor, she's new. She's been through a lot. Great girl."

"Hot as fuck, but that attitude," I say, running the towel over my hair.

"I haven't noticed."

"I call bullshit. I know Molly is your end game, but come on man, you had to notice."

"She's easy on the eyes," he concedes.

"Hot as fuck," I say again, making him laugh. "So what's her deal?"

"Not my story to tell, my man."

That's Jake, noble to a fault. "So, how are things with the beautiful Molly?"

"She's beautifully perfect. What about you? What are you getting into tonight?"

"Holding down the damn couch. You?"

"I'm at the Corner Pocket, why don't you come out?"

"Is the hot bartender working?" Sure, she has an attitude, but I could get on board with seeing her again. She's perfect as long as she doesn't talk. She's a tiny thing, with curves in all the right places. That black as night hair and those blue eyes are what fantasies are made of. I still can't believe she was running with her eyes closed. She's lucky it was me. It could have turned out worse for her.

"No. My girl and Say are having a girls' night. Movies and whatnot. They're at home."

Damn. "Oh well, I guess I get to look at your ugly ass. Let me get dressed and check in with the night nurse. Then I'll be there."

"Catch you later," he says, and the line goes dead.

Quickly getting dressed, I go in search of the night nurse. She has her own room just down from Gramps. I find her in the kitchen. "Hi, how is he?" I ask her.

"I just checked in on him. He's sleeping."

"Good. I'm going out for a while. You're going to be here, right?" I know she is, but I just want to confirm to make sure.

"Yes, sir. I'll be here all night."

"Good. You have my cell if something comes up?"

"I do."

With that, I head to the garage. Drinks with an old friend is exactly what I need right now.

TEN

Saylor

GOT UP early this morning to make a couple of pies. It's something that Elaine and I did every holiday. I have her recipes memorized. I figured I could at least contribute to the meal today. I hate to go to anything like this empty-handed. Pete used to get irritated with me, saying it was tacky. I never agreed with him, which is why I did it regardless. Just another thing I overlooked, but now looking back, I see we really weren't compatible.

I'm just sliding into my knee-high boots when my phone rings. "H-hello," I say, hopping on one foot.

"Say?" Molly asks.

"Yeah." I laugh. "Sorry, I was trying to put my boots on."

"Try sitting." I can hear the humor in her voice.

"What's the fun in that?"

"Um, maybe because you won't fall on your ass?" she says.

"Good point." I sit down on the couch and finish sliding into my boots. "What's up?"

"Just seeing how close you are to being ready."

"I'm good. But can I bother you to come and help me for a minute?"

"Sure. Jake is going to get the truck started. I'll be right over."

"Thanks." Hitting end on the phone, I grab my wristlet and make sure my debit card, cash, and license are there, and place my phone inside. Downfall to leggings, no pockets. Grabbing my scarf that's more of a fashion statement than to keep me warm, I wrap it around my neck and call it good. Running back to my room, I grab my peacoat and slip it on just as Molly knocks on the door.

"Come in!" I yell for her.

"Damn, smells good in here. What is that?"

"I baked." I smile at her.

"You bake?" she asks surprised.

"What? I don't look like a baker?" I ask, feigning hurt.

"Sorry, that's not what I meant. I just didn't know, and you didn't have to," she says apologetically.

"I know that, but I wanted to. I appreciate being included. I'm not going to know anyone there, and I just thought… " I shrug, embarrassed.

"It's going to be small. Just us, Jake's uncle, his friend, and his friend's grandson. We are kind of tight-knit."

"That's actually a relief. I was worried there would be a ton of people and I would feel awkward and out of place. Thank you again for including me."

"So what kind of pies?" she asks, changing the subject. How she knows me so well already, I'm not sure. What I am is grateful.

"Pumpkin and apple."

"Seriously? Apple is my favorite, and pumpkin is Jake's. I might have to have dessert first," she says, lifting the pie closer to her face and smelling it before placing it back on the counter.

"Get your nose away from my pie, woman," I mock scold her.

"I can't help it. They smell so damn good. I'm starving, and let me tell you, Thanksgiving is one of my favorite holidays. A holiday to eat, yes please." She laughs.

"I have to agree with you. All right, I think I have everything." With that, we each grab a pie and carry it down to the truck.

"What you got there?" Jake asks. He sniffs the air in the truck. "Wait a minute, is that pumpkin pie?" He turns to look at me in the back seat.

"Yeah, I thought I should bring something. You know, as a thank you for the invite."

"Not necessary, but damn I'm glad you did. That smells so fucking good."

Molly is laughing. "Did you seriously sniff out that she had the pumpkin?" she asks him.

"Babe, a man's nose leads him to the goods."

"Try this one." She holds up the apple so he can smell it.

He closes his eyes. "I don't know. I have pumpkin on the brain, but it smells amazing."

"It's apple," she says proudly.

"How did you do that?" he asks, looking at me in the rearview mirror.

"Do what?"

"Choose both of our favorites?"

"They're both my favorites too. Besides, you can't have Thanksgiving without pumpkin pie and apple pie. It was Elaine's favorite too. We used to make them every year."

"Say, I—" Jake starts to speak, but I cut him off.

"It's fine," I rush to say. "It's hard. This is the first holiday without her, so I'm thankful for the two of you. If you hadn't included me, I would be sitting at home alone. Missing her. I'm still missing her," I go on. "But the not being alone part helps." I take a deep breath to get my emotions in check. "So thank you," I finally say.

"You're exactly where you should be." Molly turns to look at me. "I'm really glad you're here. Not just here in the truck on the way to dinner, but here with us. I'm glad you chose the Corner Pocket that night."

"Me too, Molly, me too." The remainder of the drive is short. Jake entertains us with his singing skills as we jam along to the radio. "You missed your calling," I say with laughter as we pull into the driveway of a huge house. "Holy shit, is this your uncle's place?" I ask. The house is two stories and looks like it's big enough for a family of about fifty.

"No." Jake chuckles. "Jerry lives in a small brick ranch just outside of town, the opposite of us. This is Baxter's."

"Wow, it's beautiful."

"Right?" Molly agrees.

Climbing out of the truck, I follow behind Jake and Molly. I'm nervous never having met any of these people. Hell, I met Jake and Molly just a mere few weeks ago. Maybe I shouldn't have come? Admittedly, sitting at home sounded about as fun as a colonoscopy. Still I can't help but wonder if this was the right choice? Sure, Jake and Molly are good with it, but the others? Taking a deep breath, I slowly exhale and take the final step to the front door, right behind Molly and Jake.

"About time you got here," a deep masculine voice says, and I freeze. I know that voice.

Shit. I keep my head down as my mind races with how to handle this. He's not going to want me here. My anxiety peeks. Maybe I can tell them I'm not feeling well and Jake will let me take his truck home? I can offer to come back and pick them up later. Shit. Shit. Shit.

"Saylor," Molly says, pulling me from my mental freak-out.

Looking up, I see three sets of eyes trained on me. I don't have to look at them to know; I can feel Jake and Molly watching me. But him with the deep, masculine voice, Whiskey, his cognac eyes are boring into mine.

"You," he says.

I can't get a read on him. His face is not showing how he feels about me showing up on his doorstep. His eyes never leave mine, and I know I should look away. I want to look away; I just… can't. "Hey, Whiskey," I say, finally finding my voice. Okay, so it might have helped just a tad that Molly tapped her elbow into my arm, pulling me from my daze.

"Short Stack," he says with that deep timbre.

"You all know each other?" Molly asks.

"He, uh, he came into the bar. He came looking for Jake," I manage to say.

"Short Stack here likes to run with her eyes closed," he says, crossing his arms over his muscular chest. The muscles in his arms bulge from the movement. I'm too busy looking at the arm porn on display to hear what they're saying.

"Say!" Molly says, laughing. "Rhett is the guy you were talking about on the trails the other day?"

I look at her, then back to Whiskey. "Yeah, if that's his name. I call him Whiskey."

"Why is that?" he asks, face still void of any emotion.

Holy fuck, this guy is intimidating. "Y-you ordered whiskey that night. I just—"

"So you really didn't know who I was?" he asks, interrupting me.

"How would I?" I counter. He seems shocked.

"Let's take this inside. It's cold as hell out here." Jake puts a hand on Rhett's shoulder and pushes him back. He steps out of the doorway and allows us to enter.

"What you got there, Mol?" Rhett asks, his voice much friendlier.

She holds up the apple pie in her hands. "Say made pies for dessert."

"Do you cook with your eyes closed, Short Stack?" he asks.

"It's Saylor," I correct him.

"Right, let's try this again. Saylor Keller, this is Rhett Baxter. Rhett, this is Saylor," Molly officially introduces us.

All thoughts of leaving and not being wanted leave my mind. I'm not going to give this asshole the satisfaction of knowing he drove me away. Instead, I hold out my hand. "Nice to meet you, officially."

He stares at my hand, and just as I'm about to pull mine away, he slides his over mine. His hands are huge and warm, and the contact causes awareness to course through my veins. He's gorgeous, as long as he keeps his mouth shut. I can't help the giggle that escapes my lips thinking about how I called him pretty in my head that first night.

"What's so funny?" he asks, still holding my hand.

"Just thinking." I try to pull my hand away, but he holds strong.

"Enlighten me."

"You really don't want me to," I warn him with a smile I can't contain.

He studies me. "Didn't I just say I did?" He stares me down.

Not letting him intimidate me, I decide to tell him. "Just thinking about my first impression of you. Well, other than the one where I thought you were a complete ass."

He scoffs. "Do tell."

"I can't wait to hear this," Jake says, looking way too interested in our conversation.

I pause. I'm in his home, I should be respectful. I shake my head. I can't tell him. Sure, it's not bad, but I can guarantee it's going to piss him off.

"Scared, Short Stack?" he taunts.

"You're pretty. That's what I thought the first time I met you."

"Pretty?" he asks.

I can tell I've knocked him down a few pegs and possibly offended him. His poor ego can't handle it. "Yep." I turn to look at Molly. "Where should we put these?"

I can see the laughter in her eyes. "This way." I don't wait for further instruction, following her down the hall.

We enter a kitchen that would have had Elaine smiling from ear to ear. She loved to cook; baking was her specialty. She would have loved to have this kitchen at her disposal.

"What was all that about?" Molly asks.

I shrug. "He's arrogant."

"He's not, I mean, not usually. I've only met him a handful of times over the years, but I've never seen him act like that."

"I just bring the asshole out in men then. Look at Pete."

"Trust me, Rhett may be arrogant, but he's nothing like Pete."

"You've found one of the good ones, Mol, Hold on to him."

"I plan to."

ELEVEN

Rhett

"**Y**OU'RE PRETTY. THAT'S *what I thought the first time I met you.*" Her words flash through my mind. I wasn't expecting that, and I'll admit she knocked me off kilter just a little. I don't know if I should be insulted or thrilled that she likes what she sees. Although, pretty isn't really how I like to be referred to.

"What's with you?" Jake asks.

"Explain that," I say.

"With Saylor, what is that?"

"She's irritating. I mean, who fucking runs with their eyes closed?"

"Did you see that her eyes were closed?" he asks.

"Yeah, who does that shit?"

"Then why didn't you stop? Or better yet, go around her?" he questions.

Because she's sexy as fuck. "She needed to learn how dangerous it is to run like that."

"And it was your job to show her?"

"Better me than some sick fuck that would have done way worse than catch her fall."

69

"Uh-huh, come on, Casanova." He smirks and walks away.

"Molly, you ready to leave my nephew for me?" I hear Jerry ask.

"Fuck off, old man," Jake retorts.

Shaking off my irritation, I head that way. Jerry is greeting Saylor as I walk in.

"And this one, who might this beauty be?" he asks, pulling Saylor into a hug.

"This is Saylor; she works at the Corner Pocket," Molly tells him.

"She's living in the garage apartment," Jake adds.

"It's a pleasure to meet you. I've heard so much about you." Saylor charms him with her smile.

"We're keeping her," he announces.

Everyone laughs but me. "Do we have to?" I ask, alerting them to my presence. I rake my eyes over Saylor, as if sizing her up, trying to decide if we should keep her. It's a good show, because really, I just want to check her out. She's in those tight pants that all the ladies are wearing these days, knee-high, black, fuck-me boots, and a long sweater. Sadly, it covers most of her ass.

"Number Three, get your ass in here and meet, Saylor."

Jerry and Saylor both turn to face me, giving me a full view. Although the sweater and the scarf hide her from me, I've seen her in a tight T-shirt. I know what's underneath—well, not skin, but fuck would l like to. "We've met," I say flatly.

"Jerry Mason," he holds his out for her. Of course, she takes it with a smile on her face. Jerry really lays on the charm when he brings her hand to his lips and kisses her knuckles.

"She's too young for you, old man," I goad him.

"Doesn't mean I can't appreciate a beautiful woman." He points at Jake. "This one is too territorial of my Molly."

"Mine," Jake practically growls at his uncle.

"See what I mean?" Jerry throws his head back in laughter.

"What can we do to help?" Molly asks.

"Birds on, everything else is already in the oven. I think I have it under control, all but dessert. I forgot about that, but I found a pecan pie in the freezer. I have it thawing as we speak."

"Saylor made pies," Jake tells him.

"What? Beautiful and she bakes?" Jerry asks.

Saylor blushes and my cock twitches.

"Where's Gramps?" I ask, trying to keep my dick from joining the conversation.

"Upstairs. He's coming down to eat with us." Jerry looks at me like I'm crazy.

"He's coming down?" I ask for clarification.

"Yeah, it's Thanksgiving." He says it like I should know better.

I should, and I would if the old man would talk to me. I had breakfast with him this morning before Jerry was up, and he's still shutting me out. How the hell was I supposed to know? I don't know how much longer this freezeout is going to last.

"Rhett, did you not offer our guests a drink?" Gramps's gravelly voice says from behind me. I turn to look at him. He's still pale, but the cough is better. I still feel like this illness has taken a toll on him.

"How you doing, Mr. Baxter?" Jake asks.

"None of that 'Mr. Baxter' nonsense. I'm fine," he tells Jake.

"It's good to see you again." Molly leans in and gives him a gentle hug. Pulling back, she points to Saylor. "This is our friend, Saylor. She's working for us now at the Corner Pocket."

"S—" He coughs. "Saylor," he tries again, "nice to meet you."

"You too, Mr. Baxter. Your home is beautiful."

"It's Rhett or Baxter. Welcome."

"Or Number One," Jerry pipes up. "You know, since there are three of them and all."

"Really?" Saylor asks, surprised.

I find it hard to believe that she still doesn't know who we are. "Why so surprised?" I ask her.

"I just-" She's cut off when Gramps speaks up.

"Rhett Alexander Baxter. I'm the first, my son, his father"—he points at me—"is the second, and he's the third."

"Three generations," she says. "That's amazing."

"You made pies?" Gramps asks Jerry. Jerry is a great cook, but a baker he is not. It's usually something from the bakery for dessert. Molly did attempt to make a cake a few years ago. It was dry and tasted burnt. Not sure how she managed that, but after that, it was store bought from then on. That is until today.

Until Saylor.

"Saylor made them." Molly beams at her friend.

"That's a treat. Mason, is it time to eat? I'm famished," Gramps says, heading into the dining room to take a seat.

I stare after him dumbfounded. It's the most I've seen him talk since I've been here. Not that I needed confirmation, but it's me he's pissed at. How am I going to get him to get over this grudge he's holding?

The next half hour flies by while the girls help Jerry in the kitchen. Jake and I sit with Gramps. They talk about the bar, football, you name it. I sit there quietly, adding to the conversation here and there. Mostly, I sit stewing about how he's acting toward me. It's childish. I'm here, and I've told him I'm not going anywhere until he's ready for me to go. Hell, I even told Dad I wanted to stay a little longer to just hang out with him. Too bad it's cold or we would go fishing. I need to make plans to come back late spring or early summer so we can do that. Looking over at Gramps, he's frail and pale, not the same vibrant man I remember. I don't know how many more chances we'll have left.

"Come and get it!" Jerry yells out.

"We do things more casual," I hear him tell Saylor. "Kind of like a buffet. No point in dirtying up serving bowls when you can just walk a few feet and make your plate."

"I can definitely see the appeal," she agrees with him.

We all shuffle into the kitchen and fill our plates. Once we're seated, the sounds of forks against plates is the only noise, until Gramps breaks the silence.

"So, Saylor, are you from around here?" he asks.

"No, actually I moved here a few months ago. I'm originally from Cincinnati," she says.

"What brought you to the fine state of West Virginia?" Jerry asks.

She hesitates. "Life."

They seem to accept her answer while I'm sitting here wanting more. I want the real story of what brought her here. I remember Jake telling me she's had a hard time. What does that mean exactly? She got fired?

She's on the run? A hard time could mean anything. I find myself wanting to know the secrets of this sexy Short Stack.

"I'm sure your family is missing you today," Jerry says. "Especially with the way those pies look." He scoots his chair back from the table and smacks his protruding belly. "I'm gonna have to let that settle before I can indulge, but I'll have me a piece of both." He smiles at her.

I look to Saylor for her reaction, and what I find shocks me. Her face is somber, and if I'm not mistaken, a hint of pain shines in those blue eyes. She looks to her lap, so I can't be sure.

"Jerry, can you help me for a minute?" Jake asks, his voice hard.

I watch as he stands and stalks toward the kitchen. Jerry looks to Molly, and she nods, telling him without words that he needs to follow Jake. Molly stands at the same time as Jerry. "I need a refill, Say?" she asks, her voice chipper, but I can see the worry in her eyes.

"No thank you," she says softly. Molly gives her shoulder a gentle squeeze and follows Jerry to the kitchen.

The table is quiet, too quiet, uncomfortably so. Gramps coughs, causing Saylor to look up and at him. "Are you okay?" she asks him.

He waves a hand in the air. "I'm fine, just fighting off this pneumonia. It's taking longer to get over it than I'd like."

Silence ensures except for the mumbled voices from the kitchen. "I'm sorry," Saylor says. "They're in there because of me. I—" She stands.

"Please sit," Gramps says.

She does as asked. "I don't have any family," she whispers so low that if I hadn't been watching her, I might have missed it.

"Of course you do," Gramps says.

Fuck. Her face pales even more so, and I'm just about to ream his ass when he speaks again. "You're here with family. We're unconventional, but you are always welcome here."

I watch her as she blinks hard, fighting the moisture in her eyes. Damn this girl. She's feisty as hell, holding her own, sweet underneath, baking pies, and doing it all alone. No family. Surely there must be someone?

"Sorry about that," Jake says as they all take their seats.

I watch as Jerry leans down and kisses the top of Saylor's head. No one comments on the act. Instead, Jerry starts talking to Gramps about football. Everyone is talking, laughing, and having a good time. I hold my own, but I constantly keep going back to Saylor, watching her. Her blue eyes are so damn expressive. I see pain and sadness. It causes something deep inside of me to want to take it away, take it all away from her, so I can see the smile in her eyes. At least when she's sparring with me, I can see the spark, the sadness hidden in the shadows.

"Saylor, girl, I do believe it's time to try some of that pie." Gramps gives her a warm smile.

She stands. "I'll be right back." Molly starts to stand, I assume to help her, and Saylor waves her off. "I'll just bring them in here with some plates. I got it. It's the least I can do."

I watch her go, unable to take my eyes off that tight little ass of hers. Even under that sweater it's a sight to behold.

"See something you like?" Jerry smirks.

I shrug. That causes both him and Jake to laugh. They can see through my bullshit, but that's because they're not blind. They see what I see. Sure, Jake is wrapped up in Molly, but he sees her.

It's been a few minutes, and she's not back yet. I stand from the table and walk to the kitchen. I find Saylor on her tiptoes reaching into the cabinet. Walking up behind her, I place a hand on her hip and reach over her, grabbing the stack of dessert plates from the top shelf. "This what you need, Short Stack?" I ask, my lips next to her ear. I can feel her shiver, and my cock thickens.

"I had it," she says, a quiver in her voice.

"Uh-huh," I say, making no effort to move away from her. Gently, I move her hair that's hanging over her shoulder out of my way. I bring my lips close to her ear again. This time I can see the effect I'm having on her as goose bumps break out across her skin. "You need anything else? From me?" I add as an afterthought. I watch her throat as she swallows. Leaning in, I want to kiss her neck, right at the base where I can see her pulse pounding.

"What's taking so long?" Molly calls.

Quickly, I step to the side. Leaning against the counter, I cross my arms and legs. "Short Stack here was having trouble reaching the plates." I motion my head to where Saylor stands beside me.

"Ass," she says, loud enough that Molly can hear her. "I was working on it," she mumbles.

I bite back my retort. Instead, I stand to my full height, grab both pies, and head to the dining room. Not a minute later, Molly and Saylor emerge with plates, forks, vanilla ice cream, and whipped cream. I'm glad I'm sitting down, because seeing her holding a can of whipped cream has all kinds of naughty thoughts racing through my head. All of them starting with her stack.

TWELVE

Saylor

THE RIDE HOME is quiet. The rest of the day was a blur. I contributed to the conversation, but my mind was all over the place. Why does he affect me like he does? One minute I want to rip his head off, the other I want his hands all over me. I tried to be angry in the kitchen, but his hands on me, his hot breath against my ear… It's a reaction I've never had before. My body has never responded to a man the way it responded to Rhett.

"You awake back there?" Molly asks once we pull up in front of the house.

"Barely. I think I'm in a turkey coma," I tell her.

"A late afternoon nap is definitely in order," Jake says while yawning.

"Thank you, guys, for including me," I say, opening my door.

"Always," Molly replies.

I don't hang around for small talk. The late afternoon air has a chill to it. I just want to curl up with a blanket and sleep off this turkey. Sliding out of my boots and taking off my scarf, I settle on the couch. I'm flipping through the channels when my phone alerts me to a message.

Molly: Rhett?

What is she wanting to know?

Me: What about him?

Molly: What did I walk in on?

Me: Him being an ass.

Molly: It was more than that.

Me: Nope.

Molly: I'll let you slide for now. I'm watching you.

I laugh, because I can hear her saying that doing that thing with her index and middle fingers where she points at her eyes and then to mine.

Me: Nothing to see.

Letting my phone fall to my lap, I go back to channel surfing. I settle for a Nicholas Sparks movie. I'm just about to dose off when my phone alerts me to another message.

Molly: I'm sorry if what Jerry said upset you.

Heaviness settles in my chest. Jerry didn't mean anything by asking a simple question. I know that, but it still hurt just to think about the answer, then admitting that to Rhett and his grandfather. I was mortified until his grandfather spoke up and said I was family. It was a nice sentiment, and I took it as such. I'll always be the foster kid with no living relatives. That's just the hand I was dealt.

Me: Nothing to be sorry for. He couldn't have known. I'm used to it.

Molly: I'm sorry for that too.

Me: One day at a time, Molly. One day at a time.

Turning my phone off, I place it on the coffee table and burrow back underneath the covers. Commercials come on for all of the after Thanksgiving Day sales. Elaine and I used to go out shopping. More for the people watching than the actual deals. Sure, we would buy a few things, but we never went crazy like some. One year we saw an actual fistfight over a throw blanket of all things. I miss her so much. Tears prick my eyes, and this time, I don't fight it. I let them fall, crying myself to sleep.

I wake to the sound of knocking on the door. I must have woken up at some point and come to bed. I don't remember, letting my grief consume me. I'm still in yesterday's clothes as I rush to the door. It has to be Molly or Jake. Peeking out the window, I see Molly dancing around in the cold. I also see white, lots and lots of white. Looks like Mother Nature decided to deliver some snow. Pulling open the door, I don't get the chance to greet her as she rushes in.

"Thank God, are you okay?" she asks. I can hear the concern in her voice, and see it in the wrinkle of her brow.

"Of course I am, what's wrong?"

"I've been trying to call you for two hours. You weren't answering your phone."

That's when I remember I turned it off last night. "Sorry, I turned if off last night before bed."

She takes in my appearance. "You slept in your clothes?"

"Yeah, I, uh, fell asleep on the couch watching a movie. It must have been the turkey."

She shakes her head and smiles. "I'm glad you're okay. You had me worried."

"I'm good," I tell her. "Did you need something?"

"Shit, I forgot. Yeah, how do you feel about going sledding today. There's a good six inches of fresh snow out there."

"I don't want to intrude."

"You're not intruding if you're invited. Come on, please, Say," she begs. "I promise you'll have fun." She bats her eyelashes at me.

Laughter bubbles up as I take in the show. "Fine," I concede, like it's a huge inconvenience.

In all honesty, it's not something I've ever done before. "What time are we leaving?"

"In about an hour. Do you have thermals?" she asks.

I bite my bottom lip and shake my head.

"Okay, I have extras. Get ready. I'll go grab them and leave them on the bed for you."

"Thanks, Mol."

"Always, Say. Now go, get a shower. We have hills to slide down."

I scamper off to the shower. I'm excited but nervous all at the same time. I don't want to look like a fool, but really, how hard can it be to slide down a hill? I rush through my shower and find the thermals Molly promised sitting on the bed. I quickly put them on, sliding on a pair of jeans, long sleeve T-shirt, and a hoodie. I forgo makeup; this doesn't seem like one of those outings where I need to be all dolled up. My hair, I go for blow drying it, but first have to remove the hoodie. I didn't think that one through. Too damn hot in here. After shedding the hoodie and drying my hair, I braid it in two halves, almost like pigtails on each side. I figure this will serve dual purposes. One it will keep it out of my face with the wind, and two makes wearing a hat easier.

Hair done, I slide my hoodie back on and grab my hiking boots. They're waterproof, so hopefully these will work for today. Grabbing my coat, phone, and wristlet, I lock the door and head to the main house to meet up with Jake and Molly.

"Hey," Jake greets me.

"Hi, I feel like an Oompa-Loompa." I raise my arms. "I don't know that I've ever worn this many layers before."

"Never? Did you just freeze your ass off back in Cincy when you would go sled riding?" he asks, appalled.

"No, I've never been."

"Wait a minute." He places his hands on my shoulders from behind and turns me to face him. "You've never been? Never?" he asks.

I shake my head.

"Babe!" he yells for Molly.

"I'm right here," she says, rounding the corner from their bedroom.

"Did you know Say has never been sled riding?"

"Really?" she asks, surprised.

"Nope. Elaine had a bad hip, and it's just not something I've ever done." I shrug.

"Oh girl, you are in for a treat. It's so much fun. There's a place about two hours from here, where we go tubing. The hills are huge and you don't have to walk up. They have an escalator that you hop on with your tube and ride up the hill. We're going to have to plan to go there sometime."

"Where are we going today?" I ask. I guess I should have asked before agreeing to go, but I trust them.

"Baxter's. He has some great hills."

I still at the name. It's so damn confusing with all of them having the same name. "Is it just going to be us?" I ask, cool, calm, and collected. Well, that's how I thought I was being until Molly smirks.

"Why? You hoping we have some company?" she asks.

"Of course not."

"Uh-huh, and you're not wondering if Rhett is going to be there?"

"I'm sure Mr. Baxter is far too frail with his illness to go sled riding," I say, cheekily. I know damn good and well who she's referring to.

"Try again," she says.

I sigh. "Whiskey is welcome to come, but I don't see why that would concern me."

"Whiskey?" Jake asks.

"Rhett," Molly clarifies for him.

"What's the real reason you call him that?" Jake asks. He's cautious in his question, but I can see he's being protective of his friend.

"That's what he ordered." I pull my gloves out of my pocket and pretend to pick lint off them. Did I mention they're leather? Yeah, I'm busted.

"Oh no, I'm intrigued, do tell," Molly chimes in. She's not going to let this go.

I can feel my face heat. "His eyes," I mumble.

"Say again." Jake grins. It's a big ole, "I heard you loud and clear but want you to say it again" kind of grin.

"His eyes. I mean, come on, you have to see how gorgeous his eyes are." I'm looking at Molly, putting her in the hot seat.

"Hell yes I have." She holds her hands up for a high five.

"Hey!" Jake whines. "I'm going to pretend you didn't say that."

I smirk at him. "Payback's a bitch."

Molly throws her head back in laughter, giving me yet another high five. Jake just shakes his head at us a smile, tipping the corner of his mouth. "You ladies ready to go?" he asks.

"Yep." Molly grabs my arm and leads us out to the truck.

"Where exactly are you taking me that we need that?" I point to the

UTV on the trailer behind Jake's truck.

"Trust me, you'll be thanking me you don't have to hoof it up all those big-ass hills," Jake says.

"I'm not exactly adventurous," I tell them.

"It's going to be a great time, trust us," Molly says, releasing her hold on me to climb into the truck.

I take a seat in the back and try not to think about what I'm about to do and who I'm about to do it with.

THIRTEEN

G RAMPS HAD A good night last night, at least that's what I heard from the night nurse. Apparently, he's tired and asked to not be disturbed. I'm sitting at the kitchen island eating a bowl of cereal when my phone rings. "Hey, man," I greet Jake.

"Number Three." He laughs. "What are you doing today?"

"Nothing. Thinking about going into the distillery for a few hours. Gramps is sleeping, and even if he was awake, he wouldn't want to be around me."

"I noticed some tension. What's up with that?"

"Long-ass story. Shortened version, he's pissed I've not spent much time here. I get it, but damn, this grudge he's holding is grating on me."

"He'll come around. Listen, why don't you skip work today and let's hit the hills."

"Did it snow?" I ask him.

A deep rumble of laughter comes over the line. "Look outside, lazy ass. Are you even out of bed?" he jokes.

"Ass," I mumble. Walking to the kitchen window, I pull back the blinds, and sure enough, a blanket of white. "What time?"

"I gotta get my girl up and moving and call Say, so a couple of hours?"

"You got it, man. Just come to the main house. We'll jump on the UTV and take it to the hills."

"I'm bringing mine too. I'm not letting you have all the fun."

I laugh. "See you," I say, ending the call. A day of sledding sounds like a good time. What's better is the Short Stack will be there. I can't help the fact that I enjoy irritating her. I like the spark in her eyes, the determination I see. She thinks she can resist me.

Today should be fun.

Deciding I better check with Gramps even though I already said we could take his UTV, I head to his room. I knock lightly on the door in case he really is sleeping. He doesn't reply, so I push the door open to find him watching television. "Hey, Gramps." I take the seat next to his bed. He looks over at me, which is progress. "Jake, Molly, and Saylor want to go sled on the hills. We got about six or seven inches of snow last night. Do you mind if we take the UTV?" I ask.

"The girls are coming?"

"Yeah, they should be here in a couple of hours."

"Make sure there's gas in it. Don't want them having to walk too far in the cold."

I hide my smile, but I'm fucking stoked that he's coming around. "How you feeling today?" I ask.

He shrugs. No other reply, but I'll take it.

"Thanks, Gramps. I'll check in on you before we go." Reaching out, I give his frail arm a gentle squeeze before quietly leaving the room, shutting the door behind me.

Growing up, Gramps's place was like a playground. He has a spare bedroom filled with everything you need from swimwear for the summer to keep you warm in the winter. As I enter the room, my emotions get the best of me. Even on my too-short visits during the holidays, this room is one we would frequent. Sifting through the racks, I find some thermals to put under my shirt and jeans. I grab a ski jacket, gloves, and hat, and I should be set.

Back in my room, I lay it all on the end of the bed. No use in putting it on right away and sweating my ass off. Instead, I grab my laptop and respond to some e-mails. I tend to get lost in my work, so when the doorbell rings, it causes me to jump. Looking at the time on my computer, it's been over two hours. Setting my computer aside, I race down the stairs to answer the door. "Come on in," I say, stepping back to let the three of them pass.

"You ready?" Jake asks.

"Not exactly. I just need to change real fast, and then I'll be good to go. Give me ten minutes. Make yourselves at home." I dash upstairs and strip, just to put it all back on again. By the time I make it back downstairs, Gramps is there.

"Young lady, you can't wear that coat sledding," he tells Saylor.

"What's wrong with it?" she asks, holding out her arms to look at her coat.

"Dear, it's too nice. You don't want to ruin it."

"My wardrobe isn't exactly equipped for this kind of thing," she tells him.

"She's never been sledding before, Rhett, can you believe that?" Jake asks him.

"Never?" Gramps asks in disbelief. She shakes her head, looking at the ground. "Rhett," he calls out to me. "Take Saylor upstairs to get another coat."

I step into the room. How he knew I was creeping on their conversation, I have no idea. "Come with me." I hold my hand out for her.

She looks at my hand, then back up to me. "I'm okay, really."

"Nonsense. I have a supply for such an occasion," Gramps tells her.

I watch her as she gives him a kind smile, all her sweetness that I don't get to see shining through for him. Turning to me, the smile fades. I offer her my hand again. She doesn't take it. Instead, she says, "Lead the way."

I purposely take two steps at a time, knowing her short legs won't be able to keep up. When I reach the top, I turn around and cross my arms over my chest, leaning against the wall.

"Do you enjoy being an asshole?" she asks, shooting daggers at me as she clears the top step.

"What did I do?" I feign being offended.

"Whatever," she mumbles under her breath, and I fight a grin.

I lead her to the bedroom at the far end of the hall that's really used as the closet. Opening the door, I step back and motion for her to go on in. I'm still standing in the doorway, so she's going to have to squeeze in past me. She rolls those striking blue eyes at me, turns sideways, and slips into the room. My cock thickens from the brief touch of her body sliding past mine.

"Wow," she says under her breath. If I wasn't so focused on her, I might have missed it.

Walking over to a large dresser, I reach in and pull out some cold gear leggings and turn to face her. "Let me help you get out of those jeans," I say, slowing walking toward her. I can see the fire in her eyes. It's a mixture of anger and a little bit of desire.

"I have thermals," she snarls back.

"You should let me check, you know for the sake of that perfect ass not freezing to death."

"Trust me, my ass is just fine." She realizes immediately what she said, and her face grows crimson.

"Oh, Short Stack, I know. I'm a fan."

"Jesus," she mumbles. "A coat, Whiskey. I don't want to offend your grandfather, and as bad as I hate to admit it, he's right."

"Over there." I point to the double stacked wrack of coats. "I'll just keep an eye on that fine ass, you know, just in case it decides to put on a show."

"Unbelievable," she huffs and walks over to the racks.

My eyes follow her, her ass, her hips, her long black hair that's braided into pigtails, my eyes devour everything about her. She's fucking gorgeous, and the way her eyes fill with fire puts my dick in a constant state of "let me the fuck inside of her" anytime she's near. I watch as she pushes through the options, as if she's actually shopping. When she pulls a blue down coat from the rack, I take a step toward her. Slipping out of her coat, she tosses it over a chair in the corner. I watch as she slides one arm and then the other inside the blue down jacket that will be sure to keep her warm. Not able to resist, I take the final step, which has me standing right behind her. Gently, I gather her thick braids in my hands and pull them outside of the collar of the coat. Instead of letting them fall to cascade down her back, I toss one over each of her shoulders, bringing my lips to her ear. "Ready for a ride?" I whisper, leaning into her so she can feel how hard my cock is from just looking at her. I watch as she swallows hard, the movement of her neck mesmerizing.

She takes a step forward and turns to face me. Pointedly, she looks down at my cock. I watch as she bites her bottom lip before those baby blues lock on me. "I love a good hard ride, but I'm afraid I'm going to have to decline." The blue of the coat brings out her already stunning blue eyes.

I step toward her, hands balled into fists at my side to prevent myself from pulling her into me, rubbing my cock against her. "You sure about that?" I ask. My voice is husky, and fuck if I care that she knows she's affecting me.

"Mm-hmm," she replies.

"Let's go!" Jake calls up the stairs.

Closing my eyes, I step back. Taking a deep breath, I turn and walk toward the door.

"Hey, Whiskey," she calls out. Her voice is soft and breathy and sexy as fuck.

I stop, but don't turn around, I can't. "You can't handle me," she finally says. It's meant to be a threat, a way to goad me, get under my skin. It works, but not the way she's thinking. There is no menace behind her words. Her soft voice filled with desire washes over me. I know what she meant to say, but her physical reaction to me gave her away. She's affected just as much as I am.

I'm just about to turn around and take her right here, right now, show her how I can handle anything she wants to give me, when Jake appears in front of me.

"What's taking you all so long? We're sweating our asses off down here."

"Had a hard time finding something that would work for Short Stack. We were just headed your way." I don't bother looking behind me. Jake nods and turns to walk out of the room. I follow him, fighting the urge to look back at her.

With Jake's back to me as we descend the stairs, I adjust my aching cock with a smile on my face. Short Stack gives as good as she gets, and suddenly, this day just got a whole hell of a lot more fun.

"Much better," Gramps says, looking behind me.

"Definitely," Molly chimes in. "You ready to go sledding for the first time?" she asks Saylor.

"I'm not sure how to answer that," she laughs nervously.

Looking over, I see she's now standing beside me. Not able to stop myself, I reach out and throw my arm over her small shoulders, bringing her to me. Her head barely reaches the top of my shoulders. She's such tiny little thing. "You can ride with me, Short Stack." I pause, letting my words sink in. I'm looking down at her, gauging her reaction, when those blue glaciers look up at me. "I'll make sure it's a ride you never forget." She squints at me before pulling away and smacking my chest. She opens her mouth to tell me off, I'm sure, but Molly interrupts her.

"That's a great idea. No point in you riding alone, Rhett."

Saylor whips her head around to give Molly a "what the hell are you doing" look.

Molly grins. "Thanks, Rhett," she says, pulling on Jake's arm as they rush out of the room.

"You take care of her, boy." Gramps's gravelly voice echoes through the room.

I study him. He looks like he's feeling better, and he's talking to me. I'll take it. "Always," I tell Gramps. With that, I grab my coat, slipping my arms inside.

"Thank you for having me, Mr. Baxter," Saylor says kindly.

"You're always welcome here, sweet girl."

I place my hand on the small of her back and lead her outside.

FOURTEEN

Saylor

S EXY, INFURIATING MAN. The heat of his hand on my back feels as though it could sear my skin even through all these damn layers. Not possible, I know it's the perception of my body and my mind knowing his hands are on me.

His very large hands.

By the time we make it to the garage, Jake and Molly are speeding past us, snow flying from the tires in their wake.

"Let's get you strapped in." Rhett winks.

I roll my eyes, but climb into the passenger seat. Leaning in, he reaches behind my shoulders and grabs two straps, pulling them across my body. My breath hitches in my chest; he's close, so damn close I can feel his hot breath mingle with mine. Closing my eyes, I block out the fact that this sexy asshole has his hands on me—well, not technically, but a girl can dream. Rhett works his big hands with efficiency as he straps me in. Just as the final buckle is secured, I feel the ever-so-slight brush of his thumb across my cheek.

"You're a dream come true, strapped in, all for me."

Slowly, I open my eyes and find his whiskey-colored eyes full of heat and desire as they take me in. "Safety," I mumble. He scrambles my brain when he's this close and touching me.

Something flashes in his eyes, but it's gone before I can put a name to it. "You're safe with me," he says so softly that I'm not sure I even heard him correctly.

Leisurely, he pulls away and rounds the front of the UTV and climbs behind the wheel. I don't dare look over at him for the fear he'll see the desire written all over my face. Why do all the ones who look like him have to be assholes?

"Hold on, Say," he says before putting the UTV in gear and racing in the direction that Molly and Jake just went.

When we make it to the hill, I'm sure my knuckles are white underneath my gloves from hanging on to the handle that's attached to the dash. My smile, however, feels as though my face is going to crack open.

"Look at you," Molly says. "Fun, right?"

"So much fun," I gush. "That's... I don't know why I've never done that before."

"If you loved that, just wait," Jake says, looking past Molly from the driver's seat. "We'll go up first," Jake says, and Rhett nods.

I watch as he starts the UTV and climbs the hill, Molly all smiles and cheers beside him. I watch with rapt attention when they reach the top. Jake pulls a sled from the back and places it at the top of the hill. He takes a seat on the sled and pats between his legs. Molly doesn't hesitate to climb on and sit in front of him. She's barely seated when I see Jake push off with his foot and they come soaring down the hill. I hold my breath as I watch them until they slide right past us and eventually stop. They're both smiling from ear to ear as they walk toward us and climb in the back.

Once they're in, Rhett drives us to the top of the hill. Jake and Molly quickly climb out and get in their UTV and drive back down the hill. "It's easier this way," Rhett says. "Walking up this hill in the snow takes a toll on you. After a time or two, the desire to slide down is altered by the anguish of hoofing it back up this damn hill. We'll take turns," he explains.

"That makes sense," I say, looking down the hill at Jake and Molly. It's pretty steep.

"Since this is your first time, I'll be gentle." He smirks.

"I assure you, I can ride just fine," I retort.

Rhett smiles, climbing out and retrieving the sled from the back. It's then I realize that Jake and Molly took the other one with them. There are two sleds and four of us. Specifically, two of us at the top of this snow-covered hill and one sled. "I'll make sure you enjoy it, Short Stack." He places the sled at the top of the hill and takes a seat, sliding to the back, just as Jake did moments before. "Right here," he says, patting between his legs.

Not wanting him to see how he affects me, I climb on the sled, settling between his legs. Immediately, he moves closer, and his arm wraps around my waist. My back is to his front, and he's holding me to him. "I got you," he whispers. I can only assume it's because he can feel the slight tremble in my body. I'm sure he also thinks it's fear. He might be right, but it's not the fear of sliding down this snow-covered hill. It's the fear of being this close to him and the fact that I don't mind it, not even a little. Asshole or not, feels good to be me right now.

"There are handles on the side," he says, his lips next to my ear. "I need you to hang on." Doing as he says, I grab the handles and grip them tight. I assumed once I did so he would let go of me, but he doesn't. "I'm going to count to three and push us off. All you have to do it hold on and enjoy the ride," he says huskily.

I nod, letting him know that I heard him. I listen to him slowly count to three and push off with his foot. One hand wraps around mine on the handle, while the other stays wrapped firmly around my waist. We fly down the hill, the cold wind in our face. As we slide past Jake and Molly, they're a blur. When we finally come to a stop, Rhett wraps both arms around me and gives me a gentle squeeze. "Thanks for letting me be your first," he whispers before climbing off the back of the sled. His hand appears before my eyes. I take it, allowing him to pull me to my feet.

"Hell yes! What did you think?" Molly asks, rushing me.

"It was a lot of fun," I tell her. "You know, for an amateur, he didn't let me down," I say, keeping my face stone serious.

"Amateur?" Jake asks. "Hell, Say, we've ridden down this hill more times than I can count," he defends his friend.

Looking over at Rhett, I see he's smiling, his eyes sparking. "Get your ass up there, Jake. Looks like I have my work cut out for me," he says, climbing into the back of the UTV. I do the same, wearing a satisfied smirk. He can act like my dig didn't get to him, but I know better. His eyes never lie. Once at the top of the hill, Rhett and I load back up in his

UTV and drive to the bottom of the hill. We sit in silence as we watch our friends slide down the hill for the second time.

"Amateur, huh?" he asks when it's just he and I again standing at the top of the hill.

"I mean, it was okay." I turn my head to keep him from seeing my grin.

Rhett drops the sled at the top of the hill and takes a seat. He pats in between his legs for me, and even through I'm eager to be pressed up against him, I calmly walk toward him and take a seat. This time, there's not as much room. He's not sitting as far back as he was before. I'm just about to ask him to move back when both of his arms wrap around me. "This one's all on you, Short Stack. I'm gonna need you to hold us on this thing," he says, his breath hot against my ear.

"What about you?"

"I'm going to be otherwise occupied."

"I'm not strong enough to keep us both on here," I say, slight panic in my voice.

"You are, and if not, the worst that can happen is we tip over in the snow. No big deal. You're safe."

I want to tell him he's crazy as hell, but I'm nervous. He's huge, six four at least, and there is no way I can keep us on this thing. "Rhett, I— "

He cuts me off. "You can, and you will. His arms are still around my waist. His chin is now resting on my shoulder. "I'm going to count us off, and I need you to hold on."

I nod, gripping the handles as tight as I can. I should just get off this stupid thing, but I don't want him to know I'm scared, not so much of injury as I am of looking like a fool in front of him, Jake, and Molly. This isn't me. I've never been in this kind of position. Fighting down the panic, I squeeze tight when Rhett whispers three in my ear and kicks us off. Before his other leg is even on the sled, he removes one hand, and I feel it slide between my legs. I lean back into him, not sure of what's happening. The arm that's around my waist just holds strong as we fly down the hill.

This time when we come to a stop, Jake and Molly are not there to greet us. They're sitting on the UTV. Rhett moves his hand from between my legs, running it over my thigh. I can feel the heat through the layers of clothing from his touch. "How was that?" he says huskily.

"What did… I mean, why did—"

He knows what I'm asking, and I can hear the satisfied smirk he's wearing in his reply. "I was holding on," he says pointedly.

"But I thought I was holding on?"

"You were, but I decided I should help you."

"But what were you—" He stands, cutting off my question. Again, his hand appears in front of my face and I take it, letting him help me to my feet. My legs are shaking, but not from the ride—well, a little from the ride, the one where we rode down the snowy embankment with his hand between my legs.

"There." He points down at the sled.

Sure enough, there is a handle front and center. *How did I not notice that?* "Oh," I mumble.

"One thing you need to know about me." He pauses, waiting for me to look at him. When I do, those brown eyes of his are boring into me. "Ladies are always first." With that, he picks up the sled and walks toward the UTV. I stand there letting his words sink in. He's not talking about sledding, and secretly, an admission I can only make to myself, I want to see what he's capable of when he puts me first.

"Now it's just the girls," Molly says.

I release a sigh of relief and mentally high five my friend. I don't know how much more close contact I can take. The guys agree and leave us with both sleds while they drive to the bottom of the hill. Molly and I race down side by side, coming to stop with both guys standing, arms crossed, watching over us. Molly jumps behind the wheel and I follow her, claiming the passenger seat. The guys jump in the back and take their turn. We continue this way for another hour or so. We're all frozen and exhausted, so we head to the house to warm up and dry out.

"I'm sorry," Molly says, grinning at me sheepishly. "I meant to tell you to bring clothes."

I look down at the sweats that are so big I had to roll them at the waist several times. I still have to pick them up when I walk. And the T-shirt is so long, it looks like an oversized dress where it hits at my knees. "That would have been nice," I say, taking a sip of my hot chocolate. She giggles.

"What? You look hot in my clothes, Short Stack. I know, secretly, that's your life's goal. Go ahead and mark it off your bucket list," Rhett chimes in.

"This is really all you could find?" I ask him.

"You're welcome to go up and take a look. Actually, I should go with you. You know, in case you find something and need help changing." He places his cup on the table and starts to stand.

"I'm good," I say, resting back against the couch.

"You kids have fun?" I hear a gravelly voice say from the doorway.

Looking over, I see Rhett's grandfather standing there with a soft smile tilting his lips. He looks better today, more rested. "Yes, thank you so much," Molly and I say at the exact same time, resulting in both of us laughing.

"It was a good time," Jake says.

"What on earth are you wearing, Saylor?" his grandfather asks.

I look down at my outfit and shrug. "I forgot to bring clothes."

He looks at his grandson. "Is that all you could find her?" He raises his eyebrows in question.

"Yep." Rhett smirks behind his cup of hot chocolate.

His grandfather just shakes his head, and I swear I see a small lift at the corner of his lips. "You all done for the day?" he asks, walking further into the room.

I watch as Rhett stands from his seat in the recliner and plops down on the couch beside me. Closer than need be. His grandfather takes the recliner. "Probably. This one has to work tonight." He reaches over and taps my knee. He doesn't move his hand. Instead, he just leaves it there, resting on my knee.

Moving my legs to the floor, I place my now empty cup on a coaster and settle back on the couch, feet under me. I smile inside because I beat him at his own game. My inner smile falters as he reaches out and rests his arm on my leg, leaning in toward me on the couch. What the hell?

"Probably best," his grandfather says. "No point in risking frostbite."

Looking over at Molly, I see she's all snuggled up with Jake. I catch her eye and look toward the door. She grins but gives me a subtle nod. Thankfully.

"We should probably get going. We all have to be at the Corner Pocket tonight," Molly says, untangling herself from Jake and standing. She picks up her cup.

"Leave it. We'll take care of it," his grandfather says. Then he looks over at Rhett. "You should go hang out with them tonight. You've been working too much. Take a night to relax."

I cannot only see but feel Rhett suck in a deep breath. "Yeah, I think I might," he finally says. He sounds relieved.

I stand. "Thank you so much for today and the coat. I'll get it cleaned and bring it back to you," I offer.

"Nonsense. That's what they are here for. I'm glad you kids had a good time. Come by anytime," he tells me.

I look down at Rhett. "Thanks for these." I pull his shirt away from my skin. "I'll be sure to get them back to you."

"I'm not worried, Short Stack." He stands as well, stretching his arms over his head. I can't help but notice the strip of skin, toned muscle, and V that his sweatpants are hanging off of. "I'll see you all later?" he asks.

"Yeah, man. Thanks again," Jake calls over his shoulder as he picks up the tote bag he retrieved from his truck with dry clothes for him and Molly.

Turning to follow them, I feel Rhett place his hand on the small of my back, his thin T-shirt doing nothing to keep his heat from seeping into my skin. Rhett leans down and speaks softly, just for me. "You look good with me all over you."

"You think so?" I ask him.

He nods.

"Don't get used to it. This will be the last time you see me like this." I give him a sugary smile.

"Is that a challenge, Short Stack?"

"It's a promise." I quicken my steps to get out of his hold. When I reach the door, I look over my shoulder. "See you around, Whiskey." With that, I walk out into the cold, my coat slung over my arms. I don't even feel the brisk November air. My body is heated from his touch. Jake grabbed the trash bag with all of our wet clothes, so thankfully I don't have to worry about that. I don't say a word as I climb in the back seat of the truck and buckle in. The ride home is quiet, but I know better than to think Molly isn't going to comment about the... tension with Rhett and me today. I just wish I knew what to tell her.

FIFTEEN
Rhett

WALKING INTO THE Corner Pocket, I see Jake, Molly, and Saylor all behind the bar slinging drinks. This place is packed. Making my way through the crowd, I find an empty stool at the end of the bar. Jake makes eye contact and gives me a head nod of recognition. I settle in and watch them do their thing. They work well together.

"I'm taking these out to the floor," Saylor calls over her shoulder.

I watch her as she balances a tray full of beer mugs, a pitcher full of beer, and several shots with ease. In this crowd, that's a feat in itself. My eyes follow her as she reaches a high top of five guys who from the sound of them have already had several rounds. Saylor passes out the shots, the mugs, and then sets the pitcher of beer in the center. One of the guys says something to her, and she gives him a tight smile. It's obvious that whatever he said isn't anything she wants to hear. She makes her way back to the bar, and I turn back around in my stool. Jake is standing in front of me wearing a smirk.

"Draft?" he asks.

"Yep." He knows I always drink whatever he has on tap from my father's brewery in Tennessee.

"You know those guys?" He motions to the rowdy group Saylor was serving.

"Nope."

"Huh? I thought for sure you knew them the way you were spellbound."

"Spellbound?" I laugh. "What the fuck are you going on about?"

"You see, if you don't know that group, that means your attention was elsewhere. Then again, I think your attention was on that table and the bartender serving them?" he goads.

"She's easy on the eyes." I shrug unapologetically.

"She is. She's also not only my employee but good friends with Molly."

"Okay?" I know what he's trying to say, and I get it. However, I am going to make him say it.

"She's been through a lot, man. Not to mention, if you hurt her, Mol is going to be pissed, and so am I for that matter. She's one of the good ones."

"I was looking at her, Jake. Not fucking her. Besides, if that's what she and I decide to do as adults who can make our own decisions, you're just going to have to deal with it."

"Don't," he says sternly.

"Relax. We annoy each other, that's what we do. I knew she could feel me watching her. I was trying to annoy her. Nothing more, nothing less." I can tell by the look on his face he's not buying what I'm selling.

"On the house," he says, sliding a beer in front of me.

I wipe my finger across the frosty mug before bringing it to my lips. It tastes like home, but then this place feels more like home than Tennessee. It's funny how something like a beer, a bar, or a town can make you feel. Make all the memories come flooding back.

"Hey, Rhett." Molly waves.

It seems that she and Jake are working behind the bar, and Saylor is helping out and serving when needed. I'm mid-drink when my cell phone rings. Pulling it out of my pocket and looking at the display, I see it's Doug. "Hello," I say over the noise of the crowd.

"Baxter?"

"Hold on, let me step outside." I catch Jake's attention, holding up a finger to let him know I'll be right back, and step outside. "Hey," I say as soon as the door closes.

"Sounds like a good time," he says, laughing.

"For someone," I say. "I'm at my buddy Jake's bar. It's a packed house. What's up?"

"Calling with some news," he says.

"Okay, are you going to tell me or keep me in suspense while I freeze my balls off out here?"

He thunders a deep booming laugh. "I guess I can put you out of your misery."

"Hi, Rhett," I hear Dawn say through the line.

"Hey, D," I greet her. "Your husband's being a dick and holding out on me. I'm freezing here, man."

"You're on speaker," Doug says.

"What's going on?" I ask again.

"We're pregnant!" Dawn cheers.

Wow. "I—wow guys, that's great. Congratulations."

"Thank you," they say in unison.

I hear lips smacking, and I know they're kissing. "I'm happy for both of you." I am, I'm happy for them, but I can't help but feel a little envious yet again of what they have. That's becoming the norm when it comes to the two of them.

"When are you coming home?" Dawn asks. "I thought we could get together with drinks. Maybe invite Tessa."

"Not sure yet, and how many times do I have to tell you that Tessa and I are not happening?"

"I know," Dawn sighs. "I just want to see you happy."

"Who says I'm not happy?" I ask, trying to keep my teeth from chattering.

"I just—"

Doug interrupts her. "We just wanted to tell you. Take care, and we'll see you when you get home."

"All right, man. See you then. Congrats," I say again.

"Thanks."

I slip my phone back in my pocket and reach for the door. I step inside and am walking back to my stool in the far corner to grab my beer and get warmed up when I spot Saylor at the disorderly high top. Her stance is tense, and the guys are even more rowdy. It was a few minutes tops that I was outside. I keep my eye on her as I head to my stool, but then I see the jackass that was talking to her earlier, the one who obviously was saying something she didn't like. Yeah, that one. He puts his hand on the back of her thigh, over her skintight jeans, and pulls her into him. I'm no longer cold. My blood is boiling when I see her try to step away and he refuses, tightening his hold on her.

As I get closer to their table, I hear her say, "Let me go."

Of course, he still doesn't release her from his hold. "Take your hands off her." I step up to the table and place my hand on her waist. Drunk guy tries to stand, which causes Saylor to stumble into me. That's fine, I've got her.

"Who the fuck are you?" he asks, barely able to find the chair beneath him.

"I'm your worst nightmare if you don't take your hands off her."

This time he does stand, and he's a few inches shorter than me. A quick scan of the table tells me they all are. "Fuck you," he says with no heat. He's too damn drunk for that.

"Sit down, Ronnie," another guy says, pulling him into his seat.

"She's a cocktease anyway. You can have her," he says, chugging the rest of his beer.

Looking down at Saylor, I keep one arm around her while I cup her face with the other. "You okay, Short Stack?" I ask. I keep my attention on her, needing to make sure she's good before I throw these bastards out on their asses.

"Yeah, I'm fine. I had that handled," she says, but the slight tremble in her body tells me otherwise.

"Sure you did, sweetness. Go on back to the bar. These guys are going home."

"That's what I was just telling them. They're cut off."

"I got it," I say, giving her hip a light tap before releasing her from my hold. "Go on, I don't want you in the middle of this in case things get ugly." It's not because it's Saylor; it's any woman. No man has a right to touch them without permission. He's a poor excuse for a man.

"I can handle myself, Rhett," she says, exasperated.

"I'm sure you can, Short Stack. Thing is, you don't have to, not with assholes like these, not while I'm around. I'll take care of them. Go on back behind the bar."

"Say," Jake says. He's now standing beside us. "Go on up and help, Molly. We'll handle this." She nods and heads back behind the bar.

"Where the fuck were you?" I ask Jake.

"I was watching her. I was on my way out here when I saw you. I knew you would take care of it."

"So why are you here now?" I ask.

"She looked like she was giving you shit, and I knew she would listen to me."

It pisses me off that he's right. Surely, she knows that regardless of whatever game we have going on between us, that she's safe with me. I make mental note to talk to her, make sure she understands that above all else.

"Come on, fellas," Jake says. "It's time for you to go."

"What the fuck? She was being a prick-tease. I was just telling her what happens to girls like her."

I see fucking red. Without a thought, I reach past Jake and grab the motherfucker by his collar and lift him from the chair. "Let me tell you something, you ever lay a hand on her again, even look in her direction, you'll answer to me."

"Rhett," Jake says.

Fuck. I'm losing my shit, but this guy is pushing all my fucking buttons. Drunk prick. Now I have Jake pissed off. I know this is his bar, but dammit, he needs to defend her.

"Take him outside," he says, surprising me. "I got the others. You fella's are going to follow calmly, right?" he asks. "I know for a fact your bill is paid, so it's time for you to go."

I don't stick around for the rest of the conversation. Instead, I grab the back of dickwad's shirt and push him out the door.

Jake is right behind me with the other four guys in tow. "Listen, I don't want any problems, but you disrespected my bartender, that's unacceptable. I've called a cab." Just as he says it, the cab pulls up. "Go home, sleep it off. If this happens again, you're banned for life. Understood?" he asks, his voice booming into the night.

The four friends are not near as wasted as the one who put his hands all over Saylor. They scoop him up and the four of them pile into the cab. Luckily, it's a van. Jake and I stand with our arms crossed over our chests, legs apart, watching until the cab drives away.

"You good?" he asks.

"Yeah, I just hate pricks like that. Disrespecting women."

"Women or Saylor?" he asks. There is no teasing in his voice this time.

"Both," I admit. "I mean, we've all hung out, she's your employee, we're friends, you would have done the same."

He nods. "You're right, I would have. Although, I'm not convinced you're giving me the whole truth."

"Are we done, Dr. Phil? It's balls cold out here, and I'm sure my beer is hot by now." I'm deflecting, and I know it. It's not that I like Saylor— I mean, not the way he's thinking. She's gorgeous and we have this crazy love-hate chemistry going on. And the guy was a dick. I would like to think that no matter who it was I would have reacted the same way.

Jake just laughs and walks inside with me on his heels. He heads behind the bar, and I take my seat at the end of the bar. Before I can even sit, Saylor is there with a frosty mug filled to the brim. "Thanks for that." She motions her head toward the floor. "I know you meant well, but I really can take care of myself. Yes, I'm short"—she rolls her eyes—"but I've dealt with worse."

"I'm sure you can, and I'm sorry that you have. He's a dick. I would have done it for anyone, not just you. It was the right thing to do."

I can visibly see her relax. She doesn't say anything else, just turns and walks back to her end of the bar. Jake has taken over the floor for the night, which is a good plan on his part. I'm sure, even though she hides it, Saylor is shaken up, and no way is he putting Molly out there after what happened. Some other drunk asshole might think he can do the same. I finish my beer and leave a fifty on the bar. It's more than necessary, but technically Saylor waited on me since Jake said the first was on the house, not that I still wouldn't have paid. Something tells me she needs it. I catch Jake's eyes and point to the door. He throws his hand up in a wave, and I'm gone. I don't bother saying goodbye to Saylor or Molly; they're both slammed behind the bar. I'll see them both again soon.

SIXTEEN

I T'S SATURDAY NIGHT, and Jake made sure that the three of us were all off. Apparently, it's fight night. The bar will be buying the pay-per-view, which is sure to bring in a huge crowd. That's part of the reason I'm surprised we're all off. I volunteered to go in, but Molly shut me down. She and Jake are having people over to watch the fight, and insisted I be there. I conceded and asked what I could bring. Which leads me to my current situation—at the grocery store at ten in the morning on this dreary cold Saturday morning. It's just a week before Christmas, and the masses are out doing their last-minute shopping. I finished a couple of weeks ago. I have very few people to buy for, so it's an easy process.

Pushing my cart down the baking aisle, I look for the last few ingredients I need for my holiday baking. I have a few tins that I'm making for people, and the rest I'll just leave on the bar at work. I can't leave it in my apartment or I'll eat it all. That I don't need.

I'm almost at the end of the aisle when I hear my name. Turning, I see Pete and his baby mama, Tabitha, headed toward me. Tabitha moves her hand to her small baby bump. "Saylor, hi. How are you?" Pete asks.

"You know, living the dream," I say deadpan. Whirling around, I start to push my cart when they walk up beside me. Pete places his hand on my shoulder, and I flinch. His touch is not welcome.

"I've been calling," he says.

"Yeah, well, I'm busy and frankly have no desire to talk to you." My body is rigid. I'm not afraid of him, but I don't want to see him. I don't want to be anywhere near him. He did me a favor, I know that now, but it doesn't change the fact that just being around him has me going on the defense.

"Peter," Tabitha says in a whiny voice. "We have things to do."

He looks over at her. "Yeah, just give me a few minutes."

"Saylor, I want us to be friends."

I can't even with this guy. After everything, he's going to stand here in the middle of the grocery store with the woman he cheated on me with and tell me we need to be friends?

"Hey, babe, I got the vegetable tray. What else did we need?" a deep voice asks.

Turning, I see Rhett placing a vegetable tray in my cart. He's wearing a Baxter's Distillery T-shirt and a pair of gray sweatpants. His hair is mused, as if he just woke up. I squeeze the handle on the cart to keep from reaching out to run my hand through it.

"Who are you?" Pete asks.

"I'm hers." He points to me. "Who the hell are you?" Rhett asks, coming to stand behind me. He places his hands on my hips.

"I'm her—I mean, we're friends," Pete says.

"No we're not." I point to Tabitha. "You slept with your secretary, multiple times, while we were together. Then you knocked her up and kicked me to the curb. We're nothing."

Rhett's arm shoots around me, and he holds his hand out for Pete. Reluctantly, I see Pete take it and the slight wince as they shake hands. "Thank you," Rhett tells him. Pete furrows his brows in confusion. "If you wouldn't have fucked her over, I would have missed out on the best thing that's ever happened to me." He places his hand back on my hip.

Tabitha makes some kind of squeaking noise and stomps her foot like a toddler. Pete just stands there with his mouth hanging open. I'm not sure I've ever seen him speechless, which has a smile tilting my lips.

"Ready, baby?" Rhett asks, kissing my temple.

"Y-yes." I don't bother saying goodbye or that it was good to see them. No use in lying about it. I push the cart on shaking legs. Rhett places his hands on my shoulders and walks behind me. I walk until I reach the other side of the store then turn. It's then I notice we're in the dog food aisle.

"You all right, Short Stack?" Rhett asks, releasing me from his hold.

"Yep. You're making quite the habit of swooping in and saving the day."

"You looked like you wanted to be anywhere but there." He shrugs.

"Something like that," I agree.

"So, he's your ex?"

"Yep." I look up at the shelf, pretending to care about dog food.

"You have a dog?" he asks, amused.

"Nope. I should go. Thanks for that back there, but I had it handled."

"I know you did," he agrees. "But now he knows he fucked up. He's seen you with someone else."

I groan. "Great, now his calls are going to be more frequent."

"Possibly, but he'll know that the ship has sailed and that you've moved on. He might make a last-ditch effort, but he knows the deal."

I look up at him. "How are you so sure?"

"I'm a guy. I know that if I had a girl that looked like you and I lost her, I would try to get her back too. If I saw her with another, well, I would try even harder knowing that it's over. It's like I would have to give it one more go so I would always know I tried."

"That might be what you would do or even most guys, not Pete. He's relentless. He calls me a couple of times a week, and I just let it go to voice mail. I delete them without listening, and I ignore his texts."

"Is he stalking you?"

I laugh. "No, just annoying the hell out of me. Thanks again, I'll see you around," I say, gripping the cart and pushing it down the aisle.

"Short Stack!" he calls out.

I turn to look at him over my shoulder. "I accept all forms of sexual favors as payment." He smirks.

"Damn, and I gave my last sexual favor for the year last night." I shrug. "I guess you did this one for free." Turning back around, I push the cart to the end of the aisle. I see Pete and Tabitha are walking out the door, so I circle back around to the baking aisle to get the rest of my supplies.

When I reach the checkout, I see the vegetable tray and go ahead and get it. I'll just bring it to the fight tonight. I'm sure that's what Rhett was doing with it as well. No doubt he'll be there.

After unloading all the groceries, I put the meatballs in the Crock-Pot and start on the no-bake cookies. They're my favorite and one of the many items Elaine and I used to make every year around the holidays. I crank up the radio and get busy. By the time I'm finished, every inch of the counter, the small kitchen island, the dining room table, and two trays on the coffee table are filled with no-bake cookies. I might have gone a little overboard. I forgot that Elaine's recipe was tripled because of all the cookies she would give away. As a social worker, she became close to many families, and we always made tins full of goodies as gifts.

My phone rings, and I rush to put the pan down, wipe my hands, and find my phone under the rows and rows of cooling cookies. "Hello," I say quickly, hoping I didn't miss the call.

"Hey, Say," Tara greets me.

"Hey. How are you settling in?"

"Good. I miss you. I really wish you would come here to stay. Then at least I would have someone."

"I'm sorry. You know I can't do that."

"You can, you just refuse to," she says sarcastically.

"No, Tara, I can't. This is my life now. How is that fair to me to pack up and move just so you're not alone? Would you have done that for me?" I ask. I'm a little ticked off at her tone.

"I have Colin. You know I couldn't do that."

"Really, Tara? Do you hear yourself right now? You're pissed off that I won't move to live with you in Oregon because you're lonely. I get it, trust me I do. If anyone understands that it's me."

"You're stubborn," she snarks back.

"Stubborn? What has gotten into you?"

"Nothing. I need to go. I thought I could count on you."

"Tara, you can count on me. We're friends, but I can't just pack up my life because you're lonely. I have a life here."

"Right. You have no family, you can go anywhere."

My heart constricts at her harsh words. "I don't even know what to say to you right now," I whisper the words. How is this happening? Tara and I have been friends for years. She knows my history. How is she treating me like this?

"Whatever," she says, and the line goes dead.

Phone clutched in my hand, I step back until my body is aligned with the refrigerator. Hot tears prick my eyes. Tara has been my closest friend since I moved in with Elaine. I can't believe she would say those things. She used my history to hurt me. Why? Because I won't move across the country to live with her and her fiancé where I am guaranteed to be a third wheel the majority of the time? West Virginia is home now. Sure, I moved here with Pete, but that was after a lot of thought. We're not together, but that doesn't mean this isn't where I belong. I love working at the Corner Pocket, and I value the friendships I have with Jake and Molly. Life has taught me you depend on no one.

All I have is me.

I give myself a few minutes to let the tears fall before climbing to my feet. Feeling sorry for myself is getting me nowhere. Now more than ever I'm grateful for my decision to stay here to take the job at the Corner Pocket and the generosity of Molly and Jake. Grabbing a paper towel, I dry my eyes, wash my hands, and get back to work. Once all the cookies are dipped out onto wax paper, I head to the shower. I'm not going to think about it or let it get me down. I'm looking forward to tonight and meeting new people.

Just keep moving forward.

Grabbing a reusable shopping bag, I fill it with two containers of cookies. Luckily, the vegetable tray is sealed tight, so I tip it on its side and place it in the bag as well. I check to make sure my phone is in my pocket, as well as the key to the apartment. I know I'm just going next door, but you never know who could be lurking in the shadows. I shiver at the thought. Sliding into my coat, I throw the bag over my shoulder and grab the Crock-Pot from where I have it sitting on the table. I wanted it to cool off a little before the walk next door.

Setting the Crock-Pot on a small table that sits on the balcony of the steps, I pull the door closed and lock it before grabbing the food and starting my trek down the stairs.

"Hey," Rhett calls, climbing out of his truck. "Let me help you."

"I got it," I say. I walk right past him to the main house.

"Saylor, come on. Let me carry that," he says, catching up with me.

He puts his hand on my shoulder to stop me. I have no choice but to stop. With my hands full, I'm in no position to brush him off. Rhett takes the Crock-Pot out of my hands.

"Thanks," I mutter.

"Why are you so against people helping you?" he asks. He's not being a dick this time. I can tell from the sound of his voice, he really does want to know.

"Old habits and all that," I say, deflecting. He doesn't need to hear my life woes.

"We need to break those habits, Short Stack."

I don't comment. Instead, I knock on the front door.

"Go on in," Rhett tells me.

Before I can tell him no that it's rude, Molly answers the door. "Why are you knocking? Get in here, it's freezing out there," she says, stepping back from the door.

Rhett bends down next to my ear. "Told you."

I fight the urge to elbow him. "Do you have an open outlet where I can plug in the Crock-Pot?"

"Yeah, just set it over there." She points Rhett to an open spot beside the sink. "What's in the bag?"

"Rhett brought a vegetable tray, and I made cookies."

Molly looks between me and Rhett. "Did y'all come together?"

"Nope." I don't hesitate with my answer.

"We ran into each other at the store earlier. I left my stuff in her cart." He pulls out his wallet and hands me a twenty-dollar bill.

"Don't worry about it." I wave him off.

"Take it, Saylor," he says sternly.

"Just give it to Molly. It will be my contribution for the fight."

"I told you we were covering it. All you needed to do was bring a snack food."

"Well, I also told you I would pitch in. Now what can I do?"

"Nothing, we're good to go. Everyone else is in the living room. Let me introduce you." I nod and follow her into the living room, Rhett hot on my heels. "I want details," she whispers to me over her shoulder. I hear Rhett snicker from behind me.

"Baxter!" a deep voice calls out as we enter the living room. "Damn man, it's been too long."

"Gary, good to see you. Hey, Todd, Katherine," he greets the others.

"This is Saylor," Rhett says, placing his hand on the small of my back.

"Saylor," Molly says, looking over at Rhett with an odd expression, "works for us at the Corner Pocket. Saylor, this is Gary, Todd, and Katherine, Todd's fiancée."

"Nice to meet you." Katherine stands to shake my hand.

"You as well." Todd and Gary wave at me. Awkwardly, I wave back, feeling my face heat from embarrassment. Gary is a good-looking guy, and tall if the long legs stretched out in front of him are any indication. He has sandy blond hair, and I can see the blue of his eyes from here. They rival mine, but I have to admit the color looks better on him. His light features are night and day compared to Rhett with his dark hair and brown eyes.

"Sit wherever. Should be plenty of room," Molly says.

I survey the area. Jake is sitting in an oversized chair; Molly joins him. Katherine and Todd are cuddled up on the love seat, so that leaves the couch for me, Rhett, and Gary. Gary is already sitting on one end, so I head for the middle. I figure that will be the most comfortable for everyone, and you know sitting between two sex gods for the night isn't exactly a hardship. Maybe Rhett will be on his best behavior and not talk?

"Do you need any help getting the food out, Molly?" I ask before sitting down. Partially because that's who I am, it's what I do, and partially to delay taking my spot between Gary and Rhett, who is now sitting on the other end of the couch. The middle spot is nice and empty just for me.

"Nope, we're good."

Damn. Turning, I take the final steps and claim the center cushion.

"So, Saylor," Gary looks over at me and grins. "Are you new to town? I don't remember seeing you here or at the Corner Pocket."

"Not exactly. I've been here a few months; the Corner Pocket is more recent though."

"Nice." He looks down at my chest.

I fight the urge to roll my eyes. I try to turn my focus to the television and the preliminary fights, but I'm feeling a little out of sorts. I'm mentally going through my head, making a list of what I need to do tomorrow when I remember I forgot Rhett's clothes. Again. "Hey." I turn to look at him. "I have your clothes; I keep missing you when you're at the Corner Pocket. I meant to bring them tonight and I forgot."

He reaches out and tucks an errant piece of hair behind my ear. "No worries, Short Stack. I'll get them sometime."

"Figures," Gary mumbles.

"What?" I turn to ask him.

"Baxter got to you first," he says grumpily.

"I'm not following," I tell him.

"I'm starving. Let's eat before the main event starts," Jake says, standing. Everyone follows suit but me.

I hang back and let them go first. Rhett stands and offers me his hand. "You go ahead, I'll let the crowd die down."

Instead of walking away, he kneels in front of me. "If your ex keeps bothering you, let me know." He taps the end of my nose. "Now, come and get something to eat. Whatever you had in that Crock-Pot smelled fucking incredible." He grabs my hand and pulls me from the couch. He doesn't let go as he guides me into the kitchen with the others.

Molly notices and raises her eyebrows in question. I give her a subtle shake of my head. She mouths the word *later* and finishes making her plate.

I'm standing just inside the doorway, waiting my turn. Rhett is standing beside me. I can feel the heat radiating from him. He still has my hand in his. I try to pull away, and he holds tight.

He leans down and whispers softly, "I thought you liked my hands on you?"

I bite my tongue to keep from telling him off, but also from the contact. I'm torn; my body is telling me his touch is a good thing, a very good thing. My mind is telling me he's just another conceited asshole.

"So, Baxter," Todd says. "How long are you in town?"

Rhett turns his head to answer him, and I take that as my chance to wiggle out of his hold. I step forward, and he releases me. Grabbing a plate from the counter, I start adding a little bit of everything. I avoid eye contact and pretend to be enthralled by my finger food choices.

That was my mistake. I'm in the middle of placing two cocktail wieners on my plate when I feel him.

"What you got there?" he asks, standing way too close, looking over my shoulder.

"Cocktail wieners," I say.

He steps closer. "I like it when you talk dirty. Say it again, Short Stack."

"I-I didn't say anything." My voice sounds breathy even to me. What this guy does to me.

"You said cock," he says, pressing his into my back.

I close my eyes and take a deep breath. Thankfully, he's behind me. I don't need him to know how he affects me.

"I would give it to you, you know?" He leans in and places his lips next to my ear. "Do you want it, Saylor? Do you want my cock?" he asks cockily. No pun intended.

"Hey, Say," Molly says. "Uh, sorry, I was just checking on you," she says.

I duck under Rhett's arm, something I should have done the minute he walked up behind me. "I'm good. I'm right behind you," I say, walking toward her with my plate in one hand and a beer in the other. When I get in the living room, I heave a sigh of relief. Todd and Katherine are now on the couch. I make a mad dash to sit on the end. Leaving the open love seat spot for Rhett to sit beside Gary. The stars must be aligning in my favor tonight.

SEVENTEEN
Rhett

I FACE THE counter, not looking at Molly. Jake would kick my ass knowing my cock was saluting his girlfriend—well, not Molly, but in her direction. Saylor, though, she's got me hard as steel. She's so damn easy to rile up. Molly interrupted what I'm sure would have been a sassy comeback. It's probably a good thing she did. I shift my stance, and reaching down, I adjust my cock. Trying not to think about the throbbing in my pants, I fill my plate. Grabbing a beer from the fridge, I take a long pull.

"Baxter!" Jake yells. "Get your ass in here. It's about to start."

Thankful I wore a longer T-shirt tonight, I grab my plate and beer and head toward the living room. I'm expecting to be sitting beside her, so when I see that the only spot that remains is beside Gary, I grin. She could have sat next to him, but she chose not to. I'm not going to dwell on why that makes me happy.

Taking a seat on the love seat, I grab the pillow and place it on my lap. I set my plate on top of it as if I'm using it as a table. Thankfully, no one calls me out on it. Taking another pull of my beer, I let my eyes find her over the bottle. She's focused on the television, not paying me any attention. At least that's what she wants me and everyone else to think. I can tell by the pink of her cheeks that she's not focused on the fight on the screen. She's thinking about me. About my cock. Shit, as if on cue, I feel myself start to get worked up again. I'm going to have to carry this fucking pillow around all night.

When Jake starts yelling at the television, I turn my focus and keep it there. Me and the guys yell at the fighters and the announcers like they can hear us. We know they can't, but it makes us feel better. Katherine and Molly get in on the action in between talking about which fighters are the hottest. Jake and Todd grumble, which causes Gary and me to laugh our asses off. All the while, Saylor sits quietly. She chimes in on her picks when the girls ask her, but for the most part, she just sits back and takes it all in. She's laughing at our antics, and I like that. Her smile lights up her face, and her blue eyes sparkle, but there still seems to be something lurking just beneath the surface.

"Anyone need another?" Gary asks, holding up his empty beer bottle. After a chorus of yeses, he looks over at Saylor. "You mind helping me? I don't think I can carry all of these," he says with a laugh.

"Sure." She gives him a polite smile and follows him into the kitchen.

The fact that he's alone with her doesn't sit well with me. "I need more of those meatballs," I say, standing with my plate and heading toward the kitchen. Truthfully, they were great. I'm stuffed, but I'm willing to eat a few more just to see what they're up to.

"We should go out sometime," I hear Gary say as I walk in.

Not on my watch. "Hey, babe, I need more of those." I point to the Crock-Pot behind Saylor. "They're addicting," I tell her. She looks up at me with an odd expression on her face. I'm sure it's from the term of endearment. That's not us; that's not what we do. It just slipped out before I could stop it.

"Baxter," Gary says with grit in his voice.

"Have you tried these?" I ask, ignoring the daggers he's shooting at me. I get another big spoonful and add them to my plate. Instead of heading back into the living room, I lean against the counter, cross my legs, and start eating.

"Here," Saylor says, laughing. "You're eating like an animal." She holds up a napkin.

"What?" I say with my mouth full.

"That." She points at me. "Chew with your mouth closed." She holds the napkin up again.

I take it, letting my fingers brush hers. "Can't help it," I say, after swallowing.

"Were you raised with wolves?" she asks.

Gary snorts a laugh at the same time a round of "Ohhh's" comes from the living room. His desire to see what's happening is too strong, and he walks to the doorway to try to get a better look.

"You're right," I tell Saylor.

"About what? You being raised with wolves? I know better. Your grandpa is too nice for that."

"That I'm an animal. I could show you sometime. Help you work out some of that aggression."

"I don't sleep with animals. I'm allergic," she fires back.

"Hmmm," I muse. "I'm sure a dose of petercillin will do the trick."

She has just taken a drink, which was bad timing on my part because she laughs so hard she spits beer all over me. "I... I... I can't." She laughs. "Where do you come up with this shit?"

I fight hard to bite back my own laughter, keeping my face void of any emotion. "I'm telling you it cures what ails you. I think you should try it."

"Try what?" Gary asks, stepping back into the room.

"Short Stack makes a mean apple pie. I was just telling her that peach is better. I'm trying to get her to let me try hers," I say, not missing a beat.

Saylor just rolls those beautiful blue eyes, a smile tilting her lips. "We're missing the fight," she says, walking toward the living room.

"Really," I say, following her with my plate of meatballs. "I want to try your peach," I say, reclaiming my spot on the love seat while she takes hers on the couch.

"Fine, I'll make you a peach pie. Can we watch the fight?" she asks, exasperated.

I fight a grin. She thinks I meant pie, and I kind of did, but in the back of my mind she's the peach. Soft, pink, and I'm sure just as fucking sweet. I reach for the pillow and toss it over my lap. "You promise?" I ask her.

"Yes, Whiskey, I promise. Now hush." She points to the television and turns her attention to the fight.

Pushing thoughts of her out of my mind, I concentrate on the fight. By the time it's all over, the four of us guys are standing and yelling at the television. My guy, the underdog, won. "Hell yes." I pump my fist in the air.

"Damn," Gary mutters.

"What did you win?" Saylor asks me.

By the way I'm acting, you would think that I hit the fucking lottery. "Bragging rights." I grin. "No better winnings than bragging rights when it comes to this group."

"How old are you?" she asks.

I want to tell her that I can take her up to her apartment and show her that I'm old enough, that I'm all man, but I can't. Luckily, Saylor turns her attention to Molly.

"Do you need any help cleaning up?" she asks.

"No, I got it. We all used paper plates, so it won't take long. You headed home?"

"Yeah, thanks for having me."

"You need a ride?" Gary asks, sliding his arms into his coat.

"No thanks." She doesn't tell him that she just lives next door.

Smart girl.

Saylor disappears into the kitchen with Molly. "Good to see you." I shake Todd and Gary's hands. Leaning in, I kiss Katherine on the cheek. "You get tired of this guy… " I wink.

"That's enough. We're out." Todd places his arm over Katherine's shoulder and pushes Gary on the shoulder toward the front door. "Another fight in a couple of weeks, right after Christmas, we watching?" Todd asks.

"Let me check with Mol and I'll get back with you," Jakes tells him.

I stand back while he walks them to the door. I make myself useful and pick up a few random plates and beer bottles and carry them to the kitchen.

"What's going on?" I hear Molly ask.

"What do you mean?" Saylor asks her.

"Rhett," she says my name like that single word should tell all.

I thought I did a good job of hiding my reaction to her, but maybe not. I can't let Saylor take the heat. "Ladies," I say, announcing myself. "What can I help with?" I ask, tossing the plates and bottles into the trash.

"Thanks." Molly motions toward the trash can and the deposit I just made. "We're good."

"I'm just going to leave this. I won't eat these," Saylor says, pointing to the Crock-Pot.

Molly laughs. "Jake's got you covered there."

"I guess I'll get going." Saylor leans in and gives Molly a hug. "Thank you again for having me."

"You're always welcome here, Say."

"Especially when you bring meatballs," Jake chimes in, resting his elbows on the counter.

"I'm going to head out too. Saylor, I'll walk you out."

"I'm fine. I have, what, thirty feet?" she asks, heading to the front door, I assume to get her coat.

"I'll walk you," I say again. "Thanks, guys, this was a good time."

"Good to have you back. How long you staying?"

"Not sure yet. Gramps is doing better, but he's not ready to go back yet. I'll be here at least until after the first. I want to be here to see through the end of the year with the distillery."

"Yay, you'll be here for Christmas," Molly says.

I smile at her. "Yeah, I'll be here."

"Bye, thank you," Saylor calls out.

"Gotta go." I wave and rush to the front door. Sure enough, she's already outside. Grabbing my coat, I put it on as I jog after her. "I said I would walk you," I tell her. My long stride catches up to her quickly.

"I told you that you didn't need to. I live right outside their front door."

"Doesn't matter. It's late and dark out, and you live alone, so yeah, I'm making sure you get in okay."

"Are you going to check under my bed for monsters too?" she asks, full of sarcasm.

"Short Stack, are you trying to get me in your bed? You know I'll come willingly, so will you for that matter."

"You're impossible."

We reach the steps that lead up to her apartment. "Thank you, goodnight," she says, looking up at me.

"I'll walk you up."

"Rhett," she sighs. "This isn't necessary."

"Humor me."

Her reply is to stomp up the steps. It's dark, but the moon is bright, so I'm able to watch that tight ass of hers all the way up. It's a show worthy of an Emmy. "Door's locked," she says, making a point to show me she can't get in without her key. "You can go."

"I'll wait until you're inside." I stand there, my hands buried in my pockets to keep from reaching for her. Somehow, in between all our banter, she's dug herself just beneath the surface of my skin. I can't help but notice how beautiful she looks in the moonlight.

Once she has the door open, she steps inside and turns to face me. "Thank you, Rhett, goodnight," she says softly.

"Anything for you, Short Stack. I'll see you soon." I didn't expect the softness, for her to be nice. I was expecting snarky, sarcastic Saylor. This sweet version has me leaning in and kissing her cheek. "Goodnight," I whisper before pulling away.

She looks up at me, and although I can't see the ocean blue of her eyes, I can see the sparkle in them from the moonlight. Her lips tilt in a barely there smile before she turns to go inside. I stand there until I hear the lock click in place.

I'm halfway down the steps when I hear the door open. "Rhett," she calls out for me.

I stop immediately, turn, and jog back up the steps, my dick hard as steel, hoping she'll ask us to stay. But my heart is worried that something might be wrong once she goes inside alone. "Here," she hands me a small plastic bowl with a Christmas theme. "These are for you and your grandfather. Please tell him I said hello."

"What's this?"

"I made cookies earlier. I have way too many. It's a thank-you for making sure I made it in and for him, well, maybe it will cheer him up."

This right here is what makes her different, what makes her stand out from all of the rest. She's not out to get next to me because of my family name or the businesses. She doesn't see me as a meal ticket. Saylor is good and pure down to her soul. Suddenly, I want to know everything about her. I remember Jake telling me she's had it rough. What did her ex do other than cheat on her? It's in this moment, standing outside her door in the moonlight, holding a bowl of her homemade cookies, that I vow to find out.

"Thank you, Say. Goodnight." And because I can't help myself, I lean in and press my lips to her forehead. She grants me another kind smile when I pull back before she disappears inside and engages the lock. This time, I stand there a little longer, holding that plastic bowl like it's an extension of her. When the lights go out, I make my way down the stairs. She's getting ready for bed, I can't stand outside her door and imagine her getting naked. Nope, it's time to head home.

The house is quiet when I get home. I don't bother taking off my jacket as I make my way up to Gramps room with the bowl of cookies in hand. His door is cracked, and I can see the glow of the television. Quietly, I push open the door. "You're awake," I keep my voice low.

"Good thing or you would have woken me up."

He's still pissed, but at least he's talking to me now. "Saylor sent cookies. I wanted to see if you wanted one."

"Saylor you say?"

"Yeah, she was at Jake and Molly's tonight for the fight. I walked her home, and this was her thank-you to me and a get well to you."

"She lives above their garage," he says.

Shit. I didn't realize he knew that. "Yeah," I admit.

"Good choice," he says, holding a shaking hand out for the bowl. Grateful that he's engaging in conversation, I pull the lid off the bowl and offer it to him. "Your favorite," he says, taking one.

Looking down, I see the bowl is filled with no-bake cookies, and my mouth waters. "It's been a while since I've had one of these," I say, pulling one out and taking a big bite.

"Good," he says, shoving the rest of his into his mouth.

"Yeah," I agree, offering him another. He declines. "Right, well, I'll see you in the morning." I place the lid back on the bowl after I grab another for myself. He doesn't say anything this time, just nods and goes back to watching the television. "Night, Gramps." He doesn't reply, but then again, I didn't expect him to. He's starting to come around, I can feel it. At least I hope so. I can't leave until he's over this grudge he has toward me.

Stopping by the kitchen, I leave the cookies on the counter before heading to my room and stripping down to my boxer briefs for bed. My mind immediately goes to Saylor and what's happened in her life to keep her so guarded. I know it's not me. I can see the way her cheeks turn pink and her breathing accelerates when I'm close. It's something more, and I want to know. I need to know. I need to spend more time with her, and not while she's behind the bar. I know she won't see me on my own. That's when a though hits me. Grabbing my phone, I send a text to Jake.

Me: Hey, you all up for ice skating tomorrow?

Jake: Molly's asleep. I'll let you know in the morning.

Me: K. Invite Saylor too. I don't have her number.

I close my eyes and wait for his reply. I'm sure it will be some type of warning in regard to Saylor. She's gotten to both of them as well. They both care about her.

Jake: I'll let you know

His reply is simple and not what I expected. Maybe he's tired. Then again, maybe he just wants to issue a warning in person. Plugging my phone in, I place it on the nightstand. I fall asleep with the vision of her bathed in the moonlight.

EIGHTEEN

Saylor

"I 'M GOING TO fall on my ass," I tell Jake and Molly. I'm sitting on the back seat of Jake's truck, and we're headed to the Baxter's for a day of ice skating. "How did I let you talk me into this?" I ask them.

Jake laughs. "We'll help you. It's gonna be a good time," he assures me.

"I don't have skates, who goes ice skating without skates? Isn't it bad luck or something to wear someone else's skates?" I ask.

"No, and you have skates. I have two pair, and we're the same size. Now what?" Molly asks, turning to look at me.

I stick my tongue out at her. "Seriously, I tried roller skating once, and it was a disaster. I'll just sit on the sidelines and watch. You can show me what you're made of."

"It's going to be fine," Jake says, catching my eye in the rearview mirror.

"What if the ice is too thin and I fall in? What then?" I say, tossing out another worst-case scenario.

Jake pulls up to the house and turns to face me. "Saylor, it's safe. No way would I ever put Molly"—he reaches over and grabs Molly's hand—"or you in danger."

I nod. I know he wouldn't, but that still doesn't keep me from freaking out. "I've told you I'm not much of an adventurous girl, right?"

"We know," they say at the same time, laughing.

Before I can scold them for teasing me, Rhett comes out of the house, all bundled up with a pair of skates slung over his shoulder. He's also carrying what looks like a blanket. He climbs in the back seat beside me.

"Hey," he says in greeting. Jake and Molly reply. I, on the other hand, just stare out the window.

The more time I spend around him, the harder it is to keep up my hard-ass persona I've had with him. He may be cocky, but he's not the asshole I once thought he was. He has his moments, but he's a nice guy, and he's so damn pretty. That thought alone brightens my mood a little.

"You good?" he asks, reaching over and gently squeezing my knee.

"She's scared," Jake says. "She's never been."

"We've been over this. Y'all"—I motion to the three of them—"like to torture me." I cross my hands over my chest.

"We don't like to torture you," Molly says. I can't see her face, but I know from the sound of her voice she's rolling her eyes at me.

"Hmpf." I spend the rest of the ride looking out the window. The snow-covered landscape looks like a Christmas card or a scene from one of those holiday Hallmark movies. The truck stops just outside of a small log cabin that sits beside the large pond. "What's that?" I ask, pointing to the cabin.

"That's where we can go to stay warm," Rhett replies.

"Oh, so that's where I'll be while y'all are ice skating. Nice. This day is starting to look up."

He chuckles. "At least try it."

"Not you too," I groan.

"Come on, crazy girl," Molly says with a laugh, climbing out of the truck.

We follow Rhett to the cabin. I dance around in the cold while he unlocks the door. It's small, just a living area with a tiny kitchen, if that's what you even want to call it.

"There's a bathroom there." Rhett points to the only door.

"Here." Molly hands me a pair of skates. "Get these on, and we'll help you lace them up."

"Fine," I grumble. "Who's going to take care of me when I break my ass?" I mutter.

"I'll take care of you," Rhett says from beside me.

I was so focused on my fear, I didn't even notice that he'd taken the seat next to me.

"Right." I chuckle.

"What? You don't think I would?" he asks.

"Let's have it," I tell him.

"Have what?" He looks at me like I've lost my mind, and maybe I have.

"I know there's a sexual innuendo in there somewhere."

He throws his head back in laughter. I can't look away. He's smiling, causing his eyes to gleam. His hair falls over his eyes, and before I realize it, I reach out and push it back. His laughter dies as he watches me. "I can give you an innuendo if you want it," he says, his voice low so Molly and Jake can't hear him. "I can also assure you that if you need me, I would take care of you. No matter what the situation." He winks.

Damn him. I turn away and pull off my boots, pulling on the skates. "Is there a trick to this?" I ask loud enough everyone can hear me. "Some kind of super-secret skate tying form that I'm not aware of?"

"Let me," Rhett says. He slides off the couch and kneels in front of me.

I sit on my hands to keep from reaching out and touching him. I watch him as he carefully laces each skate.

"You'll be wobbly at first, but I'll help you." He looks up at me, and I get lost in his eyes. I've never seen anything like them before. "I won't let you fall, Say. I promise." There's conviction in his voice, and I'm reminded again that Rhett Baxter the third is one of the good guys.

"You guys ready?" Jake asks.

"Let me lace mine up," Rhett says, taking the seat next to me and slipping his sock-covered feet into his skates.

I close my eyes and try to calm my nerves. I'm not sure now if I'm more nervous about ice skating for the first time or because of Rhett. It's both, but I'm thinking a little more of Rhett now. He's managed to calm my nerves about skating. There is something in his eyes and in the conviction of his voice that makes me trust him. He saved me in the grocery store—not that I needed saving, but he helped me out of an awkward situation. Last night walking me home, when I didn't need it. He's just one of those guys that you know deep in your gut that what you see is what you get.

When I feel him stand, I open my eyes. He's holding his hand out for me. "I don't think I can do this," I tell him.

"You can. I've got you."

Reluctantly, I stand and take his hand. I wobble immediately, and he places his hands on my hips to steady me. Suddenly, this idea just got a whole lot more appealing.

"Take it slow, one small step at a time. You'll get used to it," he tells me.

"Have you never used rollerblades?" Jake calls as soon as we're out of the cabin.

"No," I yell back.

Rhett puts his arm around me, his hand resting at my hip. I'm pressed against his side, holding onto his other hand with a death grip. "I'm not going to let you fall." He chuckles when I wobble and dig my nails into the skin on his arm.

When we reach Jake and Molly, she gives me a big hug—well, me and Rhett since I refuse to let go of him. "You got her, or you want me to take her out?" Jake asks.

"I've got her," Rhett tells him. "You ready, Short Stack?"

Taking in a deep breath, the cold air burns my lungs. "Yes, as ready as I'll ever be." With that, I follow him to the edge of the pond. He steps on the ice, his arms outstretched, still holding on to me on the bank. With small wobbly steps, I move toward him.

"That's it, one at a time," he instructs.

I step onto the ice and slide into him. He immediately wraps his arms around me, hands resting on my hips. I feel him rest his chin on the top of my head. "We're going to go slow. I think, maybe, me being behind you is best so I can help guide you until you get the feel of it."

"Okay," I agree meekly.

"You stand still. I'll move behind you, and then we'll start slow."

He steps away from me, and I miss the warmth of his arms wrapped around me. He does just like he said, moves behind me and places his hands on my hips. He's close, way closer than I'm sure he needs to be, but I'm not going to say a word. His presence is making this so much better.

"Slow," he whispers, his hot breath against my cheek. "Slide one foot in front of the other."

Ever so slowly, I push one foot, just barely, then the other. Each time, I get a little braver. I wobble a little, and Rhett tightens his hold, moving in closer.

"I've got you, Say."

I nod. One foot in front of the other, I focus on the simple movement of my feet, blocking out everything else. It's not until I hear Molly cheering that I realize I'm halfway around the big-ass pond.

"Woohoo, you go girl!" she cheers.

"Don't distract me," I yell back through my laughter. I'm doing it. I'm actually ice skating. Well, if you can call it that. I do have the sexy Rhett Baxter guiding me.

"You ready to go on your own?" he asks.

My hands fly to my hips to grip his hands, causing me to stumble. Rhett pulls me tight against him, my back to his front, and steadies me. "I'll take that as a no?" he asks, amused.

"That's a hell no," I say, laughing.

"Take a spin with me," Molly says, appearing beside us.

"Molly, can you not see that I'm not exactly doing this on my own?" I ask her.

"I can guide you," she says. "Step away, Baxter." She pushes on Rhett's arm, causing me to stumble.

"Molly!" I scream, laughing. "You about made me fall."

"Yeah, but you didn't." She grins.

"You ready?" Rhett asks.

"No." I feel him slowly step away. Molly steps up beside me, linking her arm through mine. "Uh, Molly, what are you doing?"

"We're going to make a lap around."

"You need to get behind me," I tell her.

"Nope. We're going like this."

"You good, Short Stack?" Rhett asks.

"Probably not," I mumble.

"Race ya," Jake says, flying by us.

Rhett looks over at me, and I wave him on. "Go."

He takes off after Jake, leaving me and Molly with our arms linked. "Okay," she says, "let's do this."

With my arm clutching hers, we start slow. "You're doing great. Is this as bad as you thought it would be?"

"No," I admit.

"Could that have something to do with Rhett?"

"He's been... helpful."

"Right." She laughs. "He's had his hands all over you. I think he likes you."

"What?" I turn to look at her and lose my balance. She's not strong enough to stop us as we tumble to the ice. We both hit with an umpf in a tangle of limbs. We manage to roll onto our backs and fall into a fit of laughter.

"You okay?" Jake asks, offering Molly a hand.

"Up you go, Say," Rhett says, holding both of his hands out for me. He already knows that just one isn't going to be enough to get me on my feet and steady. I take his hands and allow him to pull me up. I'm like a new baby deer with wobbly legs. He wraps his arms around me and pulls me close to his chest. I take a few seconds to breathe him in. *Damn, he smells good.*

"What happened?" Jake asks.

"Nothing, we were just talking and lost our footing," Molly tells him.

"We can't leave you girls alone for five minutes," he jokes.

"Ready to go again?" Rhett asks me.

I pull away from his chest, now aware that I remained snuggled up to him. Molly's going to have a field day with that. "Do we have to?"

"Yes. If you don't get back on the horse, so to speak, you never will. Just a few more laps, and then we can go in and get warm."

"Right. Okay, let's do this." He smiles down at me, and my heart skips a beat.

He moves behind me, hands on my hips, and we're off. As we skate several more laps, I grow more confident with each one. Rhett doesn't let go, and I don't want him to. We've had a day where we've called a truce so to speak, and it's been… nice. When we're all numb, we head inside to get warm. I expected to have to light a fire, but this place has a full electric heating and cooling system. Rhett said it's nice in the summer when you go fishing and need to get cooled off or use the bathroom. I wouldn't know, that's not exactly my thing. What I do know is that his grandfather's property is amazing, and if I were him, I'd never want to leave. Then again, this might be nothing in comparison to where he lives. I don't really know much about him outside of our time here in West Virginia.

After warming up, we head back to the house to drop Rhett off. Molly and Jake are talking, engrossed in conversation, so I take the opportunity to thank Rhett. "Thanks for your help today."

"Anytime, Short Stack. You looked good out there," he says with a gleam in his eyes.

"Oh yeah, you only seen me from behind," I say, and as soon as the words leave my mouth, I know I've talked myself into a corner.

"I know." He wags his eyebrows.

He's back to being flirty Rhett. I find that I like both versions of him, so much so I don't even offer a comeback. I just wear my blush and look at the window.

"See you soon," he says, leaning into me. I don't get to reply before he's thanking Jake for the ride and hopping out of the truck.

"Tell your grandfather I said thanks and I'll be over to see him in a couple of days."

"You do that a lot?" Rhett asks through the window.

"Yeah, Jerry and I come out at least once a week. Molly comes sometimes too to keep him company."

"Right. Yeah, I'll tell him. See you later." He turns and runs to the house to get out of the cold. I watch him until he disappears behind the door. I have this nagging feeling that I should be with him. Today was unexpected and fun. Days like this have been few and far between for me lately, and I find myself wanting to hold on to it. Or is it him I want to hold on to?

NINETEEN

CAN'T BELIEVE it's already Christmas Eve. I've been here for two months. Much longer than what I had originally thought I would be, but I'm enjoying my time here. I like the work I'm doing at the distillery. It's similar to what I do for the brewery back home, but more. I'm basically Dad at the brewery. It's been a nice change of pace. Gramps is still a little distant, but each day he opens up more, forgets to be angry with me at some point throughout the day. It's to the point that it's comical. I can tell he's just being stubborn and holding out. It takes all I have not to laugh in front of him.

My parents arrive today. They're only going to be here until the day after Christmas, but it will be good to see them. The plan is for everyone to come over tonight to hang out and eat some good food. There are no small kids in the family, so there is no pretense of Santa coming. Jake and Molly will be here, as well as Jerry. Jake's parents are deceased, and Molly, well, I don't know the entire story, but I know that her home life was not the best and she doesn't really have much, if anything, to do with her parents. My mind drifts to Saylor. I know she's alone too. I made sure to tell both Jake and Molly that she was more than welcome to come with them, but now I feel like I should have made it a point to tell her myself. Make sure she knows she's welcome. I hate the thought of her sitting up in that garage apartment all alone.

The alarm at the gate buzzes, and I jump up from my place on the couch. I'm sure it's my parents. They're pulling into the circle drive just as I get the door open. Mom hops out of the car and rushes toward me.

"Slow down, woman, you're going to fall and break your neck," my dad calls after her.

She doesn't slow, so I make my way down the steps to greet her. "I've missed you," she says, wrapping her arms around me.

"Missed you too, Mom," I say, chuckling. "How was the drive?"

"Good. Beautiful actually with the snow on the trees. It's the perfect scenario—no snow on the roads, but in the scenery."

"Hey, Dad." I lean in for a quick hug and pat on the back.

"How's he doing?" Dad motions his head toward the house.

"Let's move inside before we all freeze to death," Mom says, tugging on each of our arms.

"Good. Stubborn as hell," I tell them once we're inside. "He's balking at being nice, but I see cracks in his façade every day."

They both laugh. "Sounds about right."

"What's that?" Gramps says, joining us.

"Oh nothing, just talking about the weather and the drive here," Mom says, walking toward my grandfather and giving him a hug. "How are you, Dad?" she asks.

When I was a little boy, it would confuse the hell out of me that she also called him Dad when he's my dad's dad. As I got older, I realized it was easier with all three of us being named Rhett. Sometimes she refers to him as Senior, but mostly it's Dad, and Gramps eats it up. Dad said that Mom had a lot to do with the riff between them disappearing. Gramps has a soft spot for her. Grams passed when Dad was a senior in high school. Gramps has been alone since. Regret fills me, just another reminder I should have spent more time here.

"Good to see you." Gramps returns her hug. "Son," Gramps says. Dad smiles and leans in to give him a quick hug. "Jerry and the kids will be here in about an hour," Gramps tells us.

"Son," Dad looks over at me. "Help me get our bags? We'll have just enough time to freshen up before everyone gets here."

"What about food?" Mom asks. "Is there anything that I can do?"

"Nope. Rosa was here this morning. She's got everything ready to go. We just have to heat it up," I tell her.

"Well, we stopped off at the store, and I plan on making cookies. No-bake." Mom looks at me. "I know those are your favorite, and I haven't made them in forever. I also got the ingredients for peanut butter." She winks at Gramps.

"We had some good no-bake just a few weeks ago," Gramps tells her. "Saylor made them."

"Saylor?" my parents ask in unison.

"Yeah, she's working for Jake and Molly down at the Corner Pocket. She's actually living in their garage apartment. She's alone, no family. She spent Thanksgiving with us," I explain.

"Sweet girl," Gramps says. "Val, why don't we go sit while these two bring in your things?" He looks over at me. "I had Rosa make up the room down the hall from mine for them."

I nod. It's odd, usually they're on the same side of the house as me, but I don't say anything. It's just a room; they're all great, and he's not being standoffish, so I don't want to piss him off by questioning his room assignment. It's his house after all.

Forty minutes later, the alarm buzzes again. Mom is in the kitchen baking while Gramps, Dad, and I sit at the table and watch her. She insisted we would be in the way. "I'll get it," I say, jumping to my feet. Jerry has his hand up to knock when I open the door. "'Bout time you get here, old man." I pull him into a hug. "Merry Christmas."

I greet Jake the same way, opting to lean in and kiss Molly on the cheek. Then she's there, Saylor. She's beautiful. Her hair is in big soft curls flowing down her back. Today she's wearing another pair of those legging things with a red sweater, a black scarf, and, of course, those fuck-me boots of hers that I've grown to love. Sure, they look great on her, but I've imagined her in those and nothing else. It's a new development from annoyance to desire. Over the past couple of weeks, I've visited the Corner Pocket more than I would have if she wasn't behind the bar. We still bicker back and forth, but now it's... different, as if we've called a silent truce and we're old friends just giving each other shit.

"Saylor." Her name is a whisper on my lips as I lean in and kiss her cheek. She sucks in a breath. That sound mixed with her sweet scent has my cock taking notice that she's here. I've learned my lesson around her; I wore a black button-down with a pair of jeans, opting to leave the

131

button-down untucked.

"Merry Christmas, Rhett. Thank you for having me. Are you sure I'm not intruding?" she asks.

Not able to resist, I place my arm around her and pull her into me. "You're always welcome, Short Stack." She nods, and even though I don't want to, I release her and lead them into the kitchen. I lean against the counter while my parents greet them. Then Mom turns to Saylor. I can see the hesitation in Saylor's eyes. I have to shove my hands in my pockets to keep from reaching for her to ease the worry.

"You must be Saylor?" Mom asks.

"Yes, ma'am. It's nice to meet you," she replies softly.

Mom wipes her hands on her apron and rounds the island, pulling Molly first, then Saylor into a hug. "It's so nice to not be outnumbered by these goons." She smiles with affection.

I can visibly see Saylor relax.

"I'm making cookies. I hear you're good at no-bake," Mom says to Saylor.

"I used to bake all the time with... yeah, I made some a few weeks ago."

"Perfect, I could use some help." Mom reaches into a drawer and tosses her an apron. The beaming smile that Saylor gives her in return is blinding. "Molly?" Mom asks.

"I'll supervise. You want them to be edible, right?" she jokes.

"Oh, come on now, you've baked with me before."

"She has, and remember what the kitchen looked like when you were done?" Jake asks.

Molly smacks his belly. "Hey now," she scolds him.

Jake pulls her into him and kisses her. "You know I love you," he mumbles, but we can all hear him.

"Enough of that. Shoo." Mom waves her hands. "Go bond, do manly things. Us ladies need some girl time."

Dad and Gramps are already headed toward the living room. Jake whispers something to Molly and follows them. I make eye contact with Saylor and mouth, "You okay?" She gives me a shy smile and a nod. Good enough for me. I follow Jake into the living room.

"So what's her story, man?" I ask Jake. Dad and Gramps are engrossed in conversation, not paying any attention to us.

"That's her story," Gramps grumbles.

Shit. How did he hear that? "I'm just curious," I tell him.

"Honestly, man, I don't know it all—at least I don't think I do. She's not had it easy in life. She's one of the nicest people you will ever meet." He gives me a pointed look.

"What?" I ask.

"You want to know, you get it from her," Gramps interrupts us again.

I look over at him and nod. He holds my gaze for so damn long I start to squirm. Finally, he must find what he's looking for, and he turns back to his conversation with Dad.

"So, I want to run something by you," Jake says.

"Lay it on me," I say, pushing thoughts of Saylor and her story out of my mind.

Jake looks over his shoulder toward the kitchen, then pulls a small black velvet box out of his pants pocket. With another look over his shoulder, he opens the box. A diamond solitaire shines back at me. "What do you think?" he asks.

"I think congratulations are in order."

"I've read articles where I shouldn't do it on a holiday, you know, but this isn't her gift. I just thought all of our closest people are here, and I want her to remember it."

"You doing it today?" I ask him.

"I think so. I mean, I'm nervous as hell, and I feel like I'm screwing up by not having some big elaborate proposal full of romance, but I can't think of anything except asking her, her saying yes, and spending the rest of my life with her."

I can't help but smile at that. "You two are solid. She's going to love it. You need my help with anything?"

"Fuck! Maybe. Maybe I should take her down by the pond? I mean, we've all spent so much time there over the years. She loves it there."

"Done." I stand. "Let's go get the UTV gassed up and throw in a couple of blankets. You can take her for a drive later."

He nods. "Yeah, I like that." Standing, he follows me.

We have to pass through the kitchen to get to the garage. "Smells good in here." I lean over Saylor's shoulder and look at what she's doing.

"What's that?" I ask her.

"Sugar cookies," she says as she works on cutting out shapes that look like stockings.

"We're going out to the garage," I tell them.

"Are you asking permission?" Mom asks with a grin.

Saylor's shoulders lift with her silent laughter.

I step into her, my front aligned with her back. "What's so funny?" I ask, giving her hips a gentle squeeze.

"Nothing," she says with a giggle.

Mom looks up and then down at my hands on Saylor's hips and smirks. "You're in the way. Now shoo." She waves a flour-covered hand toward the door that leads to the garage.

Reluctantly, I step away from Saylor. "You ladies be good," I say, turning for the garage. Luckily, Jake is so preoccupied with his proposal to Molly, he doesn't notice how Saylor's affecting me. The girls on the other hand—well, at least my mom, she's onto me. I don't even know what it is; there's just something about Saylor that has me wanting more. So much more, which is crazy because I don't even really know her.

TWENTY

Saylor

"**M**Y SON SEEMS quite enamored with you," Valerie says.

I choke on a laugh. "Um, we barely like each other."

"Really? You could have fooled me." She smiles kindly.

"They usually are bickering back and forth," Molly adds. "However, lately that's been less and more... friendly." She looks over at me. "What was that anyway?" she asks.

"What was what?" I play dumb. I know exactly what she's asking, and I don't have an answer for her.

"That." She points at my hips.

I shrug. "Who knows why men do the things they do?" I say, shrugging. What I don't say is that since that day at the pond when we went ice skating, there have been more soft touches. Like when he stops by the bar, he'll reach out and grab my hand or stay and walk me to my car, things like that. There's been a lot more of that. I have no clue what it means, if anything, so bringing it up isn't an option.

"Well, I know my son, and I think he likes you," Valerie chimes in.

I can feel my face heat. "He's just being nice," I counter.

"Uh-huh," she and Molly say at the same time.

"What's next?" I ask, laying the last sugar cookie on the baking sheet.

I'm changing the subject, and we all know it. Luckily, they let me.

Molly takes pity on me and launches into a story about the last time she tried to make a cake. I give her a grateful smile, and she winks. We finish up the baking a couple of hours later. The house smells amazing, so much so it's making me hungry.

"Ladies, let's take a break. We've earned it," Valerie says. Molly and I follow her into the living room where the guys are watching *A Christmas Story*.

"I love this movie," I say out loud, not meaning to.

"It's a classic," Molly agrees. She sits on the oversized chair—well, technically, she sits on Jake's lap, and he's sitting on the chair. Jerry is in the recliner beside Grandpa Rhett. Valerie joins Rhett's dad on the love seat, which leaves the couch for me and Rhett.

There's a throw blanket on the back of the couch, and I grab it, spreading it out over my lap. I wish I could kick off my boots and curl up. Instead, I train my eyes on the TV and get lost in the movie I've seen what seems like hundreds of times.

"I'm going to go take a nap before we eat," Grandpa Rhett says.

"After a long day of travel, that sounds perfect." Valerie stands and takes his arm, leading him up the steps. Rhett's dad follows his wife and father.

Then there were five.

"Me too. I'm going to find me a bed in one of these empty bedrooms and catch me a nap too. I'm not a spring chicken like I used to be," Jerry says.

And then there were four.

"Hey, babe, I thought we could take the UTV down to the pond, check it out with all the snow," Jake says.

"Do you mind?" she asks Rhett.

"Not at all. Key's in it. There are some blankets in the trunk by the door. Make sure you grab a couple and take your phones just in case."

"Thanks, man," Jake says, giving Rhett a look of relief. He must have been worried about Molly having to walk if they break down. Weird.

"You all want to come?" Molly asks.

"Actually," Rhett speaks up. "I need Short Stack to help me with something for Gramps." He looks over at me. "You don't mind, do you?"

"Not at all." I want to ask him what he needs help with, but his grandfather has been so kind to me, going as far as saying I was family to them, the least I can do is help him out when he needs it. Molly and Jake disappear into the garage.

And then there were two.

"So what do you need help with?" I ask Rhett.

"Nothing, I might have told a small white lie."

I turn to look at him. "Why?"

"Jake needed Molly alone for a little while."

"Oh," I say, not knowing what else to say. "You can go. I mean, if you have something to do, I'll be okay here with Ralphie to keep me company."

"Nope. I got nothing going on. Here." He scoots to the edge of the couch and pulls my leg onto his lap. I watch him as he slowly slides the zipper down and pulls my boot from my foot.

"Wh-what are you doing?" I ask him.

"We might as well get comfortable. I know you want to curl up to watch this." He motions with his head to the television.

"Was I that obvious?"

"Not to anyone who's not watching." He removes my other boot.

"You were watching?"

He nods. "I can't seem to help myself when it comes to you," he admits. He stands and places my boots beside the couch. He grabs the throw from my lap. "Get comfortable."

I do as he says and pull my feet up under me. Rhett waits until I'm settled before placing the throw over me. "Thank you," I say, looking up at him.

He nods. After kicking off his shoes and placing them beside mine, he sits on the couch right next to me. Instantly, I can feel his warmth even through the cover. "You good?" he asks, leaning so that his arms are resting on my legs, leaning across my lap.

"Y-yes," I stutter like an idiot. This new dynamic with us is confusing as hell. Rhett rewinds the movie so we can watch what we missed. I don't say anything as I try to focus on the movie and not on his hand that is gently rubbing my knee from where his arm is resting on my legs. It's arousing and… relaxing. It's a new concept for me. Pete was never really affectionate, and I was okay with that. Elaine was really the only person in my life to ever show me open affection.

Eventually, the caressing stops and his breathing is deep and even. He's fallen asleep. Grabbing the remote, I turn it to a random Christmas movie on the Hallmark channel. I turn down the volume, so I don't disturb him. My hand itches to run through his hair. It always looks so soft. I refrain, not wanting to wake him up. Instead, I settle for resting my hand on his back as he sleeps soundly against me. I'm sleepy, but I fight it off. I like being able to see him like this. I wish I could see his face. I imagine his features are soft and relaxed, which is not a look I'm used to seeing on him.

Turning my attention back to the television, I get engrossed with one of the many holiday movies I've watched. This is a repeat, but that's okay. They only play them this time of year. I always find myself being envious of the characters, the way their love interest loves them, fights for them, romances them. It's not something I've experienced. Looking back at what Pete and I had, I know I was settling, and that's not how I want to live my life. It's mine, and mine alone. I don't have family to run to; I need to make it what I want it to be. I have a second chance to find a Hallmark kind of love, and that's what I want. One day, I want that to be me. I want to be the one who finally lives happily ever after. Will I ever find him? My Prince Charming? My knight in shining armor?

"That feels nice," a deep, sleep-lace voice says, causing me to freeze. "Don't stop, Say," he whispers.

That's when it hits me that my hand is in his hair. I've been running my fingers through the silky stands unconsciously. *Dammit.* "I'm sorry I woke you," I say softly.

He adjusts so that he's lying sideways and his head is in my lap. His big brown eyes stare up at me. "It feels nice." He reaches for my hand and places it on his head. My fingers have a mind of their own as they begin to comb through his hair. My other hand is on the back of the couch, since I'm not sure where I should put it. Rhett reaches up and laces his fingers through mine, placing our hands on his chest. His eyes are still on mine, and I can't look away.

"You're beautiful, Saylor," he murmurs. My face heats, I feel it, and I know he sees it when his eyes sparkle. "That too," he says softly. "That blush of yours could bring a man to his knees."

"What about you?" I ask boldly. I bite my bottom lip. I can't believe I just said that. If I thought I was blushing before, it's tenfold now.

"Yeah, baby, especially me," he admits without any hesitation.

"So Whiskey, huh?" I ask him.

"Yeah, well beer actually. My father owns Baxter's Brewery in Tennessee. He and my Gramps didn't always see eye to eye, so he branched out on his own."

"Which do you like better?"

"They're both the same in my eyes. Although, growing up Gramps always said I would one day run the distillery."

"But you work for your father?"

"Yeah, after college I went to work for him. It wasn't until recently, being here I was reminded of the plans Gramps and I had as a kid."

"I love your eyes," I tell him. "Have I ever told you that?" I ask changing the subject. Partly because he seems sad and partly because his whiskey eyes are boring into mine.

"No."

"Yeah," I say, still running my fingers through his hair, not taking my eyes off his. "That's why I call you Whiskey. Your eyes, the color reminds me so much of whiskey—well, that and it was your choice of drink that first night I met you. It fit. At the time, I had no idea who you were."

"Yours remind me of a clear blue sky. They're intoxicating."

The garage door opens, and I hear footsteps. I try to pull my hand from his, but he's not having it. My hand that was in his hair is now on the arm of the couch. I feel like I'm a teenager who's just been caught in a compromising position. Ridiculous I know, but it is what it is.

"Saylor!" Molly says excitedly. She rushes to the couch, where Rhett's head is still resting on my lap, and shoves her left hand in my face. "We're getting married!"

"Wow! I'm so happy for you," I tell her. "Your ring is gorgeous."

"EEEP! Thank you! Did you know?" she asks me.

"No." I look down at Rhett, and he winks at me. I smile at him. Now I know why he wanted us to stay here. I'm glad that we did. Not sure I would have had the chance to spend one-on-one time with him if not.

Molly's smile turns smug. "What did you two get into?"

"Just watching some TV," Rhett says, not bothering to move.

"Uh-huh. You look awful cozy," Jake says from behind Molly.

Rhett turns to look up at me. "We are," he agrees.

Oh. My. God. *What is going on here?*

"What's all the commotion?" Jerry asks when he comes into the room.

"Look!" Molly shoves her hand at him.

"Bout damn time, boy." Jerry pulls Molly into a big hug. "Welcome to the family, darlin,' not that you needed this ring for that. You've been a part of our family from day one."

Tears prick my eyes.

"You okay, Say?" Rhett whispers.

"Yeah, I need to use the restroom." I can tell from the look in his eyes he doesn't believe me, but he doesn't call me out on it. Instead, he gives my hand a gentle squeeze then sits up.

I bolt off the couch and down the hall before the tears fall. Closing the bathroom door, I rest my back against it and lose the battle. Hot tears run unchecked down my cheeks. I'm happy for them, of course I am, but this family dynamic they have has me longing for what I don't have, for what I've never really had. It was Elaine and me, and I'm so grateful for everything she did for me, but I want more. I want lots of people around for the holidays. I want a list of people to shop for. I want the sense of belonging. My heart aches as the tears fall.

Knowing that I need to get myself together and get back out there, I take a deep breath and focus on breathing slow. In and out, in and out. I get my breathing under control and get the tears to subside. Grabbing a tissue, I wipe off my face. Thankfully, I don't wear a lot of makeup; some waterproof mascara is all I wore today, so that's good. My eyes are a little red, but I can blame that on being tired. After I'm as good as I'm going to be until time wipes the effects of the tears from my face, I open the door and head back to the living room. It's empty, but the laughter and conversation coming from the kitchen tells me where I need to be. With one more deep breath, I square my shoulders and follow the chatter.

"There she is," Grandpa Rhett says when I enter the kitchen. "You hungry?"

"Yes." I smile at him.

"So, for Christmas Eve, we have snack foods that Rosa always insists on making for us," Valerie explains. "We sit around snacking, sometimes we play cards, we watch movies, we just… be. Then Christmas morning, we head to the local homeless shelter and serve. We started that once Rhett was too old to believe in Santa. After that, we come home, and I make Christmas dinner."

"You coming with us tomorrow, Short Stack?" Rhett asks.

"I, uh, I don't want to intrude," I say.

"Never," he says.

"We'd love to have you, Saylor," his dad adds. "Jake and Molly go with us every year."

"I don't—" I start to say again that I don't want to intrude, but Rhett interrupts me.

"I'll swing by and pick y'all up in the morning. Be ready around nine," he says.

He's looking right at me. I give him a slight nod, and the smile that tips his lips tells me he's happy with my decision. "What can I do to help?" I ask his mom.

"Nothing, dear. It's all set up. Rosa spoiled me yet again with her preparation. Y'all grab a plate," she says.

We all gather around and fill our plates with snack foods. Rosa really did go all out. I thought we would go to the dining room, but we don't. Everyone grabs a seat in the living room. Oddly enough, we take the same seating as earlier, only this time, Rhett sits next to me instead of on the opposite end of the couch. We eat and talk. Molly and Valerie talk about the wedding, which Molly says is going to be small and intimate.

"What about you, Saylor? What kind of wedding do you want?" Valerie asks me.

"Honestly, I've never thought much about it," I tell her.

"You've never thought about it? What about with your ex?" Molly says.

I laugh. "We were together for a while, but our relationship wasn't all romance and flowers." I shrug. "We hadn't made any definite plans, and I was in no hurry to."

"Sounds like you dodged a bullet," Grandpa Rhett says.

"I think you're right," I agree with him. Pete sleeping with Tabitha and getting her knocked up might be one of the best things that's ever happened to me in my long line of bad situations.

"Who's ready for some bullshit?" Jerry asks. His face is split with his grin.

"Have you ever played?" Grandpa Rhett asks me.

"No, I have no clue," I admit.

"You're in for a treat, Short Stack," Rhett says next to my ear.

Goose bumps break out across my skin. Why is he affecting me like this? He's just a guy, a really, really good-looking guy. "Why's that?"

"These two"—he points to his gramps and Jerry—"are the best bullshitters I know."

"So, how do you play?" I ask Jerry.

"You got a poker face, darlin?" he asks.

"Um, not that I'm aware of. I've never played poker. My extent of card games stops at Go Fish and Uno."

Jerry claps his hands and rubs them together. "Sit by me, sweetheart. I'll show you the ropes."

"I don't think she needs you corrupting her," Valerie chimes in. "Us ladies will stick together."

"Okay, so here's how you play," Jake says. I listen to him explain the game, and it doesn't seem hard. I basically have to bullshit on how many cards I have. I can do this.

I follow the crowd down to the basement where there is a round professional card table set up. Valerie motions for Molly and me to sit on either side of her, claiming girl power and all that. Grandpa Rhett ends up on my other side. Jerry is beside Molly with Rhett's dad in the middle of Rhett and Jake across from us.

"Let the games begin!" Jerry exclaims with a chuckle.

And so we do. We spend a few hours playing the game that has us in a fit of laughter the entire time. I learned quickly to pay attention, to read each of them. Grandpa Rhett and Jerry are good, but not good enough. All my life I've been in the shadows. I've watched people, and I've hidden my emotions. I know better than anyone how to hide what you're feeling. I never thought that particular trait would come in handy in anything other than protecting my heart, but here I am calling bullshit on Grandpa Rhett for... I've lost count how many times. His brown eyes, not quite the cognac color of Rhett's, sparkle with laughter.

"Girlie, you're giving an old man a run for his money," he claims, laughing.

"Oh wait! We're playing for money? I better step up my game," I tease him.

The table bursts into laughter. Grandpa leans into me and whispers, "I told you you were family."

My eyes mist with tears as I give him a smile. When I look up, I find Rhett's eyes on me. He raises his eyebrows in question. I'm not sure if he wants to know if I'm okay or what it is his grandfather just whispered to me. Either way, I smile, letting him know I'm good and quickly look away.

"It's getting late. We probably ought to get home," Jake says. Jerry and Rhett's dad clean up the cards while the rest of us head upstairs. "I'm going to go start the truck." Jake kisses Molly on the cheek. He walks to the window in the front room and holds up his remote.

"So, I'll be there to get you all early in the morning. Around nine," Rhett says from his spot next to me.

"Okay. Thank you. Are you sure it's okay if I tag along?"

He reaches up and pushes my bangs out of my eyes. "Yeah, Short Stack, it's okay."

"Well, I don't think we're going to be going anywhere," Jake says from behind us. We all turn to face him.

"Why's that?" Molly asks.

"There's ice everywhere. It's too slick to drive."

"Well, we've got the space. Jake and Molly, you can stay in the room just down from Jerry. Saylor, you can stay in the room across the hall from Rhett. He'll show you where to go. The rest of you follow me," Grandpa Rhett says. "I'll dig out something for you to sleep in," he says, turning to make his way up the steps.

TWENTY ONE

STAND THERE with Saylor beside me and watch as everyone disappears up the steps. Gramps put everyone on his side of the house, except for Saylor. She's on my side. I can't help but wonder what the old man's up to. I know he likes Saylor. Me, on the other hand, he's not a fan of these days. Maybe he can sense the attraction I have for her. He's putting her on my side of the house to torture me. To know that she's sleeping right across the hall in my clothes. Yeah, he didn't offer to get her anything to sleep in. I didn't miss that either. He's fucking with me.

"This way," I say, placing my hand on the small of her back and leading her to the steps. She doesn't say anything, just lets me guide her up the stairs. "This is your room. Let me get you something to sleep in."

"Thank you, Rhett."

I nod and disappear into my room. I almost offered for her to follow me in, but I know that's a bad decision. I'm not sure I would let her leave once I got her in here. Grabbing a Baxter's Distillery T-shirt and a pair of flannel pajama pants, I hand them to her in the hallway. "There's an attached bath, so you can change in there. If you need anything, I'm just

145

across the hall." I take a step toward her.

"I'll be fine. Goodnight, Whiskey," she whispers.

Not able to resist, I lean in and press my lips to her forehead. "Goodnight, Say." Stepping back, I turn and disappear into my room.

Stripping down to my boxer briefs, I decide, with guests in the house, I better wear some pajamas as well. Grabbing a pair of flannel pants, just like the ones that I gave Saylor, I slide them on and climb into bed. When I close my eyes, all I can see is Saylor earlier on the couch. Her big blue eyes staring down at me. I can feel her fingers as they slide through my hair. My cock stirs to life. I ignore it. I refuse to take matters into my own hands when the real thing is just across the hall. It would be a poor-ass substitute for her.

I toss and turn for the better part of an hour before giving up. Throwing off the covers, I decide to go downstairs and grab a glass of milk and maybe one of those cookies to distract me. Quietly as I can, I pull open my door and step out into the hallway. The house is quiet, so the sound of her soft whimper is easy to hear. Stepping closer to her door, I lay my ear against it, listening. I don't want to go barging in, but I need to know she's okay. Sniffling and soft crying greet me. Without further thought, I tap lightly on the door. She doesn't answer. Slowly, I turn the knob. "Saylor?"

"I-I'm fine," she says with a sniff.

The sound of her cries has my chest tightening. I step into the room and shut the door behind me. "What's wrong?"

"N-n-nothing, I'm okay. I promise. Just… a rough day."

Stepping further into the room, I take a seat on the edge of the bed. I take a minute to appreciate the view. The moonlight is giving off a faint glow, just enough so I can see her hair spread out across the pillows. I can't really see her face, but I can imagine it's red, her eyes puffy from her tears. There is no doubt she's beautiful.

"Want to talk about it?" I ask her. I'm not really good at this kind of thing, but damn if I can leave her be to cry herself to sleep.

"I'm okay." She places her hand on my arm to reassure me.

It doesn't. I know she's trying to pacify me, but her touch, well, let's just say my already stiff cock is begging for attention. "Try again," I tell her.

"It's nothing. It's life." She laughs humorlessly.

"Come on, Short Stack, you can do better than that."

"Why do you call me that?" she asks. "I mean, I told you why I call you Whiskey."

I ponder whether or not I should tell her. Maybe it will distract her. "You're short," I say, reaching out and tapping her nose.

"Maybe to you. You're a damn giant," she says. "How tall are you?"

"Six four. How tall are you?"

"Five four," she laughs. "I get it."

"That's not all though."

"No?"

"Nope. These," I say, brushing my hand across her chest. "Stacked."

"Seriously?" she asks, surprised.

"Hell yes," I assure her.

"I'm average at best."

Leaning down so she can see my face, I say, "You're perfect. Now, tell me what's bothering you."

"It's hard to explain."

"I've got nothing but time." Standing I round the bed and climb in opposite of her. "Turn over," I whisper. She does as I ask. Reaching out, I tuck her hair behind her ear. "Start talking, gorgeous." She's quiet, and I'm not sure she's going to talk. I wait her out. I rest my hand on her hip, letting her know I'm still here.

"When I was two, my parents were killed in a car accident. They were both products of the foster care system, so they had no family."

Fuck me. I'm smart enough to read through the lines. I remain quiet, letting her think about what to say next.

"That left me to the same upbringing. I bounced around from home to home. Some were okay, others were... not. Don't get me wrong, I'm one of the lucky ones. I escaped before anything terrible could happen. There was some inappropriate touching above my clothes from a few of the older foster kids at my last home. I was twelve. Elaine, she was my social worker and m-my parents,'" she says, her words breaking with so much damn pain.

I want to tell her that she doesn't have to tell me, but I think she needs this. To talk about it. I need this. I have this deep-seated desire to know everything about her. I'm like a sponge soaking up as much as I can. Over the past few weeks, she's slithered her way under my skin, and now I need it all.

"She was retiring that year. Her husband passed several years earlier from cancer. It would have been too hard for her to be a single mother, but after the final incident and with her retirement, she took me. She brought me into her home as my foster mother." She takes a deep, shuddering breath. "She had a few pictures of them, of my parents. She didn't want to give them to me until I was old enough to take care of them. It's a good thing, because anything I ever had was destroyed at whatever home I was in. Most of the families took as many kids as they could house and the state not ride their case. They did it for the money. Elaine, she did it because she was that kind of person. Her heart was huge, always giving back."

Rolling over, I grab the box of tissues and hand them to her.

"She became my family. She told me my parents loved me and they were so happy when they found out about me. They went to visit her, to tell her the news." She closes her eyes. "Elaine and I, we baked every Christmas. We would make tins full of goodies to pass out to what felt like half the town." She laughs softly. "It's just hard, you know? This is my first Christmas without her."

"When did she pass?" She didn't say that's what happened, but from the way she talks about her and her being here in West Virginia all alone, that is the only answer. No way would either of them ever been without the other during the holidays, not with the way she speaks of her.

"October," she murmurs.

"Saylor." Her name is a plea from my lips. My fucking heart is cracking for this beautiful broken girl. Not able to fight it, I pull her against my chest, resting my chin on the top of her head.

"Pete, that was my ex's name, he and I decided to sell her house, since we were living here. I went back and cleaned it out, kept a few things, packed up the rest and donated. That day, the day I left her house for the last time, I was in a hurry to get home. Pete and I had dinner plans. When he got home, he was acting weird. He said we needed to talk. Basically, he told me he was getting married. He had gotten his receptionist, who we both worked with since I worked for his family's company, pregnant. He had been seeing her behind my back."

"Motherfucker," I mumble.

"He let me sell her house, my home." She sobs into my chest.

I can do nothing but hold onto her. Let her know she's not alone. She's wrecked me with her confession, so I know her pain has to be unbearable. Her body wracks with sobs, and I hold her tighter, kissing the top of her head.

"He knew," she finally says after she's calmed down. "He knew he was leaving me, and he let me sell it. I left and went to a hotel. I felt like the walls were closing in on me, so I went out. On the way to the hotel, I remembered passing a bar, and that's when I met Molly and Jake. Molly found out I needed a place to stay and a job, because no way could I go back to working with Pete and his baby mama. They helped me." She says piecing the story together the best she can through her tears.

"They're good people," I say, kissing the top of her head again.

"They are. I have a friend, Tara, back in Cincinnati. She tried to get me to move with her, but I chose not to. A few weeks later, she ended up moving to Oregon with her fiancé. She called me a few weeks ago and was angry that I wouldn't come visit her. We've been friends for years, but now that I'm looking at life from a different angle, I see it was more one sided. I'm alone, and sometimes it just gets to me, you know?" she asks through her tears.

"You're not alone, baby. You've got Molly and Jake and me and my family and Jerry; we can't forget that crazy old man," I say, trying to lighten the mood.

She laughs. "He's great," she defends him.

"He is. They all are, and you're a part of that now."

"I'm sorry," she says, lifting her head and wiping her tears from my bare chest.

"Nothing to be sorry for, Saylor."

She lays her head back on my chest. "Can you... I mean, do you think you could stay just until I fall asleep?"

Slayed. "I'm not going anywhere," I say, holding her a little tighter. Her cries begin to quiet, and her breathing becomes even. I know she's asleep, but I don't bother moving. I don't want to risk waking her. In a matter of weeks, I've went from sparring with her every chance I could get to wanting to take her pain away. The more I get to know her, the more I want her. Not just because she's this gorgeous girl who is stacked. No, it's because of who she is. She's unlike anyone I've ever met. She's so fucking strong and resilient. Her story, everything she's been through. I know there's more from her time in foster care that she didn't reveal. What she did reveal was more than enough to gut me. To make me want to track those fuckers down and teach them a lesson for touching her… I take a deep breath. I need to calm down. She's here, in my arms, safe from the craziness that was her life until she went to live with Elaine.

My mind drifts to her ex. I knew just from looking at him that day at the store he was a real piece of work, but how could he do that to her? Let her give up her home, just to turn around days later and tell her that he's marrying someone else. Fucker better be glad I didn't know then what I know now. He also better hope I never run into him again.

Saylor nuzzles closer and mumbles, "Stay."

Relaxing into the mattress, I kiss the top of her head and close my eyes. I'm not going anywhere.

TWENTY TWO
Saylor

IT'S NEW YEAR'S Eve and the Corner Pocket is packed. It's all hands on deck, so Molly and I made some snack foods for the staff to eat on all night. Molly says she does it every year to show the staff how much they appreciate them being there on a holiday.

"Hey, Say, there's a guy at the end of the bar asking for you," Morgan, one of the servers, says as she comes behind the bar to grab a clean towel.

Looking down at the bar, I see Pete waving at me. *Son of a bitch.* I really don't feel like dealing with his shit tonight. I cash out my current customer and make my way to where he stands with Tabitha standing beside him.

"Saylor, it's good to see you," Pete says.

"What can I get you?" I say. It's not good to see him, either of them, and I'm not going to pretend that it is.

"We're celebrating. We're having a boy," Pete says, pushing his chest out.

"What can I get you?" I ask again. I expected to feel pain or sadness at his confession, but all I really feel is relief. The last two months have been eye-opening for me. Especially Christmas Eve. Rhett held me while

I cried. Here's this guy who barely even likes me, one I've insulted more times than I can count, and he held me while I cried for all I've lost and will never have. Pete never once held me when Elaine died. He left me alone, stating he was giving me space to deal. Never once did he put his arms around me and just hold me. Grandpa Rhett is right, I dodged a bullet, and I couldn't be happier about it. I almost feel bad for Tabitha and their baby, almost. She knew what kind of guy he was, a cheater, before she started sleeping with him. You reap what you sew and all that.

"Just water for me," Tabitha speaks up. She has a fake smile on her face. She need not worry about me; I don't want him.

"I'll take a Bud Light," Pete says. "We're due—"

"Look," I cut him off, "I don't care. I don't want details about the baby you're having with the woman you cheated on me with, the woman who was a coworker to both of us. I don't want to know; I don't care, so stop trying to tell me about it." I turn to grab a bottle of water and his beer, placing them on the counter.

Pete slides me a twenty-dollar bill. "Keep the change," he says before grabbing their drinks and walking away. Tabitha gives me a smug look before leaving.

"What was that all about?" Molly asks.

"That was Pete being Pete," I tell her.

"Is that the baby mama?" She cranes her neck to see around the crowd.

"Yep," I say, popping the p.

"Oh, honey, you deserve so much better than him."

"Yeah," I sigh. "So, is it always this crazy on New Year's Eve?" I ask, changing the subject.

"Always, even when Jerry was running things, this has been the hangout so to speak." She gets called away to the opposite end of the bar. "Duty calls." She hip checks me and goes to wait on her customer.

Time passes quickly as we fill order after order. There is a small lag, so I take the time to grab a bottle of water and drink half of it down. "Busy night?" his deep voice greets me.

Rhett.

"Crazy," I answer. "When did you get here?" I ask, grabbing a towel and wiping down the counter.

"Couple of hours ago." He points to the back corner where Gary,

Todd, Katherine, and several others are sitting.

"You need anything?"

His eyes linger over my breasts before meeting my eyes. "Nope, just wanted to say hi."

I laugh. "I just seen you last night when you were in here."

He shrugs. "Today's a new day."

"A new year," I say cheekily.

"A new year. You have a resolution?"

"Nah, I never end up keeping them. What about you?"

"Not really a resolution, more like a plan."

"That's cryptic. Care to share?" I ask.

"Hey, can I get a Baxter's Autumn draft?" a girl asks, sliding up next to Rhett.

"Hey, I haven't seen you around." She bats her eyelashes at him, and it takes everything I have not to laugh.

"Here you go." I slide her a frosty mug.

She hands me her card, I swipe it and hand it back to her with her receipt. "You should come and sit with me and my friends." She puts her hand on his arm.

Rhett stares down at her hand, and I can tell he's annoyed. He helped me out, and I see this as my chance to repay the favor. "You mind getting your hands off my boyfriend?" I ask, standing with my arms crossed over my chest.

Rhett looks up, the corner of his lips lifting just enough for me to know he knows what I'm doing.

"Her?" she asks appalled, as if I'm not good enough for him. I happen to agree with her; Rhett is out of my league.

"Her," he confirms. He lifts his arm and her hand falls away. Blondie storms off toward her friends.

He opens his mouth to thank me I'm sure, but I interrupt him. "So, that resolution?" I ask.

He grins. It's sexy and mysterious all at once. "I'll tell you when the time is right."

"Ah, got ya. You've got some work to do."

"I'm working on it, Say. It's all I've been able to think about," he says under his breath, but I still hear him. Probably because I'm leaning over the bar, all up in his space. You have to with the noise in this place.

"Well, good luck. I'm happy to help if you need me. You've helped me out more than once."

His eyes soften. "I'm going to take you up on that," he tells me. "When the time is right, I'm going to take you up on that."

I nod and move to the next customer vying for my attention. It appears that my break is over. I stay busy filling drinks and passing food off to the servers. Rhett stays in the same spot the rest of the night. Occasionally, if there is a lag in customers, we'll talk. Jake spent some time chatting with him while slicing up more lemons. I try to ignore him, not because I hate him, it's the opposite in fact. I seem to have this weird... pull toward him. I was starting to feel it, but then after last week from the nap to him holding me while I cried, I'm unable to stop thinking about him. I try to tell myself it's because he showed me his softer side, but deep down, I know it's more. It's more, and I can't seem to shake it. I know nothing can or will come of it, so I need to get myself in check.

"Five minutes," Molly yells into the crowd, and they all cheer.

I grab the bottle of sparkling cider that the staff will be toasting with tonight and start filling up the plastic wine glasses Molly ordered just for this occasion. I set them behind the bar, so everyone can grab one. They'll start heading this way for the countdown to the new year. Looking out over the crowd, I see the couples standing close, ready to ring in the new year with a kiss. The superstition goes that if you fail to have a kiss at midnight, you will have a year of loneliness. I've had kisses at midnight, but it never took the loneliness away. So much for superstitions.

I risk a glance at Rhett, but he's no longer in his chair. His coat is still on the back of the stool, so he hasn't gone far. I assume he's in the mass of bodies finding his kiss for midnight. My chest tightens at the thought.

"Ten, nine," the crowd begins to count down. I slide past my coworkers, grab a plastic wine glass, and head toward the back hallway. I can't watch all the happy couples. I need a minute to toast to myself. I got me. When the crowd reaches five, I feel strong hands grip my hips. Spinning around, I see Rhett. It's dark, and I can't make out his facial expression.

Leaning down, he whispers, "Happy New Year, Say," and then his lips connect with mine.

His lips are soft yet firm. At first, I just stand there, shocked that this is happening. Rhett is kissing me!

"Open, Say," his deep voice rumbles.

I do as he asks, and my body takes over. Wrapping my hands around his neck, I hold on for the ride. His tongue traces my lips, causing me to moan. All too soon, he's pulling away and resting his forehead against mine.

"You have no idea how long I've wanted to do that," he says softly.

"I should get back," I say like an idiot.

He kisses me one more time, just a soft press of his lips to mine, before releasing his hold on me. Without saying a word, he grabs my hand and leads me back to the bar. With a gentle squeeze, he releases me. I stand there and watch him as he moves around the bar and takes his seat. With a deep breath, I grab a towel on the edge of the bar and go clean a few tables. I need a minute, but there's work to do. I have to process what just happened.

He kissed me.

I kissed him back.

I want more. More kisses, more of him.

Glancing behind the bar, I see Jake and Molly are swamped. Rushing back, I jump right in, taking and filling orders. All the while, I feel his eyes on me, a soft caress as he watches me.

"How are things? How much longer you plan on sticking around?" I hear Jake ask Rhett.

"Good, as far as the business goes. Gramps is still pissed. Just when I think he's going to come around, he freezes me out again."

"What about your position at the brewery?"

"Mom's filling in for me. She's loving every minute of it. She's bored to tears sitting at home. She has a few charities that she works with, but she loves working at the brewery. She and Dad started it from nothing; it's her passion. She stepped down, saying she was ready to do so, but I really think it was for my benefit when I graduated from college."

"It's good to have you in town for more than just a day or two," Jake tells him.

"Hey, guys, ready for last call?" Morgan, one of the servers, asks.

"I got it," I say. Reaching for the megaphone, I hand it to Jake.

He yells out over the crowd for last call, and the bar is swarmed. They'll have fifteen minutes to finish this last drink before Jake kicks them all out. Sure enough, fifteen minutes later, I'm on the floor picking up empty bottles, mugs, and glasses when Jake booms that it's closing time. Slowly, the crowd disappears.

I make myself busy cleaning up the tables and putting up chairs.

"We're done, Say," Jake says.

Looking up, I see that all the other staff is gone. It's just Jake, Molly, Rhett, and me left.

"I'll come by and finish mopping tomorrow. It's New Year's, let's go home and have a drink," Jake says.

"I don't mind. You all can go ahead," I tell them.

"Nope. You're done. Get your stuff," Molly says.

"Fine," I concede. I grab my coat, keys, and phone and head toward the door.

"You should let your car warm up," Rhett says.

I wave him off. "It'll be fine. I'll see you guys at home," I say over my shoulder and walk out of the bar. Normally, I would wait to walk out with them, but Rhett and the kiss, it has me on edge.

"Short Stack!" he calls after me. I don't stop, pretending to not hear him as I burrow into my coat. "Hey," he says, grabbing my arm. "You okay?"

"Of course," I tell him.

He studies me for a few seconds before giving me a brief nod. "I'll follow you home," he says, leaning down he kisses my temple. "Drive safe." He opens my door, and I climb in. I don't say anything because I can't find my words. They're lodged in the back of my throat with the emotion that I just swallowed down. With shaking hands, I put my SUV in drive and head toward home. Rhett stays behind me the entire way. When I reach the driveway, I turn in, expecting him to follow me, he doesn't. Instead, he beeps twice and drives on past.

What the hell happened tonight? I send a quick text to Molly telling her I'm exhausted and I'm going to pass on a drink. After reassuring her that I made it home okay and that I'm all right, I take a quick shower and climb into bed. Thoughts of Rhett and his lips against mine follow me in my dreams.

TWENTY THREE

T'S NEW YEAR'S Day. I've been here for two months, and Gramps is still not thawed from his anger toward me. Something has got to give. Taking the stairs to his room, I hear him coughing from just outside the door. "Morning," I say, pushing open the door.

The night nurse and the day nurse are both there. "He had kind of a rough night. He had a breathing treatment at three this morning and should have another now, before breakfast," I hear them talking.

"What happened?" I ask them.

"Sometimes this happens. It's that time of year, and he's weak."

"But he was doing so much better," I say. He was. He was happy and barely coughing just last week.

"That's emphysema," she explains.

"What can I do?" I ask them.

"Nothing you can do. We'll be here around the clock to keep an eye on him."

"Thank you."

"Mr. Baxter, I'm going to go get the machine ready for your breathing treatment. I'll be right back," she tells him.

I wait until they are both out of the room before taking a seat in the chair beside his bed. "Hey, Gramps."

"I need you to go to Vegas," he wheezes.

"What?"

"Vegas," he says, taking a deep breath. "I signed the distillery up for a convention. It's a big casino, a big customer of ours. They're having a sampling, and I signed us up. I can't go like this," he says. I can tell just that little speech exhausted him.

"Can we cancel?" Not that I'm against going to Vegas, but staying here, especially with him not feeling well, seems like the better option.

"No. I gave my word. That means something, Rhett Alexander Baxter," he says. I assume since he busted out the whole name it was meant to be scolding, but his wheezing took the heat out of it.

"Okay. So I need the details," I tell him.

"Dorothy took care of it. She can help you." He takes a deep breath. "You need to find a bartender to go with you. I was going to ask Jake and didn't get around to it."

"Why do I need a bartender?" I'm starting to wonder if he's delirious from the medications. Is he running a fever?

"It's a sampling. You need someone experienced to serve. You'll be busy talking about the company, schmoozing potential clients who will be there. You won't have time to do it all."

"Right." I agree that wouldn't be ideal. "Okay, I'll call Jake today. Anything else?"

"No, I'm tired," he says, closing his eyes, dismissing me.

"When?" I ask him, even though his eyes are closed.

"This weekend," he replies, never opening his eyes.

I sit with him anyway until the day shift nurse comes in to give him his breathing treatment.

Downstairs, I pull out my phone to text Jake.

Me: Hey, you at the bar?

Jake: Yep.

Me: Be there in fifteen.

Grabbing my keys and coat, I head to the Corner Pocket. I'm hoping that my old buddy Jake is up for a trip to Vegas.

Me: I'm here.

I'm standing outside the main entrance waiting for Jake to unlock the doors.

"Wipe your feet, man. I just mopped." He points to my snow-covered shoes.

After thoroughly wiping my feet, I take a stool behind the bar and sit to stay out of his way. "So what's up?"

"I need a favor."

"Shoot," he says, looking up at me from where he's writing something on a clipboard.

"Gramps just told me this morning that I need to be in Vegas this weekend for a sampling show he signed the distillery up for. I also need a bartender," I tell him. "You free?"

He laughs. "I wish. A trip to Vegas sounds like fun. I've got a guy coming in to install a new grill. Ours is on its last leg."

"Not to sound like a dick, but can Molly handle it?" I ask him.

"Nope. We've also got an appointment with a wedding planner." He grins. "Apparently, she has a waiting list, but had a last-minute cancellation and agreed to take us on. Mol's excited. No way am I taking that from her." He writes something else on his clipboard before looking up at me again. "Take Saylor." He says it like it's common sense.

I thought about her first, but figured she would never go for it. "You think she'd do it?"

He shrugs. "I don't see why not. We've got plenty of coverage, especially with me being here. Our meeting with the wedding planner is before we open, so I don't see an issue on my end."

A weekend in Vegas with Saylor? Hell fucking yes. "You got her number?" I ask, already pulling my phone out of my jeans pocket.

"You don't?" he asks, surprised.

"Nope."

"You two seem awful cozy lately to not have exchanged numbers."

"Are you going to give me her number or not?"

"Testy." He laughs. "Why don't you just go see her. She was home when I left."

"Fine. I'll see you later." I hop off the stool and turn to leave.

"Rhett," he calls out for me.

"Yeah." I stop and turn.

"Don't hurt her. She's had enough disappointment."

"Trust me, I'll not do what that jackass did, and if it were up to me, she'd stay a part of my family." The words fall from my lips before I can stop them. "I'm not going to hurt her," I say, trying to soften the reality of what it is I just said. I've felt protective of her since she told me her story, protective and wanting. I want to be around her all the damn time. Hence my ever-frequent visits to the Corner Pocket. Then there was last night and the kiss. I never through it would be possible, but I can still feel her lips against mine.

Fucking phenomenal.

Jake nods. "Good to know, my man. One of these days, not today because I have shit to do, you're going to explain that." He gives me a pointed look.

I laugh. "Let me work it out in my head first, then you're on." Without another word, I head outside to my truck. Time to go visit a beautiful bartender about a spur-of-the-moment trip to Vegas.

I pull up outside her apartment, which is also Jake and Molly's detached garage, and park my truck. I don't bother with my phone. I don't want any distractions when I try to convince her to go to Vegas with me in four days. I shake my head as I take the steps two at a time. Gramps sure knows how to throw some fucking curveballs my way. I reach the door and knock three times before taking a step back.

"Rhett?" she says cautiously as she brings her hand to her lips. I know exactly what she's thinking. That kiss. "What are you doing here?"

"Gramps threw something at me just a little while ago, and I wanted to ask for your help."

"Sure, come on in. Is he okay?"

I can hear the concern in her voice, and I know it's real. Saylor is that kind of person. She cares with all of her, even after everything she's been through. "Yeah, he informed me that he signed up for a taste sampling for the distillery at the end of the week. I need to take his place."

"Okay, do you want me to check in on him?"

I shove my hands in my pockets to keep from reaching out for her. She's too fucking sweet, her taste, her personality, her. "Actually, I'm in need of an experienced bartender. I'll be busy with selling the company, so to speak, so I need a professional server to offer the samples." I leave out the location on purpose. I'm taking this one step at a time.

"Did you ask Jake?"

"Yeah, he's got the new grill install and the wedding planner."

"That's right," she muses. "Are you sure I can do it?"

I take a step toward her. "I know you can, Say."

"O-okay. I'll need to make sure it doesn't interfere with my work schedule."

"It will, a little, but Jake already said it was fine."

"You asked him before me? What if I said no?" she asks, crossing her arms over her chest.

"I asked him, and he told me all the reasons he can't go. Then he suggested you. You were my first pick, honestly. I just wasn't sure I could convince you to do it."

"Oh," she mumbles. "So when and where?"

"We would leave here on Thursday, the sampling is Friday, and we would be home on Saturday."

"So it's out of town?"

"Yeah, Gramps said that Dorothy has already made the travel arrangements."

"Where are you taking me, Whiskey?"

I can't help but grin at her. Now that I know why she calls me that, I don't hate it. "Vegas."

"Vegas?" she repeats it as a question.

"Yeah, it's at a casino. They're long-time customers, and they called Gramps and invited him specifically. He says we can't cancel; I already asked."

"How is he?"

"Had a bad night. Wheezing and coughing more today. The nurse assures me that it's just symptoms of the emphysema, but at this rate, I'm not sure how he's going to ever be well enough to go back to work."

"He would hate that," she says softly.

"Yeah, he would."

"So what does that mean for the company?"

"I don't know for sure. That would be up to Gramps."

"Would you stay? I mean, would you take over for him?" She bites her bottom lip.

"At this stage in the game, it's hard to tell what he'll do. He's still angry with me for not visiting more than just a day or two at the holidays over the last several years. I used to spend every summer with him and just stopped once I graduated from high school. He's hurt, and he reminds me every day with his aloofness toward me."

"I noticed there seemed to be some distance. I'm sorry."

"It's on me, and I'm going to fix it. I don't know how, but I'm going to fix it," I say with a heavy sigh. "Anyway, back to business. Will you do it? Will you fly to Vegas with me and help me schmooze the casino owners and all the others that are sure to be there?"

"I've never traveled," she says hesitantly. "Elaine and I, we lived off of her retirement, so the money wasn't really there. I've been to two states," she adds.

Damn if her confession doesn't have me wanting to show her the whole fucking world. "I'll be right there with you."

"I've never flown in a plane, obviously." She laughs nervously.

I step closer to her. "You afraid of heights?"

"I don't know, really. I've never been in a position to find out."

She's been so sheltered, missing out on all that life has to offer. Anger boils in my veins that her jackass ex didn't help her experience more. Instead, he was too busy fucking his employees. "It's safe. Safer than driving, so they say. Vegas is great. Although it will be a quick trip, we'll find some time to walk around. Maybe catch a show. It's the city that never sleeps after all." Still chewing on her bottom lip, she was driving me and my cock crazy. "It's all expenses paid. I'll pay you two grand for the weekend in addition to expenses. Flight, hotel, food, everything is covered by the business."

"That's a lot of money."

"You're downplaying your self-worth. I need you, Saylor. I need someone who is professional and knows their way behind a bar. It's short notice as well, and you should be compensated for that."

"Sounds like you've thought of everything."

"I have. Jeans or those legging things you have will work fine with a Baxter's T-shirt. No special wardrobe; I just need you there with me. Please, Saylor you'd be saving my ass."

"Can I think about it? Just for a little while. I can give you an answer later today. I just… Can I have a little time?"

I step closer, this time not stopping until I'm standing toe to toe with her. She looks up at me, and I have to fight to not get lost in her ocean blue eyes. Reaching out, I slide my hand behind her neck, under her hair. "I'll call you later," I say, leaning down and kissing her forehead. I want to kiss those sweet, plump lips, but I have a feeling her answer would be no if I did that. I can't push her. I'll take time with Saylor any way I can get it. Without another word, I step back from her, turn on my heel, and walk out the door. One more second and I would have been all over her. I need to get my shit together when it comes to Saylor. I know what I told Jake, and I meant it. I won't hurt her.

The drive back to the house is quick. I drive on autopilot as I think about Saylor and spending a few days away with her. We'll have Thursday night to sightsee. I'll be able to show her a little of Vegas. Then Friday after the tasting, I can maybe take her to a show. I can see it now, her blue eyes wide and shining with excitement under the Vegas lights. I really hope she says yes.

Inside, I make my way upstairs to check on Gramps. He's lying on his side in bed, watching television. "Hey, how you feeling?"

"Fine," he mumbles.

"So, Jake can't go to Vegas, but he suggested that I ask Saylor. I just came from her place. She's going to give it some thought and get back with me today. I don't know what to do if she says no."

"Convince her," he says, as if it's an easy task.

"I'm working on it."

"Good."

"Anything else I need to know?"

"Dorothy will have everything you need."

"Want to watch a movie or something?"

"I'm tired, just want to take a nap," he says, closing his eyes.

I sit there and watch him. He's frail and looking every bit of his 77 years. I've missed too much time with him being wrapped up in my own life. He was my best friend growing up. Odd, but true. There was nothing that could have kept me from spending all summer with him. I refused to play summer sports because this is where I wanted to be. This house is just as much home to me as my parents' place back in Tennessee. The memories I have here are endless. I worry that I'm not going to have much time with him. The thought alone takes my breath. I can't leave here until he's over his anger. I won't leave knowing he's still upset with me.

Slipping out of his room, I quietly make my way downstairs before calling my dad.

"Hey, son," he greets me.

"Hey, Dad."

"What's wrong?"

"I can't leave here until he's no longer angry at me."

"I've been there, Rhett. That could be a long damn time." He sighs.

"I know that, but I've missed so much. He's aged, and he's angry, as he should be. I can't leave knowing that something could happen when I'm not here and he was still angry."

Dad's quiet on the other end of the phone. "I get it, I do. I've been there. He's always been stubborn as hell. We've got things covered here."

"Thanks, Dad."

"Rhett?" he asks cautiously.

"Yeah?"

"I know you love it there. When you were younger, you always said you wanted to take his place one day." He pauses. "Your mother and I, we just want you to be happy. If you choose to stay, to take over permanently, we support you."

Damn. I've thought about that very thing more than not since I've been here. I've just never said it out loud. "Thanks, Dad," I say, choking up a bit. I clear my throat. "I don't know what's going to happen, but I needed to hear that."

"We love you, son."

"Love you too, Dad. Please tell Mom I said hi and I love her too."

"Will do."

With that, I end the call. My phone rings immediately. I don't recognize the number. "Hello?"

"Rhett?"

Saylor. Her sweet voice washes over me. "Hey, Short Stack."

She laughs softly. "I'll do it. I'll go with you. However, I don't want you to pay me for it. Paying for the trip is enough. It's an opportunity I don't know if I will ever have again."

I want to tell her that I will take her anywhere and everywhere she wants to go. "I have to pay you, Saylor."

"No, please, this is my decision. You're paying for everything. I'm only missing Friday night, I was scheduled off Thursday and Saturday this week, so I'm not missing out on much."

I know if I balk at this, she's going to change her mind. I'll just lavish her with all things Vegas—shows, souvenirs, and anything else that I can think of when we get there. "Deal," I tell her.

She releases a heavy breath. "So what time do I need to be ready and where?"

"Dorothy, she's Gramps's assistant, she handled all of the reservations. I'll get with her first thing in the morning and let you know."

"Okay. I guess I'll talk to you tomorrow."

"Yeah. Thank you, Short Stack."

"You're welcome."

The line goes dead. I'm standing in the living room in front of the mantle. I see my reflection in the mirror, and I'm wearing a big goofy grin. I'm excited to spend a few days away with my Short Stack in Vegas.

TWENTY FOUR
Saylor

ODAY'S GOING TO be a day of firsts for me. First time on an airplane, first time in Las Vegas, and the first time I've ever gone away on a trip or mini vacation.

"You all packed?" Molly asks, eyeing my open suitcase on the bed.

"Not even close. What the hell do you pack for a trip?"

"Clothes, toiletries, cell phone charger, condoms." I whip my head around and she laughs. "Lighten up, Say. Did he tell you the wardrobe?"

"He said jeans or leggings with a Baxter's T-shirt was fine. I'm out of my element here."

"Okay, so normal everyday jeans and T-shirts are fine while you're there. For the event, I say a Baxter's T-shirt, your holey jeans, you know the one's I keep threatening to steal? And a pair of black heels. Casual, yet sexy."

I think about it. "Okay, I like that," I admit. "Rhett said he would bring the Baxter's T-shirts so—" I look around and take count of what I have packed. "—I think I'm good," I say, tossing in a pair of black high heels.

"As for the flight, you need to be comfortable. What you have on is perfect."

I look down at my leggings and my Ohio State Buckeyes long-sleeve T-shirt. "You sure?"

"Yes, and I would wear your Chucks, easy on and off for airport security."

"I'm a nervous wreck."

"It's going to be fine. Takeoff and landing are the worst parts. Once you're in the air, you can't even tell. Besides, you have Rhett to distract you." She wags her eyebrows.

"Stop it," I say, laughing.

"You still owe me some details," she says, lying down on the bed.

I zip up my suitcase and place it on the floor before lying down beside her. "At first we didn't get along, you know? I mean, he would say something crude, and I would volley back with my own insult. I wouldn't say I hated him, more like I hated the idea of him. He's cocky and sexy and his eyes... I love his eyes," I say wistfully.

"He does have killer eyes," she agrees. "But I know there is more you're not telling me."

"On Christmas Eve, we kind of had a moment or two," I admit.

"Go on." She nudges me with her elbow.

I proceed to tell her what happened while she was off getting engaged, then again that night, when he came to me and listened and held me. "Then there was the kiss."

"Keep going," she urges. "You can't stop there."

I laugh. "New Year's Eve at the bar, I took my drink to the back hall. I was going to go to the office for just a minute, you know celebrate alone, not like I had someone to kiss. I was feeling a little down and just needed a minute. Rhett followed me, turned me to him, and kissed me."

"That's hot," Molly says. "So, are you two together?"

"No, I mean, he kissed my forehead when he came here to ask me to go with him, but that doesn't mean anything."

"He's been at the bar every night—" she says, and I cut her off.

"That doesn't mean anything."

"Let me finish." She grins. "He's been at the bar every night you're working. He doesn't come in if you're not there."

"Really?"

She nods. "Yep. So that tells me he's interested."

"Molly… " I close my eyes, not able to look at her when I tell her what's in my head. "I have nothing to offer him. I don't even really know who I am, who my parents where. I'm floating through life, just being me, not really knowing who me is."

"Saylor." She rolls over and leans up on her elbow. "You are Saylor Keller. You're smart, beautiful, and you've been dealt a few bad hands in life. I don't know all the details of your past, but I know they don't define you. You make your life what you want it to be. You make your choices. You have everything to offer him. You have you, Saylor, and that's more than enough. It's always enough. If ever it isn't, you know it's time to move on."

"I've never felt like I was enough. Not for my foster families—well, until Elaine—not with Pete, not even with Tara. Elaine, you, and Jake. The three of you are the only people who have never tried to change me."

"Rhett," she says confidently. "From the way he looks at you and the sparks that fly when the two of you are in the same room, you can add him to that short list."

"He just wants in my pants."

"Maybe." She shrugs. "Actually, probably is more like it. He's not stupid; he knows a good thing when he sees it. However, he's already been in your bed, and did he make a move?"

"No. No, he didn't. So you see, you're wrong. He was just being nice."

"He was being a gentleman. He held you all night, Saylor. No man is going to do that for just a piece of ass."

A loud knock sounds at the door. "Shit, he's here."

"Saylor." She grabs my hand before I can slide off the bed. "Your parents, Elaine, they would want more for you. They would want you to live a full, happy life. Don't be afraid to do that. I know in your eyes people leave—"

"How do you?"

"I've only known you a few months, but I know you. I know in the past people left, but your parents and Elaine, they didn't leave you by choice. Life took them. It's a shitty hand to have been dealt, but you can live for them. Be happy for them, Say."

Another knock.

"I'll get it. I'll keep him occupied until you're ready. She slides off the bed, comes to my side, and gives me a big hug. "Have fun, Say. Let me know when you make it there, so I don't worry."

"O-okay," I say, choking back tears. I close my eyes and focus on breathing. I know I don't have a lot of time until we need to get to the airport. Inhale, slowly exhale. Opening my eyes, I steel my emotions and take one more mental inventory of what I've packed, making sure I didn't forget anything. Then I grab my suitcase and head to the living room.

Rhett's eyes snap to mine as soon as I open the door. His smile lights up his face. "Saylor."

"Hey, Whiskey." I wheel my luggage to where they're standing. "You sure about this?"

"Positive," he says immediately. "You ready to go?"

"Yeah, this is it." I look down at my small suitcase.

"You never cease to amaze me, Short Stack." He chuckles.

"What did I do?" I ask, very aware that Molly is standing beside me soaking up our conversation, our interaction, like a sponge.

"You're refreshing, Saylor. You're a fucking breath of fresh air." He grabs my bag. "I'll take this out to the truck."

We stand there and watch him leave. "Oh, honey," Molly says. "You've got that man all kinds of twisted."

"Let's go, crazy girl. I'm already nervous about flying. I don't need to add rushing through the airport to the list." She laughs and follows me out the door.

The ride to the airport is quiet. Rhett and I make small talk. I ask how his Grandpa is and his parents; otherwise we're both quiet. Not uncomfortably so, but quiet all the same. Rhett parks in long-term parking and hops out. He has both of our bags, his thrown over his shoulder and pulling mine. He holds his hand out for me, and I take it, needing the connection to hopefully calm my nerves.

I let him lead me into the busy airport. I don't say a word, just let him guide me to where we need to be. Rhett hands me a ticket once we reach security. I follow the motions, taking off my shoes, while Rhett does the same, placing our bags on the conveyor belt. Luckily, we make it through security without incident. I release a deep sigh once we're both through and cleared.

"You okay, Short Stack?" he asks, holding his hand out for me.

I take it. "Yeah, just nervous, I guess."

He gives my hand a gentle squeeze. "You want a drink before we board?"

"No, actually, I was hoping to find a restroom. I don't want to have to use the restroom on the plane."

He nods. Two minutes later, we're standing outside of the bathrooms. "I'll be right here waiting for you," he says.

Pulling out of his hold, I rush inside and take care of business. Looking at my refection, I'm shocked at what I see. You can tell I'm a little nervous, but my eyes are bright. I admit, I'm equal parts nervous and excited, and it shows. I find Rhett right where he said he would be, waiting for me. He doesn't say anything, just holds his hand out for mine. I take it, and we continue on to our gate.

"We're first class," he says, taking a seat in the waiting area outside our gate. "That means we get to board first, and we're the first off the plane."

"Is that a good thing?"

"First on, not so much, I guess. First off, I think you'll enjoy," he says.

"I'm thinking you're right."

"There's not a direct flight, so we'll have to do this all over again."

"Ugh!" I say, plopping down in the seat next to him. "You failed to tell me that."

"I admit. I was afraid you would back out."

"I wouldn't have, but I would have stressed over it, so you made a good call."

"Good to know." He leans back against his seat. "We should be boarding in thirty minutes or so. You need anything?"

"No, thanks. I'm good. My belly is too nervous."

Reaching over, he rests his hand on my knee. "It's going to be fine, Say. I promise."

"You can't promise me that."

"You're right, I can't. What I can promise is that I'll be there the entire time. I won't leave your side."

I nod. Sometimes, with the things he says, it's hard to ever remember asshole Rhett, the guy I used to throw barbs with. He's been showing up less and less. I have to admit, I like this version a whole hell of a lot.

Pulling out my phone to distract me from the flight and from Rhett, I send Molly a text.

> **Me:** Waiting to board. Apparently I have to do this again before Vegas!
>
> **Molly:** LOL. Not many direct flights from where we live.
>
> **Me:** You could have warned me.
>
> **Molly:** #sorrynotsorry Love you. Have fun!
>
> **Me:** You too.

I don't say I love you. I've only said it to one person, Elaine, and that wasn't while she was alive. Regrets, I have them in spades for that alone. I know that she knew, but I should have told her. Whispering it to her grave isn't the same thing. "You too" is all I've ever been able to convey. Molly is a great friend. I know it's only been a few months, but she's become a very important person so me. I tried to call Tara on New Year's Day. She hadn't responded to any of my texts. She didn't answer, and I didn't leave a message. Her silence tells me all I need to know.

"Saylor," Rhett says. Looking up, I see him standing. He reaches out for my hand. "It's time to board."

I let him pull me to my feet and follow him to the line. We flash our tickets and then walk down a long hallway. As soon as we pass the flight attendant, my anxiety peaks.

"You want the window or the aisle?" Rhett asks me as he steps into the first row of the plane.

"I don't know," I confess.

"Let's go window. We can shut the shade, so you don't have to look unless you want to."

"Okay," I agree meekly. I take the window seat and hurriedly pull the shade. Rhett opens the above compartment and shoves our bags inside.

"Let me help you." He reaches over and helps fasten me in my belt, then does the same to himself.

I sit quietly, watching passenger after passenger file onto the plane. Rhett pulls his phone out of his pocket and switches it to airplane mode. He holds it up to show it to me. "I turned mine off," I tell him. "I wasn't sure if I should have it on, and anyone who would call me already knows

I'm going to be in the air." I gulp at the thought.

The flight attendant introduces herself and welcomes us to the flight. She goes through safety procedures, and I listen and watch, taking it all in. "Settle in and thank you for choosing our airline," she croons with a big-ass smile. She chooses to do this on the daily. Crazy woman.

I feel the plane start to move, and I grab the arms of the seat, close my eyes, and focus on deep, even breaths.

"Saylor," Rhett says. Slowly, I open my eyes and turn my head to look at him. His whiskey eyes darken as he leans in and cups my face with his hands. He presses his lips to mine. His tongue traces my lips, taking his time tasting me. I open for him, this time without an ounce of hesitation. His hand slides under my hair, holding me to him. He takes control, caressing my tongue with his, exploring my mouth, nipping at my bottom lip, then tracing it with his tongue. It's the hottest kiss of my life. On a fucking airplane. Suddenly, I pull back, and his eyes are hooded. I watch as his tongue darts out and swipes across his bottom lip, as if he's trying to get more of me. "We're in the air, babe," he says.

"You're good," I tell him. I didn't notice takeoff at all. Nothing past the second his lips touched mine.

"I've got you, Saylor. Always," he says cryptically. "So, you want to look out?"

"Yeah, I think so." Just then, the light goes off, letting us know we can take our belts off. Rhett unbuckles his and leans over, lifting the shade just a little.

"Take a look," he says, pointing to the now partially uncovered window.

"Wow," I say, seeing the clouds below us. "That's amazing." I turn to him with a smile.

He's watching me. "It is," he agrees. "If you could go anywhere, where would it be?"

"Hawaii," I say automatically. "That's where my parents took their honeymoon. Elaine said they saved for a long time to be able to go for just a short three days. I've wanted to go there ever since."

Reaching out he grabs my hand and pulls it to his lips.

Turning back around, I feel unsettled, but not from the flight. I lift the shade completely and take in the scenery below. This flying thing isn't so bad after all. Not when you fly with Rhett Baxter.

TWENTY FIVE

Rhett

WATCHING HER EXPERIENCE flying for the first time was a riot. She stared out the window for the entire first flight. When it came time to fasten our belt to land, I effectively distracted her again. Then again on our connecting flight for both takeoff and landing. Yes, flying with Saylor is a good time for sure.

"I'll go check us in," I tell her.

She nods. "I'll be right over there." She points to a lobby of chairs a few feet from the registration desk.

I've already given her the "don't go anywhere without me" speech. I've heard of some crazy-ass things happening in Vegas. Not on my watch, not with Saylor. I'm going to be stuck to her like glue. Waiting in line, I look over my shoulder just to make sure she's still there. She's a grown woman, I know, but you hear about disappearances all the time. You can never be too cautious.

"Hi, Rhett Baxter checking in." I hand over my license and the company credit card.

"Welcome, Mr. Baxter. We have you in the presidential suite." She types furiously on her keyboard. I'm surprised by this. Gramps isn't one for flashy, unless you count the house. He always said he did that for Grams. He built her her dream home.

"There should be two rooms," I tell her.

"Yes, sir. The suite is actually a three bedroom," she says, never looking up, keeping her eyes glued to the screen.

Dorothy did me a solid. Saylor will be in my suite where I know she's safe. Paranoid, yes, but everything is different with Saylor, it's more.

"Here you are. Do you need help with your bags?" she asks, handing me a key.

"No thank you. Which elevator?"

She points across the hall to a golden set of doors. "This is the only one that will take you to the presidential suite. If you are on another floor, you'll have to ride down to catch this one. It's for security purposes," she explains.

"No complaints." I nod in thanks and turn to join Saylor. She's sitting in the same place, but now there are three guys sitting around her. One on each side and one on the table in front of her. They're about our age. The one on the left is wearing a bright green shirt with white lettering that says, "Buy this guy a shot, he's tying the knot." The other two are wearing shirts that are white with bright green lettering that says, "Groom Squad." Great, that's all I need is drunk guys trolling for pussy hitting on her.

Strolling up behind her, I place my hands on her shoulders, bend down, and kiss the top of her head. "Ready, baby?"

Titling her head back, she looks up at me, a smirk on her lips. "Yeah." She stands.

"You're leaving?" one of the groom squad asks.

"Yeah, my fiancé and I are just checking in. It's been a long flight," she says.

He mumbles "lucky bastard" under his breath but still loud enough that we can all hear him.

Sliding my arm around her waist, I pull her close. "Thanks for keeping my girl company," I say, driving the point home that she's mine. Well, not mine technically, but when it comes to them she is. I'm working on the technical part. Slow and steady wins the race.

In the elevator, there is only one button. "Uh, are we in the right one?"

Saylor asks.

"Yeah," I say, hitting the "P" button. "Apparently Dorothy booked us the Presidential Suite. It's a three bedroom."

"Wow, okay then. So we're staying in the same room?"

"Not the same bedroom. I mean, unless you want to, you know, snuggle with your fiancé." I dip my shoulder into hers, laughing.

"Hey! You were the one puffing out your chest, acting like you had to stake a claim. I was just playing along."

"They looked shady," I tell her.

She throws her head back in laughter, and two things hit me all at once. One, I want to make her laugh like that every day, and two, there is no sweeter sound.

"They did not," she says, smacking my arm playfully. "You're something else." She smiles up at me.

"I'm telling you, trust no one in this town. Stay close," I remind her.

"Yes, sir." She salutes me with a playful grin.

"So what do you want to do first?" I ask as we reach our floor.

"Um, you're asking me? The girl who has been to two states her entire life?"

"Yeah, I promised to show you around. What do you want to see?" I ask, setting our bags in the living area.

"This place is bigger than my apartment," she says, looking around.

"You can choose whichever room you want, and I'll pick what's left."

"Oh, I'll take any of them. I'm not picky."

"I know you're not, but I want this to be an adventure for you. Go look at the rooms and pick yours. I'll bring your bag once you've decided." She hesitates for a brief few seconds before going to explore the rooms.

"Rhett!" she calls out for me while still in the first room. I follow the sound of her voice and find her in sitting in the middle of a huge bathtub. "This thing can fit like eight people, and look at the shower." She points behind me. "It's huge!"

"That's what she said," I retort.

"This is my room," she says, leaning back and closing her eyes.

She didn't even notice my lewd remark; she's too excited to let it faze her. "I'll get your bag," I say, leaving her to her daydreaming.

After leaving her bag in her room and telling her she has thirty minutes to freshen up, I force myself to go choose a room of my own. Since she wasn't sure what she wants to do, we're going to go explore the city, maybe pick up a show if we can find tickets. I have no agenda, other than getting out of this suite. I can't be trusted to be in here for the rest of the night with just the two of us. Hell, sleeping is going to be hard, considering the last time she slept across the hall from me, I ended up holding her all night long.

"Ready," she calls out twenty-five minutes faster than I told her she needed to be.

She's excited, and that makes me smile. "Give me a minute," I yell back. I shake off thoughts of her sleeping in my arms and change my clothes.

"So what are we doing?" she asks when I step into the living area. She's bouncing with excitement.

"We need to grab some dinner. I thought we could walk around until we find something, and then maybe catch a show."

"It's late," she reminds me.

"This is Vegas, Short Stack, the city that never sleeps. Some of the shows don't even start until eleven."

"Wow. Okay then, let's do this." She stands and shoves her phone in her back pocket.

I do the same then hold my hand out for her. She takes it without hesitation, and that alone has this shaping up to be a great night. "Which way?" I ask when we're standing outside of our hotel.

"Left," she says, smiling.

We take off in that direction. Saylor's smile is blinding. I've been to Vegas many times, but it's like I'm experiencing it all over again for the first time through her eyes. She's fucking gorgeous on the daily, but the smile that lights up her face takes my breath away. I sound like a putz waxing poetic shit in my head, but I can't seem to prevent it when it comes to her. She's got this hold on me, like her kisses have cast a spell.

"There." She points to a sign for a burlesque show.

"That what you want to do?"

Her face turns a light shade of pink as she nods. "Yeah, it should be fun, right?" she asks hesitantly.

Unable to stop myself, I pull her into my chest and bend down to kiss the corner of her mouth. "It will be fun," I tell her. Pulling away is a feat, but I manage. We walk to the end of the block, and I'm able to secure us two tickets to tonight's show. "So we have a couple of hours. Let's go find some food." We settle on a steakhouse right on the strip. We're seated at a booth in the back of the restaurant. Saylor slides in her seat across from me, her smile still firmly in place.

"Thank you for this, Rhett."

"You're welcome, but I should be thanking you. You're doing me a solid by being here on such short notice."

"It worked out," she says, opening her menu. She doesn't say anything as she reads over her choices.

Once we've ordered, our salads are delivered and conversation flows. She asks me about the distillery and the brewery. She talks about working at the Corner Pocket and how she's happier there than she ever was at her job in human resources with her ex's family's company.

"Why do you think that is?" I ask her.

"I assume it was us, our relationship. I always felt as though I was out of place. I didn't realize it until we were broken up. When we were together, I chalked it up to never feeling like I belonged. Even with Elaine, there was always this nagging feeling that she felt sorry for me and her connection to my parents was what prompted her to take me in. I know that's irrational, but it's hard to train yourself to think otherwise."

"What about your ex?" I ask her. "He chose you."

"He did, but looking back, it's what I could bring to the table. I could work for his family's company. I fit the mold, I guess you could say."

"You deserve better," I say, barely able to keep my voice calm. Her ex is a fucking douchebag. He let the best thing that ever happened to him slip through his fingers.

"I do," she agrees. "It's just hard, you know. I have no family. Most men who are ready to settle down look for that. You know 'What's her mom look like? Because that's what you're going to be waking up next to in thirty years.'" She takes a drink of her wine. "And what if someday I have kids? I mean, I know my parents, and I have their records from the foster system. Elaine somehow pulled some strings, but that's it. I don't know if my grandparents had heart disease or diabetes. What if my kids get sick and I need that information and I can't help them?"

Reaching across the table, I rest my hand on top of hers. "Saylor, you can't worry about the unknown. When you're a mother, you will do what you have to do for your children. Okay, so you don't have that long line of family history to fall back on. You don't need that to treat heart disease or diabetes. You can't let your past control your future."

She takes another drink of wine, this time draining her glass. I grab the bottle and fill it back up. "I get that, I do." She closes her eyes and sinks back against the booth seat. "I think my fear comes from never being first choice. You know? I mean, I want a man to fall in love with me because of who I am, my past, my present, what will be my future. I want him to choose me for me, not for what I can bring to his company or how I'll look on his arm." She closes her eyes for a few seconds before opening them again and locking her gaze on me. "As far as my hypothetical children, I've never lived in a normal environment. Two loving parents, grandparents, siblings, cousins, aunts, uncles—I've never lived that life. Elaine is my only true example of how to love and nurture, and I'm scared as hell I'll fuck it all up. That not having that history will somehow taint the mother I could be. Not being able to give them that."

The waiter interrupts and drops off our steaks. I thank him and wait until he's out of earshot before replying. "Any man—" She bows her head. "Look at me, Saylor." I wait several heartbeats until she looks up at me. "Any man would be one lucky son of a bitch to get to call you his. Your family is what you make it. Nothing in your past will prevent you from being a good mother, wife, or daughter-in-law. Nothing. You have to believe in yourself. You make your dreams a reality, Say."

"Enough of the heavy." She sits forward and grabs her steak knife and fork. "This looks great."

I let her change the subject, partly because I want to shake her and kiss her at the same time. I want to prove to her that she's worthy of anything and everything she's ever dreamed of. We eat dinner, only discussing safer topics, such as tomorrow's sampling and how Gramps is doing.

"It's hard to watch them slip," she says softly.

"It is." I clear the emotion from my throat. "For me it's doubled because he's still pissed at me. I swear that man knows how to hold a grudge. He barely speaks to me, and it's been months."

"He'll come around. You have to give him time," she assures me.

"That's just it, Short Stack, what if he doesn't have time?"

"I wish I knew the answer. I wish I had words of wisdom for you. All I can say is keep trying. Never go a day without letting him know you're here and how much he means to you. If I've learned anything, I've learned that." She picks up her fork and begins eating again. We finish our meal in comfortable silence.

"You ready for this?" I ask her as we leave the restaurant.

"I am." She grins, and I feel my body relax knowing that she's happy again. We've had enough of the heavy for one night.

Instead of holding her hand, I place my arm around her shoulders and hold her close. She doesn't pull away like I expected her to. I think we both need the connection after our dinner conversation. The burlesque show is just one block down from the restaurant. I was lucky enough to snag some pretty killer seats down front. I'm not sure how, considering it was such short notice, but when I told the lady at the ticket counter I wanted the best possible, she came through for me. Maybe I looked desperate and she threw me a bone? All I do know is that I'm sitting about ten rows back from the stage at a Vegas burlesque show with my arm around the most beautiful girl in the building. Well worth whatever it is I paid for these seats. I didn't even ask, just handed her my card and told her to make it happen.

The lights go out, and Saylor leans into me. "I'm so excited," she whispers.

I chuckle at her and relax against the seat, my arm still around her shoulders. When the curtain rises and the dancers come out, she's transfixed. I can't take my eyes off of hers as they widen with the sexy dance moves and excitement of all that is Vegas. Every so often, she turns to look at me a wide grin splitting her face; every single time, I'm already looking at her. She doesn't comment. She's too damn excited to even notice that she's all I see.

"That was amazing," she says once the lights come on. She's biting her bottom lip, something she's done a lot since the dancers took the stage. I dare to think she's turned on. I know I am. My cock has been hard as one of the dancer's stilettos since we sat down. It's all Saylor. "Now what?" she asks.

"Anything you want." I stand and grab her hand, guiding her back out to the strip.

"What about the lights, you know, the fountains? I've always wanted to see that," she says hopefully.

"I think they happen every fifteen minutes at night." Looking down at my watch, I see it's half past eleven. "We have about three blocks to walk in fifteen minutes, you up for the challenge?"

"Yes!" She jumps and claps her hands. "I got my running shoes on." She sticks out her foot to show me she's wearing her Chucks—not that I didn't already know that. I've memorized every inch of her that I can see tonight.

"All right, babe, let's go." We take off at a fast walk, her hand in mine.

"Your legs are too damn long." She laughs, jogging to keep up with my brisk pace.

I stop and crouch down. "Hop on," I tell her.

"What? No. I'll hurt you."

"Really, Short Stack?" She rolls those baby blues at me.

Smiling, she climbs on, wrapping her arms and legs around me. I take off at my brisk pace, only a little faster. She clings to me, her laughter next to my ear. It makes me want to run her up and down the strip all night long. Well, it makes me want to do more than that, but my cock doesn't get to come out and play, no matter how much we both want him to.

We reach the Bellagio just as the show starts for the last time of the day. "We made it," she squeals.

Before I can stop her, she's sliding down my back and standing in front of me. She looks up and watches with rapt attention. When she looks over her shoulder at me smiling, I can't stay away from her. Stepping forward, I wrap my arms around her and bring her back to my chest. Eventually, she settles her head against my chest and enjoys the show. I've seen it before, several times in fact, but never like this. Never with my cock hard a steel, and my heart pounding so hard I feel as though it could bounce right out of my chest. Never with a beautiful woman wrapped in my arms. Never with the thoughts racing through my mind of how to keep her there.

TWENTY SIX

'M IN THE middle of a fairy tale. It has to be the magic of Vegas. Rhett has been sweet and attentive. When he pulled me into his arms, I couldn't fight it. I want to be exactly where I am. Wrapped up in him. They say what happens in Vegas stays in Vegas, and now I get it. It's a place where sex is on every corner. Many of the show posters we've passed are adult in nature. Then there's this light and fountain show. I'm sure there's a fancier name for it, but right now, all I can think of is how great it feels to be in his arms.

"Happy?" he asks. His hot breath hits my ear and causes goose bumps to break out on my skin.

"Yeah," I say wistfully. "Thank you for this." I point in front of us. His reply is to kiss my temple. We stand there until the show is over. I don't want to miss a single second of it, of being with him like this.

"Ready?" I ask, turning to face him. His arms are still wrapped tight around me. He's looking at me, and I know the magic of this place is affecting him too. "Whiskey," I whisper.

I see need flash in his eyes before his lips cover mine. The kiss is slow, but his hands are not as they pull me right against him, cupping my ass cheeks. Standing on my tiptoes, I wrap my arms around his neck and try to get closer. I need to be closer.

He growls deep in his throat. "Saylor," my name falls from his lips before they move to my neck, kissing, licking, nipping, and soothing with his tongue. It's an onslaught of emotions. I can't fight it. I don't want to. Instead, I tilt my head, giving him access. "So fucking beautiful," he mumbles before sucking gently on the base of my neck.

"Get a room!" someone slurs with laughter.

Rhett pulls his lips from my skin. His whiskey eyes are full of desire as he peers down at me. He doesn't say anything, just bends and kisses me one more time. This time it's just a quick peck before he's pulling me into his side and we start walking. I assume we're going back to the hotel, but I can't be sure. I'm reeling from his kiss, from the sensation of his lips against my skin. I don't think I could find my voice even if I knew what to say.

When we reach the door to the hotel, Rhett moves his hand to the small of my back and guides me into the building and across the lobby to the golden elevator that takes us straight to our suite. I want to say something, anything that will keep this from being awkward, but I'm so out of my element. I've never been kissed by a man the way Rhett kisses me. It's all-consuming. I can't say that it was nothing, because to me it wasn't. It was sexy, thrilling, and intense. Instead of telling him it was nothing, I want to beg him to do it again. That's my last thought when the golden doors close us inside the elevator and Rhett pushes me back against the elevator door. His lips crash to mine while he pulls my leg to wrap around his. I can feel his erection pressing into me. His lips are demanding as they mold firmly against mine. Reaching up, I bury my hands in his hair and let go. I don't think about what it means or what it doesn't. Instead, I just feel. Feel his heat pushed against me, his lips busy against mine, his tongue as it outlines my lips and battles with mine.

I just feel him.

Rhett.

All too soon, the doors are sliding open. I groan. I don't want to stop kissing him. I want more of him, more of this. I try to pull away, knowing that we need to go to our room. I squeal when Rhett bends and lifts me. Instinctively, I wrap my legs around his waist, and my arms around his neck.

"I got you," he whispers. I bury my face in his neck, placing a soft kiss just below his ear. "Saylor," he growls. It's not an angry growl; it's an "I'm going to devour you" growl. I never knew the difference until right this minute. It's empowering to know he wants me like this. I've never experienced this level of need.

"Back pocket, beautiful. We need the room key."

Keeping one hand around his neck, I slide the other down to his back pocket and pull out his wallet.

"Open it," he tells me. "It's right in the front slot." Doing as he says, I retrieve the key. "Unlock the door, Say." I can actually hear the desire in his voice. Fumbling with the key, I manage to get the door unlocked. Rhett carries me to what I assume is his room and tosses me gently on the fluffy mattress. "Wallet," he says, holding out his hand. I give it to him. I watch as he opens it and pulls out a condom then tosses his wallet to the floor. "I only have one, Say, so we need to make it count."

Heat pools in my belly. I can't take my eyes off him as he reaches behind him and pulls his shirt over his head. My eyes follow his hands as he unbuttons his jeans and slides them down his hips, letting them fall to the floor. He moves toward the bed.

"What about those?" I croak out, pointing to his boxer briefs that are doing nothing to hide his erection.

"You first. I'm close to exploding as it is. I need to get you there," he murmurs, kissing my lips.

"I'm already there," I mutter, my lips next to his ear. He growls again, and this time I feel it deep in my core.

"Off," he says, pulling at my shirt. I roll out from under him and slide off the bed. "Saylor," he warns.

"Patience," I scold him playfully.

"None. I have no fucking patience when you're no longer under me," he says. He moves to sit on the edge of the bed where he reaches out for me.

I'm faster.

"Just watch," I say, my voice husky with desire. I've never done this, been brave enough to demand what I want. It has to be the wine, or that Vegas magic. Then again, it could be Rhett. More than likely, it's a combination of all three. Slowly, I remove my shirt and toss it on the bedroom floor. His eyes follow my every move. Sliding my hands ever so slowly, painfully slow even for me, I run them across my stomach, only stopping when I reach the waistband of my jeans. I shimmy my hips until they pool at my feet. Rhett reaches for me again. This time I don't even try to evade him. With deft fingers, he slides my panties down my legs. I step of out, leaving them and my jeans in a pile on the floor.

He pulls me to stand between his legs, and he rests his forehead against my belly, holding his hands on the back of my thighs. He's breathing heavy. Not only can I see the rise and fall, but I can feel it as I run my hands up and down his back. I'm starting to worry he's changed his mind. "I'm trying really fucking hard to take this slow, Short Stack. I'm barely hanging on to my control," he says, not looking at me.

"Hey, Whiskey," I say softy, running my fingers through his hair. He raises his head to look at me. "Then don't."

He lifts me, gripping onto the back of my thighs, and tosses me on the bed. I land with a soft bounce, and I can't help the giggle that escapes.

"I love that sound," he says. "I just think we need to change it up a bit." He drops to his knees. I yelp when he pulls me to the end of the mattress and places my legs over his shoulders. "You okay with this, Short Stack? You gonna let me taste you?" he asks, running his fingers though my folds.

"Y-yes," I manage to breath the word. I lift my hips as if I'm offering myself to him. I can't control it; my body is speaking for itself.

"So fucking perfect," he says, leaning in and teasing me with his tongue.

My hands go to his hair, and I tug. It's a fantasy I've had often when it comes to Rhett; I just never thought it would come to life. He swirls his tongue around my clit, and my back arches off the bed. "Yes," I pant. "That." I hold him there. His hands grip the inside of my thighs and push my legs further apart, opening me to him. He nips at my clit then soothes it with his tongue. "I-I can't," I say, fighting the urge to push him away but wanting him to stay where he is at the same time. I'm overwhelmed with a burning sensation running through my body.

"You can," he says, barely lifting his mouth from me before going back for more.

"Rhett." His name falls from my lips. I'm gripping his hair so damn tight, holding on for the ride.

"Gonna need you to let go, Short Stack, just feel," he says, kissing the inside of my thigh.

His mouth is everywhere all at once—at least that's what it seems like. When he tongues my clit, nipping and sucking, it throws me over the edge. I make noises that sound like a wild fucking animal, but I can't seem to control it. He's giving me the most intense orgasm of my life.

When I can finally focus on what's going on around me, I feel Rhett kissing his way up my belly. Stopping at my breasts, he nips one first then the other with his teeth, causing desire to flare yet again. Not sure how it's possible with the orgasm I just had. My legs are still trembling from the onslaught of his tongue.

He settles himself beside me and pulls me into his arms. "Fucking, beautiful," he says before softly kissing the top of my head.

We lay there, quiet, neither one of us saying anything else. When my breathing slows, I come to my senses. I'm lying naked in bed with Rhett Baxter. Not willing to miss this chance with him, I run my hands over the ridged planes of his abs. I venture on until I reach his boxer briefs. The head of his cock is poking through the top. Gently, I run my finger across the tip.

He shudders. "Saylor?" There's a question in his voice.

Slipping my hand under his boxers, I grip him then give his cock a tender stroke. Before I can go any further, he's flips me onto my back and hovers over me.

He grinds his cock into my core. "You did this," he says huskily. "This is what you do to me."

"Show me." I look up at him.

"I need you to tell me exactly what that means, Say."

"I want you," I tell him, lifting my hips for more friction.

"You want me?" He bends down and kisses me. I can taste myself on his tongue. "You want my cock?" he asks huskily, grinding his hips into mine.

"Yes, all of it. Yes," I say closing my eyes, trying to memorize the feel of his weight on me. All too soon, his weight is gone and I'm opening my eyes. I watch, captivated as he slips out of his boxer briefs and strokes his cock. I moan, not able to prevent my body's reaction to him.

Leaning over the bed, he kisses me. His lips against mine is like a drug. It's not an experience I'll ever get enough of. Pulling back, he grabs the condom he took out of his wallet earlier and tears open the package. My eyes are glued to his hands and he rolls it down his length. "You're fucking me with your eyes, Saylor." His voice is gruff as he climbs back on the bed.

He hovers over me, his arms on either side of my head holding his weight. His hair falls down into his eyes, and I immediately push it back. He leans down, his lips linger over mine, and his hair tickles my face. He holds my stare, his brown eyes full of heat before he closes the small distance and slowly traces his tongue across my lips, and I open for him, craving the taste of us. It's erotic and not something I ever thought I would like. With Rhett, it's hot as hell.

"So sweet," he murmurs before pushing his tongue past my lips. His lips are firm yet soft as they connect with mine. I bury my fingers in his hair, and he moans deep in his throat at the same time as he pushes into me.

I tense at first, needing some time to adjust to his size. He doesn't move, just stays buried inside of me and deepens his kiss. Needing more, I wrap my legs around his waist and tug him into me. He pulls away from the kiss and drops his forehead to mine.

"Incredible," he murmurs as he slowly withdraws and just as slowly enters me again.

He doesn't seem to be in any kind of hurry, but I am. This fire burning inside of me is raging. It's as if my earlier orgasm was just a simple appetizer. I'm more than ready for the main course. "More," I beg. He lifts his head and thrusts a little harder. It's better, but not good enough. "Faster."

"I can't," he says, his jaw tight. "I'm not going to last, beautiful. I need you there. Touch yourself," he commands.

Releasing my grip on his hair, I slide my hand between us and circle my clit.

"That's it." He rocks his hips and gives me exactly what I asked for.

"That," I pant as he swivels his hips, never breaking rhythm. "I'm so close," I breathe.

His thrusts grow harder, faster, and I let my hand fall away, holding onto his muscular arms. "Saylor," he warns. That's as far as he gets before my second orgasm bursts inside of me. It's intense as warmth spreads through my body. His release is immediate as he throws his head back with a grunt. "Fuck me," he whispers, burying his face in my neck.

"I kinda think we just took care of that," I say, winded. I'm still trying to catch my breath.

He chuckles. "We should do it again," he says, thrusting one more time before pulling out.

"Only one condom. What kind of Boy Scout were you anyway?" I tease. I'm hoping we can avoid any awkwardness.

He slides off the bed and stands. I roll to my side to watch him. Leaning in, he kisses me and smacks my ass. "Nothing could have prepared me for you, Saylor," he says, then ambles toward the bathroom in his naked glory. Not a minute later, he strolls back out of the bathroom and sits on the edge of the bed. Sliding his hands under the covers, he puts pressure on the inside of my knee, wanting me to open for him. Apparently, when it comes to Rhett, I'm easy. I don't put up a fight and let my legs fall open. He takes a warm rag and cleans me up. When he's done, he tosses it to the floor, obviously not concerned with the carpet in this high-priced suite we're staying in.

He surprises me when he climbs into bed and slides under the covers. Immediately, he reaches for me, pulling my back to his chest. "Good night, baby," he whispers.

I should question it. I should ask him what we're doing. I should ask him what this means. However, I don't. Instead, I let his deep, even breaths lull me to sleep.

TWENTY SEVEN

OLLING OVER, I reach for her and come up empty-handed. Prying my eyes open, sure enough, I find the bed beside me is empty and cold. She left me at some point in the middle of the night. Instantly, I'm pissed off. For the first time, I wanted the woman to be next to me when I woke up, and she's not. Neither one of the reactions am I used to. Part of me wonders if it was a dream, but the images running through my mind are too vivid to not be real. Throwing back the covers, I climb out of bed. My foot hits something damp. Looking down, I see the cloth that I cleaned her with, further confirmation that last night wasn't a dream.

After a quick pit stop to the bathroom, I head out to the living area of the suit. Saylor is sitting on the couch, eating a bagel and drinking coffee.

"Morning," I say, taking the seat next to her.

"Morning," she says, way too damn chipper. "I ordered breakfast. Just bagels and pastries. I wasn't really sure what you wanted, and I know we have to be there at eleven to set up."

"What time is it?" I ask her.

"Just after ten. I was getting ready to come and wake you up."

She doesn't mention leaving me last night or early this morning. "You sleep well?" I ask her.

"Yeah, did you?"

"I did. I missed you though." Reaching over, I move her hair from her shoulder. "I expected you to be there when I woke up."

"Once I'm up, I'm up, so I went ahead and showered and got ready. I didn't want to have to rush."

I study her, trying to see if she's telling me the truth. Her voice is sincere, if not a little hesitant. I believe her, but at the same time, there is something else just below the surface.

"I should go finish getting ready."

She's looks perfect to me. Dark skintight jeans and a Baxter's Distillery T-shirt. All she needs is shoes. "Trust me, babe, you look great."

She gives me a shy smile. "I need shoes, and I want to touch up my lipstick. I should have eaten first."

She stands, and I watch her go. Her ass is fucking spectacular in those jeans. When she disappears behind her bedroom door, I know she's not coming out until she has to. I grab a bagel, slather on some cream cheese, and head to the shower. We'll get through today, and then I'll have her in my bed again. There really is no other option.

After scarfing down my bagel and a quick shower, I'm back in the living area and still no Saylor. I find myself standing outside of her bedroom door. I want to barge in and toss her on the bed and repeat every second of last night, but that has to wait. We're here for a reason, and because of that we need to go. "Saylor," I say, knocking lightly on her door. "You about ready? We need to get going." *How long does it take to reapply lipstick?*

Arms braced above the door, I stand there and wait for her. When the door finally opens, I don't move. She did more than just reapply her lipstick. Her hair that was straightened now hangs in soft curls down her back, and she's taller. I travel down to her black high heels. I have to tighten my grip on the frame to keep from locking us in her room for the rest of the day. "You trying to tempt me with those fuck-me heels?" I ask, my voice gruff.

"What?" she asks innocently. "I'm just trying to look good, you know, to sell the Baxter name." She pats my chest with both hands then slips underneath my arms.

I follow her to the living room, trying not to trip over my tongue on the way. Her ass in those jeans is epic. Her ass in those jeans and heels fuck with my head and my cock. My dick rises to the occasion, and my head is telling me to make her mine.

"Ready?" she asks, looking over her shoulder.

"Yeah, let's get this day over with," I say, placing my hand on the small of her back and leading her to the elevator.

"Why so grumpy?"

"Really, Saylor?"

"What?"

"You, that's what." I grab her hand and place it over my cock. "You did this, and looking like that"—I point to her—"I'm going to be hard all fucking day."

She takes a step closer, her heels bring her closer than ever before. "I'm sorry." She sticks out her bottom lip in a pout. "What if I promise to make it better?" she coos.

Grabbing her hips, I pull her into me. "Let's go back to the room," I say, kissing down her neck.

The elevator doors slide open, and she steps out of my hold. "Duty calls." She shrugs and prances out of the elevator.

"Son of a bitch," I mumble, following behind her. Dorothy was able to score our suite in the hotel that is connected to the casino, which means we never have to leave the building, something that I never really cared about until now. Every motherfucker we pass is checking her out. I can only imagine how bad it would be out on the strip. My irritation spikes the more stares she gets, and that irritates me too.

"So where do we set up?" she asks.

"We're going to be in the lobby of the casino with the other vendors. Dorothy shipped all of our supplies and arranged for someone to set up our booth."

"Then why did you need me? Could you not have hired someone here?"

"Honestly, I can't answer that. Gramps just said I needed an experienced bartender to come with me. I didn't question him." I should have. Now that I'm here, I'm wondering why I didn't. Then again, once

I found out Saylor was coming, I didn't care. The thought of a few days away with her was all I could think about.

We find our booth easily enough; there is a representative from the casino there to greet us.

"Rhett Baxter?" the guy asks.

"Yes." I offer him my hand. "Nice to meet you."

"You too. I'm Cliff. I have your badge for the event and everything is set up. However, I didn't get the name of your bartender."

"That would be me." Saylor raises her hand. "Saylor," she tells him.

"Nice to meet you," he says, holding her hand longer than necessary. "Give me a few minutes, and I'll be back with your badge."

"He's friendly," she says, watching him walk away.

"This is your show." I point to the table behind us, changing the subject and distracting her from Cliff. "You think you can handle it?"

"Please," she scoffs. "I've been slinging drinks for years."

"Here you go," Cliff says, handing Saylor her badge. "So the show starts at noon. It's open to the public as well as other businesses. You're free to pass out samples. Patrons are carded before being allowed access to the lobby, so you don't need to worry about that. The casino will take on that liability. The idea is to let them sample your product, hence getting people to the casino and hopefully digging into their pockets and partaking in the fun before they leave. For you, it's an opportunity to reach new customers and potential businesses to serve your brand."

"Noon to five?" I clarify.

"Yeah, after that we'll break down the booths. You can choose to take your product that's left over with you, or if you decide to leave it, it will be considered ownership of the house and dispensed as ordered," Cliff explains.

"We'll leave it. Whatever's left you can have," I tell him. I don't want to deal with shipping it back; it's not worth it.

"Great. Good luck today," Cliff says before turning to Saylor. "Maybe after we can go get a drink?" he asks her.

I slide up behind her and place my hands on her hips. He holds his hands in the air and backs away, wearing a cocky-as-fuck grin. When he turns and walks away, Saylor elbows me.

"What?" I play dumb. I know exactly what her jab was for.

"You," she huffs. "Don't think just because of last night you have some kind of claim over me," she says, her voice low yet stern.

That's exactly what it means. I just need to get her to see things my way. "Wanna bet?" I taunt her.

She rolls those big blue eyes at me. "Sure, we can bet if you feel like losing some of your money."

I place my hands back on her hips and pull her back against my front. My cock is hard, all for her. "You feel that, Say? You feel what you do to me?" I watch over her shoulder as her chest rapidly rises and falls. "You want me. I can see it in the way your body responds to mine." I run my finger down her arm that is currently covered in goose bumps. "I know what you're thinking."

"Right," she scoffs, still fighting this connection.

"My cock, deep inside you, that's what you're thinking about. That's what you want, Saylor. Admit it," I say before kissing the side of her neck.

"People are staring," she says breathlessly. Her plea is as weak as her resolve.

"I don't give a fuck. Let them see. Every motherfucker in here needs to see that you're untouchable to them."

She ignores my statement. "They're opening the doors," she says.

Releasing my hold on her, I move to stand in front of her. Bending down so we are nose to nose, our lips a breath apart, I say, "You look beautiful today. I didn't get a chance to tell you." With that, I press my lips to hers. It's brief and not nearly enough, but it will have to do until this gig is over. Then all bets are off.

The day drags on as I watch every drunk asshole in Vegas hit on her. She handles herself well, blowing off their advances. I stay close to her and give each and every one of them a warning glare. I should be out schmoozing other casino owners, but I'm not leaving her alone. If they're interested in the Baxter brand, they can come to me. Hell, we're already in most of them anyway. I still don't understand why Gramps signed up for this. He claimed it was as a favor, but was it really? Too bad his grumpy ass isn't talking to me, I might have been able to get the real story. When we get back, I'm having it out with him. Life is too short for us to go on like this.

"People love it," Saylor says, holding up a bottle of Baxter's X2; it's our most recent, eighty proof.

"I think it has more to do with who's serving than the whiskey," I tell her.

"That is why you brought me after all, right? To look pretty pouring drinks?"

"No. I asked Jake to come and he shut me down."

"Right. So I was your second choice," she says, losing some of her spark.

There's a lull in the crowd, so I take the opportunity to pull her close, snaking my arm around her waist. Her head rests on my chest. I expected a fight, but she came willingly. "Never settle for second choice, Saylor. You're so much better than that." I want to tell her she's my first choice. That she's all I think about; she's the only woman I see. This trip has proven that. There are women barely dressed everywhere, a few even trying to drum up conversation as they stop at our table. Not once was I tempted. They can't hold a candle to Saylor. I just need to figure out how to break through those walls she has built around her.

"Would you like a sample?" she asks a group of four who stop at our table.

Reluctantly, I release her from my hold, missing the feel of her in my arms. "Thirty more minutes," I tell her once the group has moved on. "What do you want to do tonight?"

"Anything." She looks up at me, eyes shining. "Maybe we can walk the strip again. I'd kind of like to see the light show at the fountain again. Fifteen minutes wasn't enough."

"We can make that happen. We'll grab dinner, and then we'll just start walking. You tell me if you see something you want to do. Deal?" I ask, holding my hand out for her to shake. Not because I need her to shake on this deal, but because I need to feel her skin against mine. Any little morsel of contact I can get from her I'm taking.

She reaches out and takes my hand. "Deal." After we shake, she hands me a shot, keeping one for herself. "To firsts," she says.

I hold my small plastic shot glass up to hers and then toss back my shot. Little did we know that toast was all too fitting for the night ahead.

TWENTY EIGHT

Saylor

THE VEGAS SUN peeking through the windows of the suite is scorching. I'm hot, too damn warm. Prying my eyes open, I blink away the sun. My head is pounding, a sure sign I drank too much last night. I knew I would regret it today, but we were having such a good time. Besides, this could be the last time I'm ever in Vegas, and they say what happens in Vegas stays in Vegas. However, this headache will be going on the plane with me for sure.

I need to pee. Groaning, I try to move and a hand clamps down on my hip. I start to panic, and then he speaks. "Stop trying to leave, baby. We're sleeping in," he mumbles, burying his face in my hair.

"I have to pee," I moan, because I seriously need to relieve my bladder.

"Fine, but come back to bed," he says, kissing my neck and releasing his hold on me. Sliding from underneath the covers, I discover I'm naked. Flashes of last night slowly filter through my mind. Me on top, Rhett hovering over me. Shaking off the memory, I run to the bathroom in all my naked glory to take care of business. Stopping at the sink to wash my hands and brush my teeth, I gasp when I see a diamond band on my ring finger. What. The. Fuck. "Rhett!" I yell.

I hear his feet thump as they hit the floor and his heavy footsteps, and then the bathroom door flies open. "What is it? What's wrong? Are you okay?" He fires off questions, running his hands through his hair.

"This!" I hold up my left hand.

"Okay, it's a ring." He shrugs.

"A ring," I scoff. "This was not here last night when we went out."

He scrunches up his forehead, as if he's thinking. "So we bought it last night," he says, still not getting what I'm saying.

"Rhett!" I stomp my foot and cringe at my own voice. "Give me your hand." I hold mine out, palm up. He places his hand in mine. "The other one," I say, holding my breath. Maybe I did just buy a ring. Although it looks real, so he would have had to of bought it for me. Hope starts to rise until he gives me his left hand and my suspicion is confirmed. "No, no, no, no," I chant, dropping his hand and rushing past him. I survey the room and see nothing out of place. Hurrying out to the living area, I scan until I see a white envelope on the counter. Rushing to it, I flip it over, and sure enough, the logo for "The Little White Wedding Chapel" adorns the font. "Fuck," I say, defeated.

"We're married," he says from behind me.

I nod. "Yeah," I confirm.

He sits on the couch and rests his elbows on his knees, burying his hands in his hair. "I remember bits and pieces of last night. That couple at the fountain, they were headed to the chapel and invited us along."

I plop down on the couch beside him and close my eyes. "Yeah," I agree as the nights starts coming back to me. "They were so excited; their enthusiasm was contagious."

"We're married," he says again.

"How do we fix this?" I ask him, opening my eyes to see him still hunched over, elbows on his knees.

He raises his head and looks at me. "Why do we have to fix it?"

"Rhett, come on. We got married. We're not even dating."

"We could be," he counters.

"But the fact remains we're not. Don't you have some fancy lawyer you can call to make this go away?"

"Yeah, I'll take care of it," he says, his voice flat. "We need to get to the airport. Our flight leaves in two hours."

"Right. When we get home, we have to figure this mess out. I'll hold on to these," I say, holding the envelope up that I'm sure holds our marriage license. Standing, I drag my hungover, newly married ass to my room to shower and pack.

Thirty minutes later, I find Rhett in the main living area, his carryon beside him. "I called a car. It's waiting to take us to the airport." He hands me a bottle of water. "You hungry?"

"I'll just grab something at the airport. The last thing we need is to miss our flight."

He nods and reaches for my bag. "I got it," I say a little more heated than necessary. This whole marriage thing is messing with me.

"Saylor," he sighs. "Let me have your bag. We need to go," he says, reaching out again.

This time I let him take it. I notice his wedding band when he does. Absentmindedly, I run my thumb over mine. I started to take it off, but it looks expensive, and I didn't want to risk losing it. Surely, he can sell it or maybe return it. "Thanks," I mumble.

The ride to the airport is quiet. I don't know what to say, and I'm sure neither does he. I mean, we got drunk and got married, what do you say to that? We make it through security and to our gate with limited talking, just enough to get us to where we need to be.

"I'm going to run and get something to eat. What do you want?" he asks me.

"Anything, and coffee, please."

He gives my knee a gentle squeeze before standing and walking away. I don't take my eyes off of him until he disappears into the crowd of people.

"Your husband's very handsome," the little lady sitting next to me says. "You all are quite the pair." She smiles warmly.

How do I explain he's not really my husband, when technically he is? It's not worth the stress of the conversation. "Thank you," I say instead. Fuck it, can't beat them, join them.

"You remind me a lot of my Harold and me when we were younger. He was the love of my life," she says. "We have four children and nine grandchildren," she boasts proudly. She continues to tell me about her grandson's graduation, which is why she's flying to West Virginia; he goes to college at Virginia Tech.

Rhett returns with two bagels and two piping hot cups of coffee. "Be careful, it's really hot," he tells me.

I want to smart off that I'm an adult and know how to drink a hot beverage, but he's being sincere. I need to keep my bad attitude in check. He didn't force me to marry him. Hell, from what I remember, I was all in on our impromptu nuptials.

"I was just telling your wife what a lovely couple you are," my new friend tells Rhett.

"Thank you." He gives her one of his panty-dropping smiles before taking his seat next to me and digging into his breakfast.

"How long have you been married?" she asks.

"Newlyweds," Rhett says before I can form an answer.

"Oh, how wonderful. My Harold and I fell fast and hard. We married after courting just four weeks. My daddy was so angry, said we were too young, but I knew he was it for me. When you know, you know." She sighs. "How long have you been together?" she asks. She's oblivious or just doesn't care that we really aren't engaging her, just answering her questions. Normally, I would be, but the topic of conversation stresses me the hell out.

"A few months," Rhett answers.

I want to give him the look, you know the one that tells him to shut his mouth, but I don't have the energy. Besides, chances are we'll never see this woman again.

"How romantic," she gushes. "Words of wisdom, never go to bed angry, and never sleep alone. I mean, you don't get married to sleep alone, right?" She wags her eyebrows.

I can't help but laugh at her antics. Thankfully, we're saved from further questioning when they call to board first class. It's terrible of me, but I hold my breath, hoping she remains seated. She does, allowing me to breathe easy.

"It was nice meeting you." Rhett stands and grabs our bags. I follow him to the line and onto the plane. "You want the window seat again?" he asks.

"I plan on sleeping, so it doesn't matter to me."

"I'll take the aisle, that way you don't have to worry about people bumping into you," he says sweetly.

I take my seat; we're in the very front row again. I immediately pull the shade closed on the window and buckle myself in. My thoughts wonder to the flight here and Rhett's means of distraction. My anxiety spikes, not really knowing what to expect for takeoff. He had me too distracted to take notice.

Rhett settles in his seat and buckles up. "You doing okay?"

"Yeah, just nervous about takeoff," I admit.

Reaching over, he laces his fingers through mine. I can feel the metal of his wedding band against my palm. "You want me to distract you?" he whispers. He's got his head resting against the seat, turned toward me. I do the same. It's an intimate position, but I need him right now. I know my fear is irrational, but it's there nonetheless.

"Maybe," I answer, not taking my eyes off his.

The flight attendant takes down her microphone and gives us her speech about safety and seat belt signs and emergency procedures. I listen but never look away from him. "Just breath, Say," he whispers as the plane begins to taxi down the runway.

As the plane starts to lift, I feel my panic grow. "K-kiss me, p-please," I say, fighting through the fear.

With one hand holding tight to mine, the other lifts and cups my cheek. He leans in, and I meet him halfway. I close my eyes and get lost in him, in Rhett, my husband. When the plane levels out, he pulls away. He brushes my hair out of my eyes. "Better?" he asks. I nod, unable to speak. With his hand on my head, he guides me to rest against his shoulder. "Sleep," he says softly.

I settle against him and close my eyes. I can't believe we got married; I'm leaning against my husband. My heart hurts that it's not real. To be able to spend my life with him. To truly be a part of his family… they're amazing, and it would be a privilege to be a part of it. Looking back, I'll be able to say I was wild and crazy and got married in Vegas.

"Miss," I hear Rhett asks. "Can I get a blanket for my wife?" he asks softly.

His wife.

My husband.

I fight to keep my eyes closed. Why is he referring to me as his wife? We're married, but it isn't real. I feel him drape the cover over me. "Sleep, baby," he says, his lips brushing across my forehead.

I'm too tired to figure it out. We can do that when we get home. Right now, I just want to sleep off the aftereffect of Vegas and snuggle up to my husband. Might be the last time I have the chance.

TWENTY NINE

Rhett

WHEN WE MAKE it back to the house, all I want to do is crash. I didn't sleep on either flight. Saylor was able to rest on both, leaning against me. Each time I asked the flight attendant for a blanket for my wife, the word cemented with me. I should have dropped her off at her place. Instead, I convinced her to come home with me so we could discuss how to get out of this mess—her words not mine. I could never consider being married to Saylor as a mess. It's impulsive and out of character for both of us with that level of commitment, but not a mess. After we boarded our connecting flight and she fell back asleep, all I thought about was how to get her to try this ruse of a marriage and see if we can make it work. Not something that I would have ever thought I'd hear myself say.

Things changed when I met Saylor.

"Come on in," I say, opening the front door and letting her pass. I could have walked on in, but I'm a starving man when it comes to her. I'll take any chance I can to touch her. Placing my hand on the small of her back, I lead her into the living room.

"How do we do this, Rhett?" she says after getting settled on the couch.

I take the seat right next to her and rest my hand on her thigh. "I don't know. I'll call my family's lawyer on Monday and see what he says. I don't even know if he handles divorces."

"I can't believe we did this," she says with a heavy sigh.

"What? You don't like being married to me?" I ask her.

"We're not really married," she counters.

"I beg to differ. Those papers in that white envelope in your bag say otherwise."

"You know what I mean. We're not in love," she says.

"Married?" a gruff voice says from the doorway.

"Shit," I mumble under my breath. "He never comes downstairs unless we have company," I tell Saylor.

"What am I?" she asks.

"My wife," I say deadpan. The more I say it, the more I like the sound of it.

"You're married?" Gramps asks, using his cane to enter the room.

I wait until he's seated in his recliner to tell him the story. "Funny story," I say before telling the tale, piece by piece. "I'm going to call the family attorney on Monday and see if he can start on the divorce process."

"I'll take care of it," Gramps says sternly. "Where is your marriage license?"

"I have it," Saylor jumps up and runs to her bag, digging around until she's holding the white envelope. "Here." She hands it to him.

"You both want this, right? You agree to end this marriage?" he asks.

"It's not real, Grandpa Rhett," Saylor says softly. "We were under the influence of alcohol. It's not a union of love," she explains.

"Saylor," I say, not really sure how to say everything that's running through my head. She turns to look at me, and all I want to do is kiss her until her smile reappears.

"We've talked about this," she says.

"Yeah," I mumble.

"All right then, I'll take care of this. Be warned this isn't something that will happen overnight. We can't just call a judge and ask for this to be erased. There will be paperwork and a court hearing. It's not an easy fix," he tells us.

"Thank you so much," Saylor says, bending to give him a hug.

"You're still family here, sweet girl. No matter what, you're always welcome."

Tears glisten in her eyes. I stand and reach out for her. I can't take her tears. "Come here." I pull her into my arms, and she comes willingly. "Why don't you just stay here tonight?"

"I really should go home," she says.

"Are you sure?" I ask her.

"Yeah. Thank you." She pulls away. "I'm ready to just go home and get some rest."

I want to ask about all the sleep she got on the plane, but I keep quiet. "Come on then, I'll take you home. Gramps, you sure you got this?"

"I'm sure. I've been laying in that bed too long. This will give me something to do since you took my job," he quips.

"You know you're not well enough to pull an all-day shift at the distillery."

"I sure as hell can call a lawyer from my bed. Frank and I are old friends; we need to catch up anyway. Besides, maybe I can use the distillery as leverage to do what he can to clean this up?"

"What do you mean?" Saylor asks.

"It would be a shame if I had to find a new attorney, now wouldn't it?" He winks at her.

"No, I don't want that. Don't let it affect your business. We can do this on our own."

"Nonsense. Let me help you. It will do me some good to have something to do other than watch mindless television. Frank will be hearing from me daily until we get this issue resolved."

"Thank you." She kisses his cheek.

Suddenly, I'm jealous of my seventy-seven-year-old grandfather. "Let's get you home," I say. Standing, I grab her bag and wait until she's slipping back into her coat. I lead her to my truck with my hand on the small of her back. I wish I could have convinced her to stay, but asking again would be more than pressing my luck.

"He'll take care of it," I say when we pull into her driveway. The drive here was quiet, both of us lost in our thoughts. "I'll keep on him."

"It's fine, Rhett. It's not like I have any pending offers that I'm rushing out to accept. I just don't want to be the reason you're held back," she confesses.

My chest tightens at her confession. "You're not holding me back, Saylor. I know it's just a piece of paper, but you don't have to worry about me being with anyone else. We have to file with the courts, so word is going to get out."

"Shit, your parents," she says, burying her face in her hands. "They're going to hate me."

"Hey." I grab her hand and pull it away from her face. "You're impossible to hate. I'll call them later and explain what's going on. Don't worry. It will all work out like it's supposed to." I fight the urge to lean in and kiss her. The pull is there like a current in the ocean. Pulling away, I climb out of the truck and retrieve her bag.

She doesn't bother to tell me she can get it this time; she's learned her lesson. I follow her up the stairs, dreading saying goodbye.

"Thank you," she says softly.

"You're welcome. I'll call you tomorrow? We should keep in touch; you know, until this is all cleared up."

"We're still friends, Rhett. This doesn't have to be awkward."

"I don't want it to be, but I can't stop thinking about being inside of you, and now you're my wife. That fucks with my head, Saylor," I say, leaning into her.

"We're both adults. We can manage," she says with mock confidence. I can see the desire in her eyes.

"Can I kiss my wife goodnight?" I ask her, my lips now hovering over hers.

"We shouldn't," she says, gripping my coat.

I eliminate the distance and press my mouth to hers. I nip at her bottom lip until she opens for me. Sliding my tongue past her lips, I get lost in the taste of her. My cock is hard as steel, remembering how she feels. Is it possible that this kiss is better than all the others? That it's sweeter knowing she's my wife? I know she's not really mine, but the thought of it somehow changes things. Sweeter, softer, more electrifying. I never would have thought it could have been possible, not with us. Every time my lips touch hers, it's explosive. Slowly, I pull away from her.

"Goodnight, Say," I whisper. Before I release my hold on her, I drop a chaste kiss to her forehead. I motion for her to go inside, handing her her bag.

"Night, Whiskey," she whispers before closing the door.

I stand there on her step, fists clenched. I want to beat the fucking door down until she lets me in, inside her house and inside of her. I need to get my head on straight where she's concerned. She's made her position clear. I just need to figure out why it bothers me so much.

THIRTY

G RABBING MY CANE as soon as the door shuts, I'm on my feet and headed toward the window. I need to make sure they're gone before I make the call. I watch until I can no longer see his truck before making my way to my office upstairs. I may be an old man, but I know a spark when I see it. Those kids have it in spades. That Saylor is a special person, and my Rhett just as much. I'm hard on him, but he needs to see there is more to life than your title and your money. I can tell that being here is doing that for him. It's been hard on me, not falling back into our old ways, laughing and joking all the time, but I'm teaching him a lesson. Like his father, he let the outside world change his rhythm of life, alter what he views as important. I think our girl Saylor is just what he needs to come back down to earth. No doubt in my mind, she'll keep him grounded just as my sweet Mary did for me, and the same as Valerie has done for my son. Behind every good man is a strong woman.

Easing myself down into my chair, I don't have to look up the number I've called numerous times over the years. I dial the phone and wait for him to pick up. "Frank," I say in greeting.

"Rhett, how you been? I heard you've been under the weather and your grandson has been filling in for you," he says.

"Dorothy gossips too much." I laugh.

"She's a keeper that one. What can I do for you?"

"I need your help with something. I'll make it worth your while," I tell him.

"I'm listening."

"First let me ask, in your scope of practice, are you able to handle a simple basic divorce? A quickie wedding that happened in Vegas?"

"I can. It's not my specialty, but if it's what your describing, just some basic paperwork and some signatures. Could have it completed and through the courts in a few weeks, month tops."

"Great. Now, what I'm about to tell you stays between us. It's not illegal, so you don't have to worry. This is where I make it worth your while. My grandson got married this weekend. The girl, well, they're perfect for each other. However, they feel as though since alcohol was involved it was a mistake. I disagree. I told them I would handle everything, and that's where you come in. I need a draft in a week or so, something that looks official, but I don't want it to be filed. If either Rhett or Saylor contacts you, you are to tell them that it's in the works and these things take time. I want to give them time to change their minds."

"Baxter, you're playing with lives here," he warns me.

"Nothing too extreme. If in three months, they have not figured out that a divorce is not what they want, then you can file the damn papers. But I'm going to need you to field questions and concerns. Make up some legal mumbo jumbo that they won't bother checking into. They just need a little time."

"Baxter, you sure about this?"

"What's a few more weeks of marriage in the grand scheme of things. You said a month, I say three. It's eight more weeks. I'll double your hourly rate." He whistles, and I know I've got him. He's a great guy, but lives for the money and expensive things. He's a great attorney, but everything I don't want my grandson to be.

"You had me at double." He laughs.

"Great. I'll be your point of contact, but if either of them reach out to you, play it off. Stall them, and we'll need something official looking in the next week or so."

"I'm all over it. I need a copy of the marriage license, and I'll get started. I'll have my courier drop something off soon. The house?"

"Yes. Talk soon," I say, ending the call.

The plan is in motion. Now I just need to sit back and enjoy the show. I'll tell them eventually, regardless of the outcome. They'll thank me when they're living happily ever after. Closing my eyes, I look toward the ceiling. "Help me guide them, Mary Bear. I love you and miss you every day." Opening my eyes, I kiss my fingers and touch the frame on my desk of my late wife.

THIRTY ONE

Saylor

AFTER RHETT DROPPED me off last night, I came in and took a long, hot shower, then went to bed. I was exhausted both mentally and physically. I was also afraid I would call him and beg him to come back. I shouldn't have let him kiss me, but my strength to resist him is nonexistent at this point. When he referred to me as his wife, my freaking ovaries exploded. It makes me wonder, what would it be like to really be his? To be married to a man like Rhett? He's got this hard exterior, but when he lets you in, he's all soft and cuddly. He's the full package.

My phone vibrates across the small kitchen table.

Molly: You up?

Me: Yep.

Molly: I'm on my way over.

Me: K

I was expecting this. I'm sure she wants to know how the trip was. I'm fairly certain she doesn't know about my predicament, or she would have

213

mentioned it. Looking at the diamond band on my hand, I know I should take it off, and I will. I'm going to see how long it takes her to notice first. Might as well have a little fun from this bizarre situation.

"Come in!" I yell when she knocks on the door.

"Hey, girl, how was the trip?" she asks, kicking off her boots and tossing her coat on the small bench by the door.

"It was good."

"I need more than that. What all did you do? See any shows?"

I nod. "Yeah, we went to a burlesque show, which was pretty wild. We watched the fountain/light show at the Bellagio both nights. The first night we got there after the last show had started. I wanted to see it again," I explain.

"I've heard it's amazing." She sighs. "I'll get there one day."

"How have you been? How did the meeting go with the wedding planner?" Flashes of my wedding roll through my mind.

"Meh, there's a lot to this wedding business. We might just do something small like Gatlinburg, or somewhere tropical, maybe even Vegas." She laughs.

If she only knew. "What do you want, Molly? Don't let the stress of planning the wedding keep you from having the wedding of your dreams."

"You know, I always thought I wanted a big wedding, but as I get older, and now that I'm engaged, I'm not so sure. I think it was just a fantasized dream of a little girl, you know? What about you?"

"I've never really planned on having a big wedding. Honestly, I think weddings are overrated," I tell her. Not just because I recently married the sexy Rhett Baxter while intoxicated in Vegas either.

"How so?" she asks.

"Think about all the money you could potentially spend on a huge wedding. All the food, the venue to house everyone, and the decorations. Me personally, I think a wedding should be just for the bride and groom. You're pledging your life to someone, and that someone is all that matters in that moment. I've just always felt weddings were frivolous. Think of the honeymoon or even down payment on a house you could have using that money differently."

"You make a good point," she agrees.

214

"Don't let me influence you. Hell, maybe it's because I've never really had family or a father to walk me down the aisle? All I know is that it's never been something I've dreamed about. For me, it was more the union, the binding myself to someone for life. Creating a family, somewhere for me to belong," I explain.

"Honestly, I've never really thought about it like that. I can see the appeal for sure, especially after our meeting. I just want to be married to Jake."

"Nothing else really matters."

"Yeah," she sighs. "I mean, now that I think about it, we've been wanting to remodel the rest of the house anyway. We could use that money and still be married. It's genius, really." She laughs.

I pull up my arm to look at my watch. "Therapy's over. I'll see you the same time next week." I laugh.

"What is that?" she asks, grabbing my hand.

"What does it look like?" I counter.

"It looks like a wedding band, a very expensive wedding band," she says, pulling my hand closer to get a better look.

"Ding, ding, ding," I sing.

"From the looks of this thing, it's new. It's all shiny and shit. Not an heirloom." With a tight grip on my hand, she looks up at me. "Are you married?"

I can see her trying to process this. "Yeah, but not for long."

"Explain," she says, dropping my hand and pulling her feet under her on the couch. I assume to settle in for the story.

"It was Saturday night," I say as I begin to tell her the details about my weekend that I'm sure she would have much rather have heard as soon as she got here. "So yeah," I say once I've finished. "Grandpa Rhett is calling his attorney and taking care of the divorce. He was pretty adamant that he would handle it."

"You're married?" she asks to clarify.

"Yep."

"To Rhett? Rhett Baxter?"

"Yep," I say again.

"Did you… I mean, have you—" I stop her there.

"Yep."

"Holy fucking shit! I need details," she says, wiggling around in excitement.

My mouth drops open. "Really, Molly?"

"Hell yes, that man is fine." She wags her eyebrows.

"That man is my husband," I say, laughing. "I tried to say it with a straight face," I tell her.

"Being under that is no laughing matter," she quips with a smile.

"Gah!"

"So you're married, but getting a divorce?"

"Yep," seems to be my answer of choice for this conversation.

"Are you dating?"

"No. It was a one-time thing—well, the first night, and then after the wedding, but that was the alcohol," I say in a rush.

"Wait, hold up," she says, doing just that and holding up her hands to stop me.

"You slept with him before you were married?"

This time all I can do is nod.

"And you're not dating."

"Nope. It was a Vegas thing, the lights, the shows, the atmosphere. It was supposed to have been left in Vegas, but we sort of brought it home with us."

"Did you discuss that specifically?"

I stop and think. "No," I say cautiously. "We're on the same page, trust me."

"Uh-huh, so when do you see your sexy husband again?" she asks. "Damn, I didn't think you would beat me down the aisle." She giggles when I smack her arm.

"Not funny," I say, trying not to laugh. I have to laugh about it; crying all day isn't an option. So we drank too much and got married. Gramps will get his guys on it and that will be that.

"Fine," she says with an exaggerated sigh. "What do you have planned for the rest of the day?"

"Nothing. I need to run to the grocery store, but other than that, a whole lot of nothing."

"I need to go too, want to ride together? We can grab lunch and make an afternoon of it," she suggests.

"Sure."

"Be ready at noon," she chirps, jumping up from the couch and heading toward the door. "Is this top secret? I mean, obviously the sex I'll keep to myself, but the marriage, can I tell Jake?"

I nod. "I don't see why not. They're friends. We didn't really discuss trying to keep it under wraps. I guess we need to have that conversation."

"It's going to get out, Saylor. You know that, right? Rhett is a good-looking guy, comes from money, his family is legend in this town. Besides, it's public record and will be reported in the local paper."

"Do people still read those?"

She smirks. "See you in a few." She waves and walks out the door.

I start to worry that Rhett will be upset that I told her and that I told her she could tell Jake. Grabbing my phone, I send him a message.

Me: Hey, I told Molly. She asked if she could tell Jake, and I told her yes.

It's mere seconds before his reply comes through.

Rhett: What exactly did you tell her?

Me: That we're married, but getting a divorce.

Not the complete truth, but the part I was feeling guilty about.

Rhett: It's cool. I'm not trying to hide it.

Rhett: I'm not ashamed to be married to you.

Rhett: Are you?

Rhett: I mean, are you ashamed to be married to me?

He fires off a round of texts.

Me: Not that we did it, but how. It was irresponsible.

Rhett: Yeah...

I wait for more, but it never comes. Tossing my phone on the couch, I head to the bedroom. It's time for a long, hot shower before trudging around in the cold to get groceries. What an exciting life I lead. You know, except for the drunken Vegas marriage.

THIRTY TWO

Rhett

HAVEN'T SEEN her since I dropped her off at her place on Saturday. Other than the text messages on Sunday, I haven't talked to her either. Is it normal for a man to go without seeing or speaking to his wife? Oh, right, we're not normal and not together in the true sense of the word married. It's fucked up, and it's fucking with my head. It's Thursday night, and I know she's working. I might have texted Jake and asked him if they all wanted to go ice skating tomorrow. He declined, saying the three of them were working tonight and the girls planned to go shopping tomorrow so skating is out.

That led me to now, sitting in my truck in the parking lot of the Corner Pocket. I have the defrost on high to keep my windows from fogging up. That's all I need is for someone to report back to Saylor I'm out here fogging up the windows with some bar fly. Sure, we're not together, but I won't embarrass her or myself like that. Cheater, I am not. Regardless of the situation.

Pulling my keys from the ignition, I make my way inside. The stool at the far end of the bar, where I've spent more nights than I care to admit in recent months, is vacant. As if the universe knew this is where I would end up tonight. Not that it was hard to figure out. It's been too fucking long since I've laid eyes on her. I'm not letting this marriage thing stop me from pursuing her. After that first night together in Vegas, I thought things were going to go my way. I was wrong, but that's okay. Nothing worth fighting for is ever easy. I'm going to give her the divorce she's asking for, and then I'm going to make her mine. If some day we get to the point of marriage, I won't hesitate to give her the wedding she deserves. I'm getting way ahead of myself putting the cart before the horse and all that. I have to convince her to date me. Then I need to make some decisions about my future. I can't ask her to leave this town, not when she's finally settling in and making a life. It's not a hard decision to make, really. I've always loved it here, and the distillery owns a special place with me. Sure, my parents might be disappointed, but from the talks I've had with Dad recently, I think he knows it's coming. I'm not doing it just for her. I'm doing it for me. I'm happier here, and I want her to be a part of that.

As I slide onto the stool, Jake spots me and gives me a head nod as he mixes a drink. Molly is at the opposite end of the bar, and I know Saylor's on the floor serving. I spotted her as soon as I came in. It's as if my eyes are trained to seek her out any time she's near. It's irrational and not like me, but this is Saylor and that makes all the difference.

"You here to check up on your wife?" Jake asks when he makes his way toward me.

"Just came for a drink," I say, fighting the urge to not look over my shoulder for Saylor.

"Keep telling yourself that," he says, pouring me a draft.

"It's been a few days since we've talked. Just thought I should give her an update on the divorce."

"I'd be happy to relay the information." He smirks.

"Fucker," I mumble, making him laugh.

"Hey," Saylor says, coming up beside us. She rambles her order to Jake and then turns to face me. "How are you? Any news from your gramps?"

I would like to pretend she means his health, and she might, but I know what she's really asking. "He made the calls, said we should have the paperwork in a few days to start the process."

"Great." Jake fills her tray with shots. "Duty calls." She smiles, grabs the tray, and takes off into the crowd.

"It's busy for a Thursday night," I comment, taking a sip of my beer.

"Yeah, it's ladies' night. We're trying out themes to see how big of a crowd they draw. Oddly enough, guys swarm to ladies' night. There are more dicks than chicks," he tells me.

Raucous laughter fills the bar, causing me to turn my head. As soon as I see Saylor with some drunk asshole gripping her arm, I'm on my feet.

"Rhett!" Jake calls out for me.

I don't stop. I reach her in a few long strides. Sliding up behind her, I place one hand on her hip and the other on the drunk asshole's shoulder and squeeze.

"What the fuck?" he says, letting go of Saylor.

She relaxes against me. "You good, babe?" I ask her. My lips next to her ear, she gives me a subtle nod.

"Get the fuck off of me. I saw her first. I got no issue with you, dude," he seethes.

Moving in front of Saylor, I lean down and get in his face. "Here's what's going to happen, motherfucker. See, you just had your hands on my wife." His eyes widen. "No man touches her but me. So the way I see it, we do have an issue." Reaching out, I grab the collar of his shirt and pull him to his feet. He's still several inches shorter than me. "You have two options, apologize to my wife and leave quietly and never come back, or I can make you."

"I know who you are," he croaks out. "W-why would your wife be working in a bar?" He laughs.

Saylor steps around me. "Saylor," I warn her, my voice low.

She raises her hands and shows him her diamond wedding band that she's still wearing. The image makes my heart do crazy things in my chest, but I swallow it down until this guy is away from her.

"He's a real man," she says, her voice strong. Not one ounce of fear remains from what I saw in her face from across the room.

Releasing the drunk fuck, I pull Saylor into my arms and kiss her temple. "We're waiting," I tell him.

"Fuck, man, just do it so we can get out of here," one of his friends urges.

"Fuck you, I'm out of here." He shoulders past me and walks right into Jake.

"You're banned." He looks up at his friends. "All of you. The next time you step foot in my bar, you'll be escorted out by the police."

"Fuck you," the drunk says, storming past Jake and out the door, his friends following behind him.

"You good, Short Stack?" I ask Saylor, my arms still wrapped around her.

She holds up her wrist and there are red marks from his fingers. I step away from her and take a step toward the door. My anger raring.

"Whiskey!" she calls, chasing after me. "Don't." She grabs my arm, halting me. She steps in front of me, wraps her arms around my waist, and rests her head against my chest. "I'm fine. Don't make it worse," she whispers.

"She's right," Jake says, clamping his hand down on my shoulder as if he can hold me back. "They're gone and not worth it. You good, Say?"

"I'm fine. He didn't hurt me. He was just one of many drunk douchebags who thinks they can put their hands wherever they want." She looks up at me. "You need a drink." She steps away and pulls me to my stool at the end of the bar, pushing me into it. I don't take my eyes off her as she rounds the bar and pours me a fresh beer and slides it in front of me. "Drink," she says, pointing to the frosty mug. She leans her elbows on the bar, watching, waiting for me to do as she says. Grabbing the mug, I bring it to my lips and drain half of it before setting it back on the bar. "Better?"

I run my fingers through my hair. "What are you doing to me?" I ask her.

She smiles softly. "Nothing more than what you're doing to me. What's with all the wife business?"

"You're my wife," I remind her.

"On paper," she whispers.

"We had a wedding night."

She looks down the bar. "Jake's getting backed up, and it looks like Molly is on the floor. I need to get back to work."

Reaching out, I grab her hand gently and run my fingers over the red marks on her wrist. My heart is racing from the rush of anger, or maybe it's just her, just Saylor. My mind is racing with flashbacks of my time with her in Vegas. I run my finger over her wedding band. Her thumb brushes over mine, our eyes meeting. Something passes between us; something…

more. I just wish I could describe it. I wish I knew what it meant.

"I need to go," she says softly.

Reluctantly, I release her and pick up my beer. I nurse the remainder the rest of the night, never taking my eyes off her while she works. Once the doors are locked, I help them put the chairs up so the floor can be mopped. I stay out of the way while they go about their nightly closing routine. Saylor assured me she was fine, that I could go, but I'll make sure she gets to her car safely. Jake's here, but I won't be satisfied if I don't see to it myself.

I catch up on a few e-mails from my phone while I wait. Saylor put her foot down at me helping any more than I already have. I gave into her, not wanting to piss her off. "I'm done," she says, pulling my attention from my phone.

"Got everything you need?" I ask her.

"Yeah," she sighs, pushing her arms into her coat. I do the same, lace her fingers with mine, and lead her out to her car. It's already running and warm. "I didn't even see you come outside," she says.

I shrug. "You were busy." Unable to resist her being this close, I pull her into my arms. "You work tomorrow?"

"No, I'm off all weekend actually."

"Have dinner with me," I say.

"What are we doing?"

"I don't know," I confess. "I know I thought about you all the time before Vegas, and now, you're all I think about."

"The weather is supposed to be bad. Why don't I make us dinner? We can talk," she says, stepping out of my hold.

"I'll bring dinner, what time?" I ask, reaching up and pushing the hair out of her eyes.

"I have nothing going on, so you tell me. What time will you leave the office?"

"I'll text you."

"Okay." She turns to open her car door, but then turns back around to face me. "Thank you, Whiskey. For standing up for me." With that, she climbs in her car and drives away.

I was more than standing up for her, and we both know it. I overreacted, but I refuse to apologize for it. Not when it comes to Saylor.

She's had more than enough pain in her life. I'll be damned if I let her be treated like some cheap piece of ass. My stomach rolls at the thought of her as a little girl, in a strange home, with sleazy older guys and possibly her foster father touching her. She alluded to as much, and I want to demand names so I can track them all down and teach them a lesson. Just the thought of someone hurting her, touching her, causes rage to flow through my veins.

My truck was warming up too. I climb behind the wheel and pull out onto the road. I take the long way home, just to make sure she makes it home safe. Apparently, this is my new normal when it comes to Saylor.

When it comes to my wife.

THIRTY THREE

'M LYING IN bed, all snuggled and warm into the blankets, thinking about getting up and facing the cold when my phone vibrates on my nightstand. With a sigh, I pull my arm out from under the blankets and grab it.

Rhett: Morning, beautiful.

I smile.

Me: Morning, Whiskey.

Rhett: Pizza for dinner tonight?

Me: You know how to show a girl a good time.

Rhett: Only the best for my wife.

He does that all the time. Refers to me as his wife. I know it's true, but it's not really, and it confuses my fragile heart. The heart that's begging me to throw caution to the wind and jump in feet first to whatever it is he's offering. My head, on the other hand, urges me to proceed with caution. I know how it feels to have your heart broken; that's the story of my life. However, having him and then losing him, I don't know how I would ever come back from that. Sure, I would pick myself up and move on, but I know I would never take the risk again. That leads me to a life of loneliness. Something I've felt less of ironically since my split with Pete.

Me: Pepperoni and Bacon?

Rhett: Anything you want.

Me: I'll be here.

Rhett: I'll be there around five.

Me: See you then. Have a good day.

Rhett: You too, Short Stack. See you soon.

Climbing out of bed, I strip my sheets and head to the laundry closet, just off the kitchen. I tell myself it's time, and it has nothing to do with the fact that Rhett will be here tonight.

Nothing at all.

Breakfast, shower, cleaning, and laundry is what fills my day. By one o'clock, I'm finished and antsy. I find myself in the kitchen in front of the pantry. When I see the container of oats, I decide to make some no-bake cookies. It has nothing to do with the fact that they're Rhett's favorite.

Nothing at all.

As usual, I make way more than I can eat, even with Rhett's help. Grabbing my phone, I call Molly.

"Hello," she says in her usual chipper voice.

"Hey, I made some cookies, y'all want some?"

"Sure, we're actually getting ready to head over to Baxter's. Jerry is there, and it's been a while since we've seen Number One. We used to visit at least once per week, but we've slacked off since Rhett has been home.

"Visiting," I correct her.

"What?"

"He's not home. He's just visiting."

"Ahh," she says. "I get it now."

"Get what?"

"Why you're keeping your husband at arm's length."

"It's just a piece of paper, Molly."

"Uh-huh," she says, appeasing me. "You want to come with us?"

Looking at the clock, I see it's a few minutes before three. "How long do you plan on staying?"

"Why? You got a hot date tonight?" she jokes.

I bite my lip. I don't know if I would call it a hot date, or even a date at all. We're just two friends getting together for dinner to talk about a common interest. Our divorce.

"You do!" she says excitedly. "Wait." The excitement falls from her voice. "I know it's just a piece of paper, but you're married and che—" I stop her there.

"Rhett's coming over. It's not a date. We're just having dinner and discussing the next steps for the divorce."

"What time?" she asks, the excitement back in her voice.

"Five."

"We can be back by then. We'll only stay an hour or so. The weather is supposed to get bad."

"Yeah, that's why we're staying in too," I admit.

"How long until you're ready?"

"I'm good now. Let me wrap up some of these cookies to take to them and you, and I'll meet you outside."

"See you in ten," she says, ending the call.

I quickly grab some Ziploc bags and fill them with cookies. I make three bags, one for Molly and Jake, one for Jerry, and one for Grandpa Rhett. Sliding into my coat, I grab the cookies and my phone, and I'm out the door.

"Perfect timing," Jake says, meeting me at the truck. "Gimme." He holds his hand out for a bag of cookies.

I laugh and hand one over before climbing in the back seat. "You better plan on sharing those." Molly reaches over and grabs the bag from his lap. Jake mumbles something that sounds like "only you" with his mouth full, causing the three of us to laugh.

"Knock, knock," Jake says, not really knocking as we walk on in to Grandpa Rhett's house like we live there.

"In here," Jerry calls out.

I follow along to the living room. "Hey, kids," Grandpa Rhett says, happier than I've seen him in a while. "Saylor," he says, his eyes lighting up. He turns to Jake. "You taking care of my girls?"

"You know it. Especially this one. She made cookies," he says, pointing at me.

"Cookies," Jerry pipes up. "No-bake?" he asks hopefully.

"Yes." I laugh. "Here." I walk toward him and hand him a bag, then give the other to Grandpa Rhett.

"Thank you, sweetheart." He pats my hand before taking the bag.

"How are you feeling?" I ask, taking a seat next to him on the couch.

"I'm getting better every day," he says, smiling.

"He's fine," Jerry interjects. "He's just enjoying that grandson of his being around again."

I look at Grandpa Rhett, and he shrugs, causing us to laugh. "I was cleared to go back to work with the promise to take it easy on Monday. I just decided on my own that I needed a little more time."

"You miss him," I say, low enough that only he can hear me.

He nods. "It's been too long," he says sadly.

"Wanna know a secret?" I ask him. He nods, and I lean in close. "He misses you too," I whisper. "He regrets staying gone so long."

"So what kind of trouble are the two of you causing today?" Jake asks.

"You see it," Jerry says, leaning back in the recliner.

"I find that hard to believe," Molly says, chuckling.

"How's the wedding planning coming?" Jerry asks. "You make sure this one gives you the wedding of your dreams."

She looks over at me. "Dreams change," she says. "I think we're going to go small, maybe destination, or who knows, maybe we'll go to Vegas." Everyone laughs but me. I do, however, bite back my grin.

"How about a game of Rummy?" Gramps asks. We all agree and head to the kitchen.

That's where Rhett finds us an hour later. "Hey," he says, greeting us. He walks over to where I'm sitting and stands behind my chair. Bending down, he kisses my cheek. "Nice surprise," he whispers. "I'm slaving away at the office and come home to a bunch of misfits," he teases everyone.

"This one"—Jerry points at me—"is a card shark. Don't trust her," he jokes.

"I take it you're winning?" Rhett asks.

Molly hands him the notebook with our scores. "She's kicking ass and taking names."

"That's my girl," Rhett says affectionately, causing my heart to flutter in my chest. "I'm going to grab a quick shower," he says, and then he's gone.

"He's enamored with you," Grandpa Rhett says, making me blush.

"He's just being nice. We're in an awkward situation."

"Your deal," Molly says, pushing the cards to Jerry.

I mouth "thank you," and she nods.

"This could be the final round," she tells us. "Say is sitting at four hundred and sixty-five points." The guys grumble, causing Molly and me to laugh at them. They hate losing, which makes my victory even sweeter.

"Rematch!" Jerry demands when I lay my final card.

"Not this time, old man," Rhett says. "We've got plans," he says, pointing at me.

"We should get going too," Molly says. "This guy"—she nudges Jake—"agreed to make me dinner."

"Raised you right," Jerry says.

"You gonna ride with me? I have to swing by and pick up dinner?" Rhett says, his lips next to my ear, causing me to shiver.

"Sure," I answer.

"You two behave," Rhett says, pointing at his grandfather and Jerry. Grabbing my hand and lacing his fingers through mine, he leads me to the door, handing me my coat.

"You going with Rhett?" Molly asks.

"Yeah, we're going to swing by and get dinner, and then we'll be home," I tell her.

"You can eat with us," she offers.

"No way, I've intruded enough on your nights off. Take the night just the two of you. We have things to discuss."

"If you change your mind, you know you're always welcome, Saylor."

I give her a hug, something I never used to do. She's rubbing off on me. "I know, and I love you for that. I do. You have fun. Maybe set a wedding date," I tell her.

"Yeah, we should probably decide for sure what we're going to do. I have been wanting to finish remodeling the house." She winks.

"Bye." I wave at them. With Rhett's hand on the small of my back, he guides me out to his truck.

THIRTY FOUR

Rhett

"**H**ERE YOU GO," I say, handing Saylor a beer and taking a seat next to her on the couch.

"How was your day?" she asks.

"Slow. I kept watching the clock, waiting to leave. I was excited to get to spend some time with you," I tell her honestly. "Yours? Aside from kicking ass in Rummy."

"I cleaned, did some laundry, oh, and I made some cookies. I gave your gramps and Jerry a bag. Jake and Molly too."

"Did you save any for us?"

"If you eat all of your dinner, I might be able to come up with dessert," she says, talking about the cookies I'm sure, but my dirty mind takes me to images altogether different. Saylor, me, her bed, and some cookie dough, maybe some icing? I adjust my position to make room for my thickening cock. I should be used to the discomfort by now. Every time I'm in her presence it happens.

"I'd love to eat your cookies," I say, winking at her. Her face turns a light shade of pink, which confirms she read through the lines. She rolls those baby blues at me. I fight the urge to lean in and steal a kiss. Don't get me wrong, I plan on stealing more than one tonight, if she'll let me, but I also want to spend time with her. I'm not risking getting thrown out on my ass just yet.

We make small talk through dinner; she tells me about how busy the bar has been and how she dodged Pete and his baby mama at the grocery store without me. This time she was able to skip out without being seen. I hate that she feels like she has to hide in her own hometown. "Guy need his ass kicked," I say.

She chuckles. "Nah, he can't hang. Trust me."

"He did you a favor, Say. You know that, right? You're so much better than what he was willing to give you."

She shrugs, and I know she doesn't believe me. "I dodged a bullet because he never would have been faithful. That goes against what I've always wanted."

"No one plans to fall for someone who's going to cheat on them."

"No," she agrees. "I just… I've always wanted a family, you know. I had Elaine, but I've always wanted big dinners and birthdays and every holiday in between. I want to be a mom one day. But I want my baby's dad to be there, to be present and involved. I want our family to be important, and looking back now, I know that never would have happened with Pete. I let myself get too close to someone who wasn't right for me."

"He tricked you."

"Not really. I mean, he wasn't the most affectionate or attentive, but I went along with it. I never spoke up and told him I wanted more. Honestly—" She pauses, taking a drink of her beer, our plates long since forgotten on the coffee table. "—with my background, I know I'm the least appealing. Who wants to be with someone who has no one? I have nothing to offer, no family gatherings, no grandparents for our kids, just me, and I never thought that was enough. So when Pete showed interest, he was a nice guy, self-absorbed, but nice, and I went with it."

Reaching over, I lace her fingers through mine. "You have you, Saylor. You're more than enough, and if the bastard who steals your heart doesn't see that, he's not worthy of you." *I see you and you're enough*, is what I really want to say.

"So, have you heard anything? About the divorce I mean?" she asks, changing the subject.

"Gramps said last night he talked to Frank, the family attorney, and he should have the papers soon."

"What were we thinking?" she asks, leaning her head back on the couch.

"I don't know about you, but I was thinking that there was a beautiful woman standing beside me, and when our new friends suggested we get married, she was on board." I pause and finish off my beer, setting the bottle on the table. Her eyes are still closed, so I forge ahead. "You have so much to offer, Saylor. You're smart, witty, and loyal. You have the biggest heart of anyone I know. You've lived through things I don't want to think about or even try to imagine, yet here you are putting one foot in front of the other. You're a fighter. A beautiful, sexy, kindhearted fighter, and I was thinking that I'd be one lucky son of a bitch to call you mine." I mimic her and rest my head against the back of the couch, only I don't close my eyes; I keep them trained on her.

Slowly, she opens them and finds me staring at her. Tentatively, she places her hand on my cheek. "I was thinking that for one brief moment in time, I would have a family. That I would be tied to this amazing, confident, sexy man with whiskey-colored eyes. I was thinking that being a part of the Baxter clan sounds better than anything I've ever heard. I wanted to be yours," she whispers.

"Come here," I say, my voice gruff. Sitting up, she turns to face me. "Closer, baby." She moves closer, and I pat my lap. I expect her to argue, but she surprises me when she crawls closer, straddling my lap. My hands immediately go to her hips, anchoring her to me.

She runs her fingers through my hair, something I've noticed she likes to do when I am deep inside of her. "Your hair is so soft," she says quietly.

My hands glide up and down her back until one finds it way under her hair, gripping the back of her neck. Gently, I pull her closer, our mouths now just a breath apart. I hesitate, waiting for her to shut me down, to shut me out. She doesn't. Closing the distance, I press my mouth to hers. I take my time savoring her, slowly gliding my tongue with hers.

"Rhett." My name falls from her lips. Longing tears through me.

"Tell me what you want, Say."

"This. You. More."

My answer is to hold her tighter, not able to get her close enough. No matter how close she is, I want her closer. My hand that's holding her neck trails down her back and under her sweater. I make quick work of unfastening her bra, never breaking our kiss. Snaking my hand to her front, I slide it under the cup of her bra and find her tight nipples. My mouth waters as I remember the taste of them on my tongue.

"That," she says, lifting the hem of her sweater and pulling it over her head.

I glide the straps of her bra off her shoulders and down her arms, tossing it behind me, not caring where it lands. "Perfect," I say before my lips latch on to her pert, perfect breast, rolling the other between my fingertips. Her head tilts back, and she moans.

"More," she breathes.

Sliding a hand between her legs, her thin yoga pants, or whatever they are, do nothing to hide her warmth. Needing to feel her heat, I slip my hand under the waistband and don't stop until I find her soaking wet. Gently, I run my thumb over her clit, causing her to rock her hips.

"Y-you're good at that," she says.

I chuckle. "It's all you, Short Stack. You're on fire." As I kiss her neck, she rocks again, a slow glide of her hips. Her face is flushed, her breasts bouncing. I memorize her every feature. I never want to forget her like this. "Take what you need, Saylor," I say, increasing the pressure on her clit with my thumb.

"Oh," she breathes.

"Tell me what you need," I whisper against her lips. She doesn't answer because her orgasm tears through her. She grunts with her release, as if she's unable to form words. I bite back a smile. I feel pretty damn smug I got her there. Gave her that. She slumps against me and buries her head in my neck. Dropping a kiss to her bare shoulder, I wrap my arms around her and hold her tight, still needing her closer.

Her phone rings, causing her to jump. Refusing to let her go, I stand, and she squeals, wrapping her legs around my waist and her arms around my neck. "Rhett." She laughs, and I love the sound.

"Not ready to let you go," I say, walking to the small kitchen table and handing her her phone. As soon as she puts it to her ear to say hello, I begin kissing down her neck. I saw that it was Jake calling when I handed it to her. I'm not worried about him knowing I'm taking care of her.

"Really?" she asks, tilting her head to the side, giving me full access.

"Uh-huh."

"What's he want, baby?" I whisper in her ear. Goose bumps break out across her skin.

"Thanks, Jake," she says and hangs up. "H-he said that the roads are getting bad. It's pretty icy out." She buries her hands in my hair.

Fuck. I don't want to leave her. Slowly, I pull back and look at her. "Tell me what you want, Saylor. I can go, or I can—" She interrupts me.

"Stay," she says so softly I barely hear her.

"Again," I say, needing to make sure that's what she wants.

"Stay. Stay here with me."

I kiss her hard. "It's time for bed," I say, heading toward the door that I assume is her bedroom. She giggles, holding on tight. Once we're in her room, I set her down on the bed. Placing my finger under her chin, I lift her face to look at me. "I don't have any expectations—well, I have one. You in my arms all night, preferably naked." She smiles, causing my heart to trip over in my chest. I place my hand there to ward off the rapid beat. "I want that, but I'll take the couch. I just want to spend time with you."

"You can sleep here," she says, patting the bed next to her.

I lean down and kiss her. "That's good enough for me. I'm going to go lock up. I'll be right back." One more chaste kiss and I head back to the living room to lock the door and turn off the lights. I grab my phone and call Gramps. "Hey," I say when he answers.

"Rhett? You okay?"

"Yeah, the roads are bad, so I'm just going to stay here tonight."

"Where is here?" he asks, sounding annoyed.

"With Saylor." I cringe, prepared for his "have you not learned your lesson" speech, but it never comes.

"Good, she shouldn't be alone if the weather is bad."

"Jake is next door," I remind him, even though I agree it should be me who comes to her rescue should she need it.

"Stay in and be safe," he says, ignoring my statement. "Bye." He hangs up.

I'm done trying to decipher his mood swings, and right now, my wife is waiting for me.

When I get back to her room, she's under the covers; they're pulled up to her chest. I kick off my boots and grab the neck of my long-sleeve

T-shirt and pull it over my head, dropping it to the floor. Grabbing my wallet, I set it on the nightstand along with both of our phones that I picked up. Unbuckling my jeans, I let them fall to the floor. I move to climb into bed, but she stops me.

"You forgot something," she says, pointing to my boxer briefs.

I didn't want to assume, so I left them on. Grabbing the sides, I slide them down my legs and kick them off. Saylor lifts the quilt and offers me a glimpse of her naked body. I stand still, my eyes roaming over every inch of her that I can see. "Perfect," I grit out.

"It's cold," she says with a nervous laugh.

Not needing more of an invitation than that, I climb into bed. I pull her tight, as close as I can get her. I can feel the hurried beat of her heart against my chest. Then again, I don't know if it's her heart or mine that echoes in my chest. I'd like to think it's ours, it's what happens when we come together.

"I'll keep you warm," I promise her.

"How?" she asks softly.

I run my hand up and down her back. "Like this."

"You're going to put me to sleep."

"I'll be here when you wake up," I assure her.

"What are we doing, Rhett? What is this?"

The room is dark, not even the shadows of the moon. "What do you want it to be?" I counter.

"Not fair," she says, poking me in the side. "I asked you first."

"I don't know if you're ready to hear what I have to say."

"Honesty. No matter what it is, I want honesty."

"I want you. I think about you all the time—what it feels like to wake up with you, to be inside of you. How much I like just being with you, at the bar, ice skating, eating pizza, it doesn't matter." I pause, letting that sink in. "I think there's something between us, but we complicated it with getting married."

"You're still wearing your ring."

"So are you," I counter.

"I don't know why," she admits.

"I know we're married, not in the sense of being in love, but on paper, and I promised you regardless of the level of commitment that I would honor that. Wearing the ring is a reminder of my promise to you. It also helps to keep other woman at bay."

"I'm sure you're ready for the divorce to be final, huh? Get back to your harem? I see the way the ladies swarm to you when you're at the Corner Pocket."

"They do. But have you seen me leave or even engage any of them?"

She's quiet for a while. I'm sure she's thinking back. "No," she whispers.

"You're all I think about."

"We're married," she says, like she can't believe it.

"We are. It's making whatever this is happening between us complicated. Regardless of the marriage, I want to see where this goes."

"You don't live here."

I can hear the hesitation in her voice. "Not yet, but I will. Gramps isn't getting any younger, and growing up, I always wanted to take over running the distillery. He would take me to work with him when I stayed here in the summers and show me the ropes. Said I would be in charge one day. I went to college and stopped visiting except for holidays, and those were just a day or two. I went to work for my parents after graduation and never looked back."

"He misses you."

"I know. I've missed him too. Dad asked me the other day if I was going to stay. At that time, I didn't know for sure."

"Now you do?"

I pull her a little closer. "Seems I have more than just Gramps and the distillery in this small town."

"When Elaine died, Pete convinced me to sell her house. We were already living here. A few weeks later, after I signed the papers, he admitted Tabitha was pregnant. I could have gone back to Cincinnati, but Tara, my closest friend was pretty wrapped up in her fiancé. Turns out she moved to Oregon a few weeks later. She's actually not talking to me because I wouldn't move there with her. She said some hurtful things. Anyway, I liked this town. Jake and Molly have been amazing."

"This is your home now."

"Yeah, I guess it is. To be honest, I'm not real sure where I belong, if anywhere."

"You're right where you belong," I say, kissing the top of her head.

"I don't want you to make this decision based on us seeing where this goes, whatever it is between us."

"I'm not, not entirely. I'll admit the thought of not being able to see you whenever I want doesn't sit well with me."

"What does your gramps think?"

"I need to talk to him, see if me taking the reins permanently is something he's okay with."

She yawns. "I'm sure he'll be excited."

"I'm not so sure. He's been cold since I've been here."

"He's protecting himself. He doesn't want to get used to you and then you leave again."

"Maybe you're right."

"Yeah," she says, yawning again.

"Sleep, beautiful." I kiss the top of her head.

"But you—" I cut her off.

"I'm right where I want to be. Get some rest."

She doesn't protest as exhaustion takes over. I continue to run my hand softly up and down her back, memorizing the feel of her skin beneath my fingertips. The past few months have been a whirlwind. I think about that first night that I met her. Never would I have imagined that this is where we would end up, but I wouldn't change it for anything.

THIRTY FIVE
Saylor

I WAKE TO soft kisses on my shoulder and back. Rhett. Our conversation last night comes flooding back. We agreed to see where this goes. He's right in saying the marriage complicates things. Once the divorce is final, if we're still whatever it is that we are, we'll be able to relax, not having our drunken mistake hanging over our heads and the knowledge that the quickie Vegas wedding isn't why we're together.

"What are you thinking about?" he asks, softly placing more tender kisses on my shoulder.

"Us."

"Mmm, my favorite."

Glancing at the clock, I see it's a few minutes before six in the morning. "Sleep well?" I ask him.

"Very."

Rolling over, I reach up and bury my hands in his hair. "You stayed."

"I told you I would."

"I wasn't sure after I ran out on you in Vegas that first night."

"I'm where I want to be, Saylor. Believe that."

"We're really doing this? We're... dating?" I need clarification for my heart and my mind. I know we said it all last night, but often times things look different in the light of day. I just need to hear it again. One more time to make sure.

"Yeah." He cups my face in his big hands. "We're dating, exclusively," he adds. "No one gets to do this but me," he whispers as his lips connect with mine.

I keep my mouth shut; I'm sure my morning breath could knock him on his ass.

"Open for me, Say," he murmurs against my lips.

I turn my head. "I need to brush my teeth."

"Fuck that, you need to kiss me," he says, trying again. This time he pushes his morning wood into my stomach, and I don't fight him. If he wants the morning dragon lady and that's what I get in return, he has a deal.

His hand roams over my thighs and up my spine, causing me to shiver. Just a simple touch from him, that's all it takes to set my body on fire. "A girl could get used to this," I say, pulling away from the kiss.

"Yeah?" he asks softly.

I nod, rolling over on my back. He doesn't waste any time running his hands over my breasts, tweaking my nipples between his fingers. We're still snuggled under the covers, hiding from the chilly morning air. He rests his weight on his elbow while his other hand explores my body. When he reaches my core, he curses under his breath. "You're wet," he says. "I need you, Saylor." He slides his head under the covers and captures my nipple between his teeth.

My hands find their way to his hair; it's one of my favorite things, to run my fingers through his silky strands. It short everywhere but on top, and I love it.

He lifts his head, causing the cold air to hit me. "Brrr." I pull the covers around us.

"Roll over, baby," he says. I start to turn to face him, but he stops me, kissing the corner of my mouth. "The other way."

I do as he says and pull the covers up to my chin, fighting off the cold. It's not normally this cold in here; then again, I don't usually sleep naked either.

I feel him pull away, but he's back in no time. It's not until I hear the rip of a foil packet that I realize what he did. He slides close behind me and pulls me against his chest. His hand roams over my ass and between my legs. "Push that sweet ass into me," he whispers. I do. He moans when my ass makes contact with his hard length. He kisses my shoulder, my back, and then his lips are next to my ear. "Open for me." He taps my leg, and I lift a little, giving him room to slide inside me.

"Rhett," I moan his name, the sensation of him being inside me like this overwhelming my senses.

He pulls out, then pushes back in. "So tight," he whispers, kissing just below my ear. "So warm. Lift your head." He slides his arm under, bringing us closer together. His other hand massages my breasts, then trails down my quivering stomach. "I need to get you there, Saylor. I'm too fucking close to losing my shit. You feel so damn good squeezing my cock." I feel a rush of heat roll through me, and I know he feels it too from the groan deep in his throat. He softly traces his thumb over my clit, teasing me.

"You're teasing me."

"What? This?" He ghosts his thumb over my clit.

"That. I need more." In a bold move, more so than I've ever been, I push his hand out of the way and replace it with mine. With my index and middle finger, I begin small circles. There is something about being with Rhett that makes me feel sexy and empowered to take what I want, to give into my desires.

"Fuck!" he says harshly, gripping my hip. His thrusts become harder, faster, more urgent than before. I stop moving my hand, enjoying the friction of the faster pace. "Don't stop, Saylor, don't you fucking dare stop." Releasing my hip, he places his hand over mine and guides me back to my core. "Touch yourself. Take what you need," he says, kissing my shoulder. He resumes his hold on my hip and thrusts hard. He doesn't stop. He pistons his hips in and out over and over.

"Close." I'm barely able to form the words.

"Together," he says, his voice rough with desire.

A sound I've never made before in my life tears from my lungs as white-hot desire courses through me. "Rhett," I mumble his name.

"That's it, baby, squeeze my cock." With one more deep thrust, his body stills as he releases inside of me. His arms wrap around me, holding me to him.

My phone rings, and he groans. Slowly, he removes himself from me then reaches back and grabs my phone. He slides his finger across the screen. "Why the fuck are you calling my girl so early in the morning?" he grumbles into the line.

My heart tips over in my chest hearing him calling me his girl. "No," he says, "I don't have to ask her. I can make a better offer." I roll over to face him. Moving the phone away from his mouth, he leans over and kisses me. "Fine, here she is." He hands me the phone. "Be right back," he says, climbing out of bed.

I place the phone next to my ear. "Hello."

"Saylor," Molly says, surprising me.

"Hey, I thought you were Jake," I tell her.

"Well, he called because I asked him too, but he wasn't getting anywhere with Rhett. I made breakfast and wanted to see if you wanted to join us."

"Did you look outside and see his truck here?"

"No, but I assumed he stayed. We went to bed early, hence the reason I'm up with the chickens."

"So you thought we would be too?"

She laughs. "It is kind of early, huh? So you all coming over to eat?"

Rhett sits next to me on the side of the bed shaking his head no. "I think we're going to pass this time. We're still in bed."

"I see. But yet you don't sound like I just woke you up," she muses.

"Next time," I say, laughing.

"Be safe." She ends the call.

"I have the shower running, let's get you cleaned up," he says, pulling back the covers and lifting me into his arms.

"You know I have two legs that carry me anywhere I want to go, right?" I wrap my arms around his neck.

"Yep, but I like you better in my arms. You're tiny, Short Stack. I could carry you around all day."

"Hey." I lightly smack his chest, pretending to be offended. The truth is, I would let him carry me anywhere. The realization hits me hard. Somehow, when I wasn't looking, I let him get close, closer than anyone, even Elaine. Only because of the intimacy between us. It took longer with Elaine, but once I realized she was in it for the long haul, I opened up to her. She gave me a chance. She gave me what little of my family history she had. I owe her everything. This feeling with Rhett is different. It's all-consuming and scary, but I'm not letting the fear stop me. One day he might walk away, or I might lose him to circumstances beyond our control, but I know deep in my gut, a little bit of time with him surpasses never having him at all.

After a shower, where Rhett took his job of cleaning me very seriously, of course that was after he dirtied me up again, we find ourselves sitting on the couch under a blanket eating leftover pizza for breakfast. "I've never done this before," I admit.

"What?" He chases his last bite of pizza with a big drink of milk.

"Had pizza for breakfast. Elaine loved to cook. She always made something for breakfast. I very rarely had cereal. We didn't eat out a lot either. It was cheaper to cook at home and better. She was a really good cook."

"She taught you to bake?" he asks, holding up a no-bake cookie before devouring most of it in one bite.

"Yeah." I laugh at him.

"So what are we doing today?"

I shrug. "This." I point to the couch. "The roads are still a mess according to the news, and I have nowhere to be."

"You're wrong," he says, sitting back against the arm of the couch.

"About what?"

"You have somewhere to be."

"And where is that?"

"Right here." He tugs on my arm and pulls me onto his lap. Reaching over, he grabs the blanket and tosses it over us. "I say we take a nap," he says, kissing my cheek.

I don't answer him for the emotion clogging my throat. I do however settle against him and let the lull of his steady heartbeat soothe me to sleep. That's how we spend the rest of the day, lounging around, napping, eating, and learning each other's bodies.

THIRTY SIX

I'S BEEN TWO weeks since we agreed to be together. Two weeks of kisses and touching her anytime I want. Two weeks, which is long enough for me to know I don't want to leave her. It's not just her, but this town. Mom and Dad are flying in this weekend. I plan to talk to them, but first I need to talk to Gramps.

I lightly tap on his door. "Come on in, boy," he grumbles.

"Hey, can I talk to you for a minute?"

"What's on your mind?"

He's been showing me glimpses of his old self, leading me to believe Saylor was right. He doesn't want me to leave again. I hope she's right, or this conversation could turn bad quick. "I wanted to run something past you," I say, taking a seat beside his bed.

"Go on." He nods.

"How would you feel about me staying here? I know we used to talk about me taking over for you one day, is that offer still open?" I ask boldly.

"Do you want it to be?"

"I do." My voice is strong and full of conviction. I have zero doubts that this is what I want.

"Because of Saylor?"

"No, not because of Saylor. She's an added bonus, yes, but it's more than that. It's this town and the distillery, and you. All the memories I have of this place. It feels more like home to me than anywhere else."

"And Saylor?" he asks again.

I chuckle. "She's perfect, Gramps."

He nods. "So you think you can fill my shoes?"

"I'd like to try," I tell him. "I was kind of hoping you'd be there to guide me."

I watch for his reaction. He swallows hard. "Your parents?"

"Dad suspects. I assume Mom does as well. They've always had a hard time pulling me away from here."

He nods again. "That they have."

"So what do you think?"

"I think that if you're serious, if you want this and you're willing to stay no matter what happens with Saylor, then nothing would make me happier."

"I want this. Like I said, it's not just because of her. Yeah, she's here, but if she ever decides she doesn't want me, I'd still want to be here, in this town, running the distillery, living close to you."

"What if you decide you no longer want her?" he counters.

I shake my head. "Not going to happen."

"You sound certain."

"I am."

"Okay. I'll have to get a few things together, legal documents and all that. We'll make this happen," he says, giving me the first genuine smile since I've been here.

"Frank?" I ask.

"Yeah, I'll get him on it."

"What about the divorce? I know we just signed the papers last week, but have you heard anything?"

"These things take time, but I'll ask him when I call today."

I hold my hand out for him to shake. He looks up at me, and I see his eyes are misty with tears. "It's good to have you home," he says, his voice gruff.

"Good to be home. I'm going to hop in the shower and then head to the Corner Pocket, Saylor's working tonight."

"Your parents fly in tomorrow?"

"Yeah, I plan to tell them then."

He nods. "Give that girl of yours a hello from me."

"Will do." I stand and go to my room. It's been a long week, and all I want to do is bury myself inside of Saylor, then fall asleep with her in my arms.

Walking into the Corner Pocket, I spot Saylor behind the bar. She sees me and grins. "Hey, Whiskey." She leans over the bar and gives me a quick kiss.

"Missed you," I tell her.

Her smile grows wider. "Long day?"

"Yes, but it's better now." My phone rings, stopping me from asking her to sneak off in the back for a real kiss. "Baxter," I say in greeting. "When?" I listen to one of my foremen explain that the line that was down for months is acting up again. "I'll be there soon." I hit end and slide my phone back in my pocket.

Saylor finishes serving a young couple before coming back to stand before me. "Everything okay?"

"One of the lines is down at the distillery. We've been having issues with it. The guy keeps coming to repair it, but the same issues keep happening. When my foreman called the company, they said they would send somebody out. I need to be there. I don't think the jackass knows what he's doing. My foreman demanded a supervisor, and they assured him one would be present. I need to let them know what's been going on. Otherwise, I need to find a new vendor."

"I'm sorry," she says sincerely.

"Jake here?"

"Yeah, he's in the back."

"Good. I don't want you walking to your car alone. I don't know how long this will take."

"Hold on." She walks to the other end of the bar and kneels down. She comes back over with a key. "Here, if I'm in bed, use this."

"You saying you want me in your bed, Short Stack?"

"You saying you don't want to be?" she counters.

I stand and lean over the bar. "If I had my way, we would never leave your bed." I kiss her softly. "I'll see you soon."

"Be safe," she says, kissing me one more time.

Grabbing my coat, I head back to the office. Before I pull out of the lot, I send Jake a text.

Me:	Had to go back to the distillery. Can you walk Say to her car tonight?
Jake:	Yep.
Me:	Thanks.

Tossing my phone in the cupholder, I head to the distillery. Not what I want to be dealing with on a Friday night, but that's part of being CEO. I've seen my dad do it many times, and even Gramps. It's on me now.

I find Cal, my foreman, and two other guys standing by the machine that's down. I hold my hand out. "Rhett Baxter," I introduce myself.

"Mr. Baxter, I'm Bobby Lee," he points to the guy beside him, "and you know Rodney."

"Thanks for coming out so late."

"That's what we're here for. I understand from Cal there have been some issues?"

"We had Rodney in here several weeks ago to repair the engine. He got it up and running, but it seems to be breaking down every other week or so. I'm concerned that it's not being fixed properly. Rodney and I have discussed if the machine is viable, and he assures me it is."

"You mind if I take a look? May take a while to diagnose."

"By all means. Every time this machine breaks down, it costs my company money. We need it fixed." I turn to look at Rodney. "Rodney claims it can be fixed. I'd like to hear your thoughts." Rodney looks green, which tells me he's been half-assing his job.

"We'll be in that office right there." I point to Cal's office. I want to be able to keep an eye on them.

"We'll get right to work," Bobby says.

Cal and I settle in his office and wait. I keep glancing at my watch. Saylor should be closing down the bar about now. Good thing she gave me a key, not sure what time this shit show is going to be over.

"Mr. Baxter." Bobby knocks on the door. "I found the issue. The machine is fixed. We have it back up and running. I apologize for any inconvenience this has caused. There are three valves in the carburetors, two easily accessible. The other is not. It seems as though Rodney didn't bother to replace that one. How he was able to get it up and running each time with his Band-Aid repair, I'm not sure. I can assure you it will be addressed, as will his employment with my company."

"Thank you." I reach out and shake his hand. "My intent is not to cause trouble, but to ensure my company has been receiving the services it's been paying for and that my machine is repaired correctly to prevent further failure."

He hands me a business card. "This has my cell number. Call me personally if there are any issues. You gentlemen have a good night."

I say a quick goodbye to Cal after checking that the machine is indeed back up and operating. Looking at the clock, it's just before two in the morning. Hopefully Saylor is already home and warming the bed when I get there. I debate on texting her, but I'll be there soon, and if she happens to be asleep, I don't want to wake her.

When I turn on her road, my heart drops. There are flashing lights, cop cars, an ambulance, and a fire truck. I search frantically to assess the situation. The fire fighters have the hoses aimed at the back of the main house. Fuck! Slamming my truck in park, I'm out and running.

"Sir, you have to stand down," an officer says, stepping in front of me.

"This is my family. My wife, my best friend and his fiancée, my wife," I say again. "I have to get to them."

"Everyone is fine. They didn't make it inside, called as soon as they arrived home and saw the flames," he explains.

I feel my heart rate slow just from knowing she's safe, but I still need to see her. "Where is she? My wife? Saylor!" I yell for her.

"The homeowner and his fiancée, as well as their tenant and her fiancé, are over by the ambulance just as a precaution, but I assure you they're fine. What does your wife look like?" he asks cautiously. "She was supposed to be here?"

"Saylor!" I shout again, and that's when I see her. She's standing in front of her motherfucking ex, Pete, and I see red. Did he cause this? "That's her." I point and jog toward her.

"Oh shit," I hear the officer say, and I know he's hot on my heels.

"Rhett," Saylor cries, and steps around Pete. He grabs her arm to stop her. "Get the fuck off of me. I told you, you're not welcome here." She shakes her hand, but he holds tight.

"Get your fucking hands off her," I say, putting my hands on her waist and pulling her from his grasp. She clings to me. I wrap her in my arms and bury my face in her neck. Glancing up, I see Jake and Molly, and they both appear to be unharmed just as the officer said. I catch Jake's eye, and he nods, confirming they are indeed okay.

"You again," Pete sneers. "Get away from him, Saylor. She's coming home with me."

"The fuck she is."

"Is there a problem here?" the officer asks.

"Yes," Pete and I say at the same time.

"This man is harassing my fiancée," Pete says, pointing to me.

Saylor is still clinging to me. "She's my wife," I sneer. "What the fuck are you doing here?" I ask him.

"Wife?" he scoffs. "As if."

"Ma'am?" the officer addresses Saylor.

"He," she points to Pete, "is my ex. We've been over for months. This man," she says, looking up at me, her blue eyes misty with tears, "is my husband."

"Are you fucking kidding me? You're married?"

"I told you that," Saylor says, exasperated.

"I thought you were just using that as an excuse not to talk to me. Trying to make me jealous."

I want to rip his head off, but I feel Saylor stand up taller, turning to face him. I keep my mouth shut and wrap my arms around her from behind, letting her know I've got her. "You cheated on me for months, you knocked up our coworker, and left me with nothing, all alone."

"I told you—" he tries to say, and she holds up her hand to stop him.

"I couldn't give a fuck what you have to say. I don't feel sorry for you, Pete. Not in the slightest. You did this. What comes around goes around, and you're getting what you deserve. Why are you even here? How did you know where I live?"

"The baby's not mine. We can fix this and be together, just like we always said," he says, not giving up. "And I stopped at the bar a few days ago. I wanted to talk to you. To tell you I now know that we belong together." Rhett growls and holds me tighter. "One of the old guys sitting at the bar told me, after I paid off his tab, where I could find you. Tonight was the first chance I had to come and see you. Come on Saylor, don't do this."

Saylor places her hands over mine. "You did me a favor, Pete. You screwing me over led me to Rhett. I'll never be able to thank you enough for that." I bend down and bury my face in her neck, needing to be closer to her. "As far as bribing a drunk old man to find out where I live, you're pathetic. You're not welcome here. This is my home," she looks over her shoulder at me. "There is nothing between us, not anymore." My heart rate slows a fraction, from its rapid pace in my chest.

"I've heard enough," the officer says. "Sir, I'm going to have to ask you to leave."

"You'll regret this, Saylor. You have no one and nothing without me," he sneers.

My head jolts up, and I'm just about to tell this motherfucker where to go when she gives my arms, which are tight around her waist, a gentle squeeze. "I have so much more," she says calmly. "I have a man who cares about me, not for what I can do for him or how I'll look on his arm, but because of who I am. I have friends who picked me up when you dropped me and never let me fall. I have their families who have become mine as well. I've never been happier or felt more wanted in my life."

Pete steps back as if he's been slapped. It's more satisfying than if my fist would have connected with his face. Watching her stand up for herself, hearing her say she knows she's more, that's she enough, and she's right where she belongs has me wanting to drop to my knees and beg her to never leave me. Instead, I turn her to face me and cup her face in my hands. I hold her gaze, and what I see is love and hope for the future I want with her. Suddenly, nothing else matters but telling her how I feel. "I love you, Saylor," I say before pressing my lips to hers.

THIRTY SEVEN

Saylor

"**E**NOUGH OF THAT,**"** Jake says as he and Molly join us. He has no idea what he's interrupting or how fast my heart is beating. I didn't say it back, he didn't give me a chance, but I want to. I've never said the words, but I want to. I don't want to regret never telling him like Elaine. I know she knew, as I'm sure Rhett does. He makes me stronger. I look at the three people standing before me, and I know without a doubt they're my family, they're my home. It's a peaceful feeling that washes over me.

"What happened?" Rhett asks, keeping me held tight against his chest.

"Electrical," Jake says, holding Molly just as tight. "They still have some investigating to do, but they think it started in the kitchen. It reached the laundry room, but nowhere else."

"That's good. None of you are hurt, right? The cop said you found it when you got home?"

"Yeah, we're good. It must have just started when we got here. Saylor called 911, and they got here fast."

"I was here first," I tell him. "They pulled in behind me, but I already had them on the line." I step out of his hold and go to Molly, who lets go of Jake and wraps me in a tight hug. "I'm so sorry," she whispers.

"We're all safe, that's all that matters," Jake says. "This," he points to the house, "can be replaced."

"You guys are coming home with me tonight," Rhett insists. "We can come back tomorrow and check the damage. Grab some clothes or whatever you need. We have the room, and you know Gramps will be pissed if he finds out you're staying somewhere else."

"Thank you," Jake says sincerely.

"Let's get you out of the cold," Rhett says, already reaching for me.

"You folks are good to go for the night. We're going to be here a while wrapping up the investigation and making sure the fire doesn't restart. It's just precaution on our part."

"Thanks, man." Jake holds out his hand.

"I'll get a hold of you tomorrow and let you know the final findings and make arrangements for you to get the report for your insurance company."

"You all need a ride?" Rhett asks them.

"Nah, we'll follow you in my truck."

"I'm going to run inside and get some clothes for me and Molly," I tell Rhett.

"I'll come with you," Molly says.

"So will we," Rhett says. "Don't." He holds up his hand when he sees I'm about to argue. "Thought I lost you, all of you. Not willing to let you out of my sight just yet. Humor me, baby."

How do I argue with that? The main power is turned off, so we use our cell phones, and I pack a bag for us. "Ready?" I ask back in the living room. Rhett steps next to me, throws the bag over his shoulder, and laces his fingers through mine.

"We'll meet you guys at the house," he says, leading me outside. Once we're in the truck, he reaches over and grabs my hand, bringing it to his lips. "I was scared, Saylor. When I saw all the lights, and my heart dropped to my feet."

"I'm fine," I say, laying my hand on his cheek. "Take me home," I whisper. Jake and Molly pull out behind us. Rhett and I don't talk during the drive, but he never lets go of my hand.

"That you, son?" Grandpa Rhett calls when we enter the house.

"Yeah, Gramps, I have guests," he calls back. After taking off our coats and setting down the bag I packed for Molly and me, he puts his hand on the small of my back and leads me to the living room, Jake and Molly following.

"What a nice surprise," Grandpa Rhett says.

"Their house caught on fire," Rhett says, sitting in the recliner and pulling me down on his lap. "What are you doing up so late?"

I look over to his grandfather, expecting to see surprise on his face, but all I see is worry. "We're fine," I assure him.

"Couldn't sleep. What happened?" he asks. Jake jumps into the story of how they think the fire started. "You'll stay here until you can go back, or forever. I have the room," he says.

"Thank you. We'll know more tomorrow," Jake says

"I'm sure you're exhausted. You can have your usual room." He looks over at me. "Saylor—"

Rhett cuts him off. "Will be with me." He leaves no room for argument, not that he was going to get one. His grandfather seems pleased by his declaration.

"All right, kids. Get some rest. I'll see you all in the morning."

"We're going to bed," Jake says, pulling Molly into him and kissing the top of her head.

"Let me give you some clothes," I tell Molly. I dig through the bag and pull out some pajamas, yoga pants, and a sweater, and hand them to her. She turns to head up the stairs, and I stop her. "Molly."

"Yeah?"

"Thank you for trusting me, for offering me a place to stay, a job, for being my friend. You've given me more than you will ever know."

"That's what family does, Saylor." She smiles.

"Ready, babe?" Jake asks.

She holds up the clothes to show him. "Yeah, night, guys," she says, heading Jake up the opposite stairs from Rhett and me.

Rhett holds his hand out for me, and I take it. Silently, he leads us up to his room. Once inside, he shuts the door. I drop my bag on a chair in the corner of the room. "Come here, baby." I walk to where he's standing beside the bed. As soon as I'm close enough, he snakes his arm around my waist and pulls me into his chest. "I was so fucking scared, Saylor. Life without you isn't something I want to experience."

"Hold me?" I ask quietly. Tonight has been emotionally draining with the fire, Pete, and Rhett telling me he loves me.

"Always," he says, kissing my temple and releasing me. "Get changed, you need a shower or anything?"

"No, just you."

He kisses my temple one more time before releasing me and going to his dresser pulling out a pair of pajama pants. He turns to look at me and shakes his head, wearing a small grin. I'm not ashamed to be busted watching him. It's my favorite pastime. "You gonna change?" he asks. That spurs me into action. Grabbing my bag, I dig out some flannel pajama pants and one of his T-shirts that he left at the house. "That's where that went," he says when I join him in bed.

"You left it."

"It looks better on you than it does on me," he says, holding his arms open for me.

I snuggle into his side. "It's too big." I chuckle.

"But it's mine, and you're in it. It's perfect. I look good on you."

We're both quiet for a while, and my thoughts are spinning. I keep hearing him tell me he loves me over and over in my head.

"Night, baby. I—" I cut him off.

"I've never said it. Not really. I told Elaine the day of her funeral, but she was gone. I never told her while she was living. She gave me my life, an opportunity to make something of myself, and I couldn't bring myself to tell her."

"I love you, Saylor. Not because I want you to say it back. I love you for who you are, the strong, incredible woman who has turned my life upside down. I love you for what's in here." He places his hand over my heart.

"I'd never heard those words, not that I can ever remember, until I moved in with Elaine. I had been there about six months. It was Christmas morning, and I caught her crying by the tree. She missed her husband. I sat with her while she cried, and she told me she loved me, that I brought joy back to her life and gave me a reason. I didn't tell her back. After that day, she told me all the time, 'love you kid,' 'love you, Say,' 'be safe, love you,' and the list goes on. Not once did I tell her back.

I was 'me too,' 'ditto,' 'same,' anything but the words."

"She knew. She didn't need the words, and neither do I."

"I realized something tonight when I was talking to Pete."

"Oh yeah?" he asks, his voice low as he runs his fingers through my hair.

"My whole life I've worried about losing those I get close to. It's a constant in my life, the worry. Then I met Jake and Molly, and I had no choice but to let them in. They offered their love and support, their friendship, freely, just like Elaine. I've never had that with anyone else. Then I met you." I pause, trying to collect my thoughts. "Tonight I realized that I would rather have five minutes with you than to have never had you at all. You make me stronger, and I've never felt the way you make me feel."

"How do I make you feel?" he whispers.

"Special, wanted, loved… " I lift up on my elbows, resting my chin on his chest. His eyes never leave mine as he hangs on every word. His whiskey-colored eyes show me exactly how he feels. I see love shining back at me. Promises full of commitment and honor. "I love you, Rhett Baxter," I say, my voice is strong and clear, not one ounce of hesitation or fear.

"Baby." He pulls me on top of him and cups my face in his hands. "You make me a better man. You make me stronger. You make me special by letting me near you. I want you in my life, and I promise I'll love you forever."

When his lips touch mine, I feel whole. For the first time in my life, I know where I am is where I'm supposed to be. I don't know what the future holds for us, but I know I'm excited to find out.

THIRTY
EIGHT

MY PARENTS FLEW out this morning. It was great to spend time with them. It was even better to see how well they get along with Saylor; Dad is just as smitten as Gramps and me. Mom is beside herself having another girl around. She made sure to pull me aside and tell me so before they left. She gushed about how sweet she is, even more so than the first time they met, and how happy she is for us. I felt a swell of pride hearing her say that. The first time they met, Saylor was still timid, not letting people get close. This time her walls were down and she was open to them, charming them just like she did me—does me, every damn day.

Even though Dad had said he expected it, I was still leery of telling them that I wasn't coming back to the brewery. They took it rather well, and we even talked about the potential of merging the two corporations. "It's all going to be yours one day, regardless," Dad had said. Gramps even seemed open to the idea when we ran it past him. Everything seems to be falling into place.

Things are even looking up for Jake and Molly. They got the news today that they can start cleaning up the house and start the repairs.

Apparently, the damage was minimal, so repairs shouldn't take that long. Cleanup is the worst of it. Saylor texted me earlier, telling me that's where she would be when I got home tonight. It's Monday, and with the new winter hours, the Corner Pocket is closed, which works out, giving them the chance to get started right away. Once I got her message, I wrapped up what I needed to at the office and headed home. I jog up the steps to say hi to Gramps before I change clothes and head over to help with cleanup. I hear his voice coming from his office, so I slow. I'm just about to knock when I hear him talking about me.

"You let me deal with my grandson. My plan is working flawlessly. He's falling for her and her him. We might not need this divorce after all," he says.

What the fuck is he talking about?

"How much longer can you stall? I'd say a few weeks and they won't care whether it goes through or not. I'll just tell them there's a delay with the county filing the papers. It'll work, trust me," he tells whoever it is he's talking to. My guess is his attorney.

Anger floods through my veins. He's been lying to us. What I don't understand is why. Why would he go through so much trouble to keep us married? In fact, I expected the opposite. I expected screaming and yelling that I didn't have a prenup.

When I hear him hang up the phone, I step into the doorway. "Mind telling me what the hell that was about?" I ask him, trying hard to keep my anger in check.

"Rhett, I didn't realize you were home."

"I gathered that. Talk. Now," I say, stepping into the room and bracing my hands on the back of the chair that sits in front of his desk. I'm barely containing my anger.

"I was just trying to help," he says. "I knew you liked her."

"I more than like her. I love her. That doesn't change the fact that you've been lying to us."

"Not exactly lying, maybe just delaying things a little. The papers you signed were legit. I just advised Frank to stall on filing them."

"Why in the hell would you do that?"

"I've seen the way the two of you look at each other. I could see it was more than you were willing to admit. I just gave you the chance to stay together a little longer."

"Bullshit. Of course it was more. I fucking love her, Gramps. Not just a crush or a quick fuck." He cringes. "I love her with everything in me. Hell fucking yes, I want to marry her. I want nothing more than to spend the rest of my life by her side, but I want to give her the choice to do so, preferably while she's sober."

"You're already married. I don't see—" I cut him off.

"Because we want a divorce. We decide our future, and being married is not what we want!" I scream at him. Taking a few deep breaths, I gain my composure. "Look," I say, this time keeping my voice calm. "I want to give her the world. I want her to know that she has the choice. Her parents were taken from her, and she was moved from home to home without a choice. When Elaine fostered her, again it was a good home, but it wasn't her choice. I want her to have the option to choose me, to choose if we get married and where and when. I want to give her everything."

He nods. "I'm sorry. I just wanted you to be happy, and selfishly, I was hoping you would want to stay."

"I talked to you about that, you knew what I wanted."

"Not until last week. I'm a lonely old man who misses his grandson. I had hopes of bringing Saylor into our family and showering her with love and giving her the family she's always wanted."

"I want that too, Gramps, more than anything, but I want her to choose that."

"I shouldn't have meddled. I'm sorry. I'll call Frank back and tell him to move forward with the divorce."

"Thank you. I love you, old man."

"Love you too."

I point to the phone, and he laughs. I wait until he's on the phone and hear him tell Frank to move forward. Once he ends the call, I nod my approval and rush to my room. I need to change and get over to Jake's and help them clean up. Then take my girl out to dinner before getting lost in her in our bed. I'll never be able to think of it as anything but ours after the last couple of nights. Saylor changed me, changed my life, and I want to do that for her. I want her to feel strong, loved, and wanted, just like she said. That's now my mission in life. That and marrying her for love, and making our own family. I rush out the door with a smile on my face, needing to see her.

THIRTY NINE
Saylor

CAN'T BELIEVE I spilled the mop water all over me. I blame Jake. He was dancing with the broom. He had me laughing so hard I was crying and didn't see the bucket. I stepped into it and it sloshed all over me, soaking not only my clothes but my shoes. That's why I'm back at Grandpa Rhett's. My other pair of snow boots are in Rhett's room. We went down to the pond yesterday, and I wore them then. I had tennis shoes on today, and I refuse to ruin another pair.

Deciding I need to say hi to Grandpa Rhett and let him know I'm here, I head up the stairs. I freeze when I hear yelling.

"Because we want a divorce. We decide our future, and being married is not what we want!"

My heart stalls in my chest. Rhett's screaming at his grandfather about not wanting to be married to me. I haven't thought much about the divorce the last several weeks. We're both still wearing our rings, and it feels... real. From the anger in his voice, I know that feeling is one sided. I know he loves me, you can't fake that kind of affection. His eyes tell me what his heart can't. It still hits me like a dagger hearing him so livid about us still being married. Placing my hand over my mouth to silence my sobs,

I rush back downstairs and up the other side to Rhett's room. I grab my boots and dash out the door. I need to get myself together before seeing him. I didn't know he was going to come home early, and he wasn't expecting me to be there.

Wrong place. Wrong time.

I let the tears fall freely. I knew we were getting divorced; I signed the damn papers. I just didn't expect him to be so adamant about it after all that we've shared, especially to yell at his grandfather like that. When I pull onto our road, I grab a napkin from the glove box and dry my face. I pull up in front of the garage and dash up to my apartment. It's freezing-ass cold, and the water is turned off so the pipes don't freeze. Taking a seat on the couch, I switch out my shoes and focus on getting my emotions in check. He didn't do anything wrong, but the pain is there. The thought that his idea of forever and mine differ is what's breaking my heart.

My cell phone rings, and it's him. I hit the side button to silence the ringer and stare at his picture as his name flashes across the screen. It stops and then starts again. I repeat the process of silencing the ringer. It doesn't ring a third time, causing me to heave a sigh of relief. I have to talk to him sooner or later and tell him what I heard. I just need time to work through my grief for what our future might be, could be. Regardless, I want him in my life. I don't need marriage if I have him. It's my fault for letting his words lead my tattered heart down the path of fairy tales and happily ever after. We can create our own kind of fairy tale.

"Saylor!" I hear him yell my name just before he pushes open the door. "Hey, I called you."

"I know," I tell him. I don't play games, and I'll never lie to him.

"Why didn't you answer?" he asks, taking a seat next to me on the couch. He cups my face in his hands, and I know the minute he feels my wet cheeks. It's dark enough in here, I'm sure he can't see them. "Have you been crying? What's wrong? Are you hurt?" he fires off questions.

"Yes, can we talk about it later? No, I'm not hurt."

"You sure?"

"Yes. What are you doing here?" I ask, changing the subject. I'm avoiding, but I just need the tears to not be so fresh before we dig into this. I'll tell him tonight what I overheard.

"I came to help, but I stopped at the house first. You'll never guess what I stumbled in on," he says. "Come here, I need to hold you." He sits back on the couch and pulls me into his side. "I was going to say hi to Gramps before changing and heard him on the phone in his office. He was talking to Frank, the attorney. I heard him tell him to stall the divorce a little longer and that he would handle blowing us off." He laughs humorlessly.

So much for waiting until later to talk about it. Looks like it's happening now. "What happened?" I ask, wanting to know more before I tell him that I heard part of the conversation. Well, not really, just what he yelled at his grandfather.

"As soon as he hung up, I stormed in his office and demanded answers. He claimed that he could see we liked each other and that he was just giving us a chance to stay together. Then he admitted he was lonely was hoping that me being tied to you would convince me to stay here."

"That's awful," I say. My heart aches for Grandpa Rhett.

"I made him call Frank and tell him to move forward with the processing."

I can't stop the sob that breaks from my chest. He holds me tighter and kisses the top of my head.

"Saylor, babe, you're killing me here. What's going on?"

"I-I heard you," I say through my tears.

"What did you hear, baby?" he asks sweetly.

"I spilled water on me, my shoes were soaked, and my boots were in your room," I explain. "I heard you yelling. You said we wanted a divorce and being married isn't what we want."

"Babe, we decided together to do this. Have you changed your mind?"

"Have you?" I counter. "You said forever, and I thought that meant—" My voice breaks again.

"Saylor," he says softly.

"I mean, if you have, it's okay," I say, sitting up and wiping my cheeks with the backs of my hands. "I love you, and I'll take you however I can get you," I tell him honestly. I probably shouldn't let him off the hook like that, but it's true. "We can just do us, you know. We can make it whatever it is you want."

"Saylor," he says, causing me to turn my head and look at him. "I love you. Not because we got married in Vegas under the influence of alcohol, not because it's convenient for me, not because I feel obligated. I love you because of who you are and how I feel when I'm with you. You didn't hear the entire conversation, baby."

"No?" I ask hopeful.

"No." He stands and sits in front of me on the coffee table, resting his hands on my knees. "You didn't hear me tell him that I want to give you the world. You didn't hear me tell him that you've had enough of your choices taken from you in your lifetime, and I want you to have that option. You get to choose to marry me. I want to get down on one knee and ask you to be my wife the right way. Then you have the choice," he says again. Reaching up, he cradles my face in the palm of his hands. "You didn't hear me tell him that I want to give you everything."

"Everything?" I ask, trying to process what he's just said.

"Baby, it's freezing-ass cold in here," he says when he sees me shiver. "Let's go to the truck, or the main house with the kerosene heater, or back to Gramps's. Let me get you out of the cold, and we can finish this."

"Okay." I agree because I feel like my toes and fingers are going to fall off from the cold.

"I want to help Jake and Molly. I told them that I would. They've been so good to me," I say.

"Then that's what we'll do. I just need to hear you say that you understand what you mean to me first. I need to hear that we're okay."

I stand and step in between his legs where he sits on the table. "We're okay."

"I love you. When we get home, we're going to talk about this until you understand the depth of that. Gramps also needs to confess to you what he did. If I had any idea that you were there, I would have called you in there with me. No secrets. I promised you that I would always be honest with you."

My phone rings. Pulling it out of my back pocket, I see Molly's smiling face. "Hey," I say, placing the phone next to my ear.

"You guys okay? You have to be freezing over there."

"Yeah, we're good. We're headed your way actually."

"That's the other reason I'm calling. We're done for the day. Even with the heater, we're freezing. This is going to be a slow process."

"We'll get you there," I tell her. "So we'll be right behind you."

"We're going to stop by Jerry's, but then we'll be there."

"Okay. Be safe."

"You too."

"They're done for the day," I tell Rhett. "So we can go home."

"I like the sound of that. Us going home, together."

"Well, this is home technically, but—" I wave him off. "—you know what I mean." My mind is all jumbled from the tears and the fear of losing him so soon.

"My home is here." He points to me. "Wherever you are, Saylor, that's where I want to be." He stands and laces his fingers through mine. "Let's get you home and warmed up."

The ride home is quiet as I process everything Rhett told me. He loves me, he wants forever with me, but it's on my terms. And Grandpa Rhett, well, he wants me too. That makes my heart swell with love. As soon as we walk into the house, Grandpa Rhett calls out for us. We find him in the living room. "I owe both of you an apology. I never should have meddled; it's not my place to interfere with your lives. It won't happen again," he says solemnly.

I take a seat next to him on the couch. "I understand why you did it and know that you wanted to include me in your family." I stop to compose myself. I'm about to step out of the box. "I love you, Grandpa Rhett. Thank you for believing in us."

"Oh, sweet girl," he says, giving me a hug.

"I think we'll take it from here, okay? We'll figure it out."

He looks up at Rhett and grins. "I know you will. I've always had a stubborn streak, just ask your dad." He grins.

"Oh, trust me, I've heard all about it. Although, I'd never really experienced it firsthand until the last couple of months."

"Sorry about that, kid."

"It's done. I'm here, we're moving forward, and I got the girl."

"Looks like life is treating you pretty damn good," Grandpa Rhett says.

"I'd have to agree." Kneeling down, Rhett leans in and kisses me softly. We spend the rest of the night watching television with Gramps. We don't talk about us, but I know as soon as we're alone, we will. I'm confident he wants this, that he wants us, and my heart is bursting with love for him that he wants me to choose. If he only knew, I would choose him every damn time.

FORTY

Rhett

"SO HOW DOES it feel to be a divorced woman?" I ask Saylor as we exit the courthouse. After Frank filed the papers, we we're given a court date for three weeks later. The separation was amicable and both parties agreed, so it was a fifteen-minute session with the judge to confirm what was listed was correct, and he signed off on the papers.

"I think I need to go out and celebrate. Drink a few beers, maybe flirt with a few good-looking guys," she says, smiling.

I stop in my tracks and pull her into me. "You're not married, but you are taken. For life." I kiss her hard on the lips and release her.

"Is that so?"

"Yep." When we reach my truck, I open the door for her and smack her ass as she climbs inside. "That'll teach you," I say, laughing. Rounding the other side, I climb behind the wheel and put the keys in the ignition, but I don't start the truck. "Hey, can you hand me that box out of the glove compartment?"

She opens the compartment and there sits a small black velvet box with a red bow on top. "Rhett." She looks at me with tears in her eyes.

"We're meeting at Gramps's to celebrate. Mom and Dad flew in this morning. Jake, Molly, and Jerry will be there too." I tap on her arm, giving

269

it a little nudge. "But before we do, you need to open that."

With shaking hands, she opens the long, slender box. Inside is a Tiffany's white gold necklace with the initial B. For the first time since the night we were married, I slide my wedding band off my finger and hand it to her. I thought you might want to hold on to this for me, you know, until we need it again."

Her smile lights up her face as a lone tear slips from her eye. "I guess I should do that too, huh?" she asks. "It's going to be weird not wearing it. I'm used to it now."

I don't comment, just wait patiently as she slips both of our wedding bands on the chain then hands it to me. "Will you put it on me?" she asks.

I take the chain from her while she gathers her hair in one hand to keep it off her neck. Once I have it fastened, I kiss her neck and pull away. "Now," I say, starting the truck. "We have a divorce party to get to." Her laughter fills the cab of the truck as we head toward home.

"I'm excited to see your parents," she says when we pull into the driveway.

"You're Mom's new favorite." I fake a pout, when really it thrills me that they get along so well.

"Girl power," she says, raising her fist in the air.

"All right, crazy girl, let's get inside." We're greeted with cheers and a banner that says "H-A-P-P-Y D-I-V-O-R-C-E." It's handmade, and I know by the way Jerry is grinning and pointing at it, he's the one responsible. Mom made dinner—fried chicken, mashed potatoes, green beans, and strawberry cheesecake for dessert.

"You told her." Saylor turns to look at me.

I shrug. "I just thought Elaine should be here, you know? What better way to honor her than to serve your favorite meal that she used to make you?"

She wraps her arms around me. "I love you, Rhett Baxter, and she would have loved you too."

"Love you, too," I say, kissing the top of her head.

"Hey now, none of that, you're divorced," Jerry calls over. Saylor's cheeks turn pink from the attention.

We all gather around the huge dining room table that only gets used on major holidays, and eat until we can't eat any more. There is a lot of love and a lot of laughter around the table. Saylor hasn't stopped smiling, and I can only hope I can keep that smile there for the rest of her life.

"We have something else to celebrate," Gramps says, standing. "As of Monday, Rhett Alexander Baxter III is the new CEO of Baxter's Distillery."

Everyone cheers and congratulates me and Gramps on his retirement.

Jake stands next, pulling Molly with him. "Since this is a party, we have some news as well." He looks down at Molly and smiles. "In about seven months, we're going to have a new addition to our clan," he says proudly.

"You're pregnant?" Saylor squeals and jumps out of her chair to give them both a hug. The rest of us follow suit.

"So, we're, uh, going to get married in two weeks," Molly says. She looks over at us and winks. "In Vegas," she announces, and we all laugh and tell them congratulations again with another round of hugs.

"I don't think this day could get any better," Gramps says.

I stand from my seat. "Actually, there is one more thing." I turn toward Saylor and drop down to one knee. "Saylor Elizabeth Keller, you've brought so much to my life in such a short amount of time." Her eyes are already welling with tears. I'm getting a little choked up myself. This is life changing; her answer could make or break me. I'd like to think I know what it's going to be, but until I hear it from her pretty pink lips, I'm going to be sweating bullets. "You make me a better man. I'm stronger with you standing next to me. I want to be the man you lean on, the one who will forever be by your side. I want to be the man that gives you choices in life, like how many babies we're going to have." I wink at her. "Saylor, will you do me the incredible honor of becoming my wife? Will you marry me?" She nods, tears streaming down her face. Standing with the open ring box in my hand, I gently wipe her tears. "I need your words, baby." She stares down at the ring, this one an actual engagement ring, not just a wedding band. This one was bought for the woman I love, while completely sober.

"Y-yes," she says, smiling, laughing, and crying all at the same time. "Yes!" she says again, her voice clear.

Taking the ring out of the box, I slide it onto her hand. It's a heart-shaped diamond with princess cut diamonds on the band, the same pattern as her wedding band from our Vegas wedding. "I love you," I whisper before pressing my lips to hers.

"I choose you," she whispers.

My fucking heart flips over in my chest, and I wrap my arms around her, holding her tight. Chaos ensues around us, as we are now the ones getting hugs and congratulations from our friends and family. The rest of the night is filled with laughter. As I sit across the room and watch my mom, my fiancée, and longtime friend talk about weddings and babies, I feel peace wash over me. There have been some changes, life-altering changes, in the last few months, and I'm excited for every single one of them.

"Ladies," Jerry calls out. "Us men folk are going downstairs to have a beer," he tells them.

They laugh and wave him off, not breaking their conversation. Pulling my eyes away from her, I turn to follow the three of them downstairs where Gramps houses his fully stocked bar in his man cave. I'm almost to the doorway when I hear her call out for me.

"Hey, Whiskey."

Looking over my shoulder, I see her smiling at me. Mom and Molly are huddled over Molly's phone a few feet away. "What's up, Short Stack?" I smirk.

"You forgot something," she says, walking toward me.

"Oh yeah, and what's that?" I ask, resting my hands on her hips once she's close enough.

"This." She stands on her tiptoes, buries her hands in my hair, and tugs me into a kiss. "I love you," she says, pulling away.

"Saylor, look at this one," Mom calls out for her.

She flashes me a grin before running back to them. She's beautifully happy, and I vow to do everything in my power to keep her that way.

FORTY ONE

Saylor

THE LAST FOUR months have been exhilarating. Rhett and I were fine with heading back to Vegas with Jake and Molly to have a double wedding; however, my future mother-in-law put her foot down. Rhett was her only baby, and she insisted we both deserved a proper wedding. We settled on the first week of June, Rhett refusing to give her more time than that. She huffed, but finally agreed.

The week after our engagement, I moved in with him and Gramps. Gramps insisted that the house was big enough for all of us. He said that us "young ins" could bring life back to the place. I fought them, but in the end, I gave in. It was Gramps's speech about family and needing to be together that convinced me. He's been doing well without the stress of the distillery. He's got a sparkle in his eyes, as does my fiancé.

"When do we get to leave?" Rhett asks me.

I stifle my laugh. "You know we're not leaving together," I remind him.

"Come on, Short Stack, that's crazy talk. How am I supposed to sleep if you're not next to me?" he whines.

"Man up," Jake says, slapping him on the shoulder.

"Fuck off," Rhett says with no heat behind his words. "You didn't have to be away from your wife when you got married," Rhett pouts.

"Should have went to Vegas." Jake gives us a big goofy grin.

"Hush you," Molly says, placing her hands on her protruding belly. I can't help but reach out and rub it.

"How you feeling, mama?" I ask her.

"Good." She grins.

"My boy being good?" Jake asks, leaning down and asking her belly.

She laughs. "He's active," she says, before turning to me. "You ready?"

I nod, trying to contain my smile.

"For what?" Jake asks her.

"Saylor and I are staying at the hotel tonight with Valerie."

"What?" Jake asks. "Babe, when did you decide this?"

She shrugs. "A while ago."

"Why didn't you tell me? I can't sleep," he mumbles.

"Man up," Rhett says, slapping him on the shoulder, looking smug. He wraps me in his arms. "I can't believe my mother is stealing you from me."

"And me," Jake adds, causing Molly and me to throw our heads back in laughter.

"You'll be fine. I'll see you tomorrow at two."

"Sayyylorrr," he whines. "Sneak out. When they go to sleep, sneak out. I'll get a room and text you the number," he says, pulling his phone out of his pocket.

"I heard that," Valerie says, joining us with Rhett's dad right behind her. "It's not even twenty-four hours." She pats his cheek.

He mumbles something about mom stealing his girl. "Fine, let's get this over with," he says, kissing my temple.

"Let her go, son," his dad says.

"I need a minute," he says, lacing his fingers through mine and pulling me out of the room and down the hall. We end up by the exit door in the same hallway as the restrooms. Rhett pushes my back against the wall and his lips land on mine. Not able to resist, I bury my hands in his hair. Slowing the kiss, he rests his forehead against mine. He's breathing heavy; then so am I. That's what he does to me. "Tomorrow you're my wife," he says softly.

"Again," I remind him.

"Just because you wear these here"—he lifts the chain that I've worn every day since the day he gave it to me—"doesn't mean you're not my wife in here." He places our joined hands over his heart. "I'll be the one down at the front, the man at the end of the aisle waiting to start our forever."

Tears prick my eyes. "I-I'll be the one in white walking toward my forever," I say, wrapping my arms around his waist.

He lifts his forehead from mine and holds me tight against his chest. "I love you, Saylor." I'm just about to tell him I love him too when he adds, "I want it all, Saylor. I want a house full of babies, vacations, sleepless nights, lazy Sunday mornings. I want it all."

"You're ready for all that?"

"More than ready. You could toss out your pills, and we could start on our wedding night."

All I can do is shake my head and smile. "What am I going to do with you?"

"Make babies with me," he winks. "I love you, Short Stack."

"I love you too, Whiskey." With one more quick kiss, we walk hand in hand back to our guests.

Molly, Valerie, and I head to the hotel. The suite is filled with snacks, chick flicks, and our dresses for tomorrow. After changing into the matching pajamas that Valerie insisted she buy for the three of us, we curl up on the couch and settle in for girl time. We're barely through the first movie, when Molly bows out.

"Sorry, ladies, this little guy has me tuckered out," she says, rubbing her belly.

"Of course, it's been a long day. Thank you for being a part of this," I say, fighting tears.

"Saylor, you're my best friend. I wouldn't have missed this for the world."

I stand to give her a hug. "Get some rest," I say, releasing her from my hold. Valerie and I settle in and finish the movie. Just as the credits roll, my phone alerts me to a new message.

Rhett: I miss you.

Me: I miss you too.

Rhett: Marry Me?

Me: How's tomorrow?

Rhett: How's today? Look at the time, baby.

Looking at the clock, I see that it's already one o'clock in the morning.

Me: Today works too.

Rhett: Thirteen hours, Short Stack.

Me: Until forever.

Rhett: Love you.

Me: Love you too.

"My son, I assume?" Valerie smiles.

"Yeah," I admit.

"Saylor, I'm so happy he found you. You bring out the best in him."

"He brings out the best in me. I never felt like I truly belonged before," I confess. "It's hard not having any family. Elaine, she chose me, you know. And she cared enough, loved me enough to give me a good home. She was my only family," I say, wiping a tear from my eye.

"Oh, sweetheart." She slides over on the couch and pulls me into a side hug. "You are family. You hear me. You belong with us, and we love you. I couldn't be happier to call you my daughter."

A sob breaks from my chest. "I love you, too," I say, smiling through my tears.

"Now, we can't have this," she says, wiping the tears from my cheeks. "We need you rested and no puffy eyes for the big day. Not to mention, if my son finds out I upset you enough to have puffy eyes, I'll never hear the end of it."

That makes me laugh. Rhett, well, he spoils me. There really is no other way to put it. "He's... everything," I say with a sigh.

She smiles, tears shimmering in her eyes as well. "Let's get some sleep." Nodding my acceptance, I stand, giving her a hug before we retreat to our rooms.

Surprisingly, I fall right to sleep. I know it's because when I wake up, I'm marrying the love of my life. Not only do I get him, but I get his amazing family. I don't let myself dwell on the fact that I invited Tara and Colin and she never returned my call or her RSVP to the invitation. It hurts, but such is life. I have to live for me, not for her, and as my friend, if she can't see that, we are better off. I think about the day I walked into the Corner Pocket. I know in my gut a stronger force was guiding me. When I lost Elaine, she and my parents led me there. To my home, to my family. I drift off to sleep with a smile on my face.

I wake to the sounds of voices in the main living area of our suite. My first thought is that my fiancé broke the rules. I'm not superstitious. The only reason I went along with it was for Valerie; she insisted we follow the ritual. Climbing out of bed, I make my way to the living area.

"There she is," Valerie says happily.

"Morning, sweetheart," Rhett's dad says. "I thought you ladies might like breakfast."

"Thank you," I say. "Where's Molly?"

"She just went to shower," Valerie says.

"What time is it?" I ask.

"Just after eight," they both say.

I take a seat across from them and grab a pastry from the box. "Does he know you're here?" I ask Rhett's dad.

He laughs. "No. I'm not crazy, Say. You know I never would have got out of the house without him. I snuck out while they were all sleeping. Left a note saying I went to get breakfast." He looks at his watch. "I should probably get back, but I wanted to talk to you for a minute."

"Sure." I set my pastry on a napkin.

"I better hop in the shower. Love you," Valerie says, leaning in for a kiss, to which my future father-in-law obliges.

He waits until she's out of the room before turning back to face me. "Saylor, I know today is hard for you. I want to thank you for humoring my wife with a big wedding."

I smile softly at him. "It's my pleasure. It will always be a day to remember."

"That it will. There's really no easy way to approach this, so I'm just going to say it." He takes a deep breath. "Saylor, you're family. I already think of you as my daughter, and it would be my incredible honor to walk you down the aisle." He hesitates before adding. "If you'll have me."

Tears run unchecked down my face as I'm swarmed with emotion.

Loved.

Wanted.

"I-I would r-really l-love that," I stammer.

He nods, swallowing hard. I can see his eyes are glassy too. "Thank you. I'll let you get ready. I need to go get snazzed up myself. It's not every day I get to walk my daughter down to my son and watch them start their lives together."

All I can do is smile through my tears. Standing, I walk around the table and wrap my arms around him in a hug.

I feel him kiss the top of my head. "Love you, sweet girl. We'll see you soon." With one more gentle squeeze, he releases me and turns to leave. "Saylor," he says looking over his shoulder. He points to the table. "There's a little something from Rhett. I was supposed to give it to you when you get to the house before the ceremony, but I thought I would go ahead and bring it. You know, before the makeup and all that."

"Thank you. I have something for him too. Valerie has it."

He nods. "See you soon."

I watch until he disappears behind the main door. Grabbing the pink envelope, I sit on the couch. Leaning back, I close my eyes. "Mom, Dad, Elaine, if you're up there listening like I think you are… thank you. Thank you for guiding me to Rhett, to his family. To Jake and Molly. Thank you for watching out for me. I love you, all three of you, so much." I sit there for a few more minutes getting my emotions under control.

Taking a deep breath, I open my eyes and turn the envelope over in my hands. Gently, I run my finger under the seal and break it open. Inside there are two tickets to Hawaii. Closer inspection tells me that we fly out tomorrow. Smiling like a love-sick fool, I unfold the note.

Saylor,

Today is the first day of our forever, and I want nothing more than to make your dreams come true. I know you've been wondering about our honeymoon, and I want it to be the first of many adventures that we have together. Our first marriage we started with Vegas. Let's start this one with a trip to Hawaii. I know that if your parents were here, they would be so damn proud of you. This trip will be the first of many as we travel this journey together.

All my love,

Your Husband

FORTY TWO

Rhett

T ODAY'S THE BIG day. Fucking finally, it feels like it's been a long
time coming. I think part of that is because she was mine and I
signed those divorce papers when I wanted to do anything but. I
knew it was the right thing to do, to give her the choice, but I thought we
would get married sooner than this, until mom stepped in. Four months
has felt like four fucking years.

"Knock, knock," Mom says, not waiting for me to tell her to come in.
She just pushes the door open.

"You look so handsome," she says, choking up.

I hold my arms open for her, and she rushes toward me. "Love you,
Mom."

She pulls back and wipes at her eyes. "I have something for you." She
holds up a gift bag that I didn't notice she was carrying.

"How is my wife?" I ask her.

"Your fiancée is doing just fine. She's breathtaking."

"Tell me something I didn't know."

"Rhett Baxter! Have you snuck to see her?" She places her hands on her hips, causing the bag to sway, and gives me her "stern mom" look.

I throw my head back and laugh. "No, Mother, I have not. Saylor takes my breath every time I look at her."

She places her hand over her heart, and her eyes mist once again. "I'm so proud of you." She wipes her eyes. "Here." She thrusts the bag at me. "I'll give you a minute." With a kiss to my cheek, she disappears behind the door, leaving me alone.

I settle on the couch, sitting the bag between my feet on the floor. Removing the tissue paper, I reach in for the small box that is labeled with the number one. Looking further, I see another box the same size with a number two. Pulling on the ribbon, it easily falls away. Carefully, I open the box, and inside rests an old antique key and a note.

> Rhett,
>
> You gave me you and, with you, your family. It's just me, and I don't have much to offer, but today, I give you the key to my heart.
>
> Love always,
>
> Saylor

I choke back the emotion that's clogging my throat. Removing the key from the box, I hold it tight in the palm of my hand. I close my eyes and take a deep breath, getting myself under control. The urge to race to the other side of the house to the room she's holed up in is burning hot. She's so close, yet so far away. Glancing at my watch, I see it's only twenty more minutes until she's walking down the aisle toward me. I suspect Mom waited until closer to the wedding on purpose. She knew I would need to see her. Sliding the key in my pocket, I reach into the bag and pull out box number two. I repeat the process, pulling on the ribbon and it falls away just as easily. Opening the lid, I see a small packet of pills. Her birth control pills. I smile as my eyes well with tears. I quickly unfold the note to see if this means what I think it means.

> Rhett,
>
> Thank you for sharing your family with me. Now it's time to start ours.
>
> All my love,
>
> Your wife

Just as I fold up the note, Dad, Jerry, Jake, and Gramps walk in. I rush to wipe the tears; my future wife has just given me everything.

"You good?" Dad asks.

"Never better. Let's do this," I say, placing both boxes back in the bag. Standing, I reach in my pocket and run my fingers over the key.

"Good. Well, I'll see you out there," Dad says, heading toward the door.

"Wait? Where are you going?" I ask him.

He stops and turns to look at me. "I went to see my daughter this morning." He grins, looking at his watch. "It appears it's time for me to walk her down the aisle."

"You did?" I swallow hard.

"Yep. You did good, son." Those are his parting words before walking out the door.

"Let's get you married," Jake says, placing his hand on my shoulder.

We make our way to the backyard of our home, the one we now share with Gramps. Mom has turned it into a fairy tale with all the flowers and the white-fabric-covered chairs adorned with lavender bows. I take my place down front, greeting the minister with a handshake. There are no bride's side and groom's side; instead, we have three small rows of chairs. I didn't even have to press the issue with Mom, she just knew. We have Jake and Molly standing up with us, Jerry, Gramps, Mom, Dad, and my mom's parents are here. That's it. Small, intimate, but assured to be a day Saylor and I will never forget.

When Train's "Marry Me" begins to play, I turn to face the aisle. Instead of splitting down the middle, Mom had them run the white runner from the back porch around a big old oak tree and down the side of the seats. I gave her hell about it, accusing her of keeping Saylor from me even longer. She laughed, patted my cheek, and assured me that wait would be worth it.

After what feels like forever, Molly appears from around the tree; she's glowing with her protruding baby belly in her lavender dress. I move my gaze to the back deck where the aisle begins. I see Dad and Saylor; she's beautiful from a distance, of course, this is my wife we're talking about. No matter the situation, she's fucking gorgeous. I watch their every step. When they round the tree on the home stretch, I get my first good look at her. Sliding one hand in my pocket, I grip the key, her heart. The other hand I bring to my mouth and bite down. I need to make sure this moment is real.

I don't blink, afraid to miss one minute of my future walking toward me. When she's close enough to touch, I remove my hand from my pocket and reach for her with both arms. Our guests chuckle, as does my father. "Not yet, son." He grins.

Saylor's beaming smile and misty eyes call to me. I don't hear the minister ask who gives her away. All I see is her, and can only hear white noise. Nothing else matters in this moment. It's not until she takes a step toward me that I shake out of my fog and reach for her. Without thinking, I pull her into my chest and wrap my arms around her. "You're beautiful," I say, my lips next to her ear.

We opted to go with short, quick traditional vows. I've never been surer of that decision like I am now. I can't think with this beautiful woman standing in front of me. I repeat like I'm supposed to; we say "I do," and I slide her diamond wedding band from Vegas on her finger. She does the same with my tungsten band. As soon as our rings are back in their rightful places, I pull her to me and kiss her. She's on her tiptoes, even in heels, so I lift her, her feet dangling in the air, and kiss her harder.

"Rhett." She laughs.

I pull away, relishing the sound. I rest my forehead against hers. "I love you, Mrs. Baxter."

"I love you too, husband." I can hear the smile on her voice.

Our friends and family are clapping and cheering us on. Instead of setting Saylor back on her feet, I scoop her up in my arms and take off toward the house. She smiles up at me and rests her head in the crook of my neck. Once inside, I head for the stairs.

"Where are we going?" she asks.

I don't answer her, as I use my shoulder to push open our bedroom door, then kick it closed behind me. Gently, I place her on the bed, and crawl on my hands and knees to hover over her. "You're gorgeous."

"What are you doing?" She laughs as I kiss down the column of her neck.

"I'm utilizing my wedding gift," I say against her neck.

"Rhett!" she scolds. "Not now, we have guests."

"Don't care," I say, pulling all the fabric from her long dress up her leg, so I can get my hands on her.

"Stop."

I freeze and pull my lips from her. Her blue eyes are shining with happiness and love. "I don't want to rush through this moment. Let's go downstairs and greet our guests." She runs her fingers through my hair. "Our family. We have our entire lives to do this."

"We're not staying here tonight," I tell her.

She raises her brow. "Why not?"

"Because I plan on being inside my wife all night long, and although Gramps's hearing isn't what it used to be, I don't want him hearing you."

"So, strangers are okay then?" She bites back her smile.

"We're on the top floor," I counter. It's not okay, but I'll choose strangers over Gramps any day. "I love you, wife."

She grins. "I love you too, husband."

EPILOGUE
One Year Later

Saylor

"**Y**OU KNOW YOU'RE going to spoil her, right?" I ask my husband. He looks at me, horrified, and places his hands over our newborn daughter's ears. "It's okay, baby girl. Mommy didn't mean it," he coos at her.

I just shake my head and smile. Grace Elaine, or Gracie as we call her, was born three days ago. We named her after my mothers, both of them. Rhett's parents weren't here for the delivery, considering I went into labor three days early. "Your parents are going to be here any minute; you think you should put a shirt on?" I ask him, partly because of his parents are coming and partly because I have at least six more weeks before I can have sex, and the sight of my husband shirtless is too damn tempting.

"Skin to skin contact, the doctor said its good for her," he argues.

Before I can give him a hard time about being a big softie where our baby girl is concerned, the doorbell rings. "Yoo-hoo," my mother-in-law calls out. "Where is she?" she asks, stepping into the living room, Rhett's dad right behind her.

"Back up, Nanna, it's Daddy time." Rhett mock glares at her.

"You're going to spoil her. Now give her here," she scolds him. He laughs but carefully transfers our baby girl over to his mother.

"Come sit, Say. You need to rest," Rhett says.

I'm tired of sitting, but I don't bother saying it because it falls on deaf ears. Since the moment I told him I was pregnant, he's been this overprotective, by the book rule enforcer. "Yes, dear," I say overly sweet.

"Look at you, miss Gracie, you're just the prettiest little thing," his mom coos at her. "Look at her little toes," she says, pulling off her socks.

"How are you feeling?" Rhett's dad asks.

"Good. This one doesn't let me do anything." I point to my husband. "So I'm getting a lot of rest."

"Look what I found," Grandpa Rhett says, joining us. He's carrying a huge pink teddy bear that's almost bigger than he is. "I bought my sweet girl a present," he says, setting the bear on the floor beside Valerie's feet. "My turn." He holds out his arms.

"Back up, Pops," Rhett's dad says. "I'm next. Get in line." He points to the empty seat beside him on the couch.

"Y'all are going to spoil her," my husband says, smirking.

"Why don't you two go grab something to eat, take a drive, take a nap, something. Take advantage of the help while we're here," my mother-in-law suggests.

"And just leave her here?" Rhett asks, horrified.

We all laugh at him. "Yes, son, leave her here. With her family who loves her just as much as you do."

"We're good. We have plenty of food in the kitchen."

"Then just go take a drive, get out of the house."

"We're good."

"Why don't we go lie down?" I suggest.

"You tired, baby?" he asks, already standing.

I'm not, but he has to be. Every little noise she makes, he's up checking on her. Not to mention, he's been waiting on me hand and foot. Literally, he carries me to the bathroom and to bed. It's ridiculous, but I wouldn't change him for the world. He has me in his arms after making his parents promise to record or photograph if she does anything cute and to not leave the house. She's three days old and already had her picture taken more times than I can count.

Once we clear the top of the stairs, he stops and presses his lips to mine. "I love you, Saylor Elizabeth Baxter. Thank you for this life you've given me."

"I love you too."

M Y WIFE IS a fucking rock star. For the last nine months, I've watched her grow with our baby girl and not once did she complain. There were many nights where she couldn't sleep, unable to find a comfortable position, but she never said a word about it. We went to Lamaze, we watched birthing videos, everything we could to be prepared for our little girl. I thought I was prepared. I knew the breathing. I knew Say's focal point to keep her calm. I read a few books.

I was ready.

I was wrong.

The minute her contractions started coming, they came fast and hard. So much so that she was unable to get an epidural. I watched my wife give birth to our daughter naturally, in obvious pain, and it killed me. I would have done anything to take her pain away.

I live by the philosophy that I tell her and show her how much she means to me every day, but after that, after watching her delivery our baby girl into the world, I don't have the words or the actions to show her what's in my heart. I guess I could show her a picture of them together. It was an experience I will never forget, for as long as I live.

"Will you lay with me?" she asks. Not able to deny her anything, I crawl into bed facing her. She immediately lifts her hand and starts running it though my hair. It's something she's always done, and it's become soothing to me.

I can feel my eyes start to get heavy, but I fight it. I need to be awake in case they need me. "When can we have another one?" I ask with a yawn.

She laughs softly. "Let me heal from this one, maybe get her out of diapers, and then we can talk."

"I want a house full of little girls who look just like their mamma," I confess.

"Yeah? I wouldn't mind having a baby boy who looks like his daddy, maybe carry on the family name?"

"Yeah, one of those too," I say, and she laughs.

"Love you, Short Stack," I mumble, pulling her closer to me. I can never seem to get her close enough. "I miss your baby bump," I say, tenderly running my finger over her now flat belly.

"Do you?" She laughs.

"I do." I can feel myself drifting off to sleep, no longer able to fight it.

"Hey, Whiskey," she whispers.

"Hmm?"

"Thank you for giving me what I always wanted."

"What's that, baby?"

"A family."

Saylor's
NO BAKE COOKIES

Ingredients:

3 Tablespoons of Coco

½ cup margarine/butter

2 cups white granulated sugar

½ milk

3 cups of Quick Oats

½ cup of peanut butter

1 teaspoon vanilla

Combine:

Coco, margarine/butter, sugar, milk, and vanilla in a medium sized sauce pan.

High heat until the mixture is at a hard boil for one full minute. Continue to stir the mixture during this process.

Once the mixture has been at a hard boil for one full minute, remove from heat and add the peanut butter. Mix until completely blended.

Slowly add the Oats, mixing them into the mixture.

Once all the oats have been added. Spoon drops of mixture (size is up to you) on wax paper. Let the cookies cool/harden before eating.

**If the cookies do not harden, they did not boil long enough

CONTACT Kaylee Ryan

Facebook: www.facebook.com/pages/Kaylee-Ryan-Author

Goodreads:
www.goodreads.com/author/show/7060310.Kaylee_Ryan

Twitter: @author_k_ryan

Instagram: Kaylee_ryan_author

Website: www.kayleeryan.com

OTHER WORKS BY
Kaylee Ryan

With You Series
Anywhere With You
More With You
Everything With You

Stand Alone Titles
Tempting Tatum
Unwrapping Tatum
Levitate
Just Say When
Unexpected Reality
I Just Want You
Reminding Avery

Soul Serenade Series
Emphatic
Assured

Southern Heart Series
Southern Pleasure
Southern Desire
Southern Attraction

ACKNOWLEDGMENTS

I'm always afraid I'm going to forget someone during this process. Sure these are my words but it takes a team of people to get them in your hands.

To my readers:

You're amazing. Not only do you buy my books and read them, you message me along the way. I love hearing from each and every one of you. I love hearing your thoughts as you read and how the story as a whole touched your life. I'm grateful for ALL of you more than you will ever know. Thank you for taking the time to read my words.

To my family:

Your continued support is beyond measure. I'm so thankful to be living this life with you. I love you.

Golden Czermak:

Your talent behind the lens is incredible. Thank you for another amazing photo/cover.

Tami Integrity Formatting:

You have a way of taking my words and turning them into a beautiful little package. As always, it's been amazing and my pleasure working with you.

Sommer Stein:

Every time, you seem to be in my head and produce a cover that fits not only my vision, but it captures the story. Thank you for another kick-ass cover!

My beta team:

Kaylee 2, Jamie, Stacy and Lauren I love you! You ladies are like family to me. I don't know where I would be without you. Ashley, Molly, and S, thank you for your honest opinions on Hey, Whiskey. It's always nice to have another authors opinion on your work.

Give Me Books:

With every release, your team works diligently to get my book in the hands of bloggers. I cannot tell you how thankful I am for your services.

Bloggers:

Thank you, doesn't seem like enough. You don't get paid to do what you do. It's from the kindness of your heart and your love of reading the fuels you. Without you, without your pages, your voice, your reviews, spreading the word it would be so much harder if not impossible to get my words in reader's hands. I can't tell you how much your never-ending support means to me. Thank you for being you, thank you for all that you do.

To my Kick Ass Crew:

The name of the group speaks for itself. You ladies truly do KICK ASS! I'm honored to have you on this journey with me. Thank you for reading, sharing, commenting, suggesting, the teasers, the messages all of it. Thank you from the bottom of my heart for all that you do. Your support is everything!

With Love,

Kaylee Ryan
AUTHOR

Made in the USA
Columbia, SC
19 July 2021

42078878R00163